Years of Dreams

Years
of
Dreams

GLORIA GOLDREICH

LITTLE, BROWN AND COMPANY

Boston   Toronto   London

FIRST EDITION

The characters and events in this book are fictitious. Any similarity to real persons,
living or dead, is coincidental and not intended by the author.

LIBRARY OF CONGRESS CATALOGING-IN-PUBLICATION DATA

Goldreich, Gloria.
    Years of dreams / Gloria Goldreich. — 1st ed.
        p.   cm.
    ISBN 0-316-31937-6
    I. Title.
    PS3557.03845Y4   1992   91-28962
    813′.54 — dc20

        10 9 8 7 6 5 4 3 2

MV-NY

Published simultaneously in Canada by
Little, Brown & Company (Canada) Limited

PRINTED IN THE UNITED STATES OF AMERICA

For Esther Weissbart

Years of Dreams

Spring 1983

THE TELEPHONE'S shrill ring pierced the quiet of the spring afternoon. Harshly, insistently, it drowned out the lilting melody of the violin. The auburn-haired musician frowned, lowered her bow, and reluctantly lifted the receiver.

"Hello. This is Merle Cunningham," she said. Her English nursemaid had cautioned her to identify herself when she answered the phone and now, decades later, she adhered to the lessons of her childhood.

She listened to the caller, absently stroking the silken gut of the violin's G string, but within moments she set the instrument down with great care. She feared to hold it because his words, uttered with such urgency and stuttering nervousness, caused her hands to tremble; she gripped the receiver tightly lest it slip from her grasp.

"No," she protested. "No. It can't be. You must have heard wrong."

Horror and incredulity replaced the irritation in her tone. Suddenly light-headed, she sank down on the green velvet chair, reached for the pad and pencil on the white table, in readiness next to the phone.

"All right, I understand," she said. "Yes, I'll write it all down."

Now he spoke very slowly. As always, her need impelled his strength. She repeated his words as she wrote.

"Fieldston Hospital. Lowell Commons. Cambridge." *But what was she doing in Cambridge? Didn't she have performances, rehearsals, in New York?* Denial had drifted into bewildered acceptance and now into a stubborn determination to wrest reason from the irrational.

But he had no answers for her. The police officer who had called him had given him only the scant facts. The time of the accident. The location of the hospital.

"Will she live?" She asked the question timorously, her voice very soft.

"They don't know."

He was honest with her, a hard-earned honesty. Briefly, bitterly, she regretted the long struggle that had preceded its acquisition. She wanted him to lie to her, to reassure her. Instead he spoke of the most direct route from Egremont to Cambridge, reminded her of the exit number that gave the easiest access to Harvard Square. She agreed that it would be wisest to take the Porsche, which handled well in highway traffic. Implicit in his suggestion, her agreement, was their shared fear. *There must not be another accident.* What had happened once that day must not happen twice. They would have to be doubly vigilant.

"You'll call the others?"

His question was a statement. He knew that she would, that already she was phrasing the words she would say to them — to Anne and to Nancy. And to Rutti. His mouth grew dry as he thought of Rutti. He had received a postcard from her that morning. A gentle watercolor of Hampstead Heath at dusk. What time was it in London? He made a swift calculation. Night had fallen. Airline ticket and travel offices would be closed. He would ask his secretary to arrange for Rutti's flight.

"Merle, I'll call Rutti myself," he said.

"Yes." Mentally, she thanked him, as she had thanked him so often for so much through the years. "I love you." The words were a talisman and she listened as he repeated them. They were the pledge of his protection. She clutched the receiver for a long moment after he hung up. She did not want to make her own calls. She wanted to spare her friends the news that now weighted her with sorrow. But she knew that she had no choice. Slowly, the pressure on each button an effort, she called Nancy in New York.

They were having an early drink when the phone rang, and they were both disinclined to answer it. The day was warm and Nancy had opened the top buttons of her turquoise silk blouse, released her heavy dark hair, streaked with silver now, from its olive-wood clip and allowed it to fan out about her shoulders. Barefoot, she stroked his trouser leg with her toes before rising to move toward the phone.

He pulled her back.

"Let it ring," he said teasingly. "I thought you were trying to seduce me. And I want to be seduced. I deserve to be seduced. Love in New York. On a spring afternoon. In the middle of the week. Why not?" He kissed her hand.

The phone rang again, the jarring tintinnabulation of authority and urgency.

"I have to answer," she said smiling, but pulling away from him. "I have one distinctly suicidal patient and another depressed enough to become suicidal at any moment. The occupational hazard psycho-analysts face in springtime. And there are the boys. The school might be calling. Or Keren. Remember, she wasn't feeling well when she called from Siena."

"And perhaps it's just a wrong number. Would you forgo love in New York on a spring afternoon for a wrong number?"

He laughed and she shook her head and hurried to the phone. Perhaps it would, after all, stop ringing before she reached it. Why hadn't she put on her answering machine? *Love in New York on a spring afternoon.* She would deal with this call swiftly. Humming, she unbuttoned yet another button, unzipped her white linen skirt.

"Merle. Hi!" Pleasure filled her voice. She was always glad to hear from Merle.

He was surprised then to see her frown and bite her lip. He moved swiftly toward her when she swayed slightly, as though she had been struck.

"I can't believe it. How horrible. Yes. Of course I'll come. The very first flight I can get to Boston—the shuttle. But what was she doing in Cambridge? All right. Fieldston Hospital. I'll find it."

She was very pale. He stood beside her, held her close, stroked her neck.

"Who?" he asked. "What happened?"

But she did not answer him. She was listening to Merle, her eyes half closed.

"Yes. Of course you must try to reach Anne. Her secretary will be able to locate her. She is part of the pact. Our pact."

She hung up then and rested heavily against him.

"Oh, it's bad," she said and her voice broke. "It's very bad."

She repeated what Merle had told her. His face contorted with fear and they clung to each other, silent because there was nothing they could say. Then she went to pack and he called Eastern Airlines and asked for information about the Boston shuttle.

The tall woman whose soft fair hair was plaited into an intricate chignon, smoothed the jacket of her pale blue crushed cotton suit and listened in disbelief as her name was broadcast throughout the Dallas airport.

"Dr. Anne Richardson. Dr. Anne Richardson. Please pick up the nearest courtesy phone."

"Excuse me." Breathlessly she intercepted a young woman in a flight attendant's uniform. "Where is there a courtesy phone?"

"Here. There. Everywhere. Every red phone without a dial." She pointed to two within paces of where they stood and hurried on.

"Thanks."

Anne picked up the receiver, setting her flight bag down.

"This is Dr. Anne Richardson," she said. "I'm answering your page." Her throat was dry, her pulse racing. *Tommy. Oh let it not be Tommy.* And it could not be Sanjit. She had spoken to him only a half hour ago. It was probably a screwup at the lab, a problem on the tissue culture so vital to the DNA experiment she was running. Her assistant knew how uptight she was about that. Of course that was it. *Tommy was fine. He had to be fine.*

"One moment. We're tryin' to get your party on the line, Doctor." The operator was unflappable, her accent a jaunty Texas twang. "OK. Here we go . . ."

"Anne. Is that you?"

"Merle. For God's sake what is it? What's happened? My plane for Mexico City leaves in half an hour. Nothing can be that important."

But it was that important. She listened, leaning against a pole for support, indifferent to the passengers who rushed past her, deaf

6

to the flight announcements that sputtered incomprehensibly from a dozen speakers.

"The police officer didn't say anything about vital signs, head trauma?" She asked the questions of her profession, but Merle had no answers. Merle was crying.

"Merle. It will be all right. Look, I'm going to book a flight to Boston. I hope my luggage has a terrific time in Mexico City. Please, Merle. Don't cry."

She hung up and waited for her heart to stop pounding, for her pulse to slow, before lifting her flight bag and heading for the desk of the nearest ticket agent.

He did not call Rutti after hanging up on Merle. Instead he called the owner of her gallery, whose phone number he had on his Rolodex as he had so many other numbers, because he was a careful man, an experienced man who never relinquished any contact. And so it was Nathaniel Evans, who had long represented Rutti in the United Kingdom, who drove from his home in Highgate to Browns Hotel where he knocked on Rutti's door, holding a thermos of strong tea and a flask of brandy.

The diminutive artist, who had been the toast of the London art world that week, was pleased to see him. She stood on tiptoe to kiss his cheek and pirouetted so that he might approve of the wool dress, the color of primroses, that she had bought that day in an elegant Kensington boutique.

"Do you like it?" she asked with the exultant triumph peculiar to women who revel in finery because they were so poorly clothed as girls.

"It's lovely," he said, but he did not smile and she knew at once that something was wrong. Of course something was wrong. Why else would Nathaniel Evans be standing at her door without previous notice?

"What is it? What's happened?" she asked and cursed herself for a fool. She had allowed her vigilance to relax. She was no longer prepared for tragedy.

And when he told her, she fell forward into his arms. She did not faint. She simply did not have the strength with which to stand.

"I must go to her," she said.

"Yes. Of course. It's arranged. All arranged. I have your tickets. I'll drive you to Heathrow now. At once."

"Will I be too late?" Her question was choked in anguish.

He did not reply. He could not bear to tell her that he did not know. "You must believe that everything will be all right," he said at last and Rutti looked up at him, grateful and disbelieving. "I was told to say that your friends are there," he added.

"Yes," she said. "Of course they are."

He watched as she removed a framed drawing of a young girl from her bedside table and placed it in her purse. That and her passport were all she took, although he draped a dark cape about her shoulders because the London night was chilly and it would surely grow cold over the Atlantic.

She did not look back as they left the room. That was one of the lessons her life had taught her. She never looked back. There was no point.

The Sixties

1

NANCY YALLON, breathless and exhilarated, her cheeks reddened by the long uphill walk from the hospital housing complex, laughed aloud as a chipmunk, with urban insouciance, scampered between the wheels of Keren's stroller and disappeared behind the towering oak that guarded the east gate to the park.

"See you around," she called gaily to the vanished animal as she paused to adjust her long red scarf so that it covered her dark hair.

She looked down at Keren, fast asleep, her chubby olive-skinned cheeks aglow as though polished by the November cold. Her irrepressible black curls escaped the white wool cap and a single dark lash rested on her ruddy cheek.

"Sleepyhead, you missed the chipmunk," Nancy said, and smiled as she lifted the lash gently onto her finger, made a silent wish, and blew it away.

Keren smiled in her sleep, a slow sweet smile that pierced Nancy's heart with joy. She bent to adjust the plaid blanket but the soft wool slid free of the slick pink nylon snowsuit and Nancy did not persist. Keren would be warm enough beneath the layers of clothing even if the temperature dropped.

"Snow, I can feel it," Dov had said that morning with the joyous excitement peculiar to those who grew up in arid regions and so throughout their lives regard the falling snow as a miracle.

"I hope so," Nancy replied, tossing him an extra pair of socks. He was on emergency room rotation and the admitting area was drafty, the tile floor cold.

She studied the sky now, as she wheeled the stroller into the park, noting the thick fleecy clouds that drifted across the pewter-colored sky. Snow would be fun. Keren was old enough to have her own small sled this year. Nancy imagined racing after Dov as he pulled Keren across plains of shining whiteness, their laughter blending as Keren's delight matched their own. It was wondrous, she thought, how having a child renewed and energized, transformed fading memory into vigorous reality.

Smiling, she wheeled the stroller past the bench where the three amiable Jamaican nannies sat, their rainbow-colored quilted nylon coats fluttering open to reveal their sparkling white uniforms. They called to their charges in pleasant, lilting voices.

"Charles." "Emmy." "Joanie." "Come here now. Now, I say."

They folded blankets, wiped plastic toys clean, tucked magazines into their plastic shopping bags. They smiled at Nancy and shook their head reprovingly because, as usual, she had arrived too late to expose Keren to the morning sunlight.

"We leave now," they sang out, almost in unison, as she paused. "Too cold. Too cold for the children. Too cold for us."

"Not so cold," Nancy replied, and they laughed appreciatively because throughout the summer months she had waved and called to them, "Too hot. Too hot for me. Too hot for the baby." Always she had waited for their answering chorus: "Not so hot."

It pleased them all that with the changing season this small rite was altered, but not forgotten. The continuity of the pleasant exchange, like other casual urban encounters, assuaged loneliness, negated anonymity. The Jamaican women returned to their tasks, moving swiftly because it was Friday and in all likelihood they had the weekend off. They rushed to claim their leisure. Nancy contemplated her own weekend. Dov would be on shift both Saturday and Sunday and she felt a guilty shiver of anticipation at the freedom his absence would grant her. She could finish her reading, perhaps even begin her paper if she claimed the sitting hours owed her by the play group.

Nancy waved and walked quickly past the swing set where, as always, a trio of pregnant women sat together, their hands clasped across their abdomens, their heads bent close. They spoke with the breathless intensity of women who anticipate each other's revelations, who acknowledge themselves to be linked by shared sensations, common experiences. Now and again they glanced toward their children who pumped themselves skyward on the swings.

"Not so high," one of them might shout, but the children never replied. They were cheerfully indifferent to mothers who were anchored so firmly by the weight of pregnancy. Still, the women called to them.

"Kevin." "Scott." "Lisa."

The air was musical with the sound of the children's names, reverberant with love and caring.

Nancy approached the four pretty young women who had played Scrabble throughout the summer and the early days of fall. They sat around their stone table now, pads and pencils clutched in their gloved hands, hunched over a game of Boggle. She wondered how they had discovered their common passion for word games. Perhaps they were childhood playmates or college friends. She felt a brief, irrational pang of envy.

She had grown up and gone to school in the Midwest and most of her girlhood friends and college classmates were scattered throughout the country. She kept up with them through the "Class Notes" column in her alumni magazine. "Keith has joined a firm in Omaha and we are having fun settling in." "Aren't we lucky that Don's residency is in Honolulu? Drop in anytime for a luau." They wrote of their children's births, of their volunteer activities, of the courses they were taking — computer literacy, French, gourmet cooking. Cheerfully, they harvested new skills and looked to the future; their optimism shielded them from transitory loneliness. This was, after all, just the beginning.

Nancy rushed past the fountain where, on summer days, dancing children arched through the sprays of water. Now leaves carpeted its concrete surface and toddlers rolled large bright red and blue balls down its graceful inclines. Nearby, a group of mothers played whiffle ball with their small children. They laughed as a chubby boy valiantly swung the yellow plastic bat and clapped excitedly when he hit the ball and scurried about the improvised bases.

It occurred to Nancy, not for the first time, that the park was an archipelago of small islands, each occupied by women with similar interests. She had made her own choice and she moved purposefully now to claim her seat on the bench beneath the dogwood tree at the edge of the sandbox. The three other benches that rimmed the small play area were already occupied and the three women who had been her silent companions for so many months glanced up and smiled pleasantly at her, although they did not speak. They had sat together on their separate benches through spring's new warmth, summer's blinding brightness, and autumn's golden-lit days, always aware of each other, yet avoiding conversation, although they smiled gently at the antics of their children and now and again exchanged knowing glances of shared amusement, shared pleasure. They mutely acknowledged that privacy was paramount to them. They were all women who had work to do and who took pleasure in that work.

They carried texts and pads in the woven bags they hung over the slat of their benches. They had not introduced themselves to each other, although they knew the names of the children and had, at various times, offered helpful assistance, extending Band-Aids and tissues, cans of apple juice. Occasionally there was a murmured comment on the beauty of the weather, the swift passing of the season. There was warmth in these brief exchanges and mutual approval. They cared about their children, they cared about their work. But never had they allowed the small crisis of a child's accident or argument to disturb their own controlled separateness.

Nancy, encountering the auburn-haired woman, Greg's mother, on the Fairway checkout line, had observed the parameters of playground etiquette and smiled without speaking. Glimpsing the diminutive blond woman, Sarah's mother, across the aisle at the Thalia, Nancy had only nodded.

"Who's that?" Dov had asked, and she noted then that the blond woman was very pretty. Her eyes were large and gray-blue in color and her features were delicate and perfectly proportioned. Sarah, her daughter, asleep on her lap in the theater, had inherited that fragile beauty, that skin, petal-soft and white. "Oh, a woman I see in the park," Nancy replied. Dov would not have understood the nuances of playground etiquette.

Carefully she set the brake on the stroller and opened her large woven bag. Her adolescent psychology text was entangled in Keren's yellow sweater; she released it, brushed it free of zwieback crumbs, and found her highlighter. If Keren slept for another half hour she could finish the chapter. If Dov had dinner at the hospital and if

Keren did not fuss but went to sleep right after her bath, she could even begin the next chapter and be caught up in time for Professor Aaronsohn's seminar. Nancy budgeted her time as other people budget their money, relegating minutes and hours to neatly imagined ledger columns, balancing each day's debits against a circumscribed credit line of scavenged freedom.

Still, she did not open her text at once, but glanced covertly at the other women and then at the group of toddlers who sat on their well-padded haunches and earnestly transferred the sand from their battered pails to their plastic dump trucks. The largest of the children, red-headed Greg, rose to fetch a stone from a corner of the sandbox. In his one-piece olive-green snowsuit, bought oversize at winter's onset to allow for the long season of growth, he careened clumsily across the uneven hillocks of sand, like a space traveler moving across the lunar terrain of a distant planet.

His mother and the other women watched him, aware of the possibility that the stone might be used as a weapon or tossed at one of the other children. They sat poised to intervene, but in the end Greg simply placed the stone atop the mound of sand and the other children, in admiration of his efforts, went off to seek out stones of their own. Relieved, the women turned from the children and once again became absorbed in their own work. They lifted the books they held on their laps, turned pages with gloved fingers, clumsily maneuvered their pens and pencils across the lined surfaces and white expanses of their open pads. Only Greg's mother, her auburn hair caping the black seaman's jacket over which she had draped a kelly-green mohair shawl, carried no book today. Instead she held a transistor radio on her lap, and although she courteously kept the volume low, they could hear the strains of Mahler's "Song of the Earth."

Intermittently, it had occurred to Nancy to introduce herself to the others. She, after all, had been the first to claim this particular island in the park, scorned by the nannies and the more sociable mothers because of the battered condition of the benches, the lack of swings and slides. The three other women had drifted in as though magnetically drawn to the communality of silence. When Greg had pushed Keren down and Keren wept inconsolably, though she was not really hurt, Nancy comforted her daughter and listened as Greg's mother spoke sternly but softly to her son. *"We do not push other children. We would not like other children to push us. We say we're sorry when we make someone cry.*" Nancy had thought of leaning forward to reassure her. She framed the words in her mind. "Keren overreacted. She's oversensitive, I think. By the way, my name is Nancy Yallon."

But Greg's mother had too swiftly turned back to the folio of sheet music she had with her that day and raised the volume of her radio. A Mozart octet. Nancy remained silent as the music drifted over the playing children, the reading mothers.

Once when the small blond woman fumbled in her bag for a pencil, Nancy had offered her own. The woman had shaken her head and wordlessly lifted her sketch pad to demonstrate her need for a drawing pencil, thick-pointed, velvet-textured. She found it at last and at once bent over the pad, working with broad, courageous strokes. Nancy had returned to her book, both relieved and disappointed.

She herself had rebuffed an overture from Anne, the very young woman who wore her sand-colored hair in a single thick plait. Nancy knew her name to be Anne because that was what the small boy, Eric, called her in his quivering voice.

"Anne, I need you. Anne, come here." Alone among the children who played so peaceably in the sandbox, Eric was a whiner, imperious in his misery, but Anne was patient with him, firm but strangely indifferent.

"Hey, can you figure this out?" Anne had asked Nancy one afternoon when only the two of them sat beside the sandbox. She extended the book. A Graduate Record Examination review book open to a complicated analog. But Nancy, who had to finish a source reading that afternoon because she had promised Dov she would type his grant proposal that night, had shaken her head without glancing at the book.

Looking at the three women now, as they shivered against the late November chill, she wondered for how much longer they would all brave the cold and take up these places beside the sandbox. And, of course, it was highly probable that when they stopped coming to the park, they might never see each other again. By next spring graduate programs and residencies might be completed, and they would move on. They would vanish, conversant with each other's habits, sensitive to each other's rituals, without knowing each other's names. How stupid, Nancy thought. I really should do something.

She opened her book and unsheathed her highlighter. The Mahler was finished and the announcer's silken voice invited them to listen to an all Bach program. Greg's shovel became wedged beneath the slats of the sandbox and his mother set the radio down on the bench and wrenched it free. A Bach quartet, majestic in its slowness and complexity began and then, quite suddenly, it stopped. Annoyed, the women glanced up and then leaned forward because the interrupted music was replaced by the announcer's voice, no longer mellifluous, but hoarse with anguish, blurred by terror and incredulity.

"This broadcast has been interrupted to bring a special announcement. A terrible announcement. Terrible." His voice trembled. He was no longer reading from a text.

Nancy closed her book. The blond woman's drawing pad slipped to the ground and she made no move to retrieve it. Anne bit the end of her braid. Greg's mother turned the volume up and they all leaned forward.

"The President of the United States, John Fitzgerald Kennedy, has been shot during a visit to Dallas, Texas. He is being rushed to the emergency room of Parkland Hospital and we await further bulletins. A doctor who spoke briefly to newsmen on the scene was not optimistic." Nancy's heart beat too rapidly. *Not optimistic.* She was a doctor's wife. She understood what that meant. She rose, released the brake on the stroller, and wheeled it back and forth as though the motion might cancel out the announcer's words.

They all stood now, clustered about the radio. They looked searchingly at each other as the announcer spattered them with details. Jacqueline Kennedy had not been hit by the assassin's bullets, although several shots had been heard. There had been a rumor that a bullet had hit Vice President Lyndon Johnson, but new reports denied that. It was Governor John Connally of Texas who had sustained injury.

"Oh, God," Anne said. "It's a nightmare."

"Let me find a news station," Greg's mother said. "What's an all-news station?" She turned the dial of her radio with nervous gestures as they struggled to remember the call letters of the nonmusic stations.

"WINS — give us twenty-two minutes and we'll give you the world," they all blurted out in chorus, and they laughed ruefully.

17

That laughter drew them together even as it faded into smiles of recognition.

"Mommy! Mommy!" The child's scream was shrill with terror and they all wheeled about to face the sandbox, stunned to have forgotten the children.

"Our reporter has just reached Parkland Hospital where Secret Service agents have cordoned off all entrances and exits. . . . " The announcer's voice trailed after them as they rushed to the children. It was Sarah who had called to them, Sarah whose hands were pressed to her face as blood streamed beneath her splayed fingers. "Mommy, Mommy," she screamed again.

"Jacqueline Kennedy is with her husband," the announcer continued, as they surrounded Sarah. "We are told that she has asked for a priest."

Sarah's mother gently removed her daughter's hands from her face and they saw, with relief, that the blood came from her nose. Nancy reached into her bag and passed her a wad of tissues. "Pack it gently into the nostrils," Anne said. "Very gently. And then apply just a little pressure. Here, let me." She knelt beside the child, who leaned against her mother as Anne worked. It surprised Nancy that Sarah offered no objection to the ministrations of a stranger, but then, of course, they were not strangers to each other.

"The doctors offer little hope. We know now that two bullets penetrated the President's skull." Anne discarded tissues saturated with blood and took up fresh ones as they heard for the first time about the motorcade, about the grassy knoll, about the storeroom of a book depository where the assassin had concealed himself.

"I didn't do anything," Greg shouted, above the announcer's voice. "Not me. She fell and hit her nose on my rock."

"I fell," Sarah screamed. "I fell and I'm bleeding."

"She fell and she's bleeding," Eric bleated, and he too began to weep.

Now Keren woke and sat up in her stroller.

"Mama?" As always when she awoke, she was bewildered, and Nancy hurried to her side before her bewilderment turned into fear.

Keren grew calm at once and Nancy felt a glow of pride at her own power, her maternal omnipotence. Oh, how wonderful it was to soothe and calm her frightened child.

"You're all right," Anne reassured Sarah. She dug into her large woven bag and distributed licorice sticks.

"Please stand by for further bulletins," the announcer intoned with a new intensity. He was no longer merely reporting the news. He was pleading with his listeners to share his grief and shock.

The women and children were shivering now, yet they huddled together, reluctant to leave. The sorrow that had swept across the country, the pain that had radiated from Dallas, was national, communal. It could not be borne alone.

"Come to my house," Greg's mother said suddenly, almost pleadingly. They looked at each other, they looked at her, and they each nodded. "Sure," Nancy said for all of them. "Of course, we'll come. Thank you."

"I live just up the street." She took Greg's hand and piled his sand toys into a large plastic bag. They followed her, leaving the park in solemn procession. An elderly sweeper nodded to them as they passed. "A terrible thing," he said and they saw that he was crying.

Traffic moved slowly on Central Park West, as though the drivers of Manhattan had organized themselves into a spontaneous, evenly paced cortege. Two elegant women in long mink coats passed them, both dabbing at their eyes with linen handkerchiefs. All along the way women wept; the faces of men were sorrowful and schoolchildren walked hurriedly, looking over their shoulders as though fearful that death and danger trailed them.

"Merle," the auburn-haired woman said, as they waited on a corner for the light to change. "My name is Merle Cunningham."

"I'm Nancy Yallon."

"Anne Richardson."

"I am called Rutti. Rutti Weisenblatt."

They offered their names shyly, like small girls at a party, and then assessed each other as though to determine, after all these months of silent watching, whether the name fit the face. Rutti Weisenblatt had a distinct accent; German or Viennese, Nancy guessed. Perhaps, like Dov, she practiced the English she used in public, carefully repeating words and phrases.

Merle's home was a newly renovated brownstone on a pleasant street just off the park. It was a narrow house, its ocher facade recently sandblasted, the rich brown trim of the arched windows freshly painted. A chinaberry hedge surrounded it, protecting it from the street, offering a semblance of privacy on the urban street.

Merle fished for her key, but before she could find it the door was opened by a tall black woman who wore a gray uniform.

"Oh, Merle, isn't it awful? Isn't it terrible? Poor Jackie, poor Caroline. And that little boy. They sent for a priest." She had been crying and her voice was thick with sorrow.

"Yes, Lottie. Awful. Terrible. Can you help my friends with their things? And take Greg and the children into the playroom. They'll want some apple juice, I think. And when you have a chance we'll have some coffee and cake. In the den. Yes, of course. In the den." Her voice was musical and her instructions, so vaguely offered, were, in fact, quite explicit. And Lottie, sniffling still, complied, expertly relieving them of their coats and jackets, finding room in the vestibule for Keren's stroller, leading the children down the hall to the play-room, and then disappearing into the kitchen.

Merle's house was scented with wealth. The thickly carpeted hallway was fragrant with a subtle commingling of lemon oil and fresh flowers, of a wood fire and scented sachets. In the den a fire did blaze in the brick-fronted fireplace and a copper bowl, set on a low rosewood table, was filled with yellow rosebuds. Nancy, who treated herself to a single rose each Friday, calculated the cost of the flowers to equal a week's grocery money for herself, Dov, and Keren. Immediately, she was ashamed. She did not want to become the kind of woman who assessed and envied the wealth of others. After all, she too had grown up in a household where out-of-season flowers filled bowls bought in distant lands. Their current situation was temporary. Her parents would be glad to supplement Dov's meager resident's salary but she, greedy for experience, would not forgo the requisite graduate student poverty, the camaraderie of potluck suppers and baby-sitting pools, the cheerful trading of children's clothing and secondhand furniture.

Anne and Rutti sat on the tweed sofa that faced the fire, Nancy settled herself, cross-legged, on the white fur rug, and Merle retreated into the canyon of a huge black leather chair. She pressed a button on the armrest and a television set slid silently out of a bookcase. Another press of her finger and the picture flashed on the screen. The facade of Parkland Hospital in Dallas appeared; a jowly, gray-haired man in a pin-striped suit stood before it, speaking to reporters.

"The President's vital signs are not encouraging," he said in the gravelly accent of the region. "Neurosurgeons have been summoned and are already with him in the operating room."

"Doctors say that the President's vital signs are not encouraging. Neurosurgeons have been summoned," a newscaster repeated.

"Oh God, are they going to parrot everything?" Merle asked. She turned down the volume and they watched the cluster of reporters confer with each other, take notes, weep.

"Neat set," Anne said. "What else can it do besides escape from walls? Is it toilet-trained?"

They all laughed and then looked at each other guiltily.

"My husband Andrew's idea," Merle replied. "He thought of it himself and drew up the design, worked with an electrician to get it right. Now he has it patented. All over America television sets are going to come slithering out of bookshelves and breakfronts."

"Is he an inventor?" Nancy asked.

"No. He just has an eye for that sort of thing," Merle said. She shifted uncomfortably and turned the volume up once again.

The hospital spokesman had reappeared on the screen. His voice was hoarse, his face ashen. "An oxygen tube has been inserted in the President's throat. He received infusions of whole blood." He read from the paper in his hands. He did not look up.

"But will he live, Doctor? Will he live?" The reporter's tone was insistent and the spokesman looked up and turned to him with the look of a teacher pondering the face of a student who cannot, who will not, learn.

"No," he said quietly. His voice cracked. "President John Fitzgerald Kennedy is dead. He died five minutes ago at one thirty-three Dallas time."

"Ach, *Gott. Gott.*" The cry came from Rutti. Tears turned her eyes the color of blue crystal, but she was a woman who cried without changing facial expression, without uttering a sob. Nancy wondered how and where she had learned to discipline her sorrow, to control her grief.

They all wept now, Merle curled up in her chair like a frightened child, her head buried in her arms; tall Anne with her snoulders heaving, her face contorted; Nancy with her arms pressed against her eyes, a gesture taught to her by her mother who was always embarrassed by tears. Keren rushed into the room just then and hurled herself at her mother.

"Stop, Mommy," the child said angrily. "I don't want Mommy to cry. Mommies don't cry."

"Come, I'll take you back to the other children." Lottie, her own face streaked with tears, set down a tray laden with mugs, a platter of golden-brown croissants, and a ceramic pot of jam. And Keren, who shied away from strangers, who screamed at the arrival of a baby-sitter, allowed the tall black woman to take her hand and lead her back to the playroom.

The women busied themselves with the coffee then, each of them lacing it with cream and sugar, although later Nancy observed that Rutti and Anne drank their coffee black and that Anne never used sugar. That afternoon they needed the comfort of sweetness. They lathered the croissants with butter and painted them with jam and they ate and drank with the strange greed of mourners at a postfuneral repast. Death haunted them but *they* were alive, *they* could taste the tartness of raspberry jam, the creamy freshness of the butter. Appetite affirmed their lives.

Always, Nancy thought, when she remembered this day — and she had no doubt that she would remember this day, that she would never forget the strains of the interrupted Bach, of the announcer's shocked and somber voice — she would think of eating croissants in front of a fire in a room she had never seen before in the company of women whose names had been revealed to her only because the President — their President — had died.

The phone rang. Merle answered it and spoke in a muffled voice.

"I know. It's terrible. Terrible. I can't believe it. Oh, Andrew, come home. Come home soon." Her voice took on the tone of a frightened child pleading with her father to hurry to comfort her. Nancy caught Anne's eye and they both looked away as though a shared thought might betray and embarrass them.

Slowly, they regained their composure. Nancy wiped her eyes. Small blond Rutti stood and tucked her white blouse into her navy blue skirt. A cotton skirt, Nancy noticed. Why was she wearing cotton in winter? It occurred to her now that Rutti had worn either that skirt or a black and red wraparound of Indian weave throughout the summer and for much of the autumn and encroaching winter. Rutti was poor then, really poor, as opposed to the genteel graduate student poverty in which she and Dov indulged.

Anne reached into her bag and took out a compact. She studied her face and carefully worked pressed powder onto her beautifully high cheekbones. She traced her eyes with a pale gray eyeliner, but she applied no lipstick. Her long fair hair was plaited into a single braid, which she smoothed now with one rapid stroke. Merle, too, after she hung up, ran a comb through her auburn hair. They were restoring themselves, reconstructing their costumes and masks.

"Andrew said that he heard a news report on the radio. A reporter said that the President's head exploded. Exploded in blood." Merle shivered.

They sat in horror, the image fixed in their minds, all of them remembering how Sarah's blood had spurted through her fingers, had been absorbed so quickly by the sand.

"I saw him once," Nancy said suddenly. "I was standing on Broadway and his motorcade passed. He was sitting on the top of the seat, or maybe he was standing, and I thought that he looked straight at me. And he waved. God, he was a beautiful man. His hair was copper-colored. He seemed so young, so radiant." She fell silent, remembering that she had been in her ninth month then — Keren had been born two weeks later. She had been heavyhearted that afternoon — a residual depression, Aaronsohn would call it — because of a quarrel with Dov. He had not wanted her to take her last exam, had argued that the trip up to Columbia would be too arduous for her.

"Why are you being so stubborn?" he asked. "Is your degree more important than the baby? Do you know what stress in the ninth month can do to a baby?"

"And do you know what stress in the ninth month can do to a mother?" she retorted. "Or doesn't that matter to you? Am I just an incubator, a baby-making machine?" Her own words shocked her. With their utterance she passed a new border; she articulated the resentment that had been growing since her pregnancy. Dov revealed his priorities, and in challenging him, she threatened the fragile foundation of their marriage, the code of reasonableness and civility on which they prided themselves. Still, she plunged on. "I want to take that exam because I took that course and I want those credits."

She harvested her graduate credits like a miserly farmer who preserves precious seed against a splendid planting season not yet arrived. She took one course, two courses a semester because she and Dov had agreed that she would study full-time for her doctorate when he completed his residency. The part-time courses, the solitary seminars represented her insurance policy, her hold on her own talent and her future.

She took the exam, and in defiance, she walked down Broadway afterward, sailing bravely on, the great protuberance of her pregnancy thrust forth. She smiled at the undergraduates who darted fearfully out of her way. She stood on a corner and saw John Fitzgerald Kennedy, aglow with youth and promise, and he waved and smiled.

She and Dov made up, of course. She cooked chicken in wine for dinner and set the table with a white cloth and lit the Dansk candles she had long been saving. Dov brought her a bouquet of roses and he held her hand when she told him about seeing the President.

Merle, who had closed her eyes as Nancy spoke, as though envisioning John Kennedy perched atop the seat of the moving vehicle, uncoiled herself from her seat and stood before the fire, her arms outstretched.

"We were married the Saturday night after his inauguration," she said. "I had a pillbox hat just like Jackie's made for my going-away suit. Pale blue," she added wistfully. "Andrew likes me in pastels." She plucked absently at the sleeve of her black turtleneck sweater, pulled it lower over her black slacks, and Nancy wondered if Merle changed before Andrew arrived home.

"I was in a room with him once," Anne volunteered. "It was a Peace Corps party or reception sort of thing. We were a special group — the first volunteers to graduate from a training program in Puerto Rico — and Sargent Shriver gave this do for us in Washington. The President came — oh, just for a few minutes, but I shook hands with him." She shivered and smiled, as though recalling the warm touch of his hand, the radiant encouragement of his smile.

They each had a memory of the fallen President, *their* President, and they exchanged them as they sat before the fire. Like new mourners, their voices were muted, their energies depleted. Rutti told them that she had become an American citizen three months before the 1960 election. She had cast her first ballot for John Kennedy. Nancy recited a fragment of his inauguration speech. She had sat before the television screen watching and listening, with Keren at her breast. "The torch has been passed to a new generation," the new President said, and she felt herself to be part of that generation, forever linked to the energetic man with the ready smile whose words filled her with hope.

It grew late. Through the arched windows they watched the long shadows of the early darkness of winter begin their shadowy descent. Merle lit one lamp, then another. The young women looked at each other and glanced at their watches. They had things to do, but they were reluctant to leave. Lottie appeared with another carafe of coffee and they refilled their cups. They spoke of the senior Kennedys, of Jackie, of Caroline and three-year-old John John. How would the children be told? Who would tell them? Nancy imagined Dov dead, she having to break the news to Keren. *Daddy won't be coming home any more. Daddy went bye-bye. Forever.* She was startled that she should have such a thought, such an unnatural, irrational projection.

And then, impelled to intimacy by the afternoon's events, by the encroaching darkness, by their recognition of each other during the long months of their carefully observed silence, they talked about themselves.

Rutti told them that she was from Vienna, that she did not live with Sarah's father. She did not say whether or not she was divorced, and they did not ask her. They would learn everything in time. She worked at odd hours in the university's social science research division, earning enough to support Sarah and herself, enough to pay part of her tuition at the Art Students League. A scholarship covered the rest. She offered the economic details of her existence without embarrassment.

"It is difficult," she said. "But it is not impossible. And surely, it will get better." She spoke with the calm optimism of one who has already endured the worst.

"Who stays with Sarah when you work?" Merle asked.

"I take her with me. No one minds. I bring her toys, a sleeping bag."

Anne was not Eric's mother but his baby-sitter. She was living with his family while she studied for her medical boards. Not an optimum arrangement, but the only one she could manage on her return from her two-year stint in the Peace Corps in Nigeria.

"They're great people," she said quickly, as though she had in some way maligned them. "Hope and Ted. They have this small advertising agency. And they're always looking for new artists," she told Rutti. "You'll have to meet them. They're really interested in new talent."

Her offer was spontaneous and generous. They were at the threshold of friendship, eager to help each other, already anticipating intimacy, reciprocity.

Nancy turned to Anne.

"My husband's a resident. We have a lot of the manuals and stuff he used for his boards. You might want to look at them."

"Sure." Anne's acceptance was automatic.

It was established, then, that they would continue meeting, that they wanted to know each other. They stood, fumbled uneasily with their bags, collected their belongings.

"Listen," Merle said. "Come over on Monday. All of you. With the kids. Lottie will do something about lunch. OK?"

They all nodded. They took out their notebooks and exchanged addresses and phone numbers. They spoke and wrote swiftly, exhilarated yet shy in this awkward, sweet beginning of friendship. The children hurtled down the hall toward them, and they bundled them once again into snowsuits and waved as they parted, going their separate ways through the wintry darkness.

2

THE WEEKEND passed slowly. Events in Dallas dominated the news and they watched television obsessively. By Sunday night Jacqueline Kennedy's blood-stained pink suit was engraven in their memories and they closed their eyes against the image of Lee Harvey Oswald, so oddly collegiate in his crewneck sweater, slumping to the ground as Jack Ruby, portly and sweating in business suit and fedora, shot him in front of a nation of viewers.

History assaulted them, disrupting their routine, invading their consciousness. They were irritable with the children and shouted at them and then, remembering brave, widowed Jackie, they were ashamed. Nancy held Keren on her lap and watched as the even-featured Kennedy brothers and sisters and cousins filed so sadly in and out of the White House.

"Was that Eunice?" Dov asked, staring at the screen.

"No, that was Jean," Nancy replied. Like the rest of the nation, they were on first-name terms with the mourners, linked to their grief.

Rutti went to work, but there was little to do. She sat at the reception desk and assured sad-eyed students and research assistants that indeed, this was a terrible time. Her accent endowed her with an odd authority. It reminded them that she had endured and survived other terrible times, perhaps worse times. No. Not worse. They shared a youthful certainty that there had never been a national loss like theirs, a grief as profound as their own.

Anne and her employers, Hope and Ted, grew quietly drunk Saturday night and fell asleep in front of the television set. They did not waken until Eric pulled at them on Sunday morning and they began to drink again when Jack Ruby killed Oswald. But they did not get drunk. Hope and Ted had a conference the next day that they had not canceled because they could not afford to jeopardize the account.

"He's a Republican," Hope said. "He wouldn't understand." She was a tall thin woman who had come to New York from Kentucky and was determined never again to go farther south than New Jersey. She and short, stocky Ted, whom she had met on the McCann Ericson trainee program, ran their fledgling agency out of one sparsely furnished room at a very good address on Madison Avenue. They met their clients at expensive restaurants, charging the meals to accounts that they juggled with wondrous dexterity.

Their cash flow problems did not faze them. They joked that they placed all their bills in a hat and plucked out one or two for payment. "If creditors get too snotty, I warn them that I won't even put their bills in the hat," Ted joked.

Anne admired them for their courage and optimism. There were weeks when they could not pay her small salary, but she never pressed them.

Merle and Andrew took Greg to the Cloisters where solemn-faced adults wandered the dimly lit corridors staring at catafalques and death vestments while children chased each other across the cold stone floors.

Dov reported that the emergency room was not crowded with the usual weekend victims of domestic anger, street stabbings, and accidents. It appeared that events in Dallas had exhausted all impulse for violence. But there was an increase of intake for Psychiatry. Police officers led in a beautiful girl who had perched on a window ledge at a Barnard dormitory weeping and pleading piteously, "Jack, don't die. Jack, don't leave me."

Dov had admitted the girl and sent her up to the psychiatric ward for observation. "A gorgeous girl," he told Nancy and listened distractedly as she told him of her meeting with the three women in the park, about Merle's invitation to lunch. "Good," he said, "good."

It worried him that Nancy was so often alone. He knew that she did not relate to the wives of his colleagues, who invited them for dinner and whom they dutifully invited back. Each young wife carried a covered dish and gaily offered recipes for meatless lasagna or grain-stretched veal loaf. Their poverty was clever and chic and, besides, it was temporary. Their husbands were doctors and prosperity stretched before them. Nancy recorded their recipes and passed them on to Glynnis and Ingrid who lived on their floor and with whom she exchanged baby-sitting hours and discussed the price of Beechnut Baby Foods at the Fairway Market. But she avoided all the women in the park and seldom joined them for coffee in the late afternoon. He was pleased that she had, at last, made contact with women whom she liked.

He turned the pages of the newspaper. The medical details of the President's death interested him. He had served in the army medical corps during the Sinai campaign and had watched a field surgeon operate on a corporal who had sustained skull wounds similar to those that crazy son of a bitch Oswald had inflicted on Kennedy. That poor bastard of a corporal had lived. A vegetable case. Dov had seen him once at the Veterans Hospital in Acco. The young American President had been luckier.

Keren went to sleep without a fuss and Nancy read her text and source material late into the night. She would, after all, be prepared for Aaronsohn's seminar.

On Monday morning Nancy, once again wheeling Keren in her stroller, met Rutti on Merle's corner. Rutti held Sarah's hand and a white bakery box perched atop her overflowing tote bag.

"I should have remembered to bring something," Nancy said, apologetically.

"It is not important." Rutti did not add that she herself was so often a guest in other people's homes, that she lived so much of her life dependent on the hospitality of others, that these small gestures had become second nature to her. Small gifts were important, she knew. Each December she sent a set of tea towels to the elderly couple who had served as her foster parents in Surrey, her first placement after leaving the children's transport that had carried her from Austria to England. And no matter what her circumstances, she sent an art book each Rosh Hashanah to Chana and Dror who had been her kibbutz parents on Beit Yair when Youth Aliyah had transferred her to Israel. Such offerings balanced her indebtedness to those who had been kind to her.

"No, it was really thoughtful of you," Nancy insisted. She smiled down at Sarah. "Hi, Sarah. Keren, say hello to Sarah."

Keren's blue-mittened hand slipped free of the stroller bar and reached out to touch Sarah, but the small blond girl pulled away. She smiled shyly and trudged on, her head lowered.

"She's a good little walker," Nancy said. "Keren should be walking more. She's really too big for the stroller. But she gets so tired."

"Oh well, Sarah is used to walking," Rutti said, yet again diminishing and disparaging the compliment. "We walk all over, Sarah and I. She goes everywhere with me — to work, to the park, to my classes."

"There's no one you could leave her with?" Nancy asked. "No friends, no family?"

"Family?" Rutti repeated the word slowly, as though it was so foreign to her existence as to be incomprehensible. "I have no family. No one. They were all killed in the war. When I was a child." She spoke very softly, her voice untinged by self-consciousness or self-pity.

"Yes. Of course. I should have realized." Nancy was flustered, apologetic.

"But how could you have realized something like that?" Rutti asked reasonably. The innocence and ignorance of Americans no longer surprised her. Americans lived at a remove from war and suffering. Their soldiers fought in distant lands and their own country was unscarred by battlefields, their cities untouched by war. The landscape of suffering and survival was foreign to them. Nancy Yallon had studied in a history text the war that had orphaned Rutti Weisenblatt. Perhaps she had watched the desert battles that had seared Rutti's adolescence, re-created on filmstrips in her suburban Hebrew school. But Rutti did not expect her to relate to her experiences. She had abandoned all such expectations.

"I should have realized because I am Jewish and because I am married to an Israeli," Nancy persisted.

Rutti did not reply, but Keren now reached forward and plucked at Sarah's sleeve. The two small girls quite suddenly began to talk to each other in high, sweet voices that caused their mothers to smile.

They had reached Merle's house. Rutti lifted Sarah so that she could ring the doorbell. The musical chimes sounded and Lottie opened the door. She took their coats, relieved Rutti of the cake box (Nancy hoped she would remember to tell Merle that Rutti had brought the cake), and led them into the den. Merle and Anne, already intently staring at the television screen, smiled at them. Greg and Eric sprawled on the floor and sorted Lego pieces into three piles according to color, announcing each decision as they worked.

"Red."

"Blue."

"Yellow."

The small boys' voices rose and fell in light counterpoint to the subdued music and grief-hushed voices that emanated from the television set. Anne and Merle resumed the positions abandoned on Friday afternoon, Merle curled up in the black armchair, her hair a bright soft aureole against the headrest, Anne seated cross-legged on the white carpet, curling the end of her long fair braid about her fingers. Merle motioned Rutti and Nancy to the low tweed couch in front of the fireplace where a newly laid fire was just beginning to blaze. The tiny tongues of flame licked at the kindling, teasing the bark of the sweet-smelling cedar logs.

"Hi — it's just beginning," Merle said.

"Eric, Greg — let Keren and Sarah play with some Legos." Anne did not shift her gaze from the screen.

The children, as though sensing the solemnity of the hour, arranged themselves in a semicircle and, as the muffled drums sounded and the caisson, on which the young President's flag-covered casket rested, pulled by six gray-white horses, moved across the screen, they continued their playful chorus.

"Red. Blue. Yellow."

Greg briefly turned his attention to the television picture.

"Mommy," he said plaintively, "no one is riding those three horses. Why isn't anyone riding them?"

"I don't know, Greg," Merle replied softly. "You'll have to ask Daddy."

Her answer satisfied him and he returned to the game. It was, Nancy suspected, an answer Merle often offered her son, deferring automatically to Andrew Cunningham's knowledge, his authority.

31

The military band played the Chopin Funeral March and, as the last sound of the slow trumpets faded, the cortege halted in front of the White House, where the Kennedy family and the international dignitaries left their limousines and began their walk to Saint Matthew's Cathedral. The Requiem Mass, the newscaster informed them, would not be televised.

Merle lowered the volume and they sat in silence as the camera roved across the faces in the crowd and focused on the world leaders. Charles de Gaulle walked beside the tall and somber Prince Philip. Stately Frederika, Queen of Greece, lifted her mourning veil briefly. Olof Palme of Sweden spoke confidingly to Golda Meir of Israel.

"God, what a horrendous weekend," Merle said.

"The worst," Nancy agreed and they all nodded.

"Crazy. Insane, both of them. Ruby and Oswald," Anne said. "Crazy killers."

"Ah, but one does not have to be insane to kill." Rutti protested. "There were men who spent the entire day killing and, when their work was done, they washed their hands, combed their hair, and went home to their families. Perhaps this Oswald thought that he could kill the President and then wash his hands, and go home to kiss his wife, his children."

"I think I know what you're talking about, Rutti," Nancy said. "You're talking about the war and however evil the war was, and the camps, it was organized evil. Those killers were part of an army, operating within a system. A horrifying system but still a system. These men — Oswald, Ruby, they're individuals acting out their own distorted impulses. I think Anne is right. I think they were — are — psychotic, pathological. They have homicidal tendencies that they couldn't control — a superego deficit." She blushed, embarrassed to have used such facile professional clichés.

"Ah, the voice of the psych major is heard in the land," Anne said. "Did I guess right, Nancy?"

"Yes. I'm a graduate student. A very part-time graduate student. One seminar this semester. I want to go back full-time when Dov — my husband — finishes his residency. We can make different child-care arrangements then." Her voice trailed off apologetically. She did not want these new friends to know that often she lay awake and wondered if she would, in fact, ever complete her graduate work.

She loved Keren, adored her, never felt as happy as when she bathed her daughter and lifted her, damp and fragrant, into her arms, but her pregnancy had been unplanned. Dov spoke often of the importance of women having children when they were young, of the wisdom of raising children who were closely spaced. Keren was three. He had looked searchingly at Nancy the night they celebrated her birthday with festive cupcakes. He made love to her that night with urgency, with persuasive tenderness. She was relieved when her menstrual flow began the following month, although it was two weeks late.

She wanted another child, but she also wanted to complete her degree. Of course, she could complete her graduate work in Israel, where they planned to settle eventually, but the language barrier frightened her. Her Hebrew, acquired in afternoon Hebrew schools and Zionist camps, was rudimentary and Dov, despite his promises, did not have time to teach her. A layer of dust covered the Linguaphone records she had bought and she could not find her Hebrew grammar and workbook. They were somewhere in the cartons they had brought from Cleveland, which they had still not unpacked. They had so little shelf space, Dov pointed out. She did not remind him that they had managed to find room for his texts.

"That's terrific — if you can do it," Anne said. "I couldn't. I know that. I'm going to put all that — marriage, kids — on hold until I finish medical school. Otherwise I know I'd never make it — I'd fall right into the trap."

"What trap?" Merle asked.

"The domestic trap. I've seen it happen with my friends. It sounds great. They get married and they agree that they'll be considerate of each other, respect each other's turf. Study, work — whatever. And then the first kid comes and the second. The man can't give up his job so the woman gets stuck. For a while. Until they can afford help or the kids are old enough so that she can do her own thing. But just for now her thing is taking care of the kids and the house and taking his suit to the cleaners and making sure the prescriptions are filled and the rest of that crap. And probably, by the time she's ready to pick up her life she's too tired or she's burned out. I mean, studying is a skill like anything else and the truth is that if you don't use it you lose it. Oh, I don't mean everyone —" She grinned at

Nancy, as though to exempt her from the grim scenario. "I mean, some people are really disciplined. I bet you are, Nancy. I mean I don't really know you but I watched you reading and taking notes in the park. . . ." She blushed, as though she had confessed to an embarrassing, clandestine act and suddenly they all laughed and their own similar confessions bubbled forth in a rush of frankness and giggles.

"I watched you work, Anne — always with those GRE books," Rutti said.

"I walked behind you once, just to see your sketch pad," Merle told Rutti. "It was a picture of the kids in the sandbox, the four of them caught in a shadow, I remember. Peacefully playing."

"Well, it's better than catching them fighting and crying," Nancy observed wryly and they all laughed.

But their laughter was brief. The mass was over and the casket was carried out of the cathedral by six servicemen. Richard Cardinal Cushing, stately in his red hat and gown, his lace surplice shining white in the pale sunlight, blessed it as the widow and her son and daughter watched. Jacqueline Kennedy had lifted her veil and the four women leaned toward the television screen, the better to see her, as though they might discern the secret of her composure, decipher the code of her dignity, by studying her pale and lovely face.

"How old is she?" Anne asked.

"Her thirties, I think," Nancy hazarded.

They watched as Jacqueline Kennedy leaned forward and whispered to her son who, like his sister, wore a pale blue dress coat. And the small boy, whose third birthday fell on the day of his father's funeral, whose birthdays would always be remembered as death-days, lifted his hand in salute and remained standing erect, his hand at his brow, as his father's casket passed. The women in the room wept. Merle's sob was audible and Lottie, who had slipped in soundlessly, went to her and encircled her in a protective embrace.

They did not move from the set until taps were played and the flag that had covered the casket was folded and given to the President's widow. They watched as, hand in hand, Jacqueline and Robert Kennedy left the cemetery. Their own hands were linked and Lottie, who stood in the doorway, lifted her voice in mournful song.

"Day is done," she sang, her rich contralto filling the room.

"Gone the sun," Merle and Anne joined in.

"From the lakes, from the hills, from the sky," Nancy too sang and Rutti hummed along.

"All is well. Safely rest."

They were all standing now, their arms about each other's waists, their faces tear-streaked. All was not well nor would all ever be well again. They wept for the widow who was of their generation, for the small boy whose birthday would always be threaded with sorrow; they wept because the bright-haired President whom they had always thought of as their own was dead.

And as they stood there, the children hurtled into the room. It was Greg who organized them so that they stood in line — Greg and Keren, Eric and Sarah, holding hands in imitation of their weeping mothers and singing too until all at once they began to giggle. And then Lottie shooed the children into the kitchen for lunch and Merle switched the television set off and pressed yet another button. A bar slid out of the breakfront and she opened a bottle of white wine, filling four glasses and passing them to her guests. Her own she lifted high.

"To Jacqueline Kennedy," she said.

"To Jacqueline," they repeated and sipped the wine, welcoming its sweet fruity flavor, its reminder of gentler seasons.

They sat together then in front of the fire and held the wine glasses by their slender stems. The firelight danced in golden shafts against the delicate crystal. Rutti, who owned a single goblet that she had bought at a rummage sale because it had cost only a dollar and because it reminded her of the glasses on her mother's Sabbath table in Vienna, passed her tongue across the thin crystal lip of the Orrefors goblet.

"Poor Jackie," Nancy said. "I feel so sorry for her."

"Why?" Anne asked harshly, impatiently. "It's sad, of course. Terrible. But she's alive. She'll survive. She'll have a good life. It's John whom they buried today. Not his wife."

"But she's all alone," Merle said.

"She has family, friends, money. She's beautiful. She's talented. She will manage without him. Women can live their lives without men. She'll go it alone — the way I do — the way Rutti does. Jackie doesn't need a man to define her. She'll define herself." Anne rose and refilled her glass. "Right, Rutti?"

The small blond woman shrugged.

"It is not easy to be alone. To be a mother alone. For me, there was no choice. We parted, Sarah's father and myself. We had no choice. We could not live together. We do not blame each other. We accept our separation because we have had to accept so much. It is history we blame. For what it did to him. For what it did to me." Her cheeks were flushed and she felt strangely light-headed. She was unused to drinking wine at midday and she had eaten very little for breakfast. Words she had never spoken before poured out with unfamiliar fluency. But it was all right. These were confidences one could share with friends and these three women had newly become her friends, the first friends she had made in New York. She smiled at the thought and was suffused with a new optimism.

Nancy turned to her, took Rutti's hand in her own, smiled. Nancy who was a Jew, who was married to an Israeli. Oh, they would have so much to say to each other. The anticipation of intimacy excited her. She had been so long alone.

"Still, you do manage alone," Anne persisted. "You even manage with a kid. We're moving toward new times. We don't have to be devastated by the loss of a man — not if we lay claim to our own lives. Not if we have a sense of ourselves. I think that's what we sense about Jackie Kennedy — that she has a sense of herself."

"Ah," said Merle, curled up again in the black leather chair, stirring the dregs of her wine with her finger and licking it like a wistful child, "the President's widow as a symbol of liberated womanhood. Self defined. Unlike yours truly. Who am I, after all — Andrew Cunningham's wife, Greg Cunningham's mother?" She shrugged and moved to refill her glass.

"Oh, come on, Merle, you're more than that," Nancy said. She was wary of the new tenor of their conversation. They were talking too quickly, revealing too much.

"Oh yes. I am also John Loring's daughter." Merle stood up on the chair, her long pale toes curled about the leather seat, and bowed from the waist. "Here I am, my new friends — my good friends — one woman defined by her relationship to three men — Merle Loring Cunningham." Rutti, Nancy, and Anne looked warily at each other but almost at once Merle sprinted from the chair onto the white rug and smiled brightly at them.

"Come on," she said, her voice reclaiming its usual enervated softness. "It's been a very long morning. Let's have some lunch."

Gratefully, they allowed her to manipulate the mood. It was her house and they played by her rules. They followed her into the dining room where a poached salmon dominated the elegantly set table, and an endive and radish salad filled a teakwood bowl. They ate ravenously as though to fill the emptiness caused by their grief. They passed each other slices of bread from the warm whole-wheat loaf that Merle carved with fine precision and they spoke as they ate, pouring words into the void of their sorrow. They wondered where Jackie Kennedy would live with her children. They wondered if Robert Kennedy would, one day, run for President. They wondered if Lee Harvey Oswald's widow, Marina, would go back to Russia. They spoke of the new Pop art show at the Guggenheim and of *The Feminine Mystique,* which had been published only a few months before.

They ate the cake that Rutti had brought and for which Merle thanked her and they drank the fragrant coffee poured from a white pitcher patterned with rosebuds. But today Rutti and Merle drank their coffee black and Anne declined sugar.

They were startled when the giggling children dashed into the room, the girls scrambling onto their mothers' laps, the boys chasing each other about the table.

"Sarah is older than Keren," Rutti's daughter said proudly.

"And always will be," Nancy agreed and they all laughed. The children clapped their hands and repeated "And always will be" amid peals of laughter, pleased to have been initiated into adult merriment.

It was time to go, but before they left they agreed that they would go together to the Guggenheim later in the week. Anne arranged to stop at Nancy's apartment to look over texts Dov might lend to her. Merle stood in the doorway holding Greg's hand and the others waved as they left. They parted with the comfortable casualness of longtime friends whose established intimacy requires no extended leave-taking, no superficial, affectionate embrace.

3

Aᴘᴜɴɪꜱʜɪɴɢ cold front from Canada descended upon the city. Wet snows fell through the nights, and mornings found the streets transformed. Adults wrapped scarves about their faces and children wore face masks. Layers of clothing, coats piled over sweaters, leg warmers concealed beneath skirts and pants, made thin men and women appear ungainly. Pedestrians drifted through the city streets like participants in a costume party.

Nancy, hurrying home from the Fairway Market, her arms laden with overflowing grocery bags, stood on a corner beside a woman whose face was lost in an upturned collar. It was only when the light changed that she recognized the bright green mohair shawl and swirl of copper-colored hair that trailed out of the black beret; it was Merle. She could not call to her because her own mouth was covered by her red wool scarf. Besides, she would see Merle the next day when they would all meet for lunch.

The park was abandoned. The empty swings slammed against one another, propelled by the fierce wind that roared through the barren branches of the trees. Merle and Nancy, Rutti and Anne met by prearrangement, gathering at the Museum of Natural History or the Guggenheim, in Merle's home or in Nancy's cluttered apartment. They arrived breathless, their hands frozen to numbness despite their thick gloves, their faces roughened and red. They smiled gratefully at each other as they knelt to unzip the children's quilted jackets, to help them change from boots to sneakers. They giggled at the children's knock knock jokes and shrugged their shoulders good-naturedly. They reveled in the newness of their friendship. It was uncluttered by shared memories, unscarred by past hurts or failed expectations. Strangers in each other's worlds, they were neither hampered by competitiveness nor restrained by a web of connections. The name of a friend or colleague, mentioned by one, was unfamiliar to the others and this vested them with freedom. They could tell each other anything — *anything*.

They became familiar with one another's schedules. They knew that Nancy's seminar on the psychological development of the adolescent met on Monday evenings and that often she reserved Monday afternoon to reread her notes or complete an assignment. Merle was at Juilliard on Wednesdays for a violin lesson. On Tuesdays and Thursdays Anne took Eric to a preschool program at the Y. Rutti eagerly filled in for absentee workers at her office and they might not see her for much of the week. She needed the money, she told them without embarrassment. Her art supplies were expensive and she received very little child support from Werner, Sarah's father.

Occasionally, then, during the week, only two or three of them would meet, but they all reserved Friday afternoons. Like quilting women, they bent their heads together and spoke softly, intent on putting together the patchwork of one another's lives. They were all skilled storytellers, all swift to recognize absurdity, to revel in each other's humor.

"If you could sleep with anyone in the world, who would it be?" Anne asked mischievously one afternoon.

"You first," Merle said.

"Robert Kennedy. Michael de Bakey and Richard Burton," Anne replied lazily.

"In that order?" Nancy asked. Stretched out on the floor, her arms folded beneath her head, she did her biking exercises, pumping vigorously.

"What are you doing?" Anne asked.

"Getting in shape so I can steal Burton from you," Nancy replied and they collapsed in laughter as Merle tossed a pillow at them.

The children's malapropisms triggered their merriment. On an afternoon when they had all complained about the "freezing" cold, Keren announced that she was "freezing" hungry. It became their code.

"I'm freezing bored," Merle whispered to Nancy as they sat side by side at an afternoon screening of *The Cardinal* and they giggled so loudly that the other patrons hushed them.

"Guess who I am," Rutti commanded, and then set her face in a toothy grimace. "Zis is your country. You all must beautify it." She overlaid her Viennese accent with a Texas drawl and blew them all kisses.

"Lady Bird!" they shouted. "Do Queen Elizabeth." Her mimicry delighted them.

Rutti clutched Anne's handbag, perched Merle's fur hat on her head.

"My husband and I are delighted to be with you," she said and the children imitated her.

"My husband and I," they shouted, improvising purses and hats, parading through the room.

Anne told them about a physician who had conducted a medical school interview. White-haired and unctuously paternal, he had studied her application, reviewed her recommendations. He had offered a series of suggestions to dissuade her. (Anne pulled her glasses down to her nose, stroked an imaginary tie, as she related this.) Finally, he said in a low voice, as though initiating her into a mystery, "My dear, I must warn you that doctors deal with a great deal of blood." And Anne had stared back at him guilelessly and said, "That's why women are prepared for medicine. We bleed every month. Why, I'm bleeding at this very moment." The interview was swiftly concluded. "He had white furniture in his consulting room," Anne said. "I guess he was afraid I'd stain the chair."

"Did you?" Merle asked and they collapsed into renewed laughter.

On a Friday, late in January, they met in Nancy's living room and sat on a blanket, spread on the floor, improvising a picnic. They had done this for the children's amusement, but the youngsters lost interest after a few moments and scampered away clutching the crusts of their peanut butter sandwiches, which they ate perched on Nancy and Dov's bed, intent on *The Magic Garden*.

The women, however, were reluctant to abandon the fantasy and did not change position. Merle, in her usual black slacks and turtle-neck, stretched out full-length, her face turned upward, like a sunbather seeking out the exact angle of solar radiance. Rutti also reclined, but leaned on one elbow so that she might feed Sarah who, now and again, drifted into the room and ate like a bird from her mother's hand. Sarah was small for four, fine boned and fair complected. She was blond, like her mother, and her hair, too, was curly and formed a cloud of gold about her face.

"How pretty you are," Merle said as Sarah plucked raisins from her mother's hand.

"Yes. Sarah is pretty," the child agreed. Always she spoke of herself in the third person. "*Sarah is hungry. Sarah wants milk. Sarah wants Keren to play.*" In lilting singsong, she distanced herself from her own needs, her own longings.

Sarah skipped off and Nancy set a tray of coffee mugs on the center of the blanket. Merle reached for one, took a sip, and then resumed her reclining position.

"She's so cute, your Sarah," she told Rutti. "You know, when I was pregnant with Greg I was sure I was carrying a girl. I wanted a daughter so badly." Her voice was wistful.

"Why?" Always it was Anne who probed cleanly, directly. Analytic, forthright, she sought answers, phrasing her questions brusquely. Nancy imagined her querying a patient, working up a case history. Anne would make an excellent doctor.

"Oh, I guess it's because I grew up in a household of men. My mother died when I was six so there was myself, my father, and my two brothers — both of them a lot older than me. I used to make believe I had a sister. I even had a name for her. Gladys. Such an ugly name, but I thought it beautiful then because a girl in my class had a sister named Gladys and I used to envy her when she said things like, 'Gladys and I are getting matching dresses this spring' or 'Gladys and I are going to the ballet with our aunt.' So I gave myself my own sister Gladys. She listened to music with me and played paper dolls with me. I even invented a voice for her — just a little bit louder than my own." She was silent for a moment, as though listening for that vanished voice of her own invention. "And then I married Andrew." She continued. "And again I was surrounded by men — Andrew's brothers and his partners and the men who work for him and the men who want to work for him. And of course, there's Greg — my darling little man. The cutest of babies . . ."

41

"Only you didn't get your daughter." Anne finished for her.

"But you'll have other children." Nancy interposed quickly, reassuringly. "You'll have a daughter."

"Oh, I wanted to have another baby right away. But Andrew thinks we should wait. Until Greg is in school all day," Merle said, and the color rose in her cheeks.

"Do you always do what Andrew says? Do you always think what Andrew thinks?" Anne asked. Rutti drew close to Merle as though to protect her from the tinge of mockery in Anne's voice.

Merle turned away and busied herself with clearing clutter from the rug. She liked Anne's strength and competence. Fearlessly, Anne succeeded on her own and could not understand the failures of others. Unlike Nancy, Anne would have difficulty understanding the decisions Merle had made, the compromises she had accepted, even welcomed. Merle had walked with Nancy down the dimly lit corridor of the Dinosaur Hall in the Museum of Natural History. They smiled proudly as Greg and Keren darted ahead of them loudly singing the alphabet song over and over. Their own children seemed to them so much more joyous, so much more vigorous than the other youngsters who tugged impatiently at their parents' hands. They burned with pride at Greg's precocity, at Keren's grace, at the thrilling voices that sang "A B C . . . " with such delight.

"They're so confident," Nancy said. "They don't even look back. They're not afraid of getting lost."

"And I was always afraid of getting lost." Merle reflected. "I could never shake the feeling, maybe because I always felt myself alone. I guess it prepared me in a way for my first year in New York. Not that it made it easier; nothing could have made it easier."

She had come to New York after studying in a conservatory in the small Michigan city where she had lived with her father and her brothers. She studied violin and composition, driving back and forth each day in the bright red convertible her father gave her for her eighteenth birthday. Her violin teacher took her out for dinner after graduation and she asked him if she could continue to study with him privately.

"There is nothing more I can teach you," he said. "And besides it is time for you to leave here. You must be in a city where music, a great deal of music, is available — concerts, recitals, orchestras, chamber groups. Chicago or New York. Perhaps Los Angeles."

"Will I ever be good enough?" she asked, forcing her voice to ask the daring question loudly, but still not daring to complete it. *Will I ever be great?* That was what she wanted to ask.

"You will never know unless you try. Emanuel Klein teaches at Juilliard. We are good friends. I will write to him. Of course, you would have to audition."

"Of course." Already she saw herself at the audition, wearing her burgundy velvet skirt, her long-sleeved white satin blouse, her bright hair tied back lest it touch the tautly drawn strings of her instrument.

She cajoled her father into a visit to New York. She wanted to shop, to go to the theater. *Please, Daddy*. She had learned that when she spoke very softly, when she lifted her eyes shyly, pleadingly, he would consent to anything. And, reluctantly, he did consent. She arranged an audition with Emanuel Klein and played for the thin, bearded master teacher in a spacious studio, so acoustically sensitive that she feared the rapid beating of her own heart was audible. She played the Mendelssohn violin concerto; she trembled with panic because her mistakes, her timing errors, were thunderous in that room. But Emanuel Klein nodded when she finished.

"I'll take you on," he said. "You'll be in the graduate program. Fill out an application. It is, of course, a formality. You will be accepted."

She was accepted, but her father grew pale when she told him of her plans.

"I won't allow it," he said angrily and she perceived the pain beneath his anger. She saw then that he was an old man. She was his youngest child. Her brothers were married. When she left he would be alone in the house, with only the housekeeper to keep him company. Merle had, for so long, been central to his life. If she left, he would be alone. Her mother had died young and Merle, slight of build, with hair the color of firelight, was so like her mother. He had to keep her safe. Love made him anxious, controlling.

Again she pleaded with him, lifting and lowering her eyes. *Please, Daddy*. When that did not work she wept, but he turned his back and strode from the room. Love made him hard and unrelenting. She slammed doors, pouted, refused to eat. He proposed a trip to Europe. Father and daughter. Or perhaps a family trip with her brothers and their wives. She wept anew. She did not want to go to Europe. She wanted to study music.

A letter from Juilliard arrived. Registration for the fall semester was commencing. She showed the letter to her father.

"Do they charge tuition at this school?" he asked.

"Yes."

"If you want to go, pay for it yourself. If you want to leave me, to live in New York, pay for everything yourself!" His tone was sharp, his anger devastating. He was a banker and this was his ultimate weapon, although her brothers and their wives had warned him against using it.

She had a small bank account of her own. Enough to buy herself a ticket to New York. Her oldest brother's wife gave her five hundred dollars in small bills. The folded currency smelled of sachet and moth balls and Merle realized that this was money her sister-in-law had hidden in her drawer, hoarded against a secret desire, a possible emergency.

She arrived in New York with six hundred dollars. When she told him her story, Emanuel Klein arranged for a reduced schedule, a student loan, and a partial scholarship. She answered an ad on the bulletin board at Juilliard and found a room to share in a student apartment on 121st Street, west of Broadway. Six girls shared three bedrooms, a minuscule living room, and a tiny kitchenette. They bought their milk in pint bottles and wrote their names on the silver paper caps. They bought two eggs at a time and chipped in to buy a container of margarine, which seemed to be always rancid. Merle gagged as she prepared her meals. She gagged when she went into the windowless bathroom, its walls coated with mildew, the wastebasket always overflowing with soiled tissues and sanitary pads. She shared her small bedroom with Tran, a beautiful Vietnamese piano student who wept all night.

"I miss my beautiful country," Tran told Merle. In the middle of the night she screamed in French. *"Laissez moi! Laissez moi!"*

"How are you?" Merle's father asked each Sunday evening when she phoned home.

"It's hard," she reported honestly.

"Of course it's hard." He was triumphant. He would not relent. She would come home.

She found a job waiting tables in a trendy restaurant near Carnegie Hall. She discovered that the patrons of trendy restaurants were not generous tippers and by the end of the month she had to work a double shift to meet even her small rent payment, one sixth of the total.

Exhausted, she attended class, practiced, went standing room to concerts. But when she dropped a tray and a carafe of hot coffee spilled on her hand, burning her fingers, Emanuel Klein intervened. First he scolded her and then he found her a job playing in a quartet at a small, elegant restaurant on Central Park West. She wore a long black skirt and a black silk blouse against which her skin was alabaster white. Her auburn hair fell to her shoulders; when she played the solo movements in the quiet selections that were considered appropriate dinner music her eyes shone like polished jade.

Andrew Cunningham took some business associates to dinner there one evening. They discussed a tricky merger over the soup, devised a strategy over the entrée, and when dessert was served, he looked up, distracted by the beauty of the music. He saw the auburn-haired violinist and stared hard at her, his gaze sharp with recognition. She seemed familiar to him, though, of course, he had never met her. He returned the next night and had dinner alone, at a table where he could see her clearly. He came again the next week and on the weekend he invited his brothers and their wives to join him.

"She's beautiful, isn't she?" he said, but he did not wait for their reply.

The following evening he had dinner alone, nursing his coffee until the lights dimmed and the musicians gathered their music and put their instruments into their cases. Dutifully, he paid his bill and waited for her on the sidewalk. She was startled to see him and briefly frightened. He was a tall man and broad of build. He stood erect, in an almost military posture, in his well-cut suit, his gleaming white shirt and silk paisley tie with a matching handkerchief tucked in his pocket. His features were craggy and although his hair was dark, his forelock was ash colored. Soon, she realized, he would be completely gray.

"I thought you played beautifully," he said.

"Thank you." How soft her voice was. He was not surprised. He had known it would be soft. *She was familiar to him.*

"May I take you home?"

"I don't think so." She was not naive. She had learned to protect herself in this city. She carried a small, very sharp knife in her purse and once, in the subway, she had flashed it at a boy who had approached her too closely in an empty car.

"My name is Andrew Cunningham. I could give you a long list of references." He could, of course, do just that. He was not unknown in this city where his father had practiced law for so many years and where he himself now ran a consulting firm. He was a man with a penchant for seeing the potential in a concept, a design, and had a talent for arranging for others to invest. He smiled and she thought his smile engaging.

"I'm Merle Loring."

"Merle Loring," he repeated. "Well, now that we are properly acquainted, may I take you home? My car is parked not far from here."

She was so very tired. It was late and she had an early lesson with Emanuel Klein the next day. He had told her his name and he had smiled. More important, she had noticed that he had smiled when they played the Sibelius. She could not be fearful of a man who smiled when he heard Sibelius.

"I live all the way uptown," she warned him. "And I can't ask you to come in. My roommate is sort of moody." She hoped that Tran would be asleep when she came in, but even so she would not want Andrew Cunningham, in his well-cut suit and snow-white shirt, to move through the crowded rooms.

"That's all right." He smiled at her reassuringly.

They spoke easily during the drive uptown. She remarked on the skill of his driving. Her brothers and her father were good drivers and always she had admired the way they maneuvered through traffic. She herself was fearful at the wheel and she considered their prowess a masculine talent, a mark of strength and control. Andrew Cunningham pulled up before her shabby building. It was spring and the windows were open. The sounds of music and excited student chatter drifted into the street.

"I'll come to hear you play again," he said. "Will you let me drive you home again?"

"I don't know." She wondered how old he was. Thirty perhaps, or thirty-five. Not too old. She had spent so much time with her father, her teacher, her brothers, that younger men bored her.

She got out of the car.

"Does your window face the street?" he asked.

She nodded.

"Which floor are you on?"

"The fourth."

"Lean out and wave when you're in your room. I want to know that you're safe."

She was moved that he should be so protective and because he was waiting she hurried up the four flights of stairs and entered the dark apartment. Everyone was out. She remembered that there had been talk of a party. Grateful for the quiet, she pushed open the door of the bedroom she shared with Tran and put the light on.

Her heart stopped and a scream swelled in her throat and became a silent tumor constricting her breath. Blood slithered across the floor and licked at her shoes. It streaked the bedclothes and soaked the mattress on which Tran lay. Tran's eyes were focused in a blank stare; her small sweet mouth was open. Tran's dark hair fanned out across the pillow; her skin was drained to the color of ivory, almost exactly matching the patterned silk pajama suit she wore. The blood came from the slits Tran had cut in her wrists, the deep neat cuts she had made with the knife that Merle had bought to keep in her purse when she traveled the subway and which she had left on her desk that evening.

Merle reeled. She moved toward Tran. Dizzy, her eyes burning, she touched the motionless girl's hand. The blood, thick and glutinous, adhered to her palm; Tran's skin was cold, clammy. Now the scream escaped at last, piercing and terrible, resonant with horror. Nor could she stop screaming although her throat ached and her head pounded. Her screams caused Andrew Cunningham to leap from his car and race up the four flights, taking the stairway two steps at a time.

It was Andrew who called the police that night and then the

Emergency Medical Services and then the dean of student life. Merle sat in the living room and listened to his voice so calm and controlled. She stood beside him as he called Tran's only relative in America, an elderly woman who lived in Baltimore. Automatically, he put his arm around Merle's shoulders, allowed her to lean against him, heard the whisper of her voice in his ear again and yet again.

"Poor Tran," she said. "Poor, poor Tran."

She could not sleep in that apartment that night. He went back into the room, afloat with blood — so much blood from those narrow cuts — and picked up her violin. It was all she wanted, he knew, all she would need. He took her home to his own house and Lottie, his housekeeper, gave her a pair of his pajamas, familiar blue-and-white striped pajamas like those her father and her brothers favored. She took a long shower in the spacious, clean guest bathroom and went to bed.

She never returned to that small student apartment. Instead Andrew and Lottie went and packed her clothing, her books. He was an efficient man. He wasted little time. She was grateful to him, and admired him.

Two months later they were married in the church where she had worshiped all her life. She was surrounded by the men of her family, her father, her brothers. But her eyes followed Andrew. It was Andrew who had known whom to call that terrible night, Andrew who knew how to arrange things. It was Andrew who steadied her, cared for her, whose plans for her and for their life together were so generous, so reasonable. She would continue her music studies. Of course, she would. Always, he was tender and considerate. Always he treated her as though she were a fragile treasure to be handled with care. Always he stilled her fears, calmed her terror.

"As a matter of fact," she told Anne now, smiling without apology, "I usually do what Andrew says and fairly often I think what Andrew thinks. He's so often right."

"But then how do you know when your thoughts are your own?" Surprisingly, the question so softly asked, came from Rutti but there was no need to answer because the children whirled into the room just then and pounced upon the women, hurling themselves into outstretched arms, yelping in glee.

"Ice cream, ice cream, we want ice cream!" Greg led the chant and the others joined in, even Keren, who disliked ice cream and seldom ate it anywhere.

Nancy scooped the ice cream onto paper plates and they settled the children in a circle on the blanket. Rutti fed Sarah, who ate very quickly, and licked the spoon clean after each mouthful. It occurred to Nancy that Sarah did not eat ice cream very often. She studied Rutti and Sarah and noted, not for the first time, how thin they both were. She wondered if they ever actually went hungry. The thought troubled her.

"Don't eat with your hands, Eric." Anne reprimanded her charge. "Use your spoon properly."

"All right." He agreed angrily. "All right."

He followed her back to the blanket, allowed her to wipe his hands and tie a napkin beneath his chin, and then he resumed eating. Anne tousled his hair but he did not look at her.

"Don't you get upset with him?" Nancy asked enviously. She tried so hard to be patient with Keren, but often she lost the battle and her own voice grew shrill with rage.

"I get annoyed but not upset," Anne replied. "Remember, in Nigeria, I had twenty kids in my nursery group."

Anne's reference to her Peace Corps experience was always casual, offhand. They knew that she had joined the Peace Corps immediately after her graduation from a small denominational college in Pennsylvania. She had read with interest John Kennedy's blueprint for the Peace Corps and imagined herself part of "that cadre of young Americans who would carry their knowledge and skill to distant corners of the world." Anne's application had been among the first submitted to the Peace Corps.

"What is the Peace Corps?" her mother had asked in bewilderment. Sophie Richardson was a stocky, pale-eyed woman who had lived all her life in the same small house, in the same small Pennsylvania town. She and Anne's father had moved in with her parents when they married and they continued to live in her girlhood room, even after her father died. She had raised Anne and Anne's sisters, Helene and Edna, in that house, running up the stairs with trays for her invalid mother. Each evening she drove across town with a hot meal for her father-in-law. She cooked dinner for her daughters and herself and cleaned the kitchen. She cooked another dinner for Anne's father, who kept his small retail clothing store open three nights a week. Late in the night Anne could hear her mother placing scoured pots back on the stove, sorting silverware and crockery.

Anne's mother never bought prepared food, never bought a cake in a bakery. She did her laundry every Monday, baked every Friday. She kept the books for Anne's father and during the holiday season or when school began, she stood behind the cash register at the store or busied herself replenishing counters and shelves. Twice a year she bought a lottery ticket. "Winning could change my life," she said as she studied the numbers that were never the lucky numbers. She was constantly exhausted but never complained. She had lived her mother's life and she expected her daughters to live her own.

Anne explained the concept of the Peace Corps to her mother, that she would be trained in Puerto Rico, that she would opt to be sent to Africa. *Africa*. The word itself thrilled her.

"But why would you want to go to Africa?" Sophie Richardson asked uneasily. She was proud of Anne who was the first in their family to finish college. She was pleased that Anne had studied chemistry. She could be a science teacher. Until she married and had children. Helene and Edna had worked in the bank until they had children.

To get away from here. To make sure I am never like you. The true answer to her mother's question remained unuttered. Anne loved her mother and pitied her. She had always loved and pitied her.

"Because it will be exciting," she said. "It will be a chance to do something for other people." Her mother would understand that. All her life Sophie had done things for other people.

And it had been exciting. The training. The encounters with other young people from all over the country, all of them fired with idealism, eager for adventure. Not everyone survived the rigorous interviews, the training program, the language-intensive courses. But Anne did. On each application she wrote "Science" and "Health Care" on the line that asked for her field of interest. At each interview she spoke of her major in chemistry, her summa cum laude degree, her interest in working in a clinic, a hospital, in helping to organize field labs. She was assigned to Nigeria, which pleased her. In Lagos, she was placed in a child care center. Three of the men in her group, who had been humanities majors in college, were assigned to a public health project. They all lived together in a hostel, Peace Corps style, with a group of Nigerian young people, sharing cooking and household tasks. The young men sat in the living room and strummed their guitars after dinner. The young women cleaned up, did the dishes, often working late into the evening because shifts varied. Anne washed pots in the Lagos kitchen and thought of her mother who had also stood before a kitchen sink, her arms plunged into greasy water, and looked out into the darkness.

She applied twice to be transferred to a health care unit. Twice her application was rejected. She had a brief affair with a bespectacled, pipe-smoking Harvard graduate who insisted that the Peace Corps was integral to the process of human liberation. "The world has to be changed," he told her earnestly. "Concepts of equality must be reassessed, the distribution of labor reevaluated."

They slept in her room, and if he left for work before she did, she made the bed and put away their things. If she left first, she returned to find the bed unmade and his laundry in the center of the room. When they ate together, she prepared the meal, washed the dishes. One night, after they had made love, he asked her to get him a cup of coffee.

"Get it yourself," she said and the harshness of her tone startled him. "I am *not* my mother." He looked at her as though she had gone mad. Was a cup of coffee such a big deal? He didn't even want the damn coffee any more. The next day she packed his things and set them in a carton outside her door. He returned to his own room, still not understanding what had happened, but then affairs in the Corps often ended in just such a manner. They were on a short-term adventure and wanted no long-term commitments.

In Lagos, Anne took a careful accounting of her position. She understood that she had been assigned to the day-care center because she was a woman. She understood, too, that the men, like her lover, who wanted to change the world, had no intention of changing their own habits, that they would forever talk and strum their guitars and read their books while women washed pots and looked out at the darkness. Just as the lottery would never change her mother's life, so the most idealistic program, proposed by the most idealistic of presidents, would not change her life. She would have to do that for herself.

She wrote away for medical school applications and began to study for the Medical College Admission Test. By the time her tour with the Peace Corps was over, her plans were formulated. The job with Hope and Ted gave her room and board and a small salary, most of which she was able to save. Her evenings were free for study and she studied hard. She scored high on the MCAT. Her college record was superb, her financial need well documented. Her work in the Peace Corps demonstrated her independence, her ability to cooperate and persevere. She knew that she would be offered a scholarship to the medical school of her choice. She imagined herself in lecture halls and laboratories; she saw herself in a starched white coat, a stethoscope dangling about her neck, striding purposefully down hospital corridors. Often she lay awake at night happily fantasizing about the life that would surely be hers, a life in which all her talents would be fulfilled, a life that would guarantee that she would never, never stand over a sink and wash pots while darkness pressed against a kitchen window.

"I can't imagine anyone taking care of twenty kids," Nancy said.

She held a plastic garbage bag open into which they cheerfully tossed remnants of their pseudo–picnic lunch, soggy paper plates and cups, thin plastic forks and spoons. They lifted the blanket carefully' so that the crumbs too fell into the bag, and grinned at each other. They were efficient women, skilled at these small domestic tasks, always prepared to turn a chore into a joke. They danced toward each other to fold the blanket and Rutti grimaced, as though she were on the beach and sand had gotten into her eyes.

"Ve must stop to vacation on Vaikiki," she said, but even as they laughed, her mood changed.

"Twenty children." She reflected soberly. "There were more than twenty children in our transport when we left Vienna. They divided us into groups of ten, I think. Or perhaps it was eight." Her voice faded as she struggled to remember.

In the bedroom the tired children grew silly and then raucous. Greg and Eric ganged up on Sarah and Keren.

"Babies. You're babies," Greg taunted them.

"Stupid babies," Eric echoed.

Keren cried, but Sarah was stubbornly defiant.

"Sarah's not a baby," she said. "Be nice to Sarah. And to Keren too," she added in as afterthought. The listening women smiled.

"Time to go," Merle said. "Definitely time to go. Listen, I want all of you to come to our house for dinner. A real sit-down dinner on a Saturday night. Grown-ups only. With Andrew. You'll bring Dov, Nancy. And if either of you wants to bring someone, feel free." She smiled shyly at Rutti and Anne. The invitation embarrassed her. She did not know if they would welcome it or resent it. It placed their friendship in a new dimension but Andrew had insisted.

"If you're spending so much time with these women, I would like to meet them," he had said in his reasonable manner.

She could think of no reason to object. It was kind of him, caring of him, as he had ever been kind and caring — since the night he had led her from that room awash with blood and enfolded her in his love.

"I'll check with Dov about a weekend when he's not on rotation," Nancy said. She wondered if Dov would want to go. She so seldom knew what he wanted to do these days, exhausted as he was by the rigors of the hospital residency. But she would insist. She could see that it was important to Merle and it would be fun. She wanted to meet Andrew Cunningham. He had recently been quoted in the *Times* business section. He predicted that Lyndon Johnson's projected Great Society would mean an exploding market for leisure time products. "A great society will want to relax, will want to have the machinery of relaxation easily accessible and streamlined. I'm talking about gas grills and home entertainment centers. I'm talking about the quality of life, about investing in that quality," he said.

Nancy recalled the television set controlled by the press of a button, of the bar that responded to the flick of a switch. Was that what a man like Andrew Cunningham meant by the "quality of life"? She studied his photograph. Handsome, square-jawed, his hair crested with gray, he stared confidently into the camera. She felt a small thrill that she was on intimate terms with the wife of a man who was quoted in the *New York Times*.

"OK. Let me know when it will be good for you," Merle said.

They dressed the children in their cumbersome snowsuits, laughing as they stumbled over each other in a new game in which they pretended that the bulky outdoor clothing was intended for space. Good humor was restored. Nancy and Keren walked down the hall with them to the elevator.

"Our spaceship is here," Greg announced when the elevator arrived, and they applauded and crowded in.

"Spaceship, spaceship, spaceship," Eric, Sarah, and Greg shouted as they pressed the buttons.

"Spaceship, spaceship," Keren sang giddily as she and Nancy walked back to the apartment.

In the living room, Nancy lifted her daughter in her arms and whirled about with her.

"We're caught in a space wind," she proclaimed. Keren laughed wildly. Nancy deposited her on the couch and exhausted, she fell asleep at once.

Nancy was slicing vegetables in the kitchen when Dov arrived home. Her face was flushed and she was smiling as she thought of what she would wear to Merle's dinner party, of how proud she would be to introduce her handsome husband to her new friends, of how Dov would approve of Merle and Anne and Rutti. Dov put his arms about her waist and led her gently into the bedroom. They made love as Keren slept on the sofa and their dinner simmered fragrantly on the stove.

4

THE SNOW began to fall in the morning; the clumsy, lazy flakes were wind tossed into gentle, teasing flurries. Slowly, the storm escalated so that by midafternoon the gray March air was striped with rods of whiteness and the broad streets of Manhattan's West Side were slick with gleaming sheaths of ice. Nancy bundled Keren into her snowsuit and they trudged up Broadway to the tiny shop where the diminutive Filipino florist stood with his face pressed against the plate glass door, his dark eyes molten with memories of the warmth of his homeland. It was Keren who selected the bouquet for Merle's dinner party, imperially pointing with her mittened hand to a cluster of tall irises, three yellow rosebuds, a cloud of baby's breath.

"I carry them," she insisted and proudly held them aloft as they made their way home through the snow that frosted their eyelashes, their heads bent against the onslaught of the frigid wind.

Nancy held her daughter's hand tightly and shivered as a siren sounded and brakes shrieked. An ambulance careened past them, its red lights flashing, en route to the hospital.

Please don't let Dov have an emergency. Please let him be home on time. She did not want to miss this evening so long in the planning. They had struggled to find a date convenient to all of them — one that would accommodate Andrew's hectic out-of-town meetings, Dov's rotations, Rutti's erratic work schedule.

She saw with relief that he was already home. She plucked his sodden loden coat from the sofa, kicked aside the boots he had discarded in the living room. "Dov," she called as she knelt to unzip

Keren's jacket. "Dov!" she called again, more loudly, as she placed the bouquet, still in its wrapping, in a vase. He did not answer and when she opened the bedroom door she saw that he had fallen asleep, fully dressed, sprawled across their bed.

"Damn," she said softly and then covered him with an afghan in atonement for her own irritation. She knew he was exhausted. She let him sleep while she gave Keren dinner, played a game of Candy Land with her, and took her down the hall at last to Ingrid's apartment where she would sleep that night, a concession Nancy had earned by allowing the baby-sitting pool to charge her double for that evening's sitting hours.

She took a bath, luxuriating in the hot water as she watched the steadily falling snow. She wondered, lazily, whether they should walk to the Cunninghams or take the bus. The thought of walking through the snow with Dov pleased her and she smiled as she soaped her breasts, her shoulders, and slid lower into the tub.

They would arrive at Merle's door, their faces bright with the cold, snow lacing their hair. They had often walked through the snow during their courtship days, during the first winter of their marriage. One afternoon they built a snow fort, and on a blindingly bright January day, they pelted each other with snowballs and then dashed back to their off-campus apartment where they made love on a nest of blankets. Perhaps it was then, as they walked through the snow drifts that covered their rural midwestern campus, that Dov told her the snowscape reminded him of Israel's Negev.

"Do you see how the drifts make you think of the moon — a kind of lunar pattern," he said. "That is so like my country's desert — the white sand sculptured into such strange formations stretching endlessly in front of you."

"Just a slight difference in climate," she replied teasingly, frightened by the wistfulness in his voice.

"Ah, you make fun of me. I will make you pay for making fun of your husband." He chased her then, across the wintry terrain, brandishing a sparkling icicle until, laughing and breathless, she turned and fell into his arms. The frigid wand passed from his gloved hand into her own as they laughed and kissed.

It had been a long time since she and Dov had laughed and played in the snow, but tonight would be different, Nancy decided.

"I want us to have fun," Merle had said earlier in the week, when they discussed the dinner.

"Fun is good," Anne had agreed amiably. "Definitely put fun on the agenda."

"Introductory Fun or Advanced Fun?" Nancy had asked.

"Remedial Fun," Merle had said decisively, and they all laughed.

Nancy emerged from the bath smiling. She dried and powdered herself, then brushed her long, dark hair so that it caped her shoulders. Smiling, she wakened Dov by trailing her fingers through his hair, blowing softly into his ear. Reluctantly, he opened his eyes.

"Hey," he said, "I'm tired. Really tired."

"I know." She kept her voice understanding, sympathetic. She *was* understanding and sympathetic. "But you know, tonight is Merle's dinner party."

"All right. All right." He heaved himself out of bed. The afghan slipped to the floor but he did not pick it up. Impatiently, he pulled his clothing off, once again leaving a trail behind him as he disappeared into the bathroom. She picked up after him — sweater and shirt, blue jeans and underpants, one blue sock and one black sock because somehow, socks disappeared at the Laundromat. His mother, who did the laundry for their entire household by hand, had never lost an item of clothing, he had told Nancy accusingly.

He left the bathroom door open and she heard the rush of the shower and then, with relief, she heard him begin to sing. The song was in Hebrew and she recognized only the words for sun and sky, which were repeated again and again in the refrain.

She began to dress then, humming softly to herself. If Dov was singing, his irritable mood was broken and perhaps he too now anticipated a pleasant and interesting evening. Surely, he wanted to meet Merle and Rutti; he had heard so much about them during the past months. He had met Anne twice — the first time when she came to borrow his textbooks and then again when he had agreed to help her with her medical school application essay.

"Did you like Anne?" Nancy had asked cautiously.

"She is to be admired," he had replied. It was only days later that Nancy realized he had not answered her question.

Dov's tread was heavy as he emerged from the shower and he did not sing as he dried himself. Naked, he moved across the room to the dressing table and stood behind Nancy as she applied her makeup. Drops of water glinted on his arms and his dark hair curled into damp ringlets. His face was puckered into the boyish pout she always found hard to resist.

"Must we go?" he asked. He slipped his hand beneath her black silk blouse, massaged her back, touched her neck with his lips. She knew his intent. He would seduce her into staying home.

"Yes. We have to go," she answered firmly, sliding free of his touch. "Besides, I want to go. We haven't been out for so long."

"All right then." He was, as always, ill tempered in defeat. He slammed the bureau drawers closed as he plucked out socks and underwear, rummaged for a blue shirt, cursed briefly because he could not find his coffee-colored V-necked sweater.

"I think the men will be wearing jackets and ties tonight," she said cautiously.

"They'll excuse me," he replied sarcastically. "Israelis do not have to wear jackets and ties. Your American friends will understand that I was born in a pioneering country and that this exempts me from conventional rules of dress. What is the problem, Nancy? Are you afraid that your husband will embarrass you?"

"Stop it, Dov," she said shortly. "Wear what you please. I'll wait for you in the living room."

She closed the bedroom door softly, controlling her urge to slam it. Her mother had never slammed doors in the face of her father's thunderous moods. Men worked hard, they returned home exhausted, they deserved to be catered to, even coddled, her mother had said. And Dov did work hard, and he was exhausted, she knew. Two residents on his shift were down with the flu and there had been the annual acceleration in patient admissions. January filled the wards with thoracic cases, pneumonia at the month's beginning and bronchitis as it ended. Angina cases were common in February and in March the flu attacked. Dov had worked double shifts and was often wakened from his snatches of sleep by emergency calls. She understood his fatigue. They would leave Merle's early and sleep late the next morning. Ingrid had agreed to keep Keren until noon.

And Dov was right. Why shouldn't he dress as he pleased, as he had always dressed? After all, he had been wearing an open-necked shirt when they met, a soft-collared shirt, sparklingly white against his sun-bronzed skin. That and his neatly ironed khaki slacks had, in fact, set him apart from the crowd of college students in their loose T-shirts and faded jeans.

She remembered how he had stood in the doorway of the camp dining room, among the young people gathered there for an inter-collegiate Zionist conference. Nancy had attended at her mother's urging.

"It will be fun," her mother said. "A lot of law students go. A lot of medical students. And you're so interested in Israel." Nancy knew that what her mother meant was *Go and meet a law student, a medical student. Go to Israel on your honeymoon.* Her mother had not anticipated Dov.

Nancy watched him from her post at the long table where she was ladling sweet red punch into paper cups. When the girl who was to relieve her arrived, she darted into the ladies' room, plaited her long dark hair into a French braid, and applied fresh lipstick and the faintest blush of rouge. She filled two more paper cups with punch and carried them to him.

"Hello," she said. "My name is Nancy."

"Shalom," he replied, without surprise, as though he had been waiting for her. Her hand trembled as he took the cup of punch from her and she saw that his eyes were amber-colored, roofed by thick dark brows that did not arch but ran almost together in a straight line. "I am called Dov. Dov Yallon."

He had been invited to the conference, he told her, to give a talk on student life in Israel.

"And I came to learn about student life in Israel," she said. "I'm thinking of doing graduate work at the Hebrew University."

It would not do to tell him that she had come to the conference at her mother's insistence and besides, it was true that she had idly played with the idea of studying in Jerusalem. She had attended a lecture given by an Israeli psychoanalyst who had spoken of the inter-relationship between emotional well-being and a purposeful life. It was his thesis that Israelis, and even those who came to the Jewish state temporarily to work or study, were imbued with the feeling that their contribution was important, that they were making a difference. This inevitably increased their sense of self-worth.

All her life, Nancy Adler had craved exactly that — a sense of purpose, which she did not perceive in her own family's life — in her father's endless business meetings, her mother's social schedule. What difference did it make if her father sat on another board, if a business deal succeeded or failed? Of what importance was it if her mother chaired yet another Hadassah luncheon? Nancy was impatient with the earnestness with which her mother addressed household matters, her interminable conversations with decorators and caterers.

"That is not the color green I ordered," Nancy would hear her mother say, her voice quivering with indignation.

So what? Nancy thought irritably.

Her father arrived home from the office looking pale and distraught. A stock had gone down. A client was making unreasonable demands. The next day he would be florid with triumph. He had made an important deal, acquired a new client.

So what? So what?

She was the youngest child, born when her sister was in high school, her brother in college. Lonely and introspective, she felt herself at a remove from her family, a spectator in the theater that was her home. She watched her brother complete his graduate training in business, join her father's firm, marry a girl who looked like their mother. Janet, her sister, married a gynecologist, shopped with their mother, argued vigorously with decorators and caterers.

"That is not the color burgundy I ordered."

"So what?" Nancy asked her.

"You'll see," Janet replied. "Things like this will be important to you too."

"No. Different things will be important to me."

Her siblings had moved effortlessly into their parents' tracks. Her own life would have a sense of purpose. She would make a contribution to the world, do something for others, be something herself.

She read biographies of distinguished women, developed a crush on the silver-haired dowager professor who taught her abnormal psychology seminar, joined a campus civil rights organization, and one autumn evening when she could not bear to be alone in her dormitory room, she had attended the lecture given by the Israeli psychoanalyst.

She wondered, that first night, if Dov Yallon would recognize the psychologist's name, if he would agree with his thesis. She noticed that Dov's eyes darkened when he moved out of the light, that his neck was unusually slender, that a small white scar formed a winged arc at his clavicle. The scar intrigued her, and although she was a shy girl, she surprised herself by reaching up and touching it. Dov had stood patiently as her finger traced its way so lightly across his skin and then he had taken her wrist and kissed it.

"A fair trade," he had said, but she reflected that it had not been fair at all. She had wanted to kiss that pale furling wound on his slender neck.

She listened to his talk the next day. Student life in Israel, he told his eager audience, was different from student life in the States. The students were older. They began university after completing army service and many of them worked full-time jobs to support themselves as they studied. But there was vibrancy and energy because they had a sense of purpose, a sense of belonging.

"Why are you in America?" The question was sly, the questioner a thin-faced law student whose arguments with Israeli students were legendary on the campus.

"Because I can obtain training here that is not available in Israel." Nancy detected the strain in Dov's voice and she was indignant with the questioner on his behalf.

Later that afternoon she and Dov walked down a mountain path to a meadow where the tall, sweet grass was threaded with woodruff. He told her then that his family lived on a small moshav, a collective settlement south of Beersheba, and grew flowers for export to Europe. His parents had settled there after emigrating from Turkey and Dov had been born in the small stucco house that his father had built with his own hands. Dov was their seventh and last child, their only son.

"Six sisters," Nancy said. "God, you must have been spoiled."

"Ah, women have always spoiled me," he admitted and laughed. "Even you will spoil me. Already, you have begun to spoil me. Did you not bring me the sweet drink last night? Will you not always bring me sweet drinks?"

"Always," she promised and plucked a long shoot of meadow grass which she brushed across his lips.

He had come to America, he told her, because he wanted to see the world beyond Israel. Yes, study had motivated him and his professors in Israel had encouraged him, but his yearning had been deeper.

"I was in the Sinai in fifty-six," he said, speaking slowly, the pain heavy on each word. "I was nineteen years old, a medic running from wounded soldier to wounded soldier. There was crossfire and an Egyptian bullet caught me in the neck. Another millimeter and it would have pierced the vein. I touched the blood and I heard myself scream and I thought 'I am nineteen years old and I am going to die. I have never seen a city larger than Tel Aviv. I have never crossed an ocean. I have never loved a woman. I will die before I have lived.' Of course, I did not die. The bullet was removed and I was left with the scar and the memory of those thoughts."

She leaned forward and kissed the pale butterfly-shaped scar that would always remind her, as surely as it reminded him, of the capriciousness of destiny, of the lurking proximity of death.

"But now you have crossed an ocean," she told him.

"Yes. I have crossed an ocean. And I have seen many cities larger than Tel Aviv. And now, at last, I love a woman." His lips were soft against her own, his breath warm and grass scented.

They were married the following spring in the garden of her parents' Shaker Heights home. Dov wore an open-necked shirt and she chose a simple white cotton dress, embroidered with blue flowers. His parents did not come to the wedding. It was the harvest season, Dov explained, but she understood that they could not afford the airfare. She felt that their poverty ennobled them. She delighted in the simplicity of their wedding reception, so unlike the lavish catered affairs held when her sister and brother were married.

"You see," she told her sister, who helped to weave long-stemmed daisies and sweet woodruff into a bridal crown (she always favored the wild meadow growth that reminded her of their first meeting) "our lives will be different from yours. Different things are important to us — to Dov and myself."

"As long as you're sure the same things are important to both of you," her sister said. It occurred to Nancy, for the first time, that her family did not like Dov.

Waiting for him now, she reflected that Dov, who could be so charming when he wished, had done very little to make them like him. His contributions to their conversations were monosyllabic. He resisted her father's advice and her mother's offers to help with Keren. But all that would change when his residency was completed, when he was no longer so tense and exhausted.

Her anger melted into sympathy and she smiled up at him as he emerged from the bedroom. He had, after all, changed into a shirt and tie and selected a tweed jacket and gray flannel slacks. Briefly, she regretted his capitulation, and in apology she embraced him, pressing her face against his neck, licking the pale protuberance of his scar in teasing promise.

Nancy carried the bouquet and lifted it now and again to inhale the sweet fragrance of spring as they walked hand in hand down the snow-silent streets to the Cunninghams' brownstone.

Lottie opened the door for them, took the flowers, their coats.

"This is Lottie," Nancy said comfortably, companionably. "Lottie, this is my husband, Dr. Yallon."

"Now I know the whole family," Lottie said cheerfully. "Your Keren is a sweetie."

"Yes." Dov was uneasy. He did not know how to balance his conversation with Lottie who seemed at once to be servant and friend. He had not, after all, grown up, as Nancy had, in a home tended by uniformed strangers to whom she related with ease and affection. Still, he smiled at Lottie and Nancy placed her hand in his.

Holding hands, they entered the brightly lit living room that hummed with talk and laughter. A fire blazed and the geometrically patterned rug in darkening shades of gold was soft beneath their feet. Platters of canapés were set on low tables and a waiter moved through the room carrying a tray laden with glasses of wine.

Anne, regal in a white woolen dress, her straight platinum hair falling to her shoulders in silken sheaths, took a glass of wine and continued her conversation with Rutti. She laughed. Rutti was clearly imitating someone. But the tall thin man who stood beside her did not even smile. His fair hair fell in untidy layers and the cuffs of his shirt jutted from the sleeves of his gray cotton jacket, flapping and frayed. He gripped his wine glass tightly and took two canapés at once, chewing them rapidly, his eyes never leaving Rutti's face.

"Nancy!" Merle, elegant in a pale blue silk dress, moved toward them. "And you are Dov, of course." Her voice was, as always, breathless and her smile, radiant and welcoming. "Andrew, come and meet Nancy and Dov."

Andrew was tall. His thick hair was graying, his gaze shrewd and controlled. Nancy observed the cut of his suit, the high gloss of his shoes; she knew that, like her father, he was a man particular of his tailor, careful with his clothing as he was surely careful of all his possessions. He would not easily tolerate imperfection.

"Nancy. Dov. I've heard so much about you." He took their hands in his own, each in turn, paternally encasing them in the envelope of his authority. Nancy was surprised at the gentleness of his touch. She had imagined Merle's husband to be a man hardened by his ascent to power, conditioned to toughness by his battle for wealth and control. She moved her hand, but Andrew Cunningham held it for a moment longer and released it at his own will. He spoke softly, as large men often do. Nancy imagined that controlled voice raised in anger and she felt a tantalizing thrill of fear. She moved closer to Dov who was answering Andrew's questions about the hospital.

"Yes," Dov assured him. "I think it is an excellent urban hospital but its intake procedure should be computerized."

"You're right. But that will take a lot of money. Still, the hospital has to keep pace."

"I'm surprised that you're so familiar with the problem," Dov said.

"I sit on the hospital board," Andrew explained.

In that, too, he was like her father, Nancy realized. Any responsibility he undertook would claim his careful attention.

"No more serious talk. You must have some wine," Merle insisted. "We're celebrating."

"What are we celebrating?" Nancy asked.

A couple she had not seen before approached them. The woman was tall and thin, her elongated face freckle-spattered, her thick sandy hair pulled carelessly back. She wore a red velvet evening skirt and her cream-colored satin blouse was studded with crimson beads. It was a thrift shop outfit, plucked from the rack by an impatient woman with little money to spend; the hem of the skirt was uneven and the crimson beads so loosely sewn that they dangled from frayed thread.

In contrast, her short stout husband was impeccably groomed, his navy blue suit jacket comfortably buttoned across his protruding stomach. Jack Spratt and his wife, Nancy thought in amusement.

"Anne's admission to medical school. She was accepted at Columbia Physicians and Surgeons. She just heard this morning. Hope and Ted are going to lose the world's most overqualified baby-sitter," Merle replied, smiling at the newcomers. "Nancy and Dov Yallon — Hope and Ted Sargent." She made the introduction with practiced ease and Nancy realized that Jack Spratt and his wife were, in fact, Eric's parents.

"Perhaps Anne can stay with us," Hope said. "We may be able to juggle our schedules and work things out." Her husky voice had a southern twang and she smiled, the broad, generous smile peculiar to women who have always relied on their intelligence and humor rather than their beauty. "What's important is that Anne's on her way." She lifted her glass and turned to Anne. "To our Anne," she said.

They all moved toward Anne, their glasses raised, and she, in turn, looked at them with confidence and affection.

"Thank you," she said. Nancy, who knew her best, understood that she was thinking, *I am not your Anne. I am my own Anne. I have molded myself and belong to myself.* Impulsively, she went up to her friend and kissed her on the cheek.

"I'm so happy for you, Anne," she said.

"I'm just waiting for you to catch up, Nancy," Anne replied.

Nancy flinched. She knew that Anne thought she should increase her course load, but Anne did not understand that she simply did not have the time. Not with all she had to do for Keren and for Dov. She turned away from Anne and saw that Rutti had taken her slender companion's hand and led him to the small sofa that faced the fire. They sat side by side, holding their empty glasses, and studied the others — quiet, wide-eyed spectators, trained to polite silence, as though fearful that their invitation was tenuous, their presence in the flower-filled, carpeted room serendipitous.

Nancy and Dov approached them.

"Dov, this is Rutti, Rutti Weisenblatt."

"Rutti." Dov's voice was very gentle, as if he had recognized Rutti at once, had known instinctively that she must be protected.

"And this is Werner, Sarah's father," Rutti said.

"Yes. Of course." Nancy smiled in recognition. Sarah had inherited her father's gray-blue eyes, his avian features and fluid gestures.

"Nancy tells me that you lived for a time in Israel," Dov said, settling himself on a leather hassock beside them.

"Yes," Werner replied. "Rutti and I met in Israel."

Rutti rose.

"If you'll excuse me for a moment — I want to check on Sarah."

She had brought Sarah to the Cunninghams the way she brought her everywhere. Rutti claimed that there was no one with whom to leave the child but she had confided to Nancy, who offered to baby-sit for Sarah, that the truth was, she could not bear the thought of leaving her child. She knew what it was like for a child to awake in a strange room. She understood the terror of abandonment.

Rutti had been only a few years older than Sarah when she had walked with her parents through the winding streets of Leopoldstadt. She was excited, she remembered, because she had seldom been out so late at night. She could recall, too, the warmth of the spring evening and the dank smell that rose from the Danube Canal. In the distance the lights of a small barge glimmered and then darkened. Rutti looked up at her mother who tightened her grip on Rutti's hand and hugged the brown paper parcel, wrapped around many times with a piece of string scavenged from a baker's box, close to her breast. The parcel contained a piece of roast chicken and an apple, which Rutti was to eat that night aboard the train. There was also a hard-boiled egg and two pieces of black bread for her breakfast the next morning. Her parents were not certain where she would be when she ate the egg and bread. Somewhere in the Loire Valley perhaps, approaching Cherbourg. They had shown her each of these places on the map, her sad and serious parents, both of them so small of stature and slight of build, their faces creased with worry.

Finally, there was a slab of cheese encased in a cardboard box, and a hard roll, to be eaten on the boat that would carry her across the Channel to the freedom of England. Again, her mother instructed her about the food as they walked toward the Ringstrasse and the Vienna railroad station. She spoke in a whisper. It was 1938, the year of shouting crowds and whispering women.

"I understand," Rutti had assured her.

"Remember — when you have eaten the cheese put the cardboard box in your valise. There is an address on it — the name and address of our friends in Zurich. We will try always to keep in contact with them — they will know where we are, what has happened to us." Her voice broke and Rutti took her mother's hand and kissed it.

They could not give her any letters or documents. The strip of cardboard would be her link to them, the name and address written in her father's firm hand a guaranty.

"I will be careful," Rutti had promised.

They wept as they kissed her good-bye in the cavernous station. She looked back as she followed the stocky gray-haired woman who led the children onto the train. Her mother clung to her father, who held her as though she might fall to the ground if he loosened his grip. Thus entangled they stood until the train pulled out of the station at last. And Rutti, crying soundlessly, watched them, her face pressed against the dirt-streaked window until she could no longer see them.

She ate the food according to her mother's instructions although she could not finish all of it. She was weary and could not sleep on the train. Her stomach hurt and by the time they reached Cherbourg she was very hot and knew that she had a fever.

"Mutti," she whispered as they boarded the Channel ferry.

She ate the hard roll and thought that she could taste her mother's touch on the golden crust. She was nauseated now but still she ate the cheese and then looked in puzzlement at the cardboard container. She was so tired, so hot, and the ceaseless rocking of the boat had given her a headache. She leaned over the rail, still clutching the cardboard, struggling to recall her mother's words. A huge breaker crashed against the ferry, thrusting her backward. Her fingers loosened. She watched the cardboard fall into the sea, watched it sail briefly on the foaming crest of a wave and vanish. And then she remembered. The nausea she had fought rose up and overwhelmed her, souring her throat and mouth. Her head was pounding. She vomited and slipped, unconscious, into the fetid pool of her own sickness.

It was in England that she had awaked hours later. She opened her eyes in a small white room in the Bournemouth hostel, unfamiliar and smelling of the antiseptic cleanser peculiar to institutions. She screamed for her mother, for her father — the train journey and the Channel crossing forgotten. The kindly matron who hurried to her bedside was a stranger who spoke a language that Rutti could not comprehend. The terror of that awakening stayed with her always.

Sarah, too, often awoke at odd hours in unfamiliar rooms, but when she shouted for Rutti ("Sarah wants Mommy"), Rutti was with her in seconds. "Mommy's right here. Here I am, Sarah. Don't be frightened." She smiled when she spoke to Sarah, when she gathered her daughter into her arms and smoothed her sleep-wrinkled face, kissed away her tears.

Werner objected, urged her to get a sitter or participate in a baby-sitting pool. "You are spoiling her. She will grow up weak, frightened."

Rutti ignored his objections. She pitied Werner but she did not heed him. From the moment of their very first meeting in the improvised underground shelter in the Jerusalem corridor, she had pitied Werner, but seldom had she heeded him. She had brought Sarah to the Cunninghams early, had put her to sleep in a cot that Merle set up beside Greg's bed.

Peacefully asleep, Sarah did not stir when she entered. It was Greg who jerked awake and sat up in bed. His curls, the color of an autumn fire, clung damply to his head. He smiled at Rutti and immediately sank back into sleep. Rutti pulled the blanket up to Sarah's neck and straightened Greg's comforter.

She returned to the living room and again stood beside Werner who was in earnest conversation with Nancy and Dov. He held a newly filled glass of wine and he spoke rapidly, almost angrily, his cheeks burning.

"Surely, you cannot think of Israel as a solution, as a safe haven for Jews," he said. "There is no safe haven. The danger of evil is everywhere and we must always be careful. Always. And especially in Israel because there the concentration of Jews is already in place. Easily found. There will be no reliance on transports, no necessity to build camps." Spittle formed on his lips and he licked it away. "All that is needed are a few well-aimed missiles."

"Werner, you misunderstood Dov," Nancy interceded gently. "He sees Israel as a challenge for Jews who want to settle there — not as a solution to problems of persecution and alienation."

"Please." Rutti put her hand on Werner's arm, playfully took his drink and sipped it herself. "We are here for a party, a pleasant evening. Merle and Andrew did not invite us here to solve the world's problems."

"Rutti's absolutely right. It really is time for us to go in to dinner. You must all be famished and you don't want me to get into trouble with Lottie." Gratefully, gracefully, Merle slid into the role of hostess.

Their answering laughter defused the tension. Of course they did not want her to get into trouble with Lottie and it was true that they were hungry. They followed her into the dining room and took their seats at the beautifully set table. Lottie had placed Nancy's bouquet in a tall crystal vase and the scent of the flowers mingled with the fragrant aroma of the leek and potato soup that had been ladled into the deep ivory-colored china dishes. Over the soup Andrew Cunningham asked Hope and Ted about their advertising agency.

"It's still pretty much a shoestring operation," Hope said cheerfully. "But things are looking up. Last month we actually managed to balance our books and come out ahead. We may even be able to hire some creative staff soon and rely less on free-lancers."

"Your clients don't mind the use of free-lancers?" Andrew asked.

"They don't know about it," Ted replied easily. "We make our presentation, show the artwork, the copy, the placement concept, the demographics. Basically, what they're buying is what Hope and I present to them. And when Hope delivers a presentation there are never any questions about staff or facilities."

"Yes," Hope agreed amiably. "They look at me and think 'sincere,' 'solid.' 'This woman has her fingers on the pulse of Middle America.'" She grinned. She was a shrewd, intelligent woman who exploited her plainness as other women exploit their beauty. She understood the rules of the game. She and Ted were a team, treading slowly, cautiously, but steadily. No one had thought they could manage it. An ad agency as a mom-and-pop operation. They knew themselves to be slightly comical, even a touch absurd. Tall, scrawny Hope with her Kentucky twang and freckled complexion, rotund Ted whose accent had been cultivated on the slope of Beacon Hill and whose intellect had been honed in New Haven.

Still, they were making it work and managing with Eric as well. Of course, they had been lucky to have Anne, and Hope was confident that she would stay with them. They would arrange it. Happily, Hope sipped her wine and turned her attention to the salad. Endive, water chestnuts, and morels on a bed of red-leaf lettuce.

"Americans are so skillful at illusions," Dov said, carving into his veal. "But then illusions are essential to this country, I think."

"Why specifically to this country?" Andrew asked. This was the sort of conversation that pleased him, an intelligent exchange of ideas, well paced, unemotional. He was proud of Merle for creating this beautiful meal, for cultivating friendships with this unusual group of women. He sliced another piece of veal and placed it on Werner's plate, vaguely surprised that the fair-haired man ate so very quickly.

"Because this country is essentially innocent," Dov replied. "It's true that you've sent men off to war but it's been a century since you confronted a war on your own soil. And because, like my own country, you are still, in historical terms, a pioneering country. A frontier raises hopes, expectations. Americans traditionally have been obsessed with a belief in goodness, a denial of evil."

"But is that necessarily illusory?" Anne asked.

"It is if facts are distorted to preserve the illusion. If instead of confronting truth, a lie that perpetuates a belief in innocence is offered."

"But surely that would be very hard to do," Merle objected. "Facts can't be distorted."

"Those with enough power can do anything. Anything." Werner spoke without lifting his eyes from his plate.

They were silent then, unwilling to answer him, unwilling to allow him to elaborate, fearful that again his hand would tremble and his voice rise with dangerous excitement. They had stumbled into dangerous conversational territory and hastily they retreated to safer shores.

Andrew lifted his wine glass and proposed a toast.

"To new friendships in new times."

They clicked glasses and drank.

"To the Great Society," Ted said, refilling his glass.

"Nah — to the greater society," Hope drawled.

"To the greatest society," they all said in unison and burst into laughter.

They were comfortable with each other now and conversation came easily. They spoke of the theater. Merle and Andrew had seen *Marat/Sade*.

"Weird," Merle said.

"What did you expect?" Anne asked, and they laughed again.

"I want to see *Royal Hunt of the Sun* or *Fiddler on the Roof*," Nancy said. "But whenever I get tickets for anything Dov is on call."

She smiled ruefully and placed her hand on his.

"Nancy thinks it's a plot," Dov said.

"Don't forget — paranoids have enemies also," Nancy retorted, grinning.

"Such a strange selection of plays this season." Rutti observed. She would not see any of them. She could not afford the tickets. But she would buy a standing room ticket for the Sadler's Wells Ballet. She would take Sarah and hold her in her arms throughout the performance or perhaps allow her to sleep on the floor beside her, in a nest fashioned of their winter coats, as she had done the previous season. Werner approved of such excursions. He approved of beauty and culture. Not that it mattered. She would do as she pleased and Werner knew that. The wine had relaxed her. She ceased to worry about Werner. The food calmed him, she knew, and, as always, he had eaten ravenously.

"Why strange?" Nancy asked.

"They are all so cruel. The subjection of the Aztecs. One culture subjugating another. And then in *Marat/Sade* one man imposes himself cruelly on another. And *Fiddler on the Roof* ends with the expulsion of the Jews from their shtetl village."

"In my field we would call it displacement." Nancy reflected. "We displace our own anxiety by contemplating the anxieties of others. Perhaps we go to the theater to flee the cruelty of our own age in a world of fantasy. Or maybe it reassures us to know that cruelty is not a recent phenomenon. Other generations have survived it."

"And what are the cruelties of our time?" Andrew asked.

"I don't think we have to look too far to find them," Anne replied. "I spent last weekend reading *Why We Can't Wait* — you know, the Martin Luther King book. He has damn good reasons for not waiting, all of them based on cruelty. Why should anyone have to wait another generation to be served at a lunch counter or use a public bathroom?"

She fell silent as Lottie entered the room, carrying the silver coffee pot. Slowly, she circled the table and filled each cup. They did not resume their conversation until she left, until Merle carefully cut and served the pecan pie, spooning a cloud of whipped cream onto each golden triangle.

"You don't have to tell me why they can't wait," Hope said. "I'm from Kentucky."

"We need change. Of course, we need change." Andrew agreed. "But there's danger in changes that come too fast."

"I'd say we're just about a century too slow," Anne countered. "But we're about to make up for lost time. No one wants to wait. Things are moving too fast and we're running out of time and out of patience. Everyone wants to get on with it, to break free. Women. The black community. The boys who might find themselves dead in a swamp in Southeast Asia if they wait too long. If we wait too long."

"And are all these reforms to take place in this decade? A heavy burden for the sixties — liberating women, guaranteeing civil rights, establishing world peace," Andrew said dryly.

"It's a beginning. We're making a beginning," Nancy said.

"One last toast — to this new beginning." Solemnly Dov lifted his coffee cup and Nancy smiled at him gratefully.

Merle rapped her cup smartly with her spoon.

"That's enough," she said. "I hereby declare an end to serious talk. Remember, we're supposed to have fun tonight."

"Did we decide on Advanced Fun or Remedial Fun?" Anne asked.

The women giggled and the men glanced at each other in puzzlement.

"Definitely Advanced Fun," Merle said. "Everyone into the living room. Advanced Fun means a game."

She glided out of her seat and led the way, a bright-haired queen who expected her court to trail after her.

"A game?" Dov's query was a whispered growl in Nancy's ear.

"Please," she said and they followed the group into the living room where they ranged themselves about the fire.

Nancy noticed how close Werner stood to the flames. He held his hands out to the leaping tongues of fire, his wrists too thin for his wide, frayed cuffs. He was a man constantly in search of elusive warmth, a man who shivered against the chill of a ravaged childhood. He was, she knew instinctively, deprived and thus emotionally needy. Only last week, sitting over coffee cups in Nancy's small kitchen, as Keren and Sarah played in the living room, Rutti had told Nancy how she and Werner had met. After the war, Rutti had left England, hoping against hope that her parents might have survived, that she might find news of them in Palestine.

"I was fifteen years old," she said, staring into the dregs of her coffee cup. "And again, I was part of a group of Jewish kids trekking across Europe. We went to Switzerland and then to Italy. The British were still limiting Jewish immigration so again we traveled without documents or passports, illegal, immigrant, stateless Jewish children on our way to a state that had not yet been declared. We reached Palestine in March of nineteen forty-eight. By April I had located neighbors from Leopoldstadt who told me that my parents were dead. Suicides. They took sleeping pills the night before they were to report for deportation. I was not surprised. I think I had felt all along that they were dead. In a way, it was a relief to know for certain. I was sent to a kibbutz in the Judaean hills. In May, when war broke out, Beit Yair was the first settlement to be attacked by the Jordanians."

The teenage refugees, untrained and unarmed, took refuge in an underground shelter along with the aged and the children. There, amid the stench of sweat and urine, the acrid scent of wasted bullets, Rutti had heard a sobbing distinct from the frightened bawling of the toddlers, the mewling wails of the infants. Interspersed with small moans, the sobs rose and fell in a curious, rhythmic pattern. She made her way through the darkness, to a tall youth whose fingers covered his tear-streaked face, whose fair hair fell in thick silken folds across his high forehead. Werner. She recognized him at once because she had seen him in Switzerland and again in Italy and caught glimpses of him at the kibbutz, although they had never spoken. That was not unusual. The youthful refugees clung fiercely to their anonymity, so conditioned were they to secrecy.

Still, she had noticed Werner and thought him very beautiful. She was fascinated by the angular contours of his face and she had sketched him once from memory. It was said that he was possessed of a rare brilliance but was subject to a frightening moodiness. It did not frighten her. She gently removed his fingers from his face and wiped his tears with her own handkerchief. She opened up her arms and pulled him toward her in comforting embrace. They did not speak as Jordanian rockets exploded about their shelter, as women comforted small children and the murmur of reassuring voices was now and again pierced by shrieks of fear. She held him close against her own small body and hummed a lullaby that had comforted her when she was a child. It comforted him, too, she knew. His terror abated and he grew calm.

When the all-clear sounded, they stumbled into the sunlight that blinded them with its brightness, supporting each other as they struggled for balance. He told her then that he, too, as a small boy, had left Vienna on a kindertransport. It did not surprise her to learn that his family had lived only blocks from her own home in Leopoldstadt. It would not have surprised her to learn that their parents had known each other. Like her, he had reached England, but whereas she had been placed with a kindly family in Surrey, Werner had spent the long war years on a work farm in Cheshire, run by a Jewish charity for the refugee children who could not be placed. He had remained there for seven years — seven years during which no one had hugged him or even held his hand — seven years of lukewarm oatmeal for breakfast, hard bread painted with marmite and fat marbled meat for lunch and dinner, served without a smile. He felt himself hungry even after he had eaten. He slept on his back, with his thin arms entwined about his shoulders, hugging himself because there was no one to hug him. The nightmares began then.

He, too, had decided to come to Palestine in quest of his parents. His search had been even briefer than Rutti's. His parents' names appeared on a published list of victims executed at Mauthausen. He wept then, for the first time it seemed to him, since leaving Vienna. Tears had not been tolerated on the work farm or perhaps he had been too intimidated and bewildered during those years to allow himself the luxury of grief. But now he wept without warning and the weeping that he could not control filled him with shame and with fear.

"Don't be ashamed. Don't be frightened," Rutti said. She was grateful to him for weeping because it seemed to her that she herself had forgotten the formula for expressing sorrow. When she and Werner made love for the first time it was not ardor they sought but comfort. They did not cling together in passion but in loneliness. They were brother and sister — orphaned children who spoke the same language, who had walked down the same narrow streets, felt the same terror of abandonment.

They were married three years later in the kibbutz social hall. Chana and Dror, the handsome Israeli couple who had served as Rutti's kibbutz "parents" since her arrival in the country, escorted her to the marriage canopy.

"You are certain?" Chana had asked Rutti the night before the wedding.

The question had startled Rutti. Surely, Chana could see that she had no choice. She and Werner were bound to each other by sorrow and loss; they were responsible for each other because truly there was no one else to be responsible for either of them.

They left the kibbutz to study in Jerusalem, she at Bezalel Art School, he at the Hebrew University. They received scholarships and small annuities in reparations from the German government. Werner completed his history degree with highest honors. They celebrated with a small party in their tiny student apartment. It seemed a miracle to them. They had friends, a home. There was enough food. Rutti made lamb stew and although Werner ate with their guests, he awoke in the middle of the night and ate the rest of the stew, plucking the cold, fat-congealed meat out of the pot with his fingers. And then quite suddenly, he began to sob, the same rhythmic, unrelenting sobs she had heard that first night in the shelter. But now she could not calm him. His misery was impervious to her embrace. At last she called a doctor who, in turn, called an ambulance.

That was the first of Werner's breakdowns, of his sudden, inexplicable withdrawals into a netherworld of darkness and grief that she could not penetrate, that the kindly psychiatrist at Hadassah Hospital could not explain away, although he could predict its progress.

"It is a pattern," he said sadly. "Such episodes will occur again and perhaps grow worse as he grows older." He had looked long and hard at Rutti, so small, so lovely, her blond hair a golden mist about her head. He himself was a survivor and the young woman who sat before him, her hands clasped, her head lowered, reminded him of his youngest sister, the only one in his family who had not survived the war. "I will speak frankly. If you were my daughter, I should advise you to divorce him. He will never be well. You have no hope of a stable life with him."

But Rutti could not divorce Werner. If he were only her husband, she could perhaps have left him. But he was her tragic twin, and siblings are linked for life.

Werner studied for his master's degree and taught high school. He was respected for his brilliance, for his teaching ability, for the learned articles he published in scholarly journals. He began each semester at each new school with enthusiasm, but inevitably he lost each job, because quite suddenly, for no discernible reason, he could not get out of bed and was again plunged into melancholia that caused him to weep endlessly, to tremble uncontrollably. A second psychiatrist advised them to leave Israel.

"The tensions of this country, the constant threat of war, the constant reminder of danger, may contribute to his condition. Go to America. Perhaps he will have a less stressful life there."

Again they packed their bags. Another country. Another continent. She was twenty-seven years old. She wanted a child.

And in New York, he did seem to be better. He found a job teaching history at an adult extension division. He published a paper and was asked to participate in seminars and sit on learned panels. She took art classes. Sarah was born. Werner exulted at her birth. Sarah had colic and Werner walked the floor with her, night after night, singing softly, talking softly. He played with the infant, sprawled across the bed, across the floor, speaking to her in all the languages of his life. It seemed to Rutti that their daughter's birth restored him to joy. She believed that he was better, that the dark times were behind them. She bought an easel and painted her first oil — Werner with Sarah in his arms.

And then one winter night she awoke to the terrible, familiar sound of his sorrow, his despair. He was not beside her in the bed and she raced down the hallway to Sarah's room. He stood in the narrow shaft of radiance cast by the night-light, Sarah in his arms, tears streaking his face.

"I won't let you live in such an evil world," he said. "Not my baby. Not my darling Sarah. How can I let you grow up in such a world?"

He approached the window and Rutti's heart stopped. The window was open and the wind whipped the curtains, the pink-and-white checked curtains she had sewn herself when she believed that after all they might have a normal life. Sarah whimpered.

"Werner!" Rutti's scream, strident with terror, frightened them both. He turned and she rushed forward, swept Sarah into her arms.

"You cannot live here," Rutti told Werner the next day, her voice firm. "You cannot be alone with Sarah. You know that."

"I know that." He was abject, depressed. Guilt-ridden, he would grant her anything. "But let me see her. Let me see you. Don't leave me. Oh Rutti, not you too."

"No," she said. "Of course not. Not me. How could I abandon you, Werner? My Werner." She spoke to him in German, in the language of their mangled childhood. Again she held him close, as she had that very first night. "But I must think of Sarah. We must both think of Sarah."

"Yes. Our Sarah." He acquiesced without argument. History had claimed his life, destroyed his life. But Sarah would be protected.

They lived apart, Rutti remaining in the railroad flat on West 103rd Street and Werner moving from furnished room to furnished room. They managed. Rutti rented a bedroom to two young actors, Mark and Dan, pleasant young men who delighted in playing with Sarah. They made the child masks and costumes and cooked savory stews, which they shared with Rutti whose own culinary efforts were perfunctory. They posed for her and she captured their grace and their kindness. They were the first subjects of the charcoal portraits that were to become her forte. Werner visited often. He had begun work on a book, a cyclical interpretation of history. Occasionally, they made love. She ministered to his misery with tenderness. She had been true to her word. She had not abandoned him. It was not odd that she had asked him to accompany her to Merle's dinner party.

"I would worry about Werner if he were alone. He is used to being with us on Saturday nights," she had told Anne.

Anne had looked at her quizzically but had said nothing. Nor had the others questioned her. They understood how to be intimate without being invasive.

She wondered now, as they grouped themselves about the fireplace, what her new friends, these strong American women who had never known war and abandonment, thought of Werner. He sat on a hassock and again stretched his hands toward the flames.

"Fun time, Merle," Hope drawled.

"Give me a second. I want to check on Greg. He had a cough this afternoon."

"Then I will look in on Sarah," Rutti said.

The two children slept peacefully, their faces turned toward each other. Merle touched Greg's brow and smiled because it was cool.

"We are charmed by Werner," she told Rutti. "He is so knowledgeable. I would imagine that he has a great future academically." She had spoken with Werner before dinner, had listened, fascinated, as he explained his cyclical theory of history.

"Yes. He's getting recognition. Columbia asked him to teach a graduate seminar in historiography." Rutti spoke softly. She did not want to wake up the sleeping children.

"There, you see. You must think about the future, Rutti. About the kind of life you could have with Werner." She could see Rutti as the wife of a successful academic, presiding over a book-lined apartment, attending learned conferences. "You could be Frau Professor Weisenblatt."

"But I would not want that, Merle," Rutti replied gently. She could not live her life through a man, build her position on his accomplishments, his status. That much her life had taught her. Even if Werner were different, if he were stable and could offer her stability in turn, still, she would want to develop her own talent, be responsible for her own life.

Merle picked up a stuffed animal that had fallen to the floor. The Babar she had bought Greg for Christmas. She loved buying toys for Greg, loved walking through F.A.O. Schwarz with him. He smiled in his sleep and she wondered if he was dreaming of the elephant who reigned in the wilderness. She had read him a Babar book before he went to bed.

"Daddy is Babar and you are Celeste and I am all the twins," he had announced.

He coughed softly and Rutti looked at her worriedly.

"It's nothing," Merle assured her. "The doctor thinks it's an allergy. Nothing contagious." She knew how obsessed Rutti was about Sarah's health.

Rutti nodded, but she shifted Sarah's position slightly so that she was at a small remove from Greg. Perhaps Werner was right — perhaps she was overprotective. She did not flinch from his condemnation nor from her friends' amusement at her concern. Sarah was all the family she had. She knew, with unquestioning certainty, that she could not bear it if anything were to happen to her daughter.

Merle turned to Rutti. "I want to have another child," she said softly.

"Then why shouldn't you?"

"Andrew wants us to wait."

"But what you want must count for something."

Merle shook her head. "It is difficult to argue with someone who is always right," she said, smiling apologetically. Rutti imagined such an argument between Merle and Andrew — Merle's wispy, pleading voice contrapuntal to Andrew's deep assertive basso. No, a recorder could not do battle with a horn — wind against brass was always overpowered, brutally silenced. Merle, the musician, knew that.

They rejoined the group in the living room. Merle sat beside Andrew on the high-backed love seat that was closest to the fireplace. She smiled at her guests. She lifted her hand to touch the diamond pendant that glittered at her throat. She wore her hair loose and Andrew curled a lock of it about his finger, then slowly loosed it.

"The game," he reminded her. He was the king, giving his consort her cue. "We've been waiting."

"Yes. Of course. The game. It's called Abstractions. Does anyone know it?"

"Sure," Ted replied. "That's where one person is 'it' and goes out of the room while everyone else agrees on the name of a subject. The person who's 'it' has to guess who it is by asking abstract questions like, if this person is a jewel, what jewel would he or she be?"

"That's it," Merle said. "Andrew and I played it at a dinner party and Andrew was 'it.' He asked what dish the person would be if he were a food and as soon as the first person said barbecued beef, Andrew guessed that it was President Johnson." She laughed and pressed Andrew's hand.

Nancy glanced at Dov. She sensed his impatience, his contempt.

"All right then. Who's to be 'it'?" Andrew took control, clapped his hands authoritatively.

"I don't mind." It was Rutti who volunteered as always; she volunteered for any unpopular task, so eager was she to please. She sprang to her feet, an obedient schoolgirl in dark skirt and white blouse, her golden hair framing her delicate face, her blue eyes glinting.

"Call me when you're ready," she said. "I'll wait outside."

When she had left, they conferred, leaning forward and keeping their voices low.

"We can pick a famous personality but we have to say whether it's contemporary or historical," Merle said.

"It'd be much more interesting," Anne responded, "if we select someone we all know. One of us perhaps."

"And a bit dangerous," Nancy said warningly, her professional instinct asserting itself.

"Oh, don't be silly. We're all adults. No one will be hurt." Andrew was intrigued by the idea. He would not mind being the subject, would not be averse to hearing how others perceived him. If he were a bird he would be an eagle — if he were an animal he would be a lion.

"Let us stick with someone in the news," Dov said. He was wary, nervous. Why were Americans always playing games? Why were they so reluctant to surrender their childhoods?

"No. It will be more fun if it's one of us." Andrew was insistent. Merle had proposed the game and it was their party. He would not surrender control.

"Why not Rutti herself?" Hope suggested.

"Fine. Rutti is the subject, then," Andrew decided and they relaxed, each pleased to have escaped, to have avoided exposure.

Nancy glanced at her watch. Good. They would play one round, select a historical personality (she had already thought of Freud — if he were a color he would be gray — if he were a piece of furniture he would be a couch), and then they could say their farewells and leave.

Merle opened the door and Rutti, a half-smile on her face, entered and stood before them, her back to the fire. Werner sat with his hands clasped beneath his chin. He did not look at Rutti but kept his eyes raised to the ceiling. Nancy reached out to touch Dov's hand, to reassure him that soon, soon, they would be on their way home.

"Is the person you are thinking about our contemporary?" Rutti asked.

"Contemporary. And not famous." Merle offered a bonus with her answer, a hint for Rutti. "Yet —"

"Ah. I see. Well, if this person were a color, what color would the person be?"

"Sky blue," Nancy said.

"Pale pink." Anne did not hesitate.

"Aqua."

"Violet."

"Yellow."

They chose the softest hues they could think of, the colors of gentleness and calm.

"Werner?" Rutti coaxed an answer from him, urged him into the game. He did not lower his eyes. He did not stir. His thin, angular body was motionless, tense.

"Black," he replied. "Black as night."

They stared at him but Rutti merely nodded and phrased her next question.

"If this person were a landscape, what sort of landscape would this person be?"

"A love garden of spring flowers," Merle said.

"A lake scene," Andrew offered. "A clear blue lake surrounded by golden forsythia."

"A meadow."

"An orchard."

"A glen."

They offered images of sweetness and harmony — of nature's gentlest scenes — images that suited soft-voiced, tiny Rutti with her aureole of angel's hair, her wide blue eyes, her skin the color of ivory.

"Werner?" She turned to him, smiling, expectant.

"A dark forest. Trees waiting for winter. Their branches bare, dying weeds entangled at their trunks."

He sat motionless, staring upward. The others looked at him, uneasy, frightened. Rutti stood very still.

"And if this person were a body of water . . . ?" Her voice was very soft and they rushed in with their answers, eager for the game to be over.

"A mountain stream."

"A pool in a glade."

"A sweet brook."

"An ocean inlet — gentle, calm."

Again it was Werner's turn.

"A stagnant waterhole," he said. "Stinking and brackish." He spat the unfamiliar words out and now he looked at her.

She understood at once. She read the commingling of love and hatred in his eyes. They were not unfamiliar to her. He hated her as he hated himself. She was his wife, his sister, the mother of his child, witness to his despair. His love had tainted her. He saw her as he saw himself — black and stripped barren, stagnant, polluted by loss.

Rutti moved toward him, gripped by fear. It was happening again. Another seizure was upon him. Within seconds his rage would reach a crescendo and shatter into paroxysms of sorrow.

"Werner," she said pleadingly. Her voice broke with sympathy. She stretched her arms out to him.

But he bolted from his chair, his face ashen, his arms raised as though to fend off her advance. His fists were clenched. Dov moved imperceptibly forward, shot a warning glance at Andrew. But Werner strode to the door. He muttered as he moved and then he turned to face them, and his mutterings exploded into a tirade.

"You don't know what it's like. You don't know what she's like. She promised me life but she gave me death. I am alone again. Alone. Alone." The word was repeated, a mournful, echoing indictment.

They looked at one another, but before anyone could respond, Lottie's steps were heard, light upon the polished parquet floor of the hallway, her voice rich and caring.

"Now you just put your coat on. Don't you upset yourself. No point in it." She spoke calmly, comfortingly, in the practiced tone of one long used to confronting misery. They wondered that he did not bury his head in the comforting mound of her breasts, that he did now allow her to engulf him in the generous warmth of her embrace. The front door opened and Lottie closed it behind him and, light-footed, made her way back down the hall.

Anne led Rutti to a seat by the fire. She looked at them and read the love and sympathy in their eyes. They surrounded her, Merle and Nancy and Anne. They comforted her with their friendship, soothed her with their acceptance.

"Now you understand," she said softly.

"Oh, yes." She had spoken to all of them but it was Merle who replied.

They understood why she did not live with him and why she could not live without him. They understood that she loved him and feared him and that always she would fear for him.

"Mama." Sarah glided into the room, her pale face sleep masked, her eyes red. "Mama, Sarah wants to go home."

Rutti gathered her daughter into her arms.

"We'll go home now, Sarah darling. Of course we'll go home."

They all prepared to leave then, restoring the evening to balance with their thanks and their good-byes.

Nancy and Dov lingered for a moment after the others left.

"It was a lovely party," Nancy said.

"Poor Rutti." Merle's voice broke with sympathy.

"She will manage." Andrew spoke with certainty and they looked at him questioningly.

"I have no doubt of it," he said. "You are extraordinary women, you know. All of you."

He put his arm on Merle's shoulder and drew her close. They stood together in the circlet of light cast by the dangling bronze lamp and waved as Nancy and Dov made their way down the high stone steps of the brownstone, glazed now with a thin sheet of brittle frost.

5

THE RHYTHMIC chimes, emanating from the hospital belfry, pierced the insular silence of the medical school library and caused the librarian to frown and look at her watch. The students who sat at the long tables or huddled in the shelter of their carrels straightened their hunched shoulders, looked up from their texts and notebooks. Anne Richardson pushed aside her biochemistry textbook and thumped her fingers lightly as each chime sounded. The Oriental student who sat opposite her grimaced and bent his head closer to his notebook.

"Damn!" Anne muttered as the twelfth chime sounded. She had meant to leave the library at eleven-thirty to join her friends for the Friday lunch that had become their end-of-the-week ritual. If she left right now she might reach the Yallon apartment within the half hour, but the bus was notoriously unreliable. She had reserved a microscope for two o'clock and the lab technician had warned her that he would not hold it for her if she were late.

"There are other students who need access to the microscope," he had reminded her sternly. "Serious students."

You mean male students, you chauvinistic bastard, Anne had thought, although she did not answer but only smiled engagingly. She had promised she'd be on time.

She would have to miss the lunch again, she realized, and she thought of her friends, relaxed and laughing as they sat at Nancy's kitchen table. They would be spooning up the vegetable soup that Nancy made from scratch and nibbling on the crispy grilled-cheese sandwiches they all favored, while the children worked at their peanut butter sculptures. Nancy gave each child a small jar, a spoon, and slices of bread on paper plates and ignored them as they rolled the peanut butter into small balls, created bunny rabbits and fed each other ears, or built houses, giggling as they ate and worked.

"Definitely anal." Nancy observed. "And definitely fun. Advanced Fun."

"Definitely disgusting," Anne retorted. "But Remedial Disgusting."

This week the children had planned a peanut butter mountain with M&M gorges. Perhaps it was just as well she was missing that, Anne thought wryly, as she left the library.

She called Nancy from a pay phone.

"Hello. Who is this?" Keren's voice was sweetly high.

"Hi, Keren. It's Anne. Let me talk to your mom."

"Mommy, it's Anne," Keren called importantly.

The phone clattered as Keren dropped the receiver. Anne heard voices in the background — Rutti and Merle laughing as they talked, the children giggling — and music. Of course. Merle had promised to bring the recording of *Man of La Mancha.* Anne imagined Rutti and Merle waltzing, Nancy dancing with the children.

"Anne. You're not coming. You're a traitor. We promised each other Fridays. Is nothing sacred?" Nancy was jokingly reproving but Anne knew she was disappointed.

"I'm sorry. I was studying for this damn biochemistry comprehensive and I lost track of time. And now I have a microscope reserved for two so it would be too crazy. But I'll be there next week for sure. At Merle's, right? I'm really sorry."

"She's really sorry," Nancy called to the others.

"She's really sorry." Sarah, Greg, and Keren took up the chant. Anne knew they were dancing about as their mothers smiled. Friday afternoons were threaded with silliness. They had triumphed through the week and were buoyed by thoughts of the weekend.

"Hey, Annie. Don't work too hard. We miss you." Merle had taken the phone.

"I miss you guys too. Don't get buried alive under the peanut butter mountain."

"You cannot possibly imagine how disgusting it is," Merle said.

"Oh, yes, I can," she retorted and laughed. She hung up, smiling, and grateful for her friends' support and understanding.

During her first year of medical school, when there were fewer labs, she had seldom missed the Friday lunches. The first-year students were coddled, almost pampered. They sat proudly through orientation and listened as a succession of professors praised them. They had been carefully selected and had the highest MCAT scores of any class ever admitted to the medical school.

"You represent a diverse group of students united by your outstanding academic achievement and your commitment to medicine," another professor informed them.

Anne glanced around the room. She did not see much evidence of diversity. The majority of the class was male, white, and young. There were four black students, one of them from Nigeria. He had been unnerved when Anne greeted him in the dialect she had learned during her days in Lagos and had avoided her ever since. A group of Oriental students sat together and took notes even during the speeches of welcome. There were perhaps a dozen women in the class and only four of them responded to Anne's suggestion that they all meet for coffee. Two of them, Kate Enderby and Jean Liebowitz, held nursing degrees and were middle-aged. Peggy Andrews and Nina Alcott were both the daughters of prominent physicians who had been roommates at Rosemary Hall and then at Radcliffe and now shared an apartment on Riverside Drive.

Peggy was tall and Nina was short, but they both favored the miniskirt that had just become fashionable and they wore their brown hair at shoulder-length which, sometime in the afternoon, they each pulled back into a ponytail. Anne imagined them opening a pediatric practice together, marrying two brothers, and living next door to each other in beautiful colonial homes. They were always very cordial to Anne, and when they invited her to join them for a study session they insisted that she come early for dinner. The dinners were so good that Anne refrained from inviting them back.

Anne was still living with Hope and Ted and caring for Eric in a very part-time way. She gave Eric breakfast, walked him to the school bus, and baby-sat occasionally, in exchange for room and board. They were all casual about food and relieved that Eric was served a hot lunch at the Riverside Country Day School. He was an extraordinarily healthy child, but when he fell ill Hope glowered darkly as she juggled her schedule.

"God is punishing me for not making casseroles with fresh vegetables," she drawled. "I am not a good mother. I am a lousy mother."

"Lousy but not the lousiest," Anne replied. "Besides, you don't get colds because of a lack of fresh vegetables."

"You're only a first-year student. They don't teach the common cold to plebes. You have to be a senior to confront the mystery of drippy noses."

"True," Anne said cheerfully and went off to play Clue with Eric.

She had, she acknowledged, learned very little about the common cold or other illnesses and their remedies the first year, but she was enraptured and absorbed by her studies. Her class in cellular neurobiology occupied two entire mornings twice a week and she was always startled when the lecturer abruptly gathered his materials and left. She would have sat on contentedly for another hour, taking notes on synapses and axons, analyzing the chemicals that trigger neurological responses. The margins of her notebooks were rimmed with question marks. But why? she thought. Why this enzyme and not another? She dared not ask. Few first-year students asked questions and none of the questioners were women. Anne mentioned this to Kate Enderby, who nodded.

"I guess we're keeping a low profile without even realizing it," the older woman said. "Conditioning, I suppose."

Anne did not press her. It did not seem important. What was important was the session in the histology laboratory. She worked swiftly, her instruments gleaming, her slides intricate collages of mysterious tissue samples.

The first year had been exhilarating although often she found herself overcome by a sudden weakness, an unexpected exhaustion.

"Anne, you must slow down." Merle would advise her gently each Friday afternoon, as Nancy brought her a sandwich and a bowl of soup, and Rutti riffled admiringly through her lab workbook, studying the drawings of nerve cells, of networks of veins, muscles, and bones. She showed Anne how to hold her pencil so that her strokes would be more fluid, how to shade her work for emphasis.

Merle organized the handout sheets distributed by almost every instructor, sometimes as a supplement and sometimes to compensate for carelessly organized, barely audible lectures.

Their Friday lunches were, for each of them, a secure island of leisure after the long workweek. And they were all working hard. Rutti was taking an extra course at the Art Students League and doing graphics on a regular basis for Hope and Ted. Merle was studying composition in addition to her violin lessons.

"I haven't told Andrew about it although I'm sure he wouldn't mind," she told her friends.

"Then why not tell him about it?" Nancy asked.

"It's not important."

"It's important enough for you not to tell him," Anne retorted, but she caught Nancy's eye and fell silent.

They observed careful parameters of privacy, but at the same time they were fiercely honest with one another. It seemed natural for Nancy to advise Rutti to spend less time with Werner, to wean him away from his dependency on her and on Sarah.

"You have every right to a life of your own."

And it was equally natural for Rutti to listen quietly and then say, "I can't. Not yet."

It was natural for them to accommodate each other, to help each other, to urge each other on, to offer encouragement. They laughed at each other's jokes.

"I will miss all of you like my two front teeth," Rutti said. "Who am I?" she challenged them.

"Bugs Bunny," Eric shouted.

"No. Lucy Baines Johnson at her bridal shower," Merle said. "I hated her presents."

"Bridal showers are tacky." Anne contributed languidly as she polished her dissecting instruments.

"Then we'll be sure to make you one," Nancy said; Anne tossed a pillow at her, which gave the children license to start a pillow fight of their own.

But Anne could not always make the Friday lunches during her second year. The pace accelerated and second-year students were expected to volunteer for clinic hours, to be available for theater presentations when a case of particular relevance to course work was discussed, to become an integral part of hospital life. Anne's class diminished. There was talk of failures and dropouts. Kate Enderby did not take her comprehensive examinations at midyear. It was Jean Liebowitz who told Anne that the good-natured, ruddy-faced woman with the ribald sense of humor had had a nervous breakdown.

"She was coping with too much," Jean said sadly. "She thought it would be OK to start med school when her kids were adolescents but then her daughter developed hepatitis and Kate just couldn't manage her schedule so that she could be with her. Plus her husband's business went sour and she felt guilty about not bringing any money in." Jean sighed. "We thought we had the system beat, Kate and me. We'd paid our dues. We did our mothering between nursing shifts, did our pre-med work while our kids were in school, and now it was supposed to be our turn. But life doesn't work out that way. I guess Kate isn't going to get her turn."

"Maybe she'll bounce back." But Anne did not believe her own words.

"No. That won't happen. You're smart to get your degree first, Anne. Before you have a family. Before real life begins."

Anne discerned the bitterness in her friend's voice. Jean's hair was streaked with gray and often, during the late afternoon biochemistry lab, her face blanched and froze into a mask of weariness. Her own son and daughter were away at college and her husband, an emergency room physician, complained that he came home to an empty house. He grumbled that Jean studied on weekends when he wanted to relax.

"It's not fair for him to complain," Anne told Jean. "It's like you said — it's your turn. Why should you feel guilty?"

"Hey, Anne, grow up, life's not fair," Jean said wearily. "My kids used to hate it when I told them that. But the truth is there's no quid pro quo in marriage. Not in my marriage, anyway. But if I can survive this year, I'll make it. Everyone says the second year is the roughest."

"We'll survive," Anne said firmly.

Still, on this Friday afternoon, as a warm spring breeze wafted through the newly opened, arch-shaped windows, their panes still smoky with wintry grime, she moved slowly, weighted by an unfamiliar pessimism. She had counted on having lunch at Nancy's and she realized that she had perhaps three dollars in her wallet. Hope and Ted had been short of cash last month and Anne had not wanted to press them for her small salary. Her tuition fees were covered by a generous combination of scholarships and loans and she kept vigilant control of her small savings account, adhering to a rigid budget.

"Everything all right, Anne?" Larry, her lanky, amiable pathology lab partner stopped her. She was startled by the concern in his voice. Immediately she flashed a smile, straightened her shoulders.

"Fine. Great. Maybe a touch of hypoglycemia. I'm just heading for the cafeteria to cure it."

"Take two cubes of sugar and call me in the morning."

"Right."

The hospital cafeteria, a cavernous, badly lit room, was crowded with both staff and visitors. By tacit agreement nurses sat in one section, doctors occupied a small balcony area, and medical students clustered about the tables in the northeast corner.

Anne made her way down the food line and settled at last for an egg salad sandwich because it was the cheapest item on the menu. At the beverage counter, she filled a Styrofoam cup with hot water. She always kept a tea bag in her wallet. She was skilled in the small tricks of economic survival. In warmer weather she took a glass of ice water and plucked lemon slices from the condiment table to concoct a free lemonade. Her tweed skirts and Shetland wool sweaters, her cotton dresses and linen blouses, were purchased at thrift shops and rummage sales. Merle, who often bought clothing that did not meet Andrew's approval, had given her the pale blue cotton blouse she wore and Hope had helped her to shorten the navy blue skirt that hugged her hips and flared gracefully about her knees.

"Anne should write a book called *How to Dress on One Hundred Dollars a Year*," Nancy said laughingly one afternoon as Anne displayed her thrift shop bargains.

"Hey, I couldn't do it without you guys."

The four friends were locked into a conspiracy of cooperative survival. Scarves and sweaters changed hands. They urged each other to try different styles and applauded when Rutti abandoned her schoolgirl white blouse and dark skirt for a peacock blue soft wool dress that Nancy tailored to fit her. Nancy basted the hem as Merle plaited Rutti's golden curls into tiny braids and Keren, giggling, tried to do the same with Sarah's fine hair.

"Anne! Over here," Dov Yallon called to her from the balcony.

A few heads turned and smiles lit the worried faces of visitors. They were pleased to see the handsome doctor call to the tall, beautiful blond woman who walked so gracefully, so purposefully. The casual exchange reminded them that spring had actually begun, that warm breezes wafted and small green purses of unfurled leaves had already appeared on the ailanthus and maple trees that lined the hospital walkways.

"Hi, Dov." Anne set her tray down and smiled as Nancy's husband nodded to the tall man who sat opposite him. He was, she knew, Charles Bingham, an oncologist who was fast gaining a national reputation. She had attended a lecture he had given and been impressed by both his approach and his daring. His war on cancer was aggressive, fired by a personal passion.

"Anne Richardson, Charles Bingham," Dov said.

"It's an honor to meet you," Anne said honestly. "I was at your lecture last Friday."

Charles Bingham, surprisingly, blushed. He was a sharp-featured, lean-faced man whose sand-colored, thinning hair was brushed back from his high forehead.

"Anne's a good friend of my wife's," Dov told him. "At least she used to be. I don't know if Nancy is going to forgive you for missing another Friday afternoon."

"I spoke to her just a few minutes ago and promised I would be there next week. Today was just impossible, Dov."

"Tell me about it." Dov leaned back in his chair and Anne saw the lines of exhaustion that were etched around his eyes. Still, his fatigue did not diminish his dark good looks and there was a sensual quality to his languid posture. He wore a blue-and-white striped rugby shirt beneath his white lab coat.

"You're looking very collegiate today, Dov," Anne said, unwrapping her sandwich and ferreting in her purse for the tea bag.

"Oh, well — when in Rome," Dov said easily. Anne wondered if he had dressed that way the previous summer when he and Keren and Nancy had visited Israel for the first time as a family. Dov had a fellowship at Hadassah Hospital and Nancy's family had insisted on paying for round-trip tickets for Keren and herself.

Nancy returned from that visit aglow with excitement, more enthusiastic than ever about living in Israel. The country was exciting, dramatic, the people warm and imbued with a sense of purpose. She had fallen in love with the landscape, and she described the arid lunar plains of the Negev, the verdancy of the Galilee. Rutti had given her a letter to Chana and Dror at Beit Yair and the Yallons spent a weekend at the kibbutz in the foothills of Judaea where Werner and Rutti had first met. Proudly, Chana showed Nancy the herb garden where she cultivated herbs indigenous to Israel, which were dried and bottled for export. Chana had initiated the project and worked to develop it.

"It is a good feeling to know that I have accomplished this, that I have made a difference," the Israeli woman said.

Nancy understood Chana's pride. She, too, wanted to feel that she had made a difference, that her life had meaning. Gratefully, she had accepted Chana's gift of a small earthenware jar filled with dried marjoram. It stood on her kitchen shelf and its sweet aroma reminded her of the dun-colored hill just beyond Jerusalem where the fragile herb grew amid sloping boulders. Chana asked about Werner and Rutti, and cautiously, Nancy told her about their lives.

They also spent a long weekend with Dov's family. His six sisters swarmed about their brother, feeding him sweet cakes, the vegetable casseroles he had favored as a child, the thick hummus, which he scooped up in envelopes of pita bread baked by his mother.

"I thought that any minute one of his sisters would pour oil on his head and anoint him king of Israel," Nancy told her friends laughingly.

Anne, watching Dov now as he picked at the hospital cafeteria salad plate special, reflected that Dov himself had said very little about that summer in Israel. The thought troubled her and she turned her attention to Charles Bingham.

"I thought your lecture was very exciting. Your approach at least offers some hope. The combination of drug and transplant should yield some interesting results," she said.

"If I can ever get enough funding to test it."

"Oh, I'm sure you'll get the funding. How could they refuse it to you." Her question was actually a statement and she averted her eyes from his startled stare.

Charles Bingham watched as Anne laced her tea with three spoonfuls of sugar.

"Excuse me," he said and rose from the table.

"I hope I didn't scare him off," Anne said to Dov, disappointed that he had left and bewildered at her own disappointment. She had only just met him and he was senior staff. Perhaps he had interpreted her remarks as fawning or presumptuous.

"I don't think so," Dov replied. "I'd hardly characterize him as timid."

"Is something wrong, Dov?" Anne asked. Dov seemed moody, distracted.

"No. Nothing. I suppose I'm upset by this new fighting between the Israelis and Jordanians in Hebron. The husbands of two of my sisters were called up. You don't know what it's like, Anne, to come from a country that is always — always — at war."

"Things aren't so peaceful here in the good old U.S. of A., in case you haven't noticed," Anne replied.

She had signed two petitions that morning as she made her way to class and then to the library. She added her name to a plea from Physicians for Moral Responsibility urging Lyndon Johnson to ban the use of napalm in Vietnam. And she signed a more ambitious document urging the entire United States Congress to press for a total withdrawal of American troops, at least from the Mekong Delta. The previous evening she watched television with Hope and Ted. The three of them sprawled across the living room floor, drinking warm beer that had been given to Ted by a potential client and watched antiwar demonstrations on a midwestern campus. The youthful voices were passionate and angry.

"Hey, hey, LBJ — how many kids did you kill today? Hell no — we won't go!" they chanted as National Guard troops armed with bully sticks and riot shields watched them sourly.

They switched channels and watched a demonstration in a southern town. Whites and blacks, arms entwined, sang "We Shall Overcome" and marched on a library. Ted switched the television set off.

"Too many causes," he said. "I get exhausted watching them."

"How exhausted?" Hope asked and she crossed the room to

perch on Ted's lap, to kiss his cheeks and tickle him beneath the chin until his chubby face exploded into laughter. Intimacy banished uneasiness. They did not want to think of the faces on their television screen. They said good night to Anne and disappeared into their bedroom. Within minutes she heard the familiar sweet whispers and long sighs through the door that did not close properly. She saluted them with her empty glass and experienced a wave of loneliness.

It threatened her now again as she listened to Dov. "It's different here," Dov said. "Vietnam doesn't touch everyone you know the way a war in Israel does. Every home Nancy and I visited last summer had a photograph of a young soldier and each of them had a story. My cousin Yehuda was killed on his nineteenth birthday when a Syrian fired down at him from the Golan Heights. My classmate Yoav was killed by a sniper as he worked the fields on his kibbutz. Of course, we worry about Vietnam but we're at a remove from it. We listen to the body count every night, but in Israel the dead aren't numbers, they're names and faces. Yoav, Yehuda."

"The boys in the body counts have names and faces, too," Anne said quietly.

"I know that. But Anne, do you yourself know anyone who died in Vietnam?"

She shook her head.

"So you see, it is different. Nancy sees the drama of Israel. She doesn't know what it is like to dream about the dead." He touched the butterfly scar at his neck, sighed, and glanced at his watch. "You'll excuse me? I have to do rounds. I'm already late."

"Of course. Go ahead." She waved him away and watched him hurry out of the cafeteria. Why was it so important to Dov that she understand, she wondered. Was she supposed to be his emissary to Nancy, to report his anxiety to his own wife? Puzzled, she stirred her tea and realized she was still hungry. She would splurge, she decided, and buy herself a dessert. She reached for her bag just as Charles Bingham returned to the table, carrying a tray that contained two slices of apple pie and two dishes of vanilla ice cream.

"I hate to eat dessert alone," he said, "it makes me feel guilty. So I took the liberty of taking two portions. But if you feel I'm imposing on you I'll just have to eat them both myself."

"I could never think of apple pie and ice cream as an imposition," she replied. Her mood lifted and she spooned up the sweet edges of crust with an almost childlike delight.

"Tell me," she said, because she found herself intensely curious about the man who sat opposite her, "how did you decide on your specialization?" He was no ordinary research physician. She had discerned his passion for his work in his presentation.

He sliced his pie with great precision, as of course he did all things, and told her that he had grown up on the Oklahoma plains. His father, a small rancher, raised a herd of desert goats, a flock of slow-moving sheep, and a few cows who were always too thin because pastureland was scarce, and even in good years grazing was difficult. His mother, a pale, exhausted, soft-spoken woman, taught school. The ranch was not a successful undertaking but his father plodded on, year after year, experimenting with new breeds, juggling their bills, fiercely determined to keep his land and to stay out of debt.

"In our part of Oklahoma the corn never got as high as an elephant's eye," Charles said as he spooned up the last of his ice cream. Anne, who ate more slowly, dropped a dollop of her own ice cream onto his plate and he grinned at her and continued to talk. His voice grew soft as he described his boyhood.

The small family was always haunted by the specter of sickness. Like many farm families, it was not their own health that concerned them but the health of their livestock. The nearest large animal veterinarian lived miles away and his fees were prohibitive. Charles read the pamphlets on animal diseases published by the Department of Agriculture. He bought a secondhand text on veterinary medicine. He attended animal husbandry workshops at Four-H conventions. When he was twelve he delivered a calf. When he was fourteen he set the broken leg of a black and white kid goat, using a splint of his own design. The next year he cut away an abscess on a horse's leg with a knife he had honed to such a sharpness that it sliced almost effortlessly through the animal's flesh. He used ice to desensitize the limb.

He studied the veterinary text until he knew it by heart. When he looked at a sick animal he could envisage every muscle, the network of veins, the pumping heart, and the draining kidneys. When a diseased animal died Charles cut open the dead beast, and with each examination he marveled anew at the intricacy of the organs, the

95

mystery of the death that claimed the life that had been. He wore high boots to wade through the scarlet rivulets of blood that drenched the straw he spread so carefully around the sawhorses across which he had spread planks of raw wood. On that crude, splintered table, he accomplished what he realized now were his first autopsies.

He saw his first carcinoma in a ewe lamb when he was sixteen years old and he recognized it at once for what it was. He stared at the tumor lodged in the lamb's left ovary; it glistened with poisonous mucus and threatening pincer claws rimmed its periphery. He knew then that he was looking at evil and he set his heart against it. When he discarded the cadaver of the lamb, he buried the tumor separately, as though even in death it had power.

The veterinarian who lectured at the Four-H Club explained cancer to the high school students. Farm animals were plagued by it in increasing numbers; years later there would be speculation that the disease was caused by wastes from the Oklahoma oil companies that used dump sites perilously close to the ranches, but the veterinarian did not consider that. He did, however, notice Charles's acumen. He took an interest in the serious youth and encouraged him to go to college, to think of a career as a veterinarian.

Charles's silent, proud father showed his son a bankbook. Despite his own financial struggle he had saved for his son's education. His mother gave piano lessons and tutored private students. Every penny she earned went into the bank account. Charles, who had always been deeply attached to her, loved her even more fiercely because she was so gentle, so uncomplaining, so tenacious in her love for him, her ambition for him.

He went to the state university and sailed through the prescribed biology and physiology classes. His instructors could teach him nothing he had not already learned poring over the veterinary textbooks. He bought himself a secondhand microscope, a beautiful instrument that he handled gently, polishing the scope after each use, making sure each screw was properly tightened, the swivel properly oiled. He carried it with him to labs and when his class work was completed he studied slides in the physiology laboratory of visual aids. He saw the cancer he had first viewed in the ewe lamb's ovary replicated in a variety of animals and organs, and each time he saw it, he was angered.

During his senior year as he sat filling out his applications for veterinary school, he received a phone call from his father. His mother was ill. There was a long silence and then his father added, "Very ill." Charles knew, then, that she was dying. He went home, cursing himself because he had noticed during his last visit that his mother was unnaturally pale, that she walked with effort and had lost a great deal of weight. But then she had always been so frail, so exhausted that he had discounted his observation. Later, much later, he realized that he had fallen victim to the denial syndrome, common to the relatives of many cancer patients.

She was in the hospital when he arrived home. She had abdominal cancer, the family physician told him. It was very grave.

"You mean it's terminal." Charles did not fear the word. Death was not unfamiliar to him. It was the cause of death that frightened him.

He sat beside his mother's hospital bed and imagined the tumor growing within her. Once again, he saw that pale mass encroaching upon the ovary of the ewe lamb. The spreading cancer pinched her tender intestines, weighted her liver, caused her to writhe in pain. Her soft voice was reduced to a pleading whisper and then became a terrible shriek as she pleaded for release.

Charles bathed and comforted her. His father, who had faced so much adversity in his life, could not confront his wife's suffering. Charles fed her the pills that were supposed to relieve her pain. He did not believe that the small white pellets could impact against the invasive spreading tumor. The cancer was no longer a dread biological phenomenon. It had assumed a persona and become his enemy, his deadly adversary whose grim triumph was assured. He had feared the disease. Now he hated it. His mother died at last, every bodily function impaired and diminished. Charles heard the death rattle constrict her throat, saw her twitch and lie still, then went out to tell his father. The taciturn rancher wept uncontrollably. Charles did not weep. He was possessed of a terrible anger, a firm purpose. He would avenge his mother's death. He declared war on cancer.

He did not go to veterinary school. He went instead to medical school. He haunted pathology laboratories, read oncology journals, spent his summers working for a pharmaceutical company that experimented with anticarcinogenic drugs. He did his internship and residency in oncology. Each patient he saw reinforced his commitment, his determination. He spoke gently to the parents of leukemic children, to the children of cancer-ridden parents. His own pain, his own loss, conditioned him to deal with their pain, their loss. He experimented with drugs, radiation, diets, transplants.

"I was Batman," he told Anne as the last of the vanilla ice cream disappeared, "and cancer was the Joker."

"You were Holmes and cancer was Moriarty," she countered.

They grinned at each other in recognition of the rapport that came so easily, so naturally. They knew then that they would never be at a loss for words with each other.

"It took me ten years to realize that I was only one of the thousands whose work would be needed if we were going to make any progress. I wanted to be part of a team. That's when I decided to come to Columbia. We have the equipment, the grants, the medical school, and enough people who aren't afraid to experiment and take risks. Oncologists. Pathologists. Pharmacologists. And all of us are convinced that we have to educate a new generation of researchers, that we have to work closely with other institutions nationally and internationally."

"The torch must be passed."

"Exactly. But we don't have to pass it on today, do we Anne? A day like today calls for a cease-fire. I doubt that the war against cancer will suffer a significant setback if you and I leave this damn hospital and take a ride. The azaleas are in bloom and each spring I make it a point to greet them personally." He smiled at her and she saw how engaging his smile was, how laugh lines crinkled about his eyes.

"Why?"

"My mother had an azalea bush. A rarity in our part of Oklahoma, which meant she loved it even more. Pink blossoms and dark leaves. I don't visit my mother's grave. After my father died there was no reason for me to go back to Oklahoma. But every spring I celebrate her life by spending a spring afternoon among the azaleas at the Botanical Garden."

Anne understood then that it was not a casual, carefree invitation he was extending to her. He was inviting her into his past. "I'd love to go with you," she said with real regret. "But I have a microscope on reserve at two and I have a biochemistry comprehensive tomorrow."

"Let's make a deal," he said. "Cancel your microscope reservation, I'll lend you my microscope, and I will personally go over the biochem material with you. I used to get five bucks an hour as a biochem tutor but in honor of springtime and the azaleas I won't even charge you."

She smiled.

"You've got yourself a deal."

"And I'll even throw in a Chinese dinner."

"Lord Bountiful."

"Little Match Girl."

Again they smiled at each other, pleased and surprised that their repartee should come with such ease when they had only just met. They talked easily as they drove north. The windows of the car were open and a soft breeze warmed their faces.

"I'd forgotten how much fun it is to play hooky," she said.

The spontaneity of the outing delighted her. The break from the grinding routine of work and study was intoxicating. She laughed giddily, guiltily, but she did not regret joining him.

Charles Bingham glanced at her, noticing how a shaft of sunlight turned her silver-blond hair the color of antique gold.

"Hooky is good," he said and they both laughed as though his remark had been wildly clever.

"Spring fever," she remarked.

Again their laughter burst forth in a foolish hilarity that embarrassed neither of them. She noticed that his blue eyes were of a rare brightness and thought that when his skin was sun bronzed, they would take on a beryl glimmer.

At the Botanical Garden they walked slowly among the azalea bushes, inhaling the subtle fragrance, marveling at the brave burst of fragile blossoms. Anne stretched out her hand to touch lightly the tiny flowers that clustered together to form huge clouds of color — bridal white and pale pink, deep fuchsia and royal purple. A strong wind had blown the previous evening and fallen blossoms littered the soft dark earth with a delicate and fragrant carpet.

Charles knelt and plucked up a spray of flowers. Pink and white, star shaped, the petals shivered in the gentle wind. Gently, he loosened Anne's head scarf and placed the flowers behind her ear, arranging the spray so that it rested against a long curl of her white gold hair. Unprotesting, submissive, she stood quite still. He placed his hands on her head and she felt their weight, their warmth. She felt she could stand forever in this flowering garden with Charles Bingham's hands resting on her head. He kissed her eyes, her cheeks, and then, at last, he took her in his arms and kissed her on the mouth.

They were unhurried in their walk back to the car, unhurried in their drive back to the city, unhurried over the exceptionally good Chinese dinner at Shun Lee West. They felt no need for intensity, for haste. They felt that they had known each other always, that they would know each other always. He drove her home and she introduced him to Hope and Ted, to Eric who pattered out of his room in pajamas and stared accusingly at Anne.

"You promised you would watch *I Love Lucy* with me," he said accusingly.

"How about we both watch it next week?" Charles Bingham asked. "I'll bring pizza."

"OK," Eric replied grudgingly, but Anne could see that he liked Charles.

"You said the magic word," Hope told him.

"I know a lot of magic words." He took Anne's hand. He would gift her with all of them.

He tutored her for the biochemistry comprehensive. He asked questions and drew diagrams. He explained enzyme interaction and counterreaction.

"I knew it," he said encouragingly. "You're a terrific med student. You'll make a great doctor."

When she fell asleep on the couch at last, he covered her with a blanket, kissed her cheek, and left.

She got an A on the exam. She reported this to him when they met for lunch. It became their habit to meet each day in the cafeteria alcove and he insisted on buying lunch for both of them, ignoring her protests.

"A guy has a right to feed his gal. That's not male chauvinism. That's my Oklahoma upbringing."

"He's wonderful," she told her friends when she met them on Friday afternoons.

Nancy, Merle, and Rutti nodded. They were happy for her. The children teased her.

"Anne's got a boyfriend. Anne's got a boyfriend." Greg dashed from the room as Anne chased after him in mock fury.

Each week she and Charles grew closer. Each night it was more difficult for them to separate. Slowly, slowly, they came to understand the pleasure of each other's touch. At last, on an evening of wind and rain, they made love. Afterward, they spoke softly, revealingly. She told him of her determination to complete her studies, of her fear that she could become like her mother, like her sisters, women whose lives were circumscribed by the needs of others, who moved like shadows through their own homes. He reassured and comforted her.

Often she spent the evening in his sparsely furnished West End Avenue apartment. They made love on a sleeping bag spread wide because his bachelor bed was so very narrow. Always, their contentment was swift and shared. Their joy peaked at the same moment and the room was reverberant with their deep, rich laughter.

"Romeo!" she shouted.

"Juliet!"

"Peter Pan!"

"Wendy!"

"Elizabeth Taylor!"

"Richard Burton. And Mike Todd. And Eddie Fisher. And Michael Wilding."

They exploded with merriment. Their foolish games delighted them. Their lovers' joy was unrestrained.

They spent every spare moment together. He told her of his research and she spoke to him about her courses, accepted his help, his suggestions. His microscope became her own and he corrected her observations, showed her nuances and shadows in slides, listened as she recited formulas. Her friends issued joint invitations to them. They drove to a state park for a picnic lunch with Rutti, Werner, and Sarah. Charles hoisted Sarah on his shoulders and he and Werner strode up a trail with her.

"Sarah likes your Charles," the child called back to Anne.

My Charles. She liked the sound of the words. *My Charles.*

Rutti, too, liked him.

"He is everything Werner is not," she told Anne.

Rutti's voice was wistful. It was true that her own work was

101

going well. She had done a charcoal sketch of Merle, and Andrew had framed it and hung it above his desk. Visitors to his office had admired it and asked Andrew about the artist. Rutti now had a steady stream of commissions, in addition to the work she did for Hope and Ted. Her sketches of family groupings and her charcoal drawings had begun to attract attention. A prestigious art magazine had run a small story on her, which had resulted in gallery inquiries.

But Werner continued to trouble her. His moods were mercurial. His depressions grew darker, but just as she despaired he was catapulted into a manic high and spoke excitedly of Hegelian synthesis, of the perfectibility of man. With equal suddenness, he sank back into almost catatonic surrender and hopelessness. He held Sarah close, wept, and asked Rutti how they had had the temerity to bring a child into a world of such evil and uncertainty. Again, she waited for this mood to pass.

By contrast, Charles Bingham was so steady, so even tempered. He captured a grasshopper and held it in his cupped palm for Sarah's delight. They laughed as it hopped free and disappeared into the long, brilliant grass. Sarah looked up as a flock of geese flew by in perfect triangular formation.

"Sarah wants to know where they are going," she said imperially.

Rutti, Werner, and Anne listened as Charles explained the migratory patterns of birds. The lilting cadence of his voice transformed them all into children and they did not want his softly told explanation to end. Rutti lay on the blanket, her head resting on Werner's shoulder, his hand gentle on the soft golden cloud of her hair.

"Charles will make a wonderful father," she said.

"Yes," he agreed.

They were forever seeking out wonderful fathers, Rutti and Werner, the refugee children who had wandered, orphaned and alone, from country to country.

6

FINAL EXAMINATIONS consumed Anne. She studied with Jean Liebowitz whose husband interrupted their intense sessions to ask questions about domestic matters. Had Jean checked with their daughter who was away at college about her summer plans? Did she realize that they were out of sugar? Anne masked her own annoyance but she saw Jean bite her lips and then hurry to phone her daughter. She heard her apologize for the lack of sugar. The next time they scheduled a cram session, it was in Anne's room at Hope and Ted's apartment. She studied with Larry, her lab partner, and noted that whereas Jean's husband intruded on their work, Kay, Larry's wife, brought them coffee, set down plates of fruit, the apples quartered, the tangerines peeled. She wondered why Kay's attention should annoy her as much as Dr. Leibowitz's interruptions.

And then at last the school year was over. Eric was sent to camp and Hope and Ted planned a vacation in Mexico. The agency had finally shown a profit. Hope was exhilarated, jubilant.

"Who says a woman can't have it all?" she asked. "We can demystify that old feminine mystique."

"You bet we can." Anne looked up from the transcript of her second-year grades. Once again she had excelled and earned a scholarship as well as an assistantship. Two years down and two years to go. She was halfway there.

"All A's," she told Charles.

"Of course," he said. In celebration her friends toasted her in champagne at their Friday lunch, crowned her with a wreath of pink roses, and presented her with a black leather appointment book. On the front page of the book Rutti had drawn a sketch of Anne in her white jacket, a stethoscope dangling about her neck. Anne was pleased. She looked at the blank pages and thought of the summer that stretched ahead of them — an expanse of stress-free golden days. She had accepted a research job in a hospital laboratory, work that would be engrossing but undemanding.

She and Charles drove Hope and Ted to the airport and returned to the large, empty apartment. Anne changed the linens on the double bed and they made love in the bedroom redolent with the scents of their friends' marital intimacy. They lay awake in the darkness and stared across the room at the framed portrait of Eric on the bureau, the photograph of Hope's father and Ted's mother flanking Hope and Ted on their wedding day, the litter of bills and invitations that Hope had tossed into a small wicker basket. Again, Charles's hand rested on Anne's head.

"So this is what it would be like," he said, and she felt herself go rigid.

"What do you mean?" she asked and girded herself for the words she did not want to hear, the question she did not want to answer. Not yet. Not when she was only halfway there.

He did not reply, and in gratitude, she kissed his eyes, closed now in the aftermath of love, and saw how his lashes, extraordinarily long for a man, swept the rise of his finely sculpted cheekbones.

It was not a golden summer. An untenable heat assaulted the city and held it in its sweltering grip. The blacktop on roadways grew sodden and bubbled; air conditioners whirred harshly and were silenced by sudden power failures. Girls in brightly colored minidresses walked very slowly through the streets, as though each step was a hard-gained triumph over the oppressive humidity that threatened their progress. Men took their jackets off and smiled grimly; their shirts were sweat stained, their hair damp.

Andrew Cunningham bought a color television and the friends gathered each Friday afternoon in the Cunningham study — because only the Cunninghams had air-conditioning — and watched the news. In Washington antiwar protesters dropped their placards and dangled their feet in the reflecting pool. In the South the temperature soared and television cameras recorded the determined faces of Martin Luther King, Jr., Dick Gregory, and Stokely Carmichael as they continued James Meredith's march from Memphis to Jackson, Mississippi. Nancy held Keren close as they watched and at night she tried to tell Dov about what she had seen, but the air-conditioning unit at the hospital had broken down and he was too exhausted by the heat and his work to listen.

The children on Rutti's street opened the hydrants and danced wildly through the spray. On a July afternoon, Merle visited Rutti after a class at Juilliard and when she reached Rutti's corner, she took off her sandals and walked barefoot through the rivulet that floated down the street, holding her violin case aloft. Rutti's front door was open and Merle entered, relieved to have arrived and newly aware of how very tired she was.

Rutti's apartment was not air-conditioned, but Mark and Dan, the young actors who boarded with her, had installed ceiling fans that whirled gently and generated a cooling stir of air. Rutti served her friend a glass of iced tea and waited for Merle to tell her why she had come. Sarah sat opposite them at the kitchen table. She bit her lip as she studied the sheet of yellow construction paper in front of her and slowly, deliberately, selected a Magic Marker. She frowned, put it aside, and took up another color, which she used with optimistic daring — her strokes broad and energetic across the bright paper. Sarah's long white T-shirt, a hand-me-down from Greg, was sweat dampened and clung to her body.

"She's a nymphet, our Sarah," Merle observed. "Lolita, watch out."

"Sarah, change into shorts and a shirt," Rutti said.

"But Sarah's so hot," the child protested.

"Then change into a bathing suit," Merle said and they all laughed as Sarah dashed off and returned, pirouetting in a blue cotton suit with a frilly skirt.

"I'm glad you stopped by, Merle," Rutti said. "It would be nice if we could manage more time — just the two of us."

There was a special bond between Rutti and Merle, perhaps because they were both in the arts. They argued issues subjectively, emotionally, while Anne and Nancy took a pragmatic, intellectual approach.

"I'd love to." Merle agreed. "And I actually thought we'd be able to manage it this summer with Greg in day camp and Andrew traveling so much but everything seems to get so complicated. Andrew is involved in a thousand different projects and he keeps leaving me lists of things to take care of."

"Lists?" Rutti asked cautiously.

"Oh, nothing major. Arrange for tickets to this — find out about reservations for that. Restaurants. Theaters. Then there are gifts to buy, repairs to the house. Andrew wants to rebuild the patio, redecorate the dining room, which means contractors, decorators. Oh, it's all petty stuff, Rutti, but it takes so much time and I just can't say no."

"Why not?"

"Because he has always said 'yes' to me. Because he has always cared and taken care of me. Because that sort of thing is my job. That is what wives do — what they are supposed to do." Merle's voice, so briefly passionate, again sounded enervated, as though Andrew's love, his constant demands and solicitude, had drained her of all natural energy.

"But there are things he does not say 'yes' to. You want to have another child. He does not say 'yes' to that," Rutti reminded her.

"That's because he's thinking about me — because he worries about me. He wants me to be ready. He wants to wait until Greg is more settled, less demanding of me. It's me he's worried about. But Rutti — I didn't come here to complain or to talk about Andrew. I wondered if you could do me a favor."

She hesitated and Rutti understood that it was difficult for the wealthy to request favors. They were more comfortable granting them; dispensation was the source of their power. "Your vish — it is my command," Rutti said amiably, self-mockingly.

"Could I work in your apartment two or three days a week — maybe the days when you're at the Art Students League?"

"Of course," Rutti said. "But you know how hot this place is and you'd have to tolerate our charming little visitors. See what I mean?" She leaned forward to step on a cockroach. "God, I hate the damn vermin. I called an exterminator but he told me to save my money. Werner says the roaches are historical survivors — tough and tenacious like all survivors. *Ve haff so much in common with them,* he

106

says." She imitated Werner's accent and intonation and Merle smiled. As always, Rutti's mimicry was accurate and clever.

"Werner identifying with a cockroach," Merle said. "How Kafka-esque."

"But he is not unlike Kafka, my Werner." Rutti's voice was heavy with pity. "In his work, he brings to trial faceless men in vanished lands."

"I don't care about the roaches or the heat. It's the privacy that I'm after. No one will call me here because no one will know where I am. I need time for my work, Rutti." Merle spoke urgently.

Rutti heard her friend's passion and recognized that it was twin to the intensity that sent her hurrying to her easel, her drawing pad, fearful that an image might be lost. It was the artist's impulse, the artist's fear, that motivated Merle.

"What are you working on?" she asked her friend.

"A long violin composition. There's an international competition that Emanuel Klein wants me to enter. He feels that if I concentrate, if I work through my theme, the piece I have been developing will be a strong concerto."

"Do you have a name for the piece?"

"I call it *A Child's Prayer*. Would you like to hear part of it?"

Rutti nodded and Merle opened her violin case. Without self-consciousness, she tucked the beautiful instrument beneath her chin, lifted her bow and brushed it across the strings, making a small adjustment to a single key. She smiled at Rutti and began to play. She had no music and needed none. She had memorized the movement, born of her own yearning, transcribed and perfected note by note.

Sarah climbed onto Rutti's lap. They heard, as Merle played, the voice of a child, the whispered plea. Merle played on, delicately, eloquently, standing barefoot beneath the ceiling fan that lifted strands of her bright hair. Mark and Dan arrived home and stood in the doorway, listening. When Merle lowered her bow, her face flushed with effort and pleasure, they all clapped and smiled. Their applause was soft, keyed to the gentle music.

"That's just the introductory theme," Merle said. "I want this piece to capture the prayer of a child of our time — the prayers of kids like Greg and Sarah, Eric and Keren — their prayers for their own lives, for the world. What do you pray for, Sarah?"

The child thought carefully. Merle's question had been serious and Sarah's answer would match it.

"Sarah prays for no more dogs," she replied. "And no more fires. And no more black mommies crying."

Rutti, who watched the evening news with Sarah, knew that her daughter was speaking of news clips they had seen just last night — shots of dogs unleashed on civil rights demonstrators in a small Alabama town, of fires raging as American planes dropped bombs on North Vietnam, of Biafran mothers keening over the skeletal bodies of their dying children. Television had altered forever the child's perception of the world. It seemed to Rutti that in a way the war-ravaged childhood that she and Werner had shared had been more innocent than their daughter's American girlhood. They had been refugees, but they had been spared the visualization of the horror that had destroyed their world. Fantasy had haunted them, but they had not been forced to confront reality on a daily basis. But Sarah and her friends witnessed the battlefields of Vietnam each evening; they viewed the swollen-bellied children of Africa and heard the taunts fired at black boys and girls, dressed in their Sunday best, who sat so quietly, so bravely at the counter of a Woolworth store. The children of the electronic generation would grow up with few illusions, armed with painful knowledge painlessly acquired. Their prayers would reflect that knowledge, and, as in Merle's music, their sadness would throb with desperate hope.

Sarah took up a blue Magic Marker and drew a winged dove perching on a wide-petaled flower.

"Write the words, Mark," she commanded. "Sarah wants the words."

And Mark, lean and elegant in his bell-bottom jeans and madras shirt, his long, brown hair falling to his shoulders, a necklace of red and blue beads at his neck, took up the marker and obediently wrote: Make Love, Not War.

"For you," Sarah said and held her drawing out to Merle, who placed it in her violin case.

"So it's all right with you if I work here?" she asked Rutti.

"Fine. I'll give you a key. But won't Andrew want to know where you are?"

"I'll check in with Lottie. Andrew thinks that I'm taking extra classes at Juilliard. It isn't that I'm deceiving him, Rutti." Merle spoke with the breathlessness of a child eager to believe her own fantasy. "I want to surprise him. That's why I haven't told him about the competition. That's why he doesn't know about this piece." She had grown used to the necessity of deceiving those she loved with rationalizations so subtle that she came to believe them herself.

"I understand," Rutti said. She was relieved that she would never have to lie to Werner. Her life was her own. Werner was included in it, but he had no right of censorship.

"We don't have to tell Greg or his daddy that Merle works here sometimes," Rutti told Sarah that night as she bathed her.

"Sarah won't tell," the child replied. "Sarah knows how to keep secrets."

"*I* won't tell," Rutti corrected her gently. "*I* know how to keep secrets. Can't you say that, Sarah?"

It was important, she knew, that Sarah abandon the habit of referring to herself in the third person. She was in grade school now and other children would tease her about it. And Nancy had pointed out that it was time for the child to stop distancing herself from her feelings — because that was clearly what she was doing.

"Sarah can but Sarah won't." Giggles mitigated her refusal and Rutti, too, laughed and toweled her daughter dry, marveling as she always did at the beauty of the small, perfectly formed body, the unusual length of her long pink toes, the soft downy hair that glinted golden on her arms and legs and that would, one day, curl softly about the smiling slit of her delicate pubis. Her child, her Sarah, in whose blue eyes she saw her father's gentleness, in whose diminutive form she saw her mother's grace — her daughter, her only link to her past and to her future.

"I love you," she whispered into the clean, delicate shell of Sarah's ear.

"And I love you," the child said. "*I* love you." Lovingly, she awarded her mother this small triumph, this large surrender.

7

ANDREW CUNNINGHAM bought the house in Egremont late in July. He had not planned to make such a purchase. He had never wanted to own a summer home and often he derided others whose lives were complicated by the ownership of two residences.

But the house in Egremont took him by surprise.

He had traveled out to the Berkshires to survey a sprawling expanse of meadowland near Stockbridge. He was in search of acreage on which a shopping mall could be constructed. Such malls, he knew, were the wave of the future. Middle-class families were flocking to the suburbs and the exurbs in increasing numbers, and they craved shopping centers within driving distance that had easily accessible parking spaces and a variety of stores in a single location.

He was disappointed in the property the broker showed him. The area was too quaint, too artsy-craftsy. Andrew had also taken note of the residents and identified·them as men and women who prided themselves on their sprawling older homes and who would fight cooperative apartment buildings and shopping centers that might encroach on their territory. He had no wish to do battle with environmentalists or historic preservationists. In fact, he quite sympathized with them.

"It's a no-go here," he told Alan Wiley, the broker. "Let's get to the airport."

It was on the drive to the airport that they passed the large white house in Egremont. Andrew noted at once the For Sale sign planted amid the buttercups on the front lawn. He also spotted the white fence at the rear of the house that surrounded an empty swimming pool. Through the car window, even at a distance, he saw the cracks in the concrete wall of the pool and noticed that a broken ladder had been cast carelessly on the lawn. The disrepair of the pool, the neglected grounds, the peeling white paint, did not displease him. It meant that the house had been on the market long enough to fall into disrepair and that, in turn, meant that the price would be negotiable.

"Are you familiar with this property?" he asked Alan Wiley.

"Oh yes. The Mayhew house. It's on our list although there's been very little activity. A beautiful house."

"Can we stop and see it?" Andrew asked.

"Of course." Alan Wiley did not reveal his intense desire to deliver Andrew Cunningham to the airport and continue on to his golf game. He had been in the real estate business long enough to know that time and courtesy were investments he could often reclaim with interest.

"I even know where the key is," he told Andrew. It was where he had placed it almost a year ago, beneath a large mossy rock. He did not, however, tell Andrew why the house had remained so long unsold.

The door swung open easily and both men sneezed violently as they entered. A fine layer of white dust covered the bare floors, clung to the dark wood molding. Spider webs, in intricate, silken configuration, dangled from ledges and cornices and scattered mounds of excrement recorded the entry of small animals — field mice or bats, Andrew supposed. And yet, the house felt clean. There was no odor of damp or mildew and the sheer expanse of the rooms, the large and welcoming windows, the natural wood floors that glowed golden when he brushed the dust away with his foot, impressed him pleasantly.

Andrew, who had lived all his life in the same West Side townhouse, moved through these rooms he had never seen before, as though he had arrived home at last. He could remember only one other intuitive flash of such intensity — the night he first saw Merle playing her violin in that restaurant when he had known at once that he would marry her. He knew now, with that same incandescent certainty, that he would live in this house, that his son would swim in the pool, and that Merle would move through these rooms, newly furnished and restored to grace.

He had no doubt that she would love this house, that she would feel about it as he did. He counted it as a given that they shared the same tastes, that the decisions he made for both of them pleased her, relieved her of responsibility. She had never given him reason to think otherwise. They could come here for weekends and thus escape the brutal heat of the city that so fatigued her and caused Greg to be sullen and irritable. They were only a few miles from Tanglewood. She would have easy access to the concerts, to the summer theater at Stockbridge, the dance recitals at Lee. And it was close enough to the city so that their friends could visit.

He imagined Merle and her friends sitting on the restored porch in white wooden chairs. Nancy, Anne, and Rutti would approve of the house. They would recognize that it would be hospitable to scholarly and artistic endeavors.

Like many successful men, Andrew admired creative work and was pleased to encourage it. He had been glad to help Rutti by buying her sketches and introducing her work to his friends. He contributed to symphonies and museums and had anonymously underwritten a grant that would fund Werner's research. Werner could easily work here. He imagined Merle playing her violin, Rutti painting, Nancy and Anne taking notes as they studied.

The scenario pleased him as he wandered through the large empty rooms, ignoring the heat and the dust. He tried to flush the toilets, but of course the water had been turned off. He stood on the balcony that led from the master bedroom. Here he and Merle could talk as they looked out at the gentle slopes of the Berkshires. It seemed to him, as he stood there, that he could hear the sound of her music, his son's gleeful laughter, the soft voices of the women as they came together at the end of a long summer day.

"What's the asking price?" He turned to Alan Wiley who realized at once that the house was sold, that Andrew Cunningham had bought it.

"Fifty-two thousand," the broker said. It was ten thousand dollars more than the listing.

"Forty-two thousand," Andrew countered. Ardor never blinded him to reality. "If you accept my price today we can close within two weeks and I won't even ask you why it's been on the market for so long."

"I accept it."

Andrew had missed his plane, but he waited patiently for the next flight. He arrived home late. Merle was already asleep but he wakened her by kissing her shoulder and pulling her toward him so that he might tell her he had bought her a present, a wonderful present.

"A house," he told her. "A house in the country."

"But I don't want a house in the country," she said, her voice thick with sleep.

He did not hear her. He had not waited for her reply. He was already in the shower, soaping himself vigorously, contemplating all that would have to be done to the new house, which he already thought of as an extension of himself.

In the morning Merle, who was still asleep when Andrew left for the office, wondered if she had dreamed their nocturnal conversation. But she did not worry about it long. A knotty composition problem had resolved itself and she wanted to capture the notes on paper and then listen to their rendition as she played.

She worked steadily all morning, concentrated on the perfection of a single phrase. Again and yet again, she adjusted the strings of her instrument for exact tautness of tone and pitch. She met Nancy for lunch and told her friend about the summer home. Nancy laughed and agreed that Merle must have been dreaming. The purchase of such a house did not sound like Andrew at all.

But she had not been dreaming. Andrew took her and Greg to Egremont that weekend to see the house. Alan Wiley had contracted with a cleaning service and the newly washed windows were flung open; the French doors that led to the overgrown garden were ajar, flooding the large room with floral fragrance and the misty golden light of a mountain summer. The floors had been vacuumed, the carpet of dust and detritus swept away so that even beneath the stubborn grime, she could see the complex pattern of the original oak that Andrew assured her could be made to shine effortlessly.

"You see the possibilities, don't you?" Andrew asked excitedly.

She had never seen him so full of enthusiasm. She did not reply but moved with him from room to room. The kitchen was enormous, but it would have to be completely gutted and new appliances purchased. Unbidden, ideas rushed at her. A butcher-block island at the room's center. Copper pots hanging on the walls. Wooden spice cabinets near the wide window, rhomboids of sunlight slithering across the glass jars.

The upstairs bedrooms were covered with faded wallpaper reduced to ribboned strips. Every wall would have to be scraped and painted. Every molding would have to be reinforced, windows replaced. The bathrooms were large but antiquated. The tubs and basins stood on marble claws, gnawed by scars, discolored by age. She did not follow Andrew up to the attic.

Greg wandered out to explore the grounds. She watched as he broke into a run across the lawn, tumbled down the incline toward the pool, climbed up laughing, clutching a stick. He was an explorer, claiming new territory for king and country. He was an astronaut newly arrived on a distant planet. There was scope here for such games; there was room to wander and dream on land of one's own. Merle watched as he swung from the low-hanging branch of an apple tree. Andrew came to stand beside her.

"You see," he said triumphantly, "such a place is so good for him. He could be happy here. We could be happy here."

She felt her resistance weaken. How could she deny her husband and her son this house, these grounds? Andrew worked so hard. He was entitled to a refuge of pastoral beauty. And Greg did need more space. Nancy herself had said that. And Charles Bingham had spoken to them only last week about the sense of freedom he had experienced during his Oklahoma boyhood. "We were poor," he said, "but I always had my space and a boy needs space for roaming and dreaming." Anne smiled at him then and Merle thought that Charles Bingham would make a remarkably good father. Would she be a remarkably bad mother if she denied Greg his space in which to roam and dream? She turned to Andrew.

"It's a wonderful house," she agreed. "And the property is marvelous. It could be made into a dream house. But Andrew, who is to do it? The furnishing, the decorating, the landscaping?"

He smiled, cupped her chin in his hand, brushed away the strand of bright hair that had fallen across her forehead.

"This is your house, Merle. Every decision will be yours. It will give you something to do. A focus."

She stared at him as though he spoke a language that was unfamiliar to her. She understood that he did not know her, that he did not comprehend her life. How could he think that she had nothing to do when she struggled each day to juggle her time, to balance her hours fairly? It seemed to her that every hour she used for her music was scavenged time, stolen from Andrew and Greg. Like a fugitive, she exploited those stolen hours in her secret hideout, Rutti's apartment. Drenched with perspiration, she hurried home to shower and change, to offer cool drinks and to listen to her husband and son tell of their days, while she thought of what she would work on next, of how she would rewrite a troublesome segue, correct an awkward phrasing.

But Andrew did not know that. She had never told him about the competition. He did not know about the concerto that Emanuel Klein himself had heard for the first time the previous week.

"You are working toward something very beautiful, very meaningful," her teacher had said. He was not a man who offered praise lightly. "But there is a great deal of work yet to be done."

"I know."

He had studied her composition book, turning the pages slowly, reading carefully, note by note, cord by cord. His fingers, veined by age, crippled by arthritis, clutched a marking pen and he covered her work with his own notations and suggestions.

"You will recopy," he said. "And then we will work together again."

"Oh, yes," she promised, her heart sinking at all the work yet to be done. But she left his studio walking on air because he liked her work and called it beautiful.

She thought of Emanuel Klein now, as she stood beside Andrew and watched Greg scramble up the tree. The old man arrived at his studio precisely at eight each morning and practiced until ten. He gave private lessons until midday when his handsome, silver-haired wife arrived carrying the large brown paper bag that contained the sandwich and vegetables he ate for lunch. He worked on his own compositions until four, when she returned with a flat white box from Café Vienna and prepared his tea. This had been his routine, his senior students and colleagues had told Merle, for more than three decades.

"What we all need is a Frau Klein to take care of us," Anne said when Merle described her teacher's workday. "We need good wives to bring us lunch and pastry. Maybe that's why there haven't been too many great women composers — a real shortage of men prepared to run across town with liverwurst and kaiser rolls sliced just so."

Greg placed a sneakered foot on a slender branch and hoisted himself up, carefully, proudly.

"He's going too high," Merle said.

"No. He's all right," Andrew said as Greg stretched his arm skyward and grasped yet another leafy limb. He had almost reached the tree's crown. His face, flushed with effort and concentration, glowed between the branches and sunlight turned his unruly curls the color of copper. Andrew's fingers tightened on her shoulder and she knew that he, too, was thinking it was a miracle that this beautiful child was theirs.

Oh, keep him safe, she thought and music danced through the thought. She knew now that she would conclude *A Child's Prayer* with a deep, sweet scherzo, "A Mother's Prayer." She swayed slightly as the music grew, and as she moved, Greg sought a foothold on an outcropping of bark, missed his step, and fell, his scream piercing the air, an audible arrow that split her heart and catapulted her, screaming, out the front door toward the apple tree.

But Andrew ran past her and reached Greg first, gathering him up from the mound of leaves on which he had landed, holding him in his arms.

"Don't touch him," she screamed because she had learned that long ago in a high school first-aid class. *Never move the victim of a serious fall. Always place ice on a burn.*

"Hey, Ma. It's OK. I'm all right."

Greg wrestled himself out of his father's arms. The shock was over. He felt like a jerk for screaming, for being so scared. The cushion of leaves had broken his fall. His knee was a little sore and his jeans were ripped, but he was OK.

His parents surrounded him, probing his body, his father touching his arms, his legs, his mother plucking twigs from his hair.

"Hey, hey, cut it out. Listen, I want to try to climb that tree again."

"Another time." Andrew's voice was firm.

"So are we going to live here part of the time? I mean, we're going to come back here a lot?"

"Do you want to?" Andrew asked him. His eyes did not leave Merle's face as the boy answered.

"Yeah. Sure. This place is neat. The pool. And there's a tennis court back there. And the trees. You know, I bet there are deer in the woods behind the house. Do you like it, Mom?"

She held him close, rested her cheek on his head, felt the throbbing of his heart.

"Yes, I like it," she said softly.

I will work something out, she thought, as they walked back to the house that would be their own. *I will manage.* She would bring a new juggling act into play, she would toss minutes and hours to the accompaniment of a raucous crescendo. It would all come together somehow. She looked up and watched a flock of swifts fly slowly northward and she wondered what instinct told them when to break their flight and seek refuge on a wooded slope.

8

Rutti sat beside the pool and watched Keren and Sarah swim toward each other, moving smoothly and effortlessly through the clear blue water like small, graceful nymphs. They linked hands and kicked fiercely in their struggle to stay afloat and at last, with wild giggles, they broke free of each other. Keren, who had learned to swim the previous summer on Israel's Mediterranean coast, swam briefly underwater, while Sarah floated on her back, staring up at the cloudless sky. Rutti held her drawing pencil poised above her pad, but when she began to work it was not the children she drew. Instead, she turned her chair so that it faced the house, and ignoring the army of workmen who scurried in and out, she concentrated on capturing the graceful lines of the structure. She frowned because she could not capture the intricate crenellations of the dormer roof, across which two lithe young men moved with acrobatic grace, replacing shingles and hurling those they discarded through the air to land softly on the lawn.

It was amazing, Rutti thought, how money could accomplish small miracles. Even before the lawyers had completed their negotiations, the aging, decrepit house had been transformed into a rejuvenated, graceful home, bridal in its new coat of white paint, its wide and welcoming porch fitted with a festive green-and-white striped sailcloth awning and newly floored with weathered wood. It was Anne who suggested that a glider and chairs that matched the awning be placed on the porch, facing the road. Nancy found the fabric and Rutti supervised the delivery.

The Egremont house became a shared project for the friends, a common cause that engaged their imaginations and involved them in a mischievous complicity. Merle told them about the house at lunch the day after she returned from seeing it for the first time and agreeing to its purchase.

"I couldn't tell Andrew I didn't want the house," she told them apologetically, and she wondered why it was that she was apologizing. Her friends looked at her with concern, not accusation, and she realized later that it was herself to whom she tendered apology. "It seemed so important to him and to Greg. But there's so much to be done and with the work on my concerto, I don't know how I'll do it."

"Andrew can't help?" Anne asked cautiously.

"Can you see Andrew negotiating with decorators, waiting for repairmen and construction crews to arrive? I can just imagine him studying fabric books, meeting with a kitchen designer." Merle giggled nervously.

"Oh, no — all that is definitely woman's work," Nancy said dryly. "Women have nothing better to do than wait for repairmen who show up three hours late — that is, if they show up at all."

"Andrew does travel a great deal," Merle said, suddenly defensive.

"Merle's right. Andrew can't help. But maybe we can." It was soft-voiced Rutti, the veteran survivor, who had set the plan in motion and drew them into a scheme that at once intrigued and delighted them. The four friends, splitting the various responsibilities, working together, would accomplish the refurbishing of the house. Each of them would go to Egremont for several days at a time and supervise the workmen, shop, await delivery of furniture and appliances.

"We'll fix the pool up first so the kids will have a place to play," Merle said. "It's a quick job, mostly cosmetic. And Andrew has already arranged for a cleanup of two of the bedrooms and baths and for temporary appliances in the kitchen that will make it workable. So that will be all right. But I know he won't like the idea of this team effort. He has a sort of mystique about my doing it."

"He doesn't have to know about it," Anne said complacently. "Let him think you're doing it on your own."

"How?"

"You said he'd be traveling a lot this summer. Send Greg off to sleep-away camp. Say you don't want him to breathe in all the construction dust. Lottie can go South to visit her family. And you can say that you're in Egremont. One of us will always be there. When Andrew calls, we'll tell him you're out and you'll call him back and then we'll call you and you can take it from there."

Anne's scenario pleased her. The secrecy excited her. She remembered a club she had belonged to in high school — five girls who had met secretly in a little-used basement. They had furnished the area themselves, hanging a Navajo rug on one wall and on the other a photograph of Sylvia Plath, whose poetry they read aloud in soulful voices to one another. They lied gracefully for each other when parents called. "She just left." "She went to the library." "She's doing homework with Lanie. I think." There had seldom been a need to lie but the small falsehoods gave them a sense of power over their parents. Just as the elaborate deception they now planned would give them an odd power over Andrew Cunningham.

"Why not?" Merle asked, and her question was her agreement. She had always regarded small deceits and harmless dissemblances as legitimate weapons for women.

Smiling she went to the piano, plucked out the tune, and sang, "The moon was all aglow and heaven was in your eyes —"

"The night that you told me those little white lies," they all crooned in unison.

Swiftly they drew up a rotation schedule, giggling as they thought of code words and warning signals. The duplicity delighted them.

"What about the kids — and what will we tell Charles and Dov — Werner?" Anne, always practical, asked.

"We'll swear them to secrecy. Kids and men love secrets. We'll tell them we're helping Merle create a surprise for Andrew," Nancy suggested.

"What a chauvinistic remark," Merle said wryly. "Chauvinistic but true. OK then — Operation Surprise is launched."

"An expensive surprise," Dov said when Nancy told him of the plan. "And one that he himself will be paying for?"

Nancy did not reply. The tone of Dov's voice, the hard look he trained on her, disturbed her.

Andrew had deposited a large sum in a special account. Merle signed checks and left the checkbook with her friends, who filled in the checks as the work progressed.

"If you have to pay more to get the damn contractors to move more quickly, just do it." Andrew instructed Merle.

"Just get it done as soon as possible." Nancy in turn instructed the kitchen planners. "We'll pay overtime if necessary."

The easy accessibility of large sums of money suffused her with an almost sensual pleasure. She remembered her father arriving home beaming and jubilant after he had successfully completed a negotiation, and she understood, for the first time, the seductive power of money. That understanding frightened her. It seemed, somehow, unfeminine. She laughed and inwardly scorned her own perception.

Nancy, Dov, and Keren stayed at the house the week the kitchen was gutted and renovated. They swam, played tennis, and cooked all their meals on the terrace grill. One night Dov spread a comforter on the grass and they made love beneath the apple tree. The night wind was warm against their bodies, moonlight silvered their skin.

"Isn't this wonderful, Nancy," Dov said. "No tension. No rushing off to classes and clinics."

She stiffened and then relaxed, chiding herself for hearing accusation rather than appreciation.

Andrew called and Nancy told him that Merle was out shopping and would call him back. Then she called Merle, who had decided to stay at the Yallon apartment that week.

"How's it going?" Merle asked.

"It's heaven here," Nancy replied. The Berkshires were wreathed in sun-streaked clouds and the fragrance of late-blooming roses filled the house. "How are you doing?"

"It's heaven here," Merle countered. She reveled in the silence that pervaded the stifling apartment. She wakened in the middle of the night and played the music she had composed that afternoon.

The absence of schedule and obligation delighted her. She filled pages in her composition book with music, ripped them out and began again. At rare intervals she shouted in delight. *Yes. Just that note. Yes. Just that cord.* She had never been happier.

She returned Andrew's call. The house was coming along wonderfully, she assured him. The kitchen was completed.

*   *   *

Anne and Charles went to Egremont to oversee the decoration of the bedrooms. Charles brought his notes for the research paper he was to deliver at the regional meeting of the American Cancer Society and Anne brought a pile of English detective novels that she read one after the other as Charles worked. The few days in Egremont were the first vacation she had taken in years and she knew that the next year at medical school would be grueling.

They shopped for fruits and vegetables at local farms and cooked them together in the beautiful new kitchen. Together they cleaned up each evening. Anne washed the dishes and Charles dried, and so they stood, side by side, looking out the window at the dark mountains regal beneath the tiara of sunset. Anne reached up with soapy fingers to touch Charles's cheek and wondered if her father had ever stood beside her mother at such an hour. She thought not and was moved to pity for her mother, anger at her father.

They went upstairs early and in the milky light of early evening they came together in quiet passion and then stood naked on the balcony and watched the slow descent of darkness. They embraced, seeking warmth against the evening chill, and naked still, went downstairs and brewed herb tea, which they drank in the living room from oversize mugs while leaning against the still-rolled Oriental rug Andrew had shipped from New York. They faced the fireplace, its brick facing cleaned and restored, its new copper andirons glistening.

"Andrew and Merle will build wonderful fires. They'll sit here and talk and watch the flames," Anne said dreamily.

"Naked?" Charles stroked the white-gold hair coiled at the nape of her neck, the white gold hair curled at her pubis.

"Never naked. Andrew in a V-necked cashmere sweater and gray slacks. Merle in a loose silk pastel robe. Her Andrew costume." She shivered. "It would be nice, though, to sit naked in front of a fire and feel the flames against your skin."

"I have a fireplace," he said. "Come live with me, Anne, and be my love and we will sit naked in front of my fire and feel the flames against our skin." He was half-mocking, half-serious, but she heard his plea.

"Charles. Don't. I told you I didn't want to marry until I finished medical school."

"I wasn't talking marriage. Do you want me to talk marriage?"

"No. No marriage. No living together. We agreed. Not until I have my degree."

"We didn't agree. You declared and I accepted. Because I love you."

"And I love you."

She kissed him quickly, then, as though to stifle any words that might weaken her resolve. *He had to understand. She was almost there. She could not take any chances. Not now. Not when she was so very close.*

Rutti was responsible for the living room. She and Sarah drove to the house with Keren and Merle. She had not wanted Werner to spend the vacation week with them. A familiar melancholia gripped him. It was possible that he would come for the weekend. Andrew had recommended a new psychiatrist who spoke of mood elevators, of drugs that controlled depression, anxiety, of chemical imbalance. *Not chemical imbalance,* Rutti had wanted to shout. *Historical imbalance.* She had not shouted. She had bought the small white pills and left for Egremont.

Together she and Merle shopped for a sofa, a rosewood coffee table, an antique bookcase, a rolltop desk. Merle left for New York and Rutti supervised the delivery and placement of the furniture, waited for the floor polisher, the glazier. Keren and Sarah danced through the empty rooms, invited Rutti to picnics on the patio, sat importantly at the desk and played "office."

The drawing of the house at which she was now at work would hang over the desk. She would have it matted and framed and give it to Merle and Andrew as a gift. It irritated and frustrated her that she could not capture the shape of the roof correctly. She ripped the sheet from her pad, crumbled it, and began again.

"You're not getting it because you're not seated at the proper angle."

Startled, she turned and saw a bearded man watching her, smiling at her. He wore paint-stained jeans and a plaid shirt and leaned comfortably on a blackthorn walking stick.

"I know, because I tried to draw the house from where you're sitting and then I realized that was wrong," he continued pleasantly, companionably. "You have to be more to the right — like this." Without warning he lifted the chair holding Rutti and placed it a few feet away, across the wand of a shadow.

He was right. She saw that at once, despite her indignation. From this new perspective she could discern the lines of the roof as the architect had planned them. She could imagine the beams in skeletal form, before they were covered and shingled. She moved her pencil with new ease, new certainty.

"Ah, you're getting it now."

He stood close by, watching as she worked. She frowned.

"I don't want to be rude," she said. "But I do not know you. I think perhaps it would be best if you left." She glanced nervously at the pool where Keren and Sarah were taking turns jumping from the low diving board.

"I'm sorry," he said. "I should have introduced myself. I am a neighbor. My name is David Lorenzo."

"David Lorenzo," she repeated. It had a familiar ring. Of course. He was the children's book author and illustrator whose work had won a Newbery the previous year and a Caldecott the year before that. He had been profiled in *Art News* and questioned about his use of mythical creatures, his execution of fearsome monsters that slowly became attractive and lovable as his story evolved. During that interview he had said that he drew the nightmares of children so that they might confront them and watch them slowly become reassuring dreams. The idea had interested her and she had checked out two of his books from the library and read them aloud to Sarah. It was important that Werner's child understand the shadows of secret fears, that she learn that such fears can be harnessed and controlled, that dark fantasy could be a weapon as well as a threat.

"I do know your work," she said. "I like your books very much."

"Thank you. I live perhaps a half mile down the road and it has been my habit for years now to walk to this house and then into the woods just beyond it. There are wonderful trees there and a clearing where the light is especially good. Sometimes I carry my watercolors and work there. In season, I gather up some of the apples that have fallen from your wonderful tree. The house was empty for so long and the apples were orphaned so I adopted them and put them to good use. I made applesauce and apple butter and apple jams and jellies."

"You're a man of many talents," Rutti said. She closed her pad. It was clear to her that she would not do any more work while David Lorenzo sat beside her.

"Now, of course, it is your house and I will ask your permission to cross your property so that I can visit the woods. And I will not pick the apples since they are no longer orphans." He smiled at her, a brilliant wide smile that broke between the soft glossy fur of his chestnut-colored beard and mustache and creased his ruddy face with merriment. "And now perhaps you will tell me your name and how you came to buy this house and how you have managed to accomplish such miracles with it in so short a time. I have been waiting half a year for the roofer, three weeks for the plumber. Do you speak a secret language that they understand? Will you perhaps teach it to me, in exchange for an apple pie baked with your own apples?"

Rutti laughed. His charm, his easy humor, had a contagious quality.

"I'm Rutti Weisenblatt and I am not the owner of the house. My friends Merle and Andrew Cunningham have bought it. I'm just helping them by staying here for a few days to accept furniture deliveries and that sort of thing. As for the apples — I guess you can continue to adopt them for a while. I don't think Merle anticipates any baking or canning this year. You'll have to ask Andrew about the roofer and the plumber. He'll be here this weekend. Perhaps you can come over then and I'll introduce you."

"That would be very kind of you." He stretched out on the grass, his arms beneath his head, and looked up at the cloudless sky. "Will it disturb your work if I stay here for a while?"

"As you can see, my work is going to be disturbed in any case," Rutti said.

Keren and Sarah, each wrapped in a large patterned towel, approached them. Despite the heat of the day the girls were shivering. Sarah's lips were blue and Rutti hurried to her daughter, rubbed her dry, and despite her squealing protests wrapped her in a terry cloth robe she had left to warm on the lawn. Sarah caught cold so easily and the child's slightest illness thrust Rutti into a small panic.

"Oh, Mom, leave me alone," Sarah said irritably. She was not a baby. She could dry herself as Keren was doing and put on her own robe just the same way Keren was putting on her sweat suit.

"All right. I'm sorry," Rutti said. She was pleased that Sarah resisted her efforts, that she did not call herself by name. Slowly, slowly, her daughter was emerging into a new independence. "Mr. Lorenzo, this is my daughter, Sarah, and our friend, Keren Yallon."

"Keren. Sarah." He took each small hand into his own large one and looked searchingly into each child's face. "You may call me David because neighbors should call each other by their first names. It is more neighborly, I think."

"David," the girls said in unison and giggled.

"You must make a wish," David told them. "You must close your eyes and make a wish. That is the rule when you speak as one."

Obediently, they closed their eyes and lifted their faces to the sun. Sarah's lips moved and Rutti wished that she could read her daughter's thoughts. Was Sarah wishing that Werner would be released of his sadness and restored to them? She so seldom spoke of her father and, often when he visited, she looked at him warily.

Keren opened her eyes and looked at David expectantly.

"What should we do now?" she asked. Within minutes, without effort, he had been accepted as leader and friend.

"Would you like to explore the woods with me?" David suggested. "I'm an excellent guide."

"Sarah, David is the artist who did the drawings in *Dragon Dreams* and *The Goblins' Journey*," Rutti said.

"Are you going to write a book about the woods?" Sarah asked.

"I may," David replied. "Perhaps you will give me an idea."

"I have an idea for a book," Keren said importantly. "A prince meets a princess. But they are from different countries and they fight about whose country they are going to live in. After the quarrel they each run away and the prince goes to the princess's country and the princess goes to the prince's country and they each wait there for the other but they never meet and they live unhappily ever after." Keren giggled wildly and Sarah clapped her hands.

"What made you think of that story, Keren?" Rutti asked.

"I don't know. It just came to me. Come on. Let's go into the woods." Keren was now bored with her own story. She hopped impatiently from one foot to the other because she loved the feel of the soft grass.

"Put your sneakers on," Rutti told them. "And make sure the laces are tied." She restrained herself from kneeling beside Sarah and double-knotting the bow. She had to liberate her daughter from her own overprotectiveness. Werner was right. Nancy was right.

The girls danced ahead of them along the woodland path.

"She's very beautiful, your daughter," David Lorenzo said. "She looks like you."

"She has her father's eyes."

"Her father. Your husband."

"My husband." She would call Werner that night. She had not heard from him for several days and as always concern for him haunted her. Last night she had awakened thinking she heard him sobbing in the darkness, and then realized that her own cheeks were wet with tears. She was suffused with sorrow for Werner, for Sarah, for herself.

"His name is Werner," she added and she felt the curiosity in David Lorenzo's gaze, although he asked her no questions. There would be time enough to tell him about Werner. Instinctively, she knew that she would be seeing him again. And again.

As they trailed behind the girls, following a track of sunlight, David told her that he had lived in Egremont for almost ten years. He had bought his small cottage with the royalties earned from his first book, a collection of Ladino folktales that had, against all odds, achieved a trendy popularity. He was a Sephardic Jew and his grandmother, who had come from Lisbon, had told him the stories that he illustrated. His wife had loved the small house. She planted flowers along the narrow front path, perennials that blossomed still — tulips and daffodils in the spring, pale roses in the summer, and russet zinnias to celebrate the cool of autumn.

She had been dead for five years. He had to remind himself each morning that she was gone, that he slept alone in the huge bed that had been their very first purchase after moving into the cottage. Kathya she was called, a tall, lean woman whose pale coloring contrasted with his own ruddiness. She was a dedicated and competent teacher of autistic children. When she became pregnant with their first child, she resigned her position, and they winterized the cottage that they had originally bought as a summer retreat. They would raise their family in this quiet town, far from the city and its dangers.

Blueberry bushes grew wild across the road and in the early hours of a fog-swathed evening, Kathya went to pick fresh fruit for their dessert. David watched her crossing back, holding the overflowing baskets, sailing forth with the sweet pride and confidence of a woman in her first joyous pregnancy. And then his heart stopped as a car driven by a teenager had careened down the road. The driver, as he testified later, never saw Kathya. All he saw, through the swirling fog, was the broken body of a woman, briefly suspended in air and then slowly, slowly falling. The youth did remember the impact of his car against her body just before he fainted and she, whose falling form would haunt him forever, died.

"How terrible." She reached for David's hand.

He did not reply, but in the pressure of his grip she felt the extremity of his grief and she marveled that there had been no bitterness in his voice as he told the story, no anger. He was a man who assimilated his sorrow, addressed the agony of loss, and then again took control of his life. Gently but firmly, he closed the door upon sadnesses past and moved forward. He accepted grief, but bitterness was a stranger to him — unlike Werner, for whom bitterness had become a way of life.

He paused now, before the towering evergreen, the tallest of the trees in this copse. "Meet Father Pine," he said. "Doesn't he seem protective and paternal to you, the courageous and upright protector of his forest family? The flowers and shrubs are his children — the young firs his most valuable companions. You see how his arms wave so warningly?"

"It's wonderful the way you see the personality in growing things," Rutti said with professional admiration. She remembered a desert scene in *The Goblins' Journey* where the goblins, cavorting among the cacti, had become indistinguishable from the desert plants. "There's a goblin," Sarah had cried. "No, no, it's a cactus." Rutti corrected her, and sometimes they were both right and sometimes they were both wrong. She had marveled with a collegial admiration at the illustrator's skill.

"I see people in plants and animals, yes." He acknowledged.

"And very often, I see plants and animals in people. Your daughter and her friend, for instance. I see them as twittering sparrows. See how they chatter and skitter along on thin and fragile legs — just as sparrows do before they take first flight."

"I see," Rutti said and even as she spoke Keren flapped her arms and danced around Sarah, who rushed forward to escape her friend's winged embrace.

"And you, of course, are a flower — a full-hearted flower with petals the color of sunlight." He smiled down at Rutti but she darted forward and caught up with Keren and Sarah.

She walked between the two girls, who danced their way through the patches of radiance scattered across the forest's fragrant needled floor. Behind them, David suddenly began to sing.

"Oh give to me the life I love . . ." His strong baritone rang out through the forest's stillness and he waited as they, in turn, picked up the tune, the line.

"Oh give to me the life I love," they sang together as they passed the birch whose leaves quivered in the gentle breeze. If David Lorenzo knew Werner, Rutti thought, he would see him in that pale tree, so bent with the weight of passing seasons. Pale Werner, always burdened by the weight of his loss, by the intensity of his unremitting search.

David Lorenzo met Werner that weekend. At Rutti's insistence Werner drove to Egremont with Merle and Andrew late Friday evening and Rutti invited David to lunch on Saturday.

The mood at the house was celebratory. Smiling with proprietary satisfaction, Andrew patrolled the newly landscaped grounds and moved through rooms that were freshly painted, sparsely but subtly furnished.

"Isn't it remarkable that Merle has been able to accomplish so much in so short a time?" he said again and again. He put his arm around his wife's shoulders and looked at her proudly. "No one thought we'd be able to pull it off. They all said that it would take months, maybe years, to get this house livable but look how Merle has managed. Even with commuting to the city for her lessons with Klein. That's some gal I married." He beamed. Her achievement was a reflection of his own success, his own singular judgment and prescience.

Keren and Sarah giggled at each other and glanced knowingly at Rutti. They were delighted to be coconspirators with their mothers, but she was troubled that the small girls had been involved in their deception. Of course she and Nancy had explained it carefully. "We are helping Merle to surprise Andrew," they told Keren and Sarah.

"Well, surprise is a nicer word than deceive," Nancy observed wryly, acknowledging their shared unease at the message they were sending their daughters.

Rutti was grateful today that David did not betray them, although he shot her a quizzical glance as Andrew commented on the rock garden.

"Only Merle could have thought of placing it here," he said, and kissed his wife.

David had heard Rutti conferring with the landscape architect about the exact location of the rock garden and he had helped her to plant the beds of herbs in the carefully sectored area. He remained silent when Andrew complimented Merle on the beautifully prepared lunch, although he himself had driven Rutti into Stockbridge to pick up the pasta salad and poached salmon at the caterer. He smiled and the women smiled back at him, admitting him into their complicity.

"We must give a party — a large house party — a housewarming," Andrew said as he spread dill sauce across his salmon.

"It will be beautiful here in May and June," Rutti said. "When the daffodils and peonies bloom."

"It's wonderful up here in the spring." David agreed. His response was automatic. He would agree with anything Rutti Weisenblatt said. He smiled when she spoke.

"And I can see that it is wonderful here in the summer as well," Werner said suddenly. He had taken note of David's smile.

"Yes. Yes, it is," David replied.

"Do you find it wonderful here, Rutti?" Werner asked. He was thinner than ever; his gray-blue eyes were sunk deeply into his pale, elongated face. His nails were bitten down and, although the day was warm, he did not remove his gray cardigan.

"Oh, Daddy, it is wonderful here. Come, watch me swim in the pool." Sarah pulled at Werner's arm, coaxed him out of his seat, and led him to the pool, holding his hand and chattering up at him. She propelled him forward, as though he were a blind man and he, in turn, smiled down at his daughter and touched her golden hair. They all watched as Werner settled himself on a poolside chair, as he clapped when Sarah dived in, as, after a few minutes, he removed his sweater and lifted his face to the sunlight.

"You see," Rutti said aloud. "Only she can make him smile."

"And you, you, too, can do that." Andrew reminded her. He had a peculiar attachment to Werner. He was impressed by his intellect and, like many strong men, he felt a protective tenderness toward a man who was weak and less fortunate than himself.

David poured himself another cup of coffee and watched as Rutti, too, rose and went to the pool where she sat beside Werner.

"Who is he?" Werner asked, speaking to her in German.

"An artist. A widower. He lives nearby. We met only a few days ago."

"A good artist?"

"Very good."

He took her hand and held it to his lips, leaning very close to her.

"You won't abandon me, will you, Rutti?" She heard his words, felt the moist heat of his breath, saw the luminescent bone that jutted out at his wrist. He had grown so thin. Her heart turned with love and with pity.

"Never. I promised. I will keep my promise. But you must take better care of yourself. You must eat, sleep. You must not work so hard."

"But you don't understand," he said excitedly. "I am following a new direction. A Hegelian approach. I trace the good and evil in history in constant tension. I have written to Marcuse about my theory. I see clues, Rutti, real clues. Soon I will break through — I will understand." His eyes burned and his voice trembled with passion.

"Yes, Werner. Of course you will. I know you will."

She feared for him when he reached this peak, when such manic absorption overtook him, enveloping intellect and emotion, causing him to read and write at a frenetic pace. Experience had taught her to track each symptom, each action and reaction. Now there was exhilaration and feverish intensity. His work would be brilliant; his colleagues and students would tell her that. Editors of learned journals would publish his articles, academics would argue his theories. He would not sleep. Ideas would ambush him when he closed his eyes and he would leap from bed to transcribe them until, at last, utterly exhausted, he would find that he could not think, he could not write. Then he would be possessed of wild fears, anxious thoughts. "*Wo bin ich?*" (Where am I?) She had heard him shout the question before. She would hear it again, she knew.

Tears would follow then, and the uncontrollable hysteria that might or might not lead to an uncontrollable rage. There would be a period of calm and then the cycle would begin again.

She held his hand tightly, smoothed his lank fair hair, and kissed his face, as their daughter swam effortlessly through the clear blue water.

"Look at me, Mama, look at me, Papa."

"I need you, Rutti."

"I know."

And David Lorenzo watched them as he spoke with Merle and Andrew of the charms of Egremont, as he told, in all truthfulness, how delighted he was that they would be neighbors.

"He needs me," she told David. "And, in a way, I need him."

They walked through the woods at the twilight hour. Andrew and Werner had driven off, taking Keren with them. Rutti had said that she and Sarah would stay an extra day to keep Merle company. The lies came easier now. She accepted Andrew's gratitude as though it were her due.

"Why do you need him?" David asked.

"There is a great deal between us. More than you would understand."

"Try me."

"No." She sensed the hurt in his silence. "Not yet." She amended her abrupt reply.

They paused beneath the towering evergreen that he had named Father Pine. In the shelter of its long shadow, she moved into his arms. His lips brushed hers. Lightly, gently. His hands rested on her shoulders. Lightly, gently. She closed her eyes and his lips were soft against her lids.

She called Werner late that night. She waited as the phone rang again and again, but when he picked it up at last, she hung up without speaking. She did not want to talk to him. She wanted only to know that he was all right, that he was safe. Again she closed her eyes, and fell asleep remembering David Lorenzo's tenderness, his gentle acceptance of all that she had told him.

9

THE UNRELENTING rain of late March streaked the narrow window of the small room that had been assigned to Nancy by the Upper West Side Counseling Service. Nancy sat in the circlet of light cast by the floor lamp that stood beside her easy chair and stared into the oppressive dimness. Irritably she closed her Hebrew grammar, glanced at her watch, and straightened the white paper towel spread across the back of the chair that faced her own. A new box of tissues was in place on the low table and she slit it open so that it would stand in readiness for her three o'clock patient who was now fifteen minutes late. Enid London had never been late before and Nancy acknowledged that in all probability she was not coming at all. She doubted if she would ever come again. Dr. Aaronsohn, who was supervising Nancy's treatment of the young Barnard student, had told Nancy as much when she described her last session with Enid.

"You moved too quickly. You were too open, too forceful. You should have allowed her to arrive at the insights herself. A therapist never rushes in where a patient fears to tread." The bearded, bespectacled professor spoke calmly, without anger or irritation. He was a teacher and Nancy was his student. Still, she knew that he was displeased and she wondered if he regretted assigning patients to her this early in her training.

He had been encouraging, almost insistent, when he asked her to begin seeing patients at the onset of the fall semester.

"If you are going to complete your training in Israel, it's important that you get as much practical experience as possible here. You

134

must begin to develop your own techniques, your own patterns and you can only do that by seeing patients. Under careful supervision, of course."

She had agreed. Dov would complete his residency this year and, although he spoke of undertaking additional training, she was hopeful that he would opt to do that at Hadassah Hospital in Jerusalem. She was eager for them to begin their lives in Israel. Adventure awaited them. She wanted to move on as her friends were doing, each of them exhilarated by their work, excited by their own progress.

Rutti's work was on exhibit at a small SoHo gallery. Werner had been briefly hospitalized that fall for depression and Rutti, carrying the Mahler recordings that soothed him, went to see him after her classes at the Art Students League. She showed him her newly completed sketches of Sarah and sat beside him and held his hand as he listened to the music and studied his daughter's delicate face. Afterward, it was not unusual for her to meet David Lorenzo for a late supper.

The bearded illustrator came into the city often, although his work schedule was hectic and he was arranging for an addition to his Egremont house. He told Rutti that he planned a studio and that one wall, which faced the mountains, would be of insulated glass — in effect, an enormous window through which an artist at work could watch shifting shadows. "Two artists at work," he corrected himself. The room would be very large.

"It's the closest he ever came to pressuring me," Rutti had told Nancy.

"I don't know how you manage," Nancy had replied wonderingly. "You lead two lives."

"Only two?" Rutti asked wryly. "Actually, I think most women lead several lives. Maybe we're born with a gene that helps us to compartmentalize, to separate our different lives. Like Merle — society hostess, mother, violinist, composer."

Merle had submitted her concerto on schedule, working fiercely through the autumn. She played the completed work for her friends on a Friday afternoon in late November, as the first snow of winter fell in large, moist flakes that formed fragile stars against the windowpanes. Nancy, Rutti, and Anne sat on the floor and listened intently. The children waltzed playfully to the music, but they too sat quietly as Merle performed the final movement, the bright rondo that captured the child's dream, the mother's fear and hope. They clapped softly as she lowered her bow and smiled at them shyly, proudly. It would be months before the outcome of the competition was published, but Merle was taking a composition class at Juilliard and working with renewed intensity. Her work was maturing, Emanuel Klein had told her. There was a new depth to her phrasing. Yes. She moved forward. Steadily forward.

They were all moving steadily forward. Anne, in her third year of medical school, was doggedly surviving the surgery rotation taught by a professor who was brutally demanding.

"Peter Forbes is not normal. He's a sadist," she had complained to her friends and to Charles Bingham.

Her friends sympathized, but Charles's response was predictably level.

"No. He's a professor of surgery who has to be certain that everyone he trains knows how to cut into flesh, saw into bone, with a fair degree of accuracy," he corrected her firmly.

"You doctors — you're all in a conspiracy of self-protection," Anne had retorted.

She did not tell Charles that Peter Forbes was especially harsh with female students, badgering them unmercifully as they stood beside him at the operating table working with their retractors. He barked questions out at them, pointing to organs with his scalpel.

"Hold that muscle wall back, damn it," he had shouted at Anne. "This is an operating room, not a beauty parlor."

Grimly Anne obeyed him.

"That bastard," she had told Jean Liebowitz in the locker room, but Jean, pale and red-eyed, had not answered her.

Still, Anne persevered, working harder than ever, determined not only to survive but to excel.

"I can do it," she told Nancy. "And I'm going to."

Nancy did not doubt her. But she was not endowed with her friends' certainty, their confidence. It was her own self she doubted. She went to the window and looked down at the street that was, as always, deserted. The falling rain darkened the stone stoops, which were pocked with holes and graffiti scarred. Dov had not wanted her to accept the clinic assignment because of the location.

"It's a dangerous neighborhood, a dangerous building," he had argued.

"Run-down but not dangerous," Nancy had replied. She had proceeded to schedule her appointments, to make afterschool arrangements for Keren. A nonconfrontational defense — the pattern of her marriage. Her silence wore Dov down, diminished his arguments. His anger no longer frightened her. It came with the territory. Like Werner's illness. Like Andrew's single-minded dominance. She coped in her own way. As Rutti did. As Merle did.

A woman wearing a bright red slicker, her body bent against the wind, came down the street. Nancy watched her progress, reasonably certain that the woman was not Enid London, who moved swiftly and who never, during all her months in therapy, had worn a bright color.

She thought of calling Enid, but she knew that would be the wrong move. Aaronsohn would not approve. Again and again he had advised his students that patients called therapists. Therapists only returned calls. To call Enid, to show her that she was worried, would make Nancy vulnerable and thus ineffective. Enid would sense her worry, her concern, and, in the throes of transference, might see that concern as love. Aaronsohn had explained all this very carefully, but, then, Aaronsohn was not God. He was not infallible. In fact, he had in all probability erred when he asked Nancy to see Enid London.

"I think you will understand her," he told Nancy when he described the young woman after his initial intake conference. "She is at war with her own background, rejecting her parents' values, struggling mightily to come into her own."

Afterward, Nancy had wondered why it was that her professor had thought Nancy would have a particular empathy with Enid. Did he perceive Nancy herself as a woman in unresolved conflict with her family, her background? Was it possible that he saw a similarity between Nancy who was always so organized, so carefully groomed and bedraggled Enid in her loose and unironed black-and-gray cotton shirts and jeans, her fair hair pulled back into a straggly ponytail? *Damn Aaronsohn,* Nancy thought and glanced again at her watch. Enid was now twenty-five minutes late. Half of her fifty-minute hour was gone.

Nancy turned from the window. The Hebrew grammar lay open

on her desk, but she did not reach for it. Instead she dialed Charles Bingham's number because she knew Anne was studying at his apartment. Anne answered the phone on the first ring, her voice dispirited.

"Don't tell me you have the March blahs too," Nancy said.

"Don't project, Madame Therapist. What's going on?" Nancy knew Anne had immediately detected the depression in her tone.

"My three o'clock appointment didn't show. I think I really messed up with her during our last session. I came on too strong, too directly. I'm beginning to think I don't have what it takes to make it as a therapist. I don't know why I'm knocking myself out. What if I'm no good at it, Anne, no good at all?"

She waited as Anne considered her question. She knew her friend would not offer facile or meaningless reassurances. Anne never skirted the truth. That was why Nancy had called her.

"How many clinic patients are you seeing now, Nancy?"

"Three."

"And how are you doing with the other two?"

"One slow but steady. Signs of gain. The second I'm seeing for a situational problem. Very short-term. I think she'll only need a few more sessions and Aaronsohn agrees with me."

"So you're doing OK with two out of three?"

"I guess."

"You know, two out of three isn't a bad track record, Nancy. You're never going to have a hundred percent success record. You don't need Aaronsohn to tell you that."

"No. I needed you to tell me that," Nancy said. "Thanks! So how are you doing, Anne?"

"Working hard. Trying to survive this surgery rotation. Trying not to murder Peter Forbes with his own scalpel. That mad-dog chauvinist son of a bitch."

"Easy, Anne."

"I am not paranoid. Charles doesn't agree with me, but even he says I'm not paranoid."

"Ah, Charles the Objective. Charles the Uninvolved. And how is Charles?"

"Charles the Wonderful." Anne's voice was soft as she said her lover's name. "If not for Charles, I would first kill Peter Forbes and then myself."

"Contain your violent impulses. Assimilate your supposedly non-existent paranoia," Nancy said with mock sternness.

"I refuse to accept counseling from someone who doesn't even think she can make it as a therapist," Anne retorted, and they both laughed. The humor and honesty of their conversation had broken the tension. "Well, I must get back to my study of the human skeleton now. Tomorrow I get me a brand-new cadaver. How shall I carve him — let me count the ways."

"Carve him to the length and breadth and height your scalpel can reach," Nancy said laughing. Still laughing, she replaced the phone and just as she did so, the door to her office opened. Enid London, wearing a man's long dark raincoat and a plastic kerchief, stood in the doorway.

The young woman's eyes were red-rimmed. How long had she wept alone, Nancy wondered, before deciding to return to the clinic? Pity for Enid overwhelmed her, but she fought it. It did not do to feel sorry for a patient. Compassion could impede treatment; certainly it distorted objectivity.

"I wasn't going to come today." Enid's voice was sullen, her eyes downcast.

"But you are here," Nancy replied coolly, hoping that Enid would not notice the slight tremor in her fingers as she picked up her notebook and settled herself in her easy chair. She watched as Enid hung the rain-soaked coat on the sagging coatrack and slowly sank into the seat opposite her, leaning her head wearily against the white paper towel. Nancy took note of the small bruise above Enid's right eye, of the frayed navy blue cashmere cardigan, most of its pearl buttons missing. She sat back and waited for Enid to speak.

Enid London had grown up in the small, prosperous town of Bala-Cynwyd on Philadelphia's Main Line. Her father was a prominent attorney and her mother volunteered at the Bryn Mawr Alumnae Book Store.

The Londons were Quakers and Enid joined the Quaker contingent in Martin Luther King's march on Washington. That day in the nation's capital exhilarated her. She stood in the crowd of two hundred thousand gathered on the lawn around the reflecting pool at the Lincoln Memorial and listened to Dr. King's mellifluous voice. "I have a dream," he said, and his dream became Enid's own. She held hands with two strangers and swayed with them as they sang "We Shall Overcome." Their voices rose in powerful, optimistic chorus.

On the bus ride home, she sat next to an intense, exceedingly thin black Penn junior who told her that their generation would change the world. At the Delaware border, he kissed her. His name was Timothy and she invited him to Sunday dinner. Her parents were cordial, but when he left, her father looked at her gravely.

"It's not a good idea for you to see Timothy again," he said.

"Why not?"

"You're too young for him. You're too different from each other."

"You mean he's too black and I'm too white."

She slept with Timothy on her seventeenth birthday after which she smoked her first reefer while the radio played "Help! Help me, Rhonda!"

He transferred to Berkeley and almost at once she became involved with Barry Lewis, a Columbia political science major. Barry was energized by ideas, invigorated by anger. He was angry at his middle-class parents because they were middle class. He was angry at his country for being in Vietnam and at Columbia for insisting he take required courses. He belonged to Students for a Democratic Society and spoke of Abbie and Jerry with confident intimacy.

Enid did not mind that his breath had the sweetly sick taste of marijuana. She loved the way his thick dark hair fell to his shoulders and laughed when she ran her fingers through it and dark tendrils caught in the diamond cocktail ring that had been her grandmother's. Because of Barry she went to Barnard. She cooked spaghetti dinners for his friends and washed dishes while they made plans for demonstrations, sit-ins, teach-ins. She wakened in the night to comfort him because he had a recurring nightmare in which he saw his own body lying on a jungle floor and then transferred into a black plastic body bag — not as a whole, but limb by limb — legs, torso, arms. He dropped out of Columbia and lost his student deferment. He said that he would not answer his draft notice. He and Enid would flee to Canada. He did not ask her. He told her.

She fell into a deep depression and a Barnard friend referred her to the Upper West Side Counseling Service, where Nancy became her therapist. Their rapport had been immediate, although their progress was slow and painstaking. And then Barry received his induction notice and tore the apartment apart, breaking crockery, filling duffel bags with books and clothing.

"We're going to Canada. We've got to get the hell out of this country," he shouted. He pawned her grandmother's ring and counted the money with shaking hands.

"What should I do?" Enid asked Nancy, who had arranged an emergency appointment.

And Nancy, breaking every rule of therapy, said, "You must leave him. You must not see him again."

"Just like that?" Enid asked angrily. She slammed out of the office, although her session was not over.

Nancy knew that she had gone too far too fast.

"Of course you were wrong," Professor Aaronsohn had said. "Your job was to help her understand her reaction, not to deliver an ultimatum. You are a therapist, not a decisionmaker."

He did not comfort Nancy. It was his job to teach. It was not improbable, he told her, that Enid would abandon therapy. It was not improbable that she might even go to Canada with Barry.

But he had been wrong. Enid was here, sullen and angry. Barry had left and she felt herself at once betrayer and betrayed. She was alone. She spoke so softly that Nancy leaned forward to catch each word. Nancy listened, never speaking, terminating the session at exactly three-fifty.

"Next week," she told Enid.

"Next week," Enid agreed.

The door closed behind her and Nancy sank back, weak with relief. The rain had stopped and the room was very quiet. She lifted the phone. She thought to call Dov, but he was at the hospital and would be annoyed if she intruded on him there. She called Rutti instead. Rutti would listen and Rutti would understand.

10

A HARSH fluorescence illuminated the operating theater in which Peter Forbes performed an appendectomy. His students sat in the glass-walled balcony and looked down at the procedure, but Anne and Jean pressed their faces to the glass and stood so that they might better observe his every movement.

"You've got to give it to him — the son of a bitch is one hell of a surgeon," Jean told Anne as Forbes bellowed for additional sutures. "I couldn't sew a hem as fast as he's closing that incision."

"What a sexist parallel, Jean," Anne murmured, and they both smiled as the surgeon stared up at them for a split second. Anne read the satisfaction in his glare. He had seen them talking, seen them smile, and that observation would be used against them.

She did not mind the stringency of Peter Forbes's demands. She admired his demonstrated competence. He had been on the faculty of the medical school for over twenty-five years. In its service his hair had grown iron-gray and his body corpulent. His facial expression alternated between anger and surly discontent. It was rumored that his wife was an invalid, his only son retarded.

Nor did Anne object to his demand for perfection. Charles was right. Surgery was a discipline that left no margin for error; the slightest lapse in technique or judgment could lead to disaster or death. Rather, it was his undisguised bias against women students and colleagues that was offensive.

"He's of another generation," Charles pointed out patiently. "He doesn't understand where you're coming from. He's experienced the world of medicine as a man's world. If there were three women in his medical school class, that would have been a lot."

She herself was not intimidated by Peter Forbes, but she knew that he terrified the other women in her class. He had twice caused Nina Alcott to cry — once challenging an answer that she had given him, although the answer had been correct.

"How do I control this bleeding?" he shouted to Nina as she assisted him during a splenectomy.

"With clamps," she replied.

"Why the hell would you use clamps?" he countered harshly.

"Perhaps I wouldn't." Her voice was barely audible.

He had seized the clamps and stanched the bleeding.

In a class discussion afterward, he had reviewed her performance with angry sarcasm.

"An operating room is not a boutique. You are not shopping for a dress. You cannot change your mind every few minutes. If you cannot make a swift, informed decision, Miss Alcott, you do not belong in medical school. Trade in your hospital identification for a Lord and Taylor charge card, which is probably what you will do in a few years anyway. But no matter what you do — do not waste my time!"

His voice had quivered with indignation and Nina had fled the classroom in tears.

Jean Liebowitz had suffered more devastating humiliation. She was a diligent student, but when he barked a question at her she grew too flustered to respond.

"Why are you in medical school, Mrs. Liebowitz?" he challenged her on one such occasion. "This is not an institute for menopausal matrons seeking a new lease on life. You already have your doctor-husband. And God knows we need competent scrub nurses more than we need the kind of doctor you will become, if by some miracle you ever manage to graduate."

Jean had flushed hotly, but she had not replied. It was Anne who seethed with anger. Each day, she realized, Jean looked more exhausted. Each time she served as second assistant in surgery her movements were less certain, her voice more hesitant. Often the retractor trembled in her hand.

"Come on, Jean, it's our third year and it's almost over," Anne encouraged her friend, but Jean's despondency did not lift.

Now Peter Forbes strode up to the balcony and confronted the class.

"All right. Let's review some aspects of this very routine surgery. What did I do immediately upon opening?"

"You studied the peritoneum," Larry offered.

"Why did I do that, Miss Richardson?"

"For signs of peritonitis," Anne replied easily. The question was basic, the answer simple.

"Signs of peritonitis, Mrs. Liebowitz."

Jean shifted in her seat. She knew the answer, but as always the harshness of his voice paralyzed her.

"I would hope that you wouldn't have to pause if you were performing the procedure and you saw a sign of peritonitis. There would be no time for an exchange with your girlfriend then, would there? But perhaps you and Miss Richardson were discussing important matters as I closed. Her new haircut — your new shoes?" His tone was biting.

Jean's face was bright red.

"Perhaps you can enlighten us, Miss Richardson. It seemed such an urgent discussion."

"It was so unimportant that I've forgotten," Anne said. Then, galvanized by anger, she retorted, "I do not think I've been asked a question like that in a class since the fifth grade, Professor."

She heard the intake of breath, saw her classmates glance at her and then at Peter Forbes, who ripped off his gown and let it fall to the floor.

"This class is dismissed. I will see you in my office at six o'clock this evening, Miss Richardson. Precisely at six." He stalked out of the enclosure, thrusting himself against the swinging doors and ignoring the student nurse on her way in.

"A gutsy move, Anne," Larry said as they left. "Stupid but gutsy."

Jean walked with her to the cafeteria, her face flushed, her expression grim.

"I'll get us both coffee," she said. "I owe you."

Anne sat down at an empty table. She felt suddenly weak. Larry was right. She had been stupid. She should have made something up to appease Forbes. Or she could have just told the truth. Jean had been admiring his skill.

"Hey, Anne." Nina Alcott paused at her table. "We all owe you a thank-you. That chauvinistic bastard."

"I may need more than a thank-you," Anne said. "Maybe a whole new identity. Possibly a head transplant. Oh, if you're looking for Peggy, she just left."

"No. I'm meeting someone," Nina said, and color rushed to her cheeks.

Too swiftly she walked on and Anne watched as she mounted the steps to the balcony and sat down at a table opposite Dov Yallon. She noted that Dov had a strawberry yogurt and a glass of milk in readiness. She watched as Nina took a sip of the milk, as Dov took up a napkin and wiped away the white mustache that formed above her lip. She heard Nina laugh. She turned away. She did not want to think about Dov Yallon and Nina Alcott. There was no reason to think about them. It was not unusual for a resident and a medical student to form a casual friendship.

"So what are you going to say to Forbes?" Jean asked as she set the coffee down.

"I'll wait and see what he says to me. Six o'clock is two hours away. Enough time for him to cool down and consider what an ass he made of himself. I'm not some stupid kid he can call into the principal's office for insubordination. Anyway, I'll play it by ear. Don't worry about it."

"Oh, I worry about everything," Jean said ruefully. "I want this year to be over. And then I want next year to be over. The kids are coming home for the weekend and Jeffrey thinks we should have a big family dinner on Saturday night, go to a matinee on Sunday. Damn it — I have a unit exam."

"Go out for dinner Saturday night. Let him take them to the Sunday matinee while you study," Anne suggested.

"It's not that easy." Jean was rueful. "I am nudged by my constant companion. Dame Guilt. Maternal Guilt. Wifely Guilt. You'll see."

Anne did not reply. She would not see. She would not be a wife or a mother before she was Dr. Anne Richardson. It was understood.

"Take it easy," she said to Jean, who gathered her books and rummaged through her purse for her marketing list. "Give them TV dinners. Call a caterer."

"Anne." Dov slipped into the seat opposite her. "Nina told me about Forbes."

"I'll work it out," Anne said stiffly.

"You have to understand. He's a terrific surgeon, but an unhappy man. He has a very difficult home life."

"Not too many people have happy home lives," Anne retorted. "That doesn't give them a license to kill."

"That's true." Dov looked hard at her and as usual she felt uneasy with him. She always felt that he was judging her, judging all of them. She recalled an autumn afternoon when they had all sat on the lawn of the Egremont house, celebrating with Hope and Ted because their advertising agency had at last signed enough accounts to be installed in its own suite of offices.

"I feel like the little engine that could," Hope said in her Kentucky twang. "Everyone said that it couldn't be done but we went ahead and we did it."

"Oh, you will all go ahead and do it — of that I have no doubt," Dov replied, looking at his wife and her friends who sat in a semicircle on their white lawn chairs, their faces lifted to the pale autumn sunlight. "But what casualties will you cause as you puff your way up the track and will it be worth it in the end?"

Anne stared hard at him then and she had not felt comfortable with him since. It annoyed her that she still thought him attractive.

"I wish you would do something for me," he said now.

"I will if I can." She waited for him to ask her not to tell Nancy that she had seen him with Nina Alcott. But then what would she tell Nancy? "I saw Dov with a classmate of mine. They laughed and he wiped milk from her mouth."

"I wish you would persuade Nancy to give up seeing clinic patients at that counseling service."

"But Dov, she needs that experience. It's wonderful that she was asked to do it. That sort of assignment is usually reserved for doctoral students." His request shocked her, although Nancy had told her that Dov was uneasy about the clinic's location.

"I don't object to the work. But the neighborhood is dangerous. I don't want my wife to become a statistic. You're her friend. You don't want anything to happen to her, do you?" His voice was dark, almost accusatory.

"I'm sure you've discussed this with Nancy yourself."

"Nancy has developed a technique. She allows me to talk myself out and then she does as she pleases. That's why I'm asking you to talk to her."

"I wouldn't presume to tell Nancy where she should work," Anne said coldly.

Dov stared at her angrily.

"You're a marvelous group, you four. Devoted accomplices. How skillful you were in deceiving Andrew Cunningham. Look at the support you all give poor Rutti with Werner. It is all very admirable. The power of sisterhood. But if I ask you for help it is not forthcoming. A man is excluded from the magic circle of your friendship." He spat the words out bitterly, tearing a paper napkin into strips as he spoke.

"We'll both forget what you just said, Dov," Anne said. "You're tired. I'm tired. I don't think you have to worry about Nancy. She'll be all right."

"You will all be all right. All four of you. Haven't I always said that? I have no doubt of that."

"Thank you."

He glanced at his watch and walked rapidly away. She wondered if Nina Alcott was waiting for him and she was ashamed that the thought came so easily and seemed so credible.

She spent the rest of the afternoon studying in the library and shortly before six she went to the women's room. She washed her face and looked at herself in the mirror, startled to see how fatigue had masked it with pallor. Carefully she outlined her eyes, applied blush to her cheeks, a touch of vaseline to her lips, because she never used lipstick. She loosened her hair and brushed it so that it fell to her shoulders in silvery folds and knotted a brightly patterned silk scarf about her neck. Charles had spoken of going out for dinner, but because her appointment with Forbes was so late, there would be no time to change. The scarf would at least relieve the starkness of her black skirt and sweater. She dotted her wrists with fragrance from the pocket atomizer of *Joie* that Merle had given each of them at summer's end; then she hurried down the corridor to Peter Forbes's office. The hallways were silent and deserted at this early evening hour. A Pakistani orderly pushed a wet mop wearily across the scarred linoleum floor and nodded at her.

She knocked at the office door. There was no answer. It occurred to her with relief that the surgeon had forgotten the entire foolish incident and had gone home. She knocked again more vigorously and turned to leave just as the door swung open.

"Come in, Miss Richardson," Peter Forbes said. "Come in and sit down. I just need a moment to check something."

He motioned her to the chair before his desk and sat opposite her, turning the pages of a textbook. At last he found the diagram and text for which he had been searching. He opened a patient chart, studied it, consulted the text and made a note. He was, she knew, a careful surgeon. His preoperative preparation was impeccable. Finally, he closed the chart and the book and looked at her.

"We have a problem, Miss Richardson," he said. "You and I. I am not happy with your performance in my class."

"And I think my work on your rotation has been satisfactory. Certainly your evaluations reflect that," she replied. Her voice was firm, but she sat with her hands tightly clasped so that he would not see them tremble.

"Our problem is not related to your work. You are an extremely competent student. I have graded you fairly, I think. And I know that I have taught you well."

"Yes. Of course you have."

"And yet today you addressed me in an impertinent, insubordinate manner. In front of your classmates." His tone was angry. Her heart beat faster and she clasped her hands even more tightly. Still, she would not retreat.

"If I was impertinent — and perhaps I was — then I apologize," she said. "But I do think you are unduly harsh and punitive toward women students. I do not deny that I see that as a problem between us."

"Have you ever given thought as to why I am so harsh — as to why some of my colleagues — myself included — are not overly congenial to the idea of women students in the medical school?" he asked.

"Perhaps you can enlighten me." Anne was polite, formal. They were playing an odd cat-and-mouse game, she and this middle-aged professor who leaned across his desk, his hands spread open. Surgeons' hands, large, the muscular fingers tensile even at rest, the nails expertly manicured. She thought of the strength and dexterity of those fingers. He was a surgeon who grew impatient with his instruments. She had seen him plunge his hands into an open stomach cavity to pry loose a nodule, to probe a mass.

"We have a limited number of places in our medical school. I sit on the admissions committee. We receive many applications and we read them carefully and try to act without personal prejudice. My own nephew applied three years ago and was rejected, although he was a good student and will make a good doctor. He is studying in Mexico now. When Kate Enderby dropped out of your class, it occurred to me that perhaps the place she held could have been taken by my nephew, who would not have dropped out. You will think me chauvinistic, perhaps."

"Men dropped out of our class as well," Anne countered.

"Ah, but not as many and for different reasons. Hear me out, please. You know that we must take some women. As we must take some Jews and some black students and some Orientals. Quotas. An unpleasant and unpopular concept but it exists. I do not deny it. Still, we are careful, very careful, and most of the students we admit do survive the rigors of medical school. Most of them have long and valuable careers. And the women we admit tend to be excellent students. Those who do complete the course of study."

"Is there any real proof that women drop out of medical school in disproportionate percentages?" Anne asked dryly.

"Perhaps such statistics exist but I have not seen them. I rely on my experience. I have seen women complete their training and then have families. They work fewer hours. Perhaps they take a year off, perhaps two years. They want to nurture their families. I do not blame them. But some leave practice entirely. Their training has been wasted. My time has been wasted and they have deprived other applicants of the opportunity to study."

"And you think that is sufficient reason to harass women students?" Anne was incredulous.

"I do not harass them. I am demanding of them."

"You don't want them in your class. You don't want them in the medical school."

He did not deny her words.

"It is because I recognize the special qualities of women that I do not want them to expose themselves to a life of such rigor, of such exertion. Should a woman in a delicate state of pregnancy be asked to work the emergency room? Should a menopausal woman or a premenstrual woman inflict her mood swings on a support staff? I do not question the talent and ability of my female students. I question their hormones." He smiled at her solicitously and his voice was unctuous.

She looked at him with curiosity rather than dislike. Charles was right. Peter Forbes was a fossil, a leftover from another generation. She did not forgive him but she began to understand him.

"A good endocrinologist might challenge your assumption about hormones. Women have always made good doctors, marvelous doctors. You could probably name a few yourself. And maybe women did leave the profession at one time, but things are different today. There are new alternatives for child care — we're talking about a day-care center right here at the medical center. And there is a new generation of men who are ready to nurture their children and help to raise their families as equal partners." Her retort was sharp, impersonal. She spoke as though she were offering the rebuttal in a debate; her control masked her gathering anger. "You say that you feel protective of women. If that is so, protect us from your sarcasm and your patronization. Don't speak to us as though we are small children in a grade-school class. As you did today."

She awaited his reply, his anger and outrage, but he was silent. He stared at her dreamily through narrowed eyes. She rose. Their business was done. She had apologized and expressed her anger. He had tried to justify his position. Neither would persuade the other. He too stood and moved to her side. His breath rasped unpleasantly.

"Let me help you with your jacket."

"That's all right." She shrugged her jacket on, took up her purse, her book bag. He walked her to the door, and as she touched the knob, he placed his hand on her own.

"Miss Richardson, Anne." His voice was hoarse, his body blocked the door.

She trembled. Her mouth was dry and for a split second she feared that she might faint. She clutched her book bag, gripped her purse; her heart pounded arrhythmically. His powerful fingers touched the silk scarf at her throat, trailed down her shoulders, rested caressingly on the rise of her breasts.

"You knew what you were doing when you came here," he said harshly. "Arguing, teasing. You dressed for it. Why the scarf, the makeup, the perfume? You talk about new times, but you practice old tricks."

He pressed himself against her, pulling her forward. Fury and revulsion galvanized her. She thrust her knee against the bulge of his engorged penis. His face contorted into a grimace of pain and he bent almost double, spewing obscenities. She opened the door and raced down the hall, past the Pakistani orderly now languidly pushing a floor polisher, past a clerk wheeling a trolley of files. Panting, sweat soaked, she reached the exit and breathed in the cool fresh air of the March evening.

She did not tell Charles what had happened. She feared his anger and did not want his protection. She called him to cancel their dinner date, saying that she had a headache and was exhausted. It was true. Her fatigue was so profound that she barely had the energy to peel off her clothes as she filled the large claw-footed bathtub in Hope and Ted's bathroom. She made the water as hot as she could bear it and added Hope's bath salts. She wanted her body to have an unfamiliar odor. During her Peace Corps days in Lagos, she had heard an African student speak of the way small animals on the run from predators often rolled in unfamiliar foliage to mask their own scent. The thought filled her with a wild hysteria and she laughed and wept as she submerged herself in the aromatic bathwater and watched her skin pucker pinkly.

She wrote a letter to Peter Forbes, which she handed to him the next day as she left his classroom. She wrote that there were witnesses who had seen her run from his office the previous evening. She wrote that she would refrain from bringing charges of sexual molestation against him on the condition that he cease to harass the women students in her class. She gave him the letter on a Friday and she did not sleep the entire weekend. She took two showers a day and wept without reason.

"Med school exhaustion — maybe the beginning of a flu," Charles told Hope, who nodded but looked at Anne with tacit understanding. She brought her hot tea laced with bourbon. Her sister had brought her such a drink once, in their grandmother's finest china cup, the afternoon Hope had arrived home weeping because two men had chased her down the Cumberland highway.

On Monday Peter Forbes walked by Anne without speaking. He never called on her again and he virtually ignored the other women in the class.

"What did you do to him?" Jean Liebowitz asked.

"I seduced him," Anne replied, and they both laughed.

Later she realized that her answer was not inaccurate. She had seduced him with the power of her truth. She had reversed their roles and filled him with fear. And she had survived. She was almost there. One more year. Only one more year.

11

ON A warm May evening, David Lorenzo and Rutti Weisenblatt sat cross-legged on the floor of his Manhattan studio and ate Chinese food out of cardboard containers as they watched the evening news on television. In companionable silence, they watched Queen Elizabeth and Prince Philip arrive in Ottawa for the centennial celebration. How innocent the royal couple looked as they smiled toothily into the camera. Rutti imitated the bored, regal expression, copied the Queen's intonation. "My husband and I . . . ," she parroted, and David laughed. Her gift for mimicry delighted him. He leaned over and kissed her cheek as the news clip switched to American bombers en route to Hanoi. They watched Joan Baez sing at a peace demonstration. "What have they done to the rain?" Her voice was clear and bell-like and her beautiful, delicate face was mournful. But it was only when Abba Eban's moon-shaped face appeared on the screen that Rutti turned up the volume and leaned forward attentively.

Israel's foreign minister looked exhausted. He had flown to the United States that day from England where his talks with Macmillan had been no more productive than his exchange with De Gaulle the week before. Still, his replies to the interviewer's questions were unhesitating, delivered in his mellifluous, Oxford-accented tone. Yes, he acknowledged, it was true that Israel had ordered a general mobilization, but Israel did not want a war. He had assured U Thant of that at a meeting at the United Nations that morning. He had given similar assurances to President Johnson, who had relayed them to Premier Kosygin. Still, Nasser had insisted that United Nations Emergency

Forces leave Gaza and, of greater import, he had closed the Straits of Tiran to Israeli ships. The closing of an international waterway was an act of war, but Israel would refrain from reacting to Egyptian aggression. Every diplomatic avenue was being explored, he said.

Rutti switched the set off.

"Do you think there will be a war?" David asked.

"Dov Yallon is almost certain of it. Nancy told me that he has had letters from his family telling him that his brothers-in-law have been called up. His sisters have been cooking and baking for weeks. The Jewish response to war. Nasser says he will drive Israel into the sea and the women of Israel rush to the grocery stores." Her own mother had placed the parcel of food into her hands at the Vienna train station. She felt a stirring of nausea and leaned against David, pushing away the soggy cardboard container, still half full of vegetable lo mein.

"What will Dov do if war breaks out?" David asked.

"Nancy says that if he's called back he will go."

"And Werner?" He uttered her husband's name hesitantly.

"Does one ever know with Werner?" she responded, matching his question with her own, wondering that she could so easily speak to her lover about her husband.

She had told David about her relationship with Werner before they became lovers. She remembered how moonlight had silvered the pool as they spoke and how an owl had hooted softly in the woodland they had come to think of as their own special province.

It was summer's end and to mark the season's passing and their imminent return to the city, they had taken Sarah out for dinner in Lenox and then to see *Born Free*. She wanted to go to Africa, Sarah told them sleepily on the way home. She too wanted to raise a lion. Sarah was asleep when they reached the house. David carried her up to bed and he watched as Rutti covered her daughter and kissed her lightly on the forehead. Then he took Rutti's hand and led her outside. Hand in hand, they walked across the lawn, seeking out the exact spot where they had first spoken.

"I should like to draw you with Sarah. There is such tenderness in your face when you look at her," he said, speaking very softly in the darkness. He held her hand in his own and their shoulders touched as they sat side by side on the white bench.

"She is all I have," Rutti replied. "Oh, yes, there are my friends, my wonderful friends. But Sarah is my only family."

"There is Werner."

"Yes. There is Werner." She spoke his name with sadness.

Weeks had passed since David's meeting with Werner. Rutti had delayed her return to the city. She was taking no classes at the Art Students League and she had given up her job at Columbia months earlier when it became clear that she could support herself on her commissions. She had improvised a studio in the sunroom that over-looked the garden. The wide-windowed room remained unfurnished at Andrew's request.

"I have my own ideas for that room," he told them, and they understood that to be an edict and so left it empty.

She worked well there and Sarah played happily each morning. She swam the length of the pool and told herself stories as she whirled about the garden. Like many only children, she was skillful at amus-ing herself. They spent their afternoons with David. They walked with him through the woodland and visited his cottage, sitting in his pleasant kitchen while he cooked. Like an aproned sorcerer, he conjured up meals for them or cooked the spicy lamb stews and egg-plant dishes from the recipes passed on to him by his Portuguese grandmother.

Vegetables delighted him and Sarah trailed after him in his ver-dant kitchen garden, obediently plucking feathery-haired carrots, snapping beans from slender vines, ferreting through the dark earth for knobby red radishes.

They walked single file along the woodland path. They were Indians on the prowl.

"You are Princess Golden Hair," David told Sarah.

"And me?" Rutti asked.

"You are Queen Golden Hair."

"And you," Rutti told him, "are Big Chief No Imagination."

They laughed then, Sarah giggling the hardest, although she did not understand the joke.

David told them about his work, his family, of his visit to his grandmother's village in Portugal. Rutti spoke of her life on the kib-butz, of the warmth she had found with her adoptive family on Beit Yair, Chana and Dror's kindness, their son Ari's friendship.

Because they were artists, they talked of light and shadow, technique and perspective. But although he had talked about his life, she had never told him of Werner. Not until that night as they watched silver shafts of moonlight skid across the water and felt the beginning of the autumn cool.

"You said," he reminded her gently then, "that there was a great deal between you and Werner. And this I must know. Is there love between you?"

"Not the love of a man and a woman for each other. Not the love of passion." She hesitated, discontented with the words she had used, unable to find the right ones. "My English is so bad," she said apologetically. "How do I say it?"

"I know what you mean. You speak of the love I feel for you." He offered the words generously, to help her explain herself. He said them because he felt them so deeply and because he had longed for days to say them. "You are my love, my flower." He spoke aloud the words he had repeated so often to himself at night as he lay waiting for sleep and thinking of her.

She turned to him and he thought that she would protest, but she did not. Instead she lifted her finger to his lips, a plea for silence, a gentle reminder that he must listen to her, that he must hear her. She told him about Werner's childhood and her own, how they had been exiled and orphaned and how at last they had come together, bonded by shared sorrow and loss.

"We are more than husband and wife," she said into the darkness. She thought of how Werner trembled when she held him, of the taste of his tears upon her tongue.

"You are not even husband and wife," David corrected her. "You do not live together. You do not share a life."

"That is only because I am frightened for Sarah."

"And you are protecting her?" He did not speak harshly. He strained to understand. He marveled at her loyalty and admired her tenacity.

"I am trying. That is all I can do." Her parents could not even do that much for her. All they could do was put her on a train at the Vienna train station and pray for her safety.

"What would happen to Werner if you divorced him?" David persisted.

"He would be destroyed." Flat and certain, her answer fell into the darkness.

"He would not be destroyed."

"You don't know. You don't understand. You have not seen him when he is ill — really ill. You have not spoken to the doctors. If you love me, do not ask me to do what I cannot do." Her voice broke.

"I love you." How quietly he spoke those words: gravity and certainty weighted each syllable.

"David." She said his name and he heard the love in her voice. He kissed her, held her to him. His flower. He buried his face in the soft petals of her golden hair. He picked her up. So small she was and so light that he carried her in his arms like a child. He set her down on the grass; her golden hair fanned out against its fragrant darkness, and there was a new incandescence in her eyes. They made love for the first time, encased in an envelope of silver moonlight, listening as the owl's hoot grew fainter and fainter. They heard only the beat of their own hearts, the whisper of their own breath, the lilt of their wondering voices calling each other's names louder and louder and louder still.

She returned to New York, but he came to the city from Egremont several times a month. He had to see his publishers and meet with his agent and gallery directors. One winter evening he gave a reading at PEN, "The Child's Fantasy and the Artist's Vision." It pleased Rutti that he was famous. She showed Sarah his photograph in *Art News*. He stared out at them from the glossy page, bearded, serious, but smiling widely, as he always smiled. She cut out the picture and placed it in her wallet. An adolescent gesture, she knew, but she forgave herself. After all, she had never had an adolescence.

"Rutti, I think we must talk about Werner," he said now.

"No." She stood and, carefully closing each one, carried the soggy cartons into the kitchenette.

"What are you doing?" he asked as she opened the refrigerator.

"Putting these away. It's getting late. I have to pick up Sarah at the Yallons'."

"There's no point in saving any of it. When would we eat it?" He was returning to Egremont the next day and the West 12th studio would be empty for at least another week. "Leftovers are not for lovers." He tossed a carton into the garbage.

"David!" The waste of food triggered an angry reaction. She wrapped scraps in aluminum foil, encased bits of sandwich in plastic bags. She could not forget the rationing in England, her foster mother returning pale and exhausted with a tin of beans, a loaf of bread, and three eggs that she held as though they were fragile ornaments. Nor would she forget the austerity of war-ravaged Israel — the soups of sorrel grass that Chana cooked over a kerosene burner, the still-unripened dates and figs they plucked from the trees, eating them too quickly so that they would have something, anything, in their stomachs.

"Stop throwing it out. I'll take it home."

"And will you feed it to Werner, carry it to him in your weekly care package?"

She had not seen him cruel before, had not imagined him capable of it.

"You promised," she said accusingly. "That first night. You promised."

"What did I promise?" But his voice was soft now, as he remembered the moonlight gliding across the pool, the anguish in her voice when she spoke to him of her childhood, of Werner's, of their marriage and Werner's illness. *Damn him,* David thought, and at once he was ashamed. Werner was damned. History had damned him.

"You promised that you would never pressure me to do what I cannot do." She averted her face so that he would not see her, but gently, firmly, he cupped her chin in his hand and forced her to look at him, to read the regret in his eyes.

"Rutti. I'm sorry. But it's so hard to live this way. I want to be with you always, to live with you. I want to marry you."

"But you knew from the beginning what my situation was — is."

"I knew. And I understand your feeling for Werner. But Rutti, even if you divorced him and we married, he could still see you, see Sarah. You know that. What would be different? You don't live together now. You don't make love."

"I know."

She and Werner had not made love since the summer in Egremont. Werner had not mentioned David Lorenzo. He had not asked Sarah who had given her the watercolor of a lioness that hung above her bed. One afternoon Rutti had found him slowly turning the pages of the *The Goblins' Journey,* but he had closed the book at once when she entered.

"Werner would see divorce as abandonment — and he has been so often abandoned. I can't tell what it would do to him. Oh, David, I don't want to hurt him."

"But you are hurting me, Rutti. Every day that we are not together you are hurting me."

"You are strong. Werner would be destroyed."

There was no doubt in her voice. David was resilient. He had loved Kathya. She had died and he had grieved for her, and then he had purposefully picked up the pieces of his life and forged on. His laughter was deep and rich, his body strong, energized by confidence and passion. When she lay beside him, she marveled at the muscles that rippled through his arms, at the nut-gold hue of his skin, only a shade lighter than his soft thick beard, his curly hair. In the summer his face glowed like burnished bronze. Life engaged him. She painted a portrait of a smiling child, with tanned skin and clear green eyes. *David As a Boy* she had called it, but she had not shown it to him. Once she had painted a portrait of a skeleton-faced child, fair hair falling in scattered wisps across his forehead, his skin ghostly pale, his eyes cavernous and dark rimmed. *Werner As a Boy* she had called that portrait, which she had given to Chana who had hung it in her small living room after she and Werner had left the kibbutz. Werner himself had never seen it.

"All right," David said, "you are right. I said I wouldn't pressure you and I won't. I love you too much, Rutti. Let me go with you to Nancy's."

They talked softly, easily, as they made their way uptown. David spoke of the beauty of Egremont as it wakened to the new warmth. The flowers Kathya had planted were in blossom. Graceful daffodils and narcissi swayed before him as he walked to his cottage.

Rutti asked him about the garden that she and Merle had planned together. He told her that the rosebushes now rimmed the rock garden she had designed and forsythia replaced the stunted hedges.

"It's hard to believe that house once belonged to the Mayhews," David said.

"Who are the Mayhews?" Rutti asked.

"Oh, a sort of gothic family," he replied too casually.

Nancy was watching the news when they arrived at the apartment, her body taut, her expression worried. Keren and Sarah ran forward to greet them.

"There's going to be a war in Israel," Sarah announced.

"What a thing to say. How do you know?" Rutti asked, automatically reaching out to wipe a streak of chocolate ice cream from her daughter's chin.

"Dov said so. Didn't he, Nancy? Didn't he?"

"He did, Mommy, he did." Keren's voice was shrill, insistent.

Rutti and Nancy stared at each other over the children's heads. They read the fear in each other's eyes and swiftly turned away. David gave each girl a ride on his broad shoulders and laughed his full rich laugh.

Nasser was not simply rattling his sabres. Werner, who listened to the news every hour on the hour, recognized that. He listened to the Hebrew newscast on WEVD as he ate his solitary dinner in his furnished room.

It's classic, Werner thought, as he spooned up the cold noodles. He did not bother to heat up the meals Rutti brought him.

"Hot? Cold? What difference does it make?" he asked irritably when she protested.

She did not reply. She knew that such questions, such behavior, were only symptomatic. As always at the times when his mood darkened, he grew careless in dress. His body reeked dankly of neglect. She waited fearfully for his despair to deepen until at last it overwhelmed him and he surrendered to the ministrations of psychiatrists and their gem-colored tranquilizers. In the interim her own sadness gathered.

"Depression is contagious," Nancy had explained to her. "A reasonably happy person who has daily contact with a depressive sometimes develops the same symptoms. Try to separate out, Rutti."

Rutti visited less frequently, but she phoned him daily. She called now as he shoved his empty plate away and turned up the volume. The newscaster reported on Israeli reactions to events in Egypt. "I can't talk, Rutti," he said. "I am listening to the news." He hung up and gnawed his fist. It was all as he had predicted. The historic pattern repeated itself.

He spread his manuscript on the table and reread his words, reconsidered his own ideas. Yes, yes, it was all clear. The call for new heroes was consistent with the Jewish historical experience when messianic yearnings followed cataclysmic events. In every era as the dark shadows of history converged upon them, Jews had sought for light in the form of transitory heroes, sent by heaven. After all, had not Isaac been bound and stretched upon the altar, and then saved by an angel? The descendants of Abraham had watched the smoke rise from the chimneys of Auschwitz and waited for the leader who would carry them to the land of Israel so that they might pluck golden oranges from laden boughs. And now again they marched through the streets of Jerusalem and Tel Aviv shouting the names of the heroes who would be their saviors — Ben-Gurion, Dayan, Allon, Yadin — their messiahs in mufti, the armed angels in human form who would stay the destroyer's sword.

"It all fits," Werner muttered.

A new excitement seized him. He took up a blank sheet of paper and began to write, his pen moving swiftly because he found it difficult to keep apace with the ideas that poured forth. He wove old theories into new themes. Patterns became clear. He saw how his cyclical theory of history meshed with a causal philosophy that had long intrigued him. Soon, soon he would pierce the mystery of evil. He wrote deep into the night and fell asleep even as he worked, his head resting on the kitchen table, littered with closely written sheets.

Dov Yallon also listened to the Hebrew newscast each night. He translated for Nancy, and Keren hovered fearfully in the doorway, listening as her father spoke. Incendiary shells had destroyed five hundred acres of wheat at Kibbutz Nachal Oz. He spread open a map of Israel and showed Nancy and Keren how close Nachal Oz was to his parents' moshav.

"What can we do?" Nancy asked worriedly.

"Write checks. Send telegrams to Johnson. Demonstrate at the United Nations. Pray for the messiah," he said bitterly. "Prayer seems to be molding foreign policy these days. Nasser takes his instructions from Allah. Westmoreland tells a joint session of Congress how desperate the situation in Vietnam is and Johnson lifts his eyes to heaven and decides to send in more troops." His voice was brittle.

They watched television that night, lying side by side but not touching.

"Dov, why don't we just pack up and go," she said. "Your residency is finished. Another year is optional. You're a doctor. You'll be needed if there's a war."

"And what about your patients — your precious patients? Could you leave them? And your seminar — your research paper? Would you leave them to huddle in a bomb shelter with my mother and my sisters and their children? And would you leave your friends — break up the Fabulous Four? Who would help Merle to deceive Andrew, Rutti to nurse Werner?"

The mocking anger in his voice startled and wounded her. He was unfair. Dov knew that he and Keren were her priorities, that her commitment to Israel was profound. His irrational reaction was a result of tension. Of course. That was it. He was worried about Israel and his family, fatigued by his hospital schedule and the specter of his boards.

"Yes. Yes. I would leave them. I would leave everything," she protested and arched her body against his. She would will him, with her love, with her passion, to believe her, to understand her, to comprehend the depth of her feeling for him. She caressed his arms, his shoulders, pressed her lips against the scar shaped like a butterfly that glinted palely in the darkness.

"I am tired, Nancy. So very tired." His voice was heavy, his body inert, unresponsive to her touch.

She moved away and lay beside him listening to the familiar night sounds of the apartment. The hum of the refrigerator, the susurration of the plumbing, the turning of a latchkey in the apartment next door. Ingrid's husband was home. They would make love. He always wakened her to make love after his late shift at the hospital, Ingrid had told Nancy, half boastingly, half angrily. It was weeks, Nancy realized, since she and Dov had made love. One emergency after another had kept him at the hospital so late that he was seldom home for dinner and often she was asleep when he arrived at last.

And unlike Ingrid's husband, he would not awaken her. Dov could not help his irritability, his exhaustion.

They needed some time alone together, free of work and schedules. Free even of Keren. Perhaps Merle could let them have the Egremont house for the weekend and Keren could stay with Rutti and Sarah. She turned and kissed him on the cheek to demonstrate that she understood. But he did not open his eyes, although she was certain that he was not asleep.

Merle would lend them the house. Merle would do anything for anyone. Her voice jubilant, her cheeks aglow, light-headed with happiness, she whirled Nancy about the room, hugged Lottie, danced off to leave a message with Rutti's answering service and to shout her news at Charles Bingham so that he might relay it to Anne.

"I won," she exulted. "I really won."

She had not won first place. *A Child's Prayer* had been awarded third place in the competition, but its selection was a triumph. There had been more than four hundred entries.

"And all of them were from the best conservatories. The Eastman School. The New England Conservatory. Yale." Like a true victor, she measured her conquest against the strength of those she had vanquished.

"Have you told Andrew?" Nancy asked.

"Of course. I've told everyone. The mailman. The garbageman. Why wouldn't I tell Andrew? Oh, he was so proud, so happy. He Xeroxed the telegram and took it to his office."

"He wasn't angry he didn't know about the competition from the beginning?" Nancy asked. She imagined Andrew going to a business meeting, displaying the telegram like a father showing off an exemplary report card. *Look what my clever wife has done.* The thought irritated and disturbed her. Remembering Andrew's generosity to all of them, she reproached herself. Like Dov, she was on edge.

"Of course he wasn't angry," Merle replied. "I explained that I wanted to surprise him." She smiled. She had not guessed wrong. Andrew did not mind deception if the deception was designed for his pleasure.

"You told him how we arranged to get everything set in the Egremont house?"

"No. Of course not. Why did he have to know that?" Merle's smile was indulgent. Tossing her auburn hair, she beckoned Nancy into innocent conspiracy, mischievously urging her to acknowledge that it was all right to practice small feminine subterfuges that harmed no one and led to happy endings.

"Can you believe that I won?" she asked yet again. Oh, she wanted to play her concerto through right now. There would be a recital for the three prizewinners at the New England Conservatory. She thought that she would buy a dress of emerald green and wear her hair in a French braid entwined with green velvet ribbon.

"Have a terrific weekend," she told Nancy. "I hope Anne and Charles can come." She wanted all her friends to be as happy as she was — as secure, as protected.

"No, this weekend's impossible," Anne said regretfully when Nancy called. "Charles is running an experiment and he'll be working all weekend. I'd love to be at Egremont. It's going to be hard to get there at all this summer."

She had been awarded a research assistantship for the summer at the National Institutes of Health in Washington. Many of her classmates were also applying for summer placement. Larry would be at Johns Hopkins and Nina Alcott would be doing an externship at Peter Bent Brigham in Boston. But the NIH appointment was a real plum. She had been surprised to learn that it was Peter Forbes who had submitted her name for consideration and that he had written a laudatory recommendation on her behalf. She had not thanked him for it. Nor had she consulted Charles before accepting the position. It was understood between them that their relationship would never stand in the way of their work. Still, she did see disappointment flash across his face when she told him about the appointment, although almost at once he reorganized his own summer. He would manage frequent trips to Washington.

"You don't know how lucky you are," Jean Liebowitz said when Anne told her about Charles's reaction.

But Anne did know how lucky she was. Often she lay awake in

the dark and thought about Charles, her face wreathed in a smile, her heart pounding joyously because he was part of her life, because he understood so well who she was and what she wanted.

"Well, perhaps Rutti will be with David this weekend. I'll ask them to have dinner with us," Nancy said. It had become oddly important to her that another couple be involved in this weekend, to serve as a buffer between Dov and herself, to break the intensity of their mood. David with his deep, pleasant laughter and quirky insights, Rutti with her gift for mimicry and gentle humor could do just that.

"Rutti won't leave Werner now," Anne warned her.

"I had forgotten." Nancy was apologetic. She knew that Werner was going through a difficult period, that again he tottered on the precipice of collapse. Poor Rutti, she thought. Poor Werner. Sympathy for her friends gave her perspective on her own problems. All she and Dov needed was a relief from work, a brief respite.

But there was to be no respite.

"Out of the question," Dov said brusquely when she told him of her weekend plans that night. Again his eyes were riveted on the television screen. The news from Israel was bad. Egyptian MIGs had made yet another overflight, sweeping across Israel from the Dead Sea toward El Arish.

Nancy switched off the set and stood in front of it.

"Dov, don't use what's going on in Israel as an excuse to tune me out."

"And don't speak to me in your professional psychobabble," he retorted angrily.

"You're not on call this weekend. I checked your schedule. Look, we need some time alone together." She hated the pleading note that had crept into her voice but her anger had frightened her. "You must learn how to be angry," she told Enid London at their last session, but she herself had yet to learn that lesson. Men had always been familiar with rage, but women had relied on tears for too long.

"Why? What miracle will time together accomplish for us? You have to change, Nancy. You're so caught up with your work — your patients and your course work — that you've forgotten what I need, what Keren needs. What did Keren have for dinner tonight? Pizza. Again."

"Sorry. I've grown a little slack. No gourmet meals in the middle of the week."

"I'm not asking for gourmet meals. I'm asking you to get your priorities straight." His voice was dangerously loud. His face was frozen into a mask of fury.

"Mommy, Daddy — " Keren, wakened from sleep, stood in the doorway. Her long dark hair was tangled and the white flannel nightgown, grown too short, trailed about her knees. She looked from Nancy to Dov and rubbed her eyes. "I like pizza, Daddy," she said. She went to stand beside Nancy, to put her hand protectively on her mother's shoulder.

"Of course you do, darling. Daddy was only joking."

"Just joking," Dov agreed.

Gently Nancy took her daughter's hand and led her back to bed. Keren's fear had shamed them both.

"Sorry," Dov said when she returned. "I was wrong."

"You're tired," she replied. She curled up beside him, clearing the bed of her books and papers, not caring for once that index cards fell out of place. "Overwrought. The work. The news. I understand." She sought to soothe him, to soothe herself. "And you're not wrong. I am overextended, I suppose. It's been a tough year — good but tough."

She could not, she would not, deny how valuable the experience she had gained had been to her. She felt the thrill of achievement with her clinic patients. She saw how her professional intervention could make a difference in their lives. With pleasure, with subdued pride, she heard the new determination in Enid London's voice. She shook hands with a young man who came to her for short-term treatment and who then left her, having come to terms with his problem. She recognized her own talent, her own slowly emerging skill. And she recognized, too, the price that had to be paid for honing that skill. "That's why I thought it would be good for us to get away for the weekend," she continued.

"I wish I could." Now his tone was altered. Anger became regret. "But there's been a change in schedules. I meant to tell you. We have two residents out sick. I had to take a double shift. I won't even be able to get home." He was apologetic. "I'll make it up to you."

"Hey," she said. "It's not that big a deal. It's only a weekend, Dov. There'll be other weekends."

He held her close, his hand gently stroking her back, the gesture he so often used when Keren, frightened, awakened from a nightmare and needed to be comforted.

"It's all right," she assured him. "I'll use Saturday afternoon to get some work done."

And she was working on Saturday afternoon, her index cards spread across the table, when the phone rang.

"It's Rutti." Keren, who had lifted the receiver, called to her. "And she sounds funny."

"Nancy. I'm at Werner's. And I'm frightened. Very frightened." Rutti's voice was very faint.

Nancy gripped the receiver. She knew that Werner was riding the tide of a new and terrible depression. Rutti had described it and she had seen it for herself when she brought Werner the Hebrew newspapers that Dov routinely passed on to him. He had been disheveled, his eyes bloodshot, his fingers ink stained and blood rimmed where he had bitten his nails to the quick. Pages of manuscript and pyramids of books had littered every surface and were scattered across the floor of his room. Nancy had stepped over open texts spangled with newspaper clippings, some recent, some yellow with age.

She had asked Werner if she could stay. If perhaps he could make her a cup of tea. But he had refused. He had too much to do. He had no time. Thoughts assaulted him, he had explained, and he must rush to write them down. Only the narrowest divide separated him from the solution to the historic riddle that had eluded him for so long. He would pierce the mystery of the role of evil in history. He would know why his parents had been murdered. He would know whether his Sarah could live safely in the world. His conviction, she had seen, was manic; he had lost the thread of intellectual reality.

"I must work now, Nancy. I must write it all down. I see the connection between Hitler and Nasser. They are one and the same. Demiurges who would have the history of Israel end."

"Of course, you must write it down." She had spoken in her professional tone, soothing and credulous, but she had been deeply troubled.

That was a week ago. In the intervening days Rutti had assured her that he had grown calmer, more rational.

But now Rutti could barely speak so profound was her fear.

"Werner's not here, Nancy. I came with Sarah. We brought his groceries, his laundry. He knew we were coming. I told him again and again that we would be here on Saturday morning. But when we rang there was no answer. The super opened the door for us."

"And?" Nancy trembled as she waited for the answer. She imagined Werner dead, lying on the floor of the room, shrouded in the ink-spattered pages of his manuscript.

"I told you — he's not here. He's not here!"

"Rutti." She breathed easier. "He just went out. Maybe to the library or the university. Maybe to see his psychiatrist."

"No. He left a note for me. It's here on his desk."

"Read it to me."

"I am doing what I must do." Rutti read slowly. "I have been called to battle against evil. This time we will triumph. Sarah must live in peace. Do not be afraid, my Rutti. I am not alone. Your love goes with me." Rutti's voice broke. "Oh, Nancy, Nancy."

"Rutti. Stay there. Just stay there. I'll be right over. Just wait for me."

"Keren, we have to go out." Nancy struggled to keep her voice calm, to find her purse. Keren stared at her in surprise as Nancy hailed a taxi. They never took taxis. She perched on the edge of the cracked plastic seat, prepared for excitement, prepared for adventure.

"Are we going to Israel, Mommy?" she asked.

"We're not going to Israel, you silly Keren. We're just going to Werner's room. Sarah will be there. You'll play with her. All right, sweetie?"

Rutti was waiting for them, clutching the letter. Sarah, her golden hair plaited into braids and tied with ribbons that matched her sky-blue dress, stood at the window, her face pressed against the grimy glass.

"He'll come soon, Mommy," the small girl said. "Sarah will see him. Listen to Sarah." It was the first time in months that Nancy had heard Sarah refer to herself that way, but the reversion did not surprise her. Sarah needed every protective device she could summon.

A Good Humor truck sounded its bell on the street. Nancy fumbled in her purse for coins, a dollar bill.

"Go on down, girls. Get yourselves some popsicles."

"I want a sundae," Keren said.

"All right. A sundae. But go quickly before the truck takes off."

Sarah put her hand on her mother's shoulder.

"He'll come soon. You'll see."

"Of course, he will," Nancy said. False reassurances were becoming habit with her, she thought. She told Dov that everything would be all right. She told Keren that the argument that had awakened her was only a small joke.

The children hurried down the stairs. Keren shouted raucously after the Good Humor man.

"Hey, hey, don't go away — we want to buy a sundae." Miraculously, wondrously, Sarah laughed. Rutti pointed to a cigar box that stood open on Werner's cluttered worktable.

"He took his passport," she said. She lifted two bankbooks. "He withdrew every penny from the bank. Not that he had much to withdraw. A little over a thousand dollars in one account — about five hundred in another. Enough to buy an air ticket."

"To Israel."

"Of course to Israel."

"Did he take clothing — a valise?"

"The valise is gone and he took some clothing, I think. It's hard to tell in this mess. But he definitely took his manuscript." Her arms flew across the table. The worn boxes of typing paper in which Werner had kept his manuscript were gone. "He wouldn't leave without it. It has the formula. The solution to the riddle. He is bringing his secret weapon to Moshe Dayan. My Werner — my poor Werner — the savior of his people." She laughed hysterically.

"Rutti, stop it. Stop it! He will be all right."

"No. He won't be all right," Rutti said, her voice dulled by despair. "Oh, Nancy, do you know what frightens me the most? He wrote that he was not going alone — that my love went with him. But he didn't have even that. Not even that."

She wept and Nancy stood beside her, her hand on the golden cloud of Rutti's hair, and then she moved to the phone. She had to call Anne and Merle. Together the three of them would take care of their friend. They would contact the airlines, the Israeli consulate. Dov would know what to do. She dialed the hospital.

"Please page Dr. Dov Yallon," she said. This was only the second time she had called him during a shift. The first time had been a year ago when Keren had a fever of a hundred and four.

"Dr. Yallon is not at the hospital," the switchboard operator said. "His name is not on the roster."

"Oh, but he is," Nancy protested. "He's overseeing the emergency room."

"Dr. Rodriguez is supervising ER." The switchboard operator grew irritated.

"Look, this is Mrs. Yallon. Could you just have him paged?"

"I'll try." Sullenly she agreed.

Nancy stood clutching the phone as Keren and Sarah returned, eating their sundaes with wooden spoons.

"I got vanilla. Sarah got chocolate," Keren said. "Can we go to the park on the corner?"

Nancy glanced at Rutti, who nodded.

"I just want to put the rest of my ice cream in the freezer," said Sarah. "For my father. He likes chocolate." She stood on tiptoe and shoved the cardboard cup into the tiny freezer compartment, sliding it between the grimy stalactites of ice that curtained the door.

The hospital operator returned to the line.

"Mrs. Yallon, we've run the page a couple of times. No answer. But Dr. Yallon did leave a number with the registry in case he had to be reached over the weekend. Do you want it?"

"Please," Nancy said.

"It's in Boston." She read the numbers off and repeated them.

"Thank you." Boston. They didn't know anyone in Boston. What was Dov doing in Boston? Her heart sank and her fingers trembled as she dialed Anne's number. Succinctly she told Anne about Werner. Anne was in control at once. Hope and Ted were away and she had promised to stay with Eric. Why didn't Nancy and Rutti bring the girls there? She would call Merle. Andrew had so many contacts. And Charles would call Werner's psychiatrist.

Rutti looked around the room before they left.

"He took the pictures," she said.

"What pictures?"

"The charcoal sketches of Sarah that I did. I had them framed for his birthday. He took them."

"That doesn't mean anything," Nancy said sharply. They would have to be very careful now, not to assign significance to the insignificant.

They picked up the girls at the playground and took another cab to Hope and Ted's. This time Keren did not ask if they were going to Israel. This time Keren worked at distracting Sarah. "Do you think we'll make that light, Sarah? Look at that fat woman walking that tiny dog, Sarah." Keren had graduated into friendship.

Merle was already there when they arrived. She had brought strawberries and raspberries, a container of whipped cream. Rutti could not eat. Anne gave her a sedative and insisted that she lie down on the large double bed in Hope and Ted's room.

Andrew phoned. His office staff was calling airlines, hospitals, police stations. Charles Bingham arrived carrying Chinese food, which they heated up. Werner's psychiatrist had not been helpful.

"We should know something soon," Merle assured them, and they trembled because they feared the knowledge. Merle organized a Monopoly game with the girls but before they could distribute the money Sarah burst into tears.

"I want my father. Sarah wants her father." Her voice was plaintive but she spoke softly because she did not want to waken her mother.

They ate the Chinese food, startled that they should be so hungry. They thrust pots onto the stove and slammed utensils down. They recognized the ferocity of their anger. How could Werner have done this to Rutti and Sarah? At once they were repentant, weak with compassion. Poor Werner. He was ill. He could not help it that his illness contaminated all of them. Yet they could not forgive him, nor, as the evening wore on, could Nancy forgive Dov. He had lied to her. There was no way she could rationalize his deception.

Mark and Dan, Rutti's boarders, arrived to take Rutti and Sarah home. The lean, graceful men spoke gently. They were skilled comfort-givers; they had comforted each other so often.

At last Nancy and Keren returned to their apartment. She put Keren to bed and then dialed the number in Boston. She listened as the unfamiliar voice of a young woman said, "Hello — hello," and then she gently replaced the receiver. Her arms and legs felt unbearably heavy; misery had metastasized in her limbs.

Merle called early the next morning. Werner's name appeared on a Swiss Air passenger manifesto. He had boarded a flight for Lydda. He was in Israel.

12

WERNER DID not sleep at all during the long flight to Israel.

He went directly from the airport to Kibbutz Beit Yair to Chana and Dror's small bungalow. It occurred to him that just twenty years ago, carrying a small cardboard satchel, he had taken the same path, fascinated then as he was now by the star-shaped shadows cast by the leaves of the ash tree, the sun's brightness.

He knocked at the door but there was no answer. He opened the door and went in. Little had changed in the neat little sitting room with its austere Swedish couch and chairs of pale wood frames and woven seats, its laden bookcases and tile floor. The stereo system was new and he was pleased to see it. Dror loved opera and Chana was partial to chamber music. The pictures on the wall were familiar: a seascape of Acre Harbor, a sketch of a Prague street. Chana and Dror were both Czech. On the far wall was an Anna Ticho etching and next to it a painting of a blond youth — the face skeletal, the eyes cavernous. It was Rutti's work, he knew, but it was unfamiliar to him, and he averted his eyes and looked instead at the photographs. Noah, the Ravivs' oldest son, who had been killed in the Sinai campaign. He had been twenty-one. He would be twenty-one forever. Ari, their younger son, standing beside Yaffa, his wife. Yaffa had been a child when Werner and Rutti left the kibbutz. She was a nurse now, Rutti had told him. And there was a picture of Rutti and himself, Sarah seated between them. He was touched that Chana had framed it, that she displayed it beside the photos of her sons. But then she had told them often that she considered herself their mother.

"You will always have a home here," Chana had said, and he, who had no other home, had never forgotten her words. He stretched out on the narrow couch and almost at once, he fell asleep. It was there that Chana found him when she returned from her herb garden, carrying fragrant bundles of newly blooming marjoram and thyme.

She was a tall woman, round of face and figure, famous on the kibbutz for her competence and her strength. It was said that very little astonished her, but she was taken aback by the sight of Werner asleep on her couch. Filled with trepidation, she stared at him, seeing in the man's face the pale and frightened boy whose portrait had hung for so long in her home.

He was thin, almost emaciated, his skin drained to a chalky pallor.

"Werner." Softly she said his name, remembering that while other youngsters had taken Hebrew names he had clung to his German name. It had been given him by his parents, he had explained. He had nothing else that was of their giving.

"Ima." He called her "Mother," as had Rutti.

They were her own, her adopted son and daughter who were husband and wife, the familial bond between all of them forged by history.

"Come," she said.

She led him to the shower, turned it on for him as she had when he was a boy, tested the warmth of the water, handed him towels, soap.

As he showered, she opened his battered valise in search of clean clothing. She found only the two boxes of manuscripts and two charcoal portraits in a Lucite frame. She recognized Rutti's work and, of course, the small girl in the portraits, so delicate of feature, her hair fanning her face in an aureole of softness, was Sarah. Chana kissed each drawing and her heart grew heavier still. She went to the small chest where she kept her son's clothing, selected a plaid shirt, green work pants.

"I laid out clean clothing for you," she called to Werner. "Ari's things."

"Where are Ari and Dror?" Werner asked when he had changed and sat beside her on the couch, his damp hair darkly golden as it always was just after a shower.

"They've been called up. You know that we are preparing for an Arab attack against us."

"Of course I know. That is why I came. I've brought the secret with me. The secret of this war, of all wars. We will end evil."

"I see." She spoke gently, sadly.

"I am afraid that Werner is ill, very ill," Nancy Yallon, Rutti's good friend, had told her when she visited two years earlier. Chana saw now that the American psychologist had not erred.

She prepared dinner for him, scrambled eggs and yogurt, the soft, easily digestible food of the invalid. She offered him warm cocoa. He ate and drank without protest. She made up the narrow couch with clean linens, covered him with the afghan he had favored as a youth. When he was asleep she went to the kibbutz office and tried to call Rutti in New York. An exasperated operator told her there were no lines available for international calls, neither incoming nor outgoing.

"But this is an emergency," Chana protested.

"Everyone in Israel has had an emergency today," the operator snapped back. The next morning Werner sat beside Chana as she listened to the newscast. Her hand gripped his. And he rose when she rose. There was work to be done.

He went with her to the fields and the gardens and worked beside her.

Every radio on the kibbutz played throughout the day. News blared from the windows of the bungalows and the communal children's house, was amplified by loudspeaker into the fields, the barns, the chicken houses. The kibbutz members exulted that first day in the stunning victory of their air force; yet they remained apprehensive. They understood that many battles would yet be fought.

Werner trembled. Evil threatened Israel on three fronts. Death rained down from the heights of the Golan. Jerusalem itself was in jeopardy and the sands of the desert were caked with blood. He waited for a sign that would tell him where he should go, where it was ordained that he do battle with evil, confront it at its source. A clue would come. Of that he was certain. And he would recognize it when it arrived.

Meanwhile he helped with the filling of sandbags. He carried cartons of food, sleeping bags, canteens into the shelters. The war was only miles from the peaceful fields of the kibbutz. From their watchtower they could see the armor moving down the sinuous highway to mount a defense against the heavy reinforcements the Arab Legion was sending from the West Bank to the Jerusalem promontory.

Late in the afternoon Werner heard the message meant for him. Israeli troops had ascended the Hill of Evil Counsel. The fighting was fierce. *The Hill of Evil Counsel*. Of course. He had deciphered the code. It was on that hill that the battle between good and evil was being fought. On that harsh outcropping of rock where once malevolence had ruled. Here, where evil had spoken, evil would be routed out of history and then the world would be safe and he would no longer have to fear for his Sarah, for his golden angel, the child of his heart.

He recognized the enormity of the task at hand. He was already late. He had to move swiftly, to join the forces that would at last claim the final triumph in the penultimate struggle between light and darkness, good and evil. The dialectical process was irreversible. Werner had traced it in text after text, source after source. He had refuted other historians. Hegel himself had erred, but then Hegel had not been orphaned by history as Werner had been. Hegel had not been forced to delve into its mystery so that he might protect an innocent child. His Sarah. Named for the mother of his nation. He would do anything for her, anything.

Twilight hovered over the kibbutz. He hurried to Chana's bungalow. One of Ari's uniforms, newly laundered and pressed, hung in the closet, and Werner put it on, buttoning the officer's field jacket emblazoned with the epaulets of the armored infantry. He found Ari's maroon beret in a drawer, laced up Ari's boots. He took Chana's pistol. In the drawer of the bedside table he found the bullets hidden among her sweaters. He removed the charcoal portraits of Sarah from the Lucite frame and tucked them into the inner pocket of the jacket. And then he left the bungalow and ran until he reached the highway where he flagged down a passing jeep.

"I need a lift to my unit — the Jerusalem Brigade," he shouted. The driver saw the officer's epaulets on the field jacket, heard the perfect German-accented Hebrew, and opened the door.

"Just tell me where you want to get out," he said to Werner as they approached the city. "I'll slow down."

Werner studied the streets. And then he saw the sign, a simple marker that separated one neighborhood from another, but he recognized it. He understood that it brought a message to him. *Geulah,* it read. *Redemption.* That was his mission. He would redeem his people from evil.

"Here! Here!" he shouted.

The driver slowed down. He jumped off and ran, drawing closer to the border, closer to the Hill of Evil Counsel. Ari's boots blistered his feet and he rested briefly in the courtyard of a yeshiva. He fell asleep until the pounding of feet awakened him, the tympanic reverberation of soldier's boots quick-marching across the cobblestones of Jerusalem. Startled he looked up and saw that the sky was ablaze with stars. He hesitated for a moment at the entry of the courtyard and then fell in with the Israeli soldiers. He raced with them through the narrow streets of Geulah, the alleyways of Mea Shearim, past the Mandelbaum Gate, into the Old City of Jerusalem.

Bullets spat at them from the windows of Arab houses, from the parapets of balconies. Sirens screeched and voices shrill with hatred shouted their pledges of fury. "Death to the Jews!" He grasped Chana's revolver tightly, held it high as he ran. An Israeli soldier darted ahead of him, a boy so young that his face was smooth, unshadowed by the beard of manhood. Werner saw the heavy wooden door of a courtyard open, saw a Jordanian Legionnaire wheel about, his machine gun trained on the youth who forged on, unaware of the danger. Werner took aim, his hand very steady. He knew that he had to destroy this evil; that was why he had come to Israel. He pulled the trigger and, as in his dream, he watched the Legionnaire pitch forward; he watched the Israeli soldier run on, turn a corner. And then from the roof of the house within the courtyard, another shot rang out. Werner felt a searing pain at his heart; he lifted his hand, thrust it into his jacket, felt the stiffness of paper, the thick, hot moisture of blood. Pain coursed through him, his legs buckled, and he fell.

He looked up at the stars and thought that he had never seen a sky more beautiful. He writhed against the pain, but he did not move his fingers. They rested on the drawing of his daughter, his Sarah, for whom he had fought, for whom he would die.

*   *   *

Because Ari's name was sewn into the lining of the jacket, Werner's body was taken to Beit Yair. And it was in the Beit Yair cemetery beneath a cypress tree that he was buried on the fourth day of the war that lasted only six days.

Chana clipped a branch from that tree and sent it to Sarah. To Rutti she sent the charcoal sketches of Sarah, in full face and profile, creased now and rust-edged with traces of Werner's blood.

13

WERNER'S DEATH slowed their pace. Grief and shock hobbled the friends; they moved more slowly, more hesitantly. They recognized the unpredictability of the future toward which they had rushed with such zeal and purpose. Their vulnerability was revealed and they felt angry, betrayed. Rutti was too young to be a widow. A *widow*. The word fascinated and repelled them, vested them with new wisdom, new recognition. Her loss could not be reversed and that terrible finality and irreversibility caused them to reconsider their own choices.

They were not surprised then that Anne decided to accept an extension of her National Institutes of Health grant and take a year's leave from medical school. Washington throbbed with excitement and her DNA research excited and absorbed her.

"What about Charles?" Merle asked.

"Charles says he is going to single-handedly raise the value of stocks in airlines with Washington routes. You'd better warn Andrew."

They all laughed, pleased with Charles for being so understanding, pleased with themselves for being in the vanguard of a generation of women whose decisions were not dependent on men.

Merle spent the summer at the Egremont house and they joined her there when they could. Rutti allowed Sarah to go to Egremont with Keren and Nancy, although she herself came rarely to visit. She had a great deal to do, she explained. There was Werner's room to deal with, his books and papers to be sorted and distributed.

"We'll help," Nancy offered.

"No. No." Rutti's objections were uttered in a vague, but firm, tone of voice.

"Let me help." David's suggestion was hesitant, gentle. He understood the currents of mourning and navigated them skillfully.

"No. Please no!" The ferocity of her refusal startled him, although she had stayed aloof from him since Werner's death. He had excused that aloofness. She needed her solitude. He schooled himself to understanding. He worked with renewed intensity on the illustrations for his new book.

On a warm afternoon Anne and Nancy walked through the woodland. They paused to watch two cardinals perched amid the forsythia, their crimson bodies delicately balanced on a fragile branch. The birds danced teasingly toward each other through the golden flowers and flew off at the same moment, scissoring their way in tandem through the cloudless blue sky.

"Dov is having an affair," Nancy said. She spoke matter-of-factly, without looking at her friend. Anne plucked a blueberry. It was still unripe and sour in her mouth, but she ate it as though to punish herself with its bitterness. "Did you know?" Nancy asked her.

"I didn't know," Anne replied hesitantly. She spat out the fruit, crushed the pulpy blueness beneath her foot.

"But you guessed."

"I had a vague feeling. There were rumors. Stupid hospital gossip."

Nancy sat down on a fallen tree and Anne sat beside her.

"Would you have told me if you knew — if you were sure?"

"I don't know," Anne replied. She thought for a moment. Anne watched her friend pluck a daisy and pull it apart, petal by petal.

"Yes." She corrected herself. "If I had known for certain, I probably would have told you."

"Do you know who she is?" Nancy asked.

"I think it may be a woman in my class. Nina Alcott."

"Is she in Boston now?"

"She has a grant at Brigham for the summer."

"Then it is her. What do you know about her?"

"I've seen them together at the hospital. That's all," Anne said. "But I did have a feeling about them."

"Your feeling was right on target."

"How do you know?"

Nancy told her how she had tried to reach Dov at the hospital, how the operator had given her the Boston number.

"What did Dov say when you told him?"

"I didn't tell him."

She had meant to tell him. Throughout that long weekend, as they comforted Rutti, as they struggled to distract Sarah, she had rehearsed the speeches she would make, the accusations she would utter, the ultimatums she would demand. Late Sunday night she had even packed his clothing into a suitcase and contemplated placing a note on it telling him to take it and leave their apartment, leave their life. She and Keren would go to Merle's or to Anne's or even to Rutti's apartment. It had buoyed her to know that so many refuges were available to her, that her friends, no matter what her distress, would welcome her, support her. It did not occur to her to call her family in Ohio. Her friends, the women with whom she had shared so much, understood her in a way that her family could not. She realized then that friendship had become the fulcrum of her life, the safe center into which she could plunge for comfort.

She even wrote the note. "Dov, I know you have lied to me. We cannot go on living together." She tore that one up and wrote another. "Dov, I want a divorce. I think you will know why." But would he know why? Did she herself know why? She wept because she could not be certain and because she felt so betrayed, so frightened. She held both notes above an ashtray, lit a match, and watched them burn; the thin paper sheets curled into a winding strip of gray ash that seared and blistered her finger before she dropped it.

When Merle called the next day to tell her that Werner was dead, she unpacked the suitcase and replaced Dov's things in the drawers and closet. She understood that she must move very slowly, that she needed time, that she had to be absolutely certain of what she wanted to do. She told him about Werner's death when he returned and watched his face collapse.

"Poor bastard." His arms encircled her. He buried his face in her shoulder for comfort. "I'm sorry. God, I'm so sorry." His voice was husky.

181

She pulled away.

"Don't feel guilty," she said. "I know everything." She turned her back, busied herself at the sink. He sat at the kitchen table.

"What do you know?" Fear compounded his grief.

"I know that you didn't want to go back to Israel. Not for this war. That probably you don't want to go back — not ever." Of that much she could accuse him. That far she could go. She heard his hiss of relief above the running water.

"That's an oversimplification. My feelings about returning to Israel are very complicated."

"We'll talk about it when we aren't so upset."

He shrugged in agreement and relief.

They would talk about it, she had decided, when she was ready, when she knew exactly what she wanted to do. The next week she told Professor Aaronsohn that she wanted to go into intensive therapy. He had not been surprised. He referred her to Mina Sieberg, a distinguished analyst. Her fees were prohibitive but she adjusted them for Nancy.

"When will you tell Dov that you know?" Anne asked.

"I may never tell him. But if I do it will be because I choose to, because I want to." From the earliest days of their courtship, they had always followed Dov's timetables, his needs had claimed priority. Now she would set the pace; she would reclaim the tempo of her life.

"Good for you," Anne said.

A single cardinal returned to the forsythia bush. The two friends watched it as it flew from branch to branch.

That week Nancy had her last appointment with Enid London. Enid was going to England to read literature at Cambridge for a year.

"It's wonderful to be doing what I want to do because *I* want to do it," Enid told her.

"Yes, it must be," Nancy replied. Her patient did not recognize the wistfulness in her voice, but Mina Sieberg, to whom she repeated Enid's words, nodded in recognition.

"That is a goal you want then — to do what you want because *you* want to do it — not because Dov wants it or Keren wants it or your family wants it," Mina Sieberg said. "Given the strictures of life."

It seemed to Nancy that the silver-haired analyst had done exactly that. She herself radiated a rare serenity. Her life was wonderfully organized. Her consulting room was part of her spacious East Side apartment, and occasionally Nancy heard the voices of teenagers, the slamming of doors. Once rock music was playing too loudly; Mina Sieberg excused herself and within minutes the music ceased. Fresh flowers filled her vases, her floors were waxed to a high glow, and the fragrance of cooking and baking sometimes drifted into the room. Her husband taught philosophy at a suburban campus. Nancy acknowledged that her analyst had the life she wanted. A happy family, an orderly, beautiful home, meaningful work. Was it so much to ask for? she wondered.

The strictures of life. Nancy repeated the phrase to herself again and again that summer as she arranged for their move to a larger, more convenient apartment, as she interviewed baby-sitters who would be on hand when Keren returned from school.

"Who will pay for all this?" Dov asked.

"You'll be seeing private patients. There are my clinic fees. We'll manage."

Her new decisiveness, her new claims, frightened him. But the freedom she claimed emancipated him as well.

"I'll be home late," he told her. Because she offered no explanations, neither did he.

She cut her long hair so that it hugged her head in a sleek dark helmet. He did not recognize her. She was no longer the pony-tailed coed he had courted on a midwestern campus, the young bride to whom he had told stories of the desert town of his boyhood, whose long fingers had lightly, wonderingly, traced the butterfly scar that had brought him close to death. He stared at her, placed his hand on her head, and fingered the satin caplet of her hair.

"Do you like it?" she asked.

"I like it. I'm just surprised that you never mentioned you were thinking of cutting it — never asked me about it."

"It's my hair." Her petulance angered and aroused him.

"Of course, it's your hair."

Roughly he pulled her to him, kissed her with his hands clasped about her head, about the thick, luxuriant layers of her hair, and then moved his hands down across the contours of her body as though to assure himself that the rise of her breasts and indentation of her waist remained a familiar fortress, that he still had dominion over her.

"I'm tired," she said. "Very tired."

She extricated herself from his embrace and he watched her walk from the room. He had forgotten the grace of her long stride. He called Nina Alcott that night and told her that he could not after all arrange to go to Boston that weekend. He was undisturbed when Nina cried softly into the phone. He was the brother of many sisters and he had heard each of them, in turn, weep quietly, through the long days and nights of his boyhood.

Rutti came to Egremont for a week at summer's end. Her work in the city was completed. She had gathered Werner's clothing together and folded each item carefully before placing it in the cartons Mark and Dan scavenged from West Side liquor stores. The garments that were soiled or stained she washed by hand, ignoring Mark's reminder that there was a Laundromat nearby. She scrubbed furiously at tiny spots. She soaked the sheets and towels in the bathtub and draped them across the fire escape to dry. The physical effort and the exhaustion it brought gave her an odd satisfaction. She filled three cartons with Werner's notebooks and gave them to a historian he had respected. Chana had sent his manuscript. It would be carefully read, Werner's colleague assured her. There was a possibility of a posthumous publication.

She and Nancy took Werner's battered pots and pans, his chipped dishes and cutlery, to a women's shelter and placed them on a long table amid the debris of other households beneath a sign that read: Take What You Can. Use What You Take. She watched as a young woman wearing a long Indian print dress, a baby in a woven sling dangling at her breast, plucked up the blue pot Chana had given them when they left the kibbutz.

She returned for a last time to Werner's room, stripped now of all reminders of him, and, perched on the windowsill, she sketched in charcoal the table, the chairs, the sagging wardrobe, the narrow bed. The completed drawing was stark, haunting in its simplicity. It was a new genre for her, but she knew that she would sketch other rooms in other houses, rooms waiting for lives to inhabit them.

She showed the drawing to David as they sat in his garden that last week of summer, noting that the leaves of the maple trees were already fringed with crimson. She had not wanted to go into his house. She did not want to see the studio he had built, large enough to accommodate two easels, two drawing tables, two artists at work.

He lifted the sketch to the light.

"It's very lonely," he said. "A lonely room, as Werner was lonely."

"He did not know how lonely he was," she replied. "He did not know how far I had gone from him."

"Do you punish yourself for that, Rutti?"

She remained silent, although briefly her hand moved to cover his.

"I, too, have been lonely, Rutti," he said at last. "You have punished me as well."

He could no longer maintain the silence he had kept through the long days of that strange and terrible summer. Alone he had worked in his studio, walked in the woodland. Alone he had watched television late at night and viewed the cities of the nation afire with hatred, watched riots in Detroit, Watts, Cleveland. He listened to the body count from Vietnam. The youthful leaders of the sixties were grown older and tired. The decade that began with such hard work and high hopes, with marches and songs, was careening to an end in screams of rage, shards of shattered glass, and angry flames. Late at night, heavyhearted, he occasionally phoned Rutti in New York, but always her voice was distant, muffled in private grief.

He had willed himself to patience, but now, at last, his own loneliness had burst forth and recklessly he confronted her with it.

"I know. I know and I'm sorry." She spoke so quietly that he felt an implosion of fear strangle the words he had meant to utter. He cautioned himself to silence, waited for her to continue talking, although he already rebelled against her words, her decision. "David, I thought a great deal this summer. About Werner. About Sarah. About you. But mostly I thought about myself. I know how selfish that must sound."

She paused as though inviting his interruption, but still he said nothing. She clasped her hands on her lap. She wore the same pale blue sundress she had been wearing the first day he saw her. She looked like a schoolgirl reciting a lesson for which she had prepared long and hard, but in the end, not well enough. He touched her hair, curled a golden tendril about his finger. She breathed deeply and then continued.

"Here's how I have been thinking, what I have been thinking. I have never in my life been free to be myself. Always I worried and waited. When I was a child in England, I waited for the war to end, I worried about my parents, I thought only about searching for them. And when that was over, there was Werner and once again I worried, I waited, I searched. Year after year. In Israel and then in New York. It was as though shadows and fear were stitched together into a cloak that I could not shake loose. And I felt guilty because I wanted to be free of it. And now I am free. I don't wake up thinking, 'will this be a good day for Werner or a bad day for him?' It is only Sarah I must think about — Sarah and myself. And that is what I want to do now, David. I want to live my own life, build my own life. I want to feel that feedom. I want to know how it is to live without wearing that cloak, that terrible, heavy cloak."

"I'm sorry, Rutti, I don't believe you." He would not surrender without a fight. "It's been different with you and me. There's been no shadow. No burden. I love you, Rutti. I want to take care of you. I want to marry you."

"But you don't understand — I want to take care of myself."

"No. I think you feel guilty. You blame yourself because you think that Werner felt himself more alone, more vulnerable because you and I were together. And that may even be true."

"It was true," she said sadly.

"All right. But whatever happened would have happened even if you and I had not been lovers. Werner was sick before we ever met. It wasn't your fault. It wasn't my fault."

"David, it's no good to talk about it. I've thought about it all carefully. I must be myself for a while. I must find out who I am. I don't want to go from being Werner's widow to being your wife." She was resolute. He could not dissuade her.

"But you love me, Rutti," he said. There was certainty in his voice. She turned her head, clasped and unclasped her hands. But she did not deny his words.

"Listen to me, Rutti." He spoke very slowly. It was important that she understood him clearly. "I love you. I want us to be together.

And I will be waiting for you when you are ready to accept my love, when you forgive yourself."

"You don't understand," she said miserably. "Even the thought of you waiting — that becomes my responsibility — a shadow, another shadow. A new cloak."

"Please, Rutti. Don't ask me to say that I don't love you. That would be too much. Much too much."

She nodded, not in surrender but in acknowledgment. He put his arm around her, held her close.

Evening shadows drifted across the long grass and a chill edged the gentle wind. She rested her head on his shoulder and they sat quietly and waited for the darkness as once they had clung to each other and waited for the light.

14

BECAUSE CHARLES Bingham was working on the final draft of the paper on adoptive immunotherapy he was to present at the annual meeting of the Oncology Research Forum, he was at home that cold December afternoon to answer the phone. He picked up on the second ring because he was concerned about Chet, a small boy whom he was treating for a tumor that was oddly lodged behind the bile duct. Surgery had proven ineffective and Charles was treating the child with an experimental drug.

"Am I going to be all right, Dr. Bingham?" Chet asked him at the conclusion of each visit. He was a large-eyed child. Freckles peppered his long thin face and, although he was often in pain, he struggled to smile for his parents. His brush of rust-colored hair was worn thin by the assault of chemicals and his pink scalp shone through the sparse layer that remained.

"We're going to fight it as hard as we can, Chet," Charles replied. He passed his hand across the child's head. "Hey, I think I owe you a Mets cap." He could not promise the child life, but a vendor on the corner did sell Mets caps.

Chet had been especially weak the previous evening and Charles had been summoned to the hospital in the middle of the night.

"Can't the resident take care of it?" Anne asked sleepily.

"I don't want to take any chances," he replied.

"Of course not." She respected his commitment, his dedication. Only that afternoon she had overheard a group of oncology residents discuss Charles as they sat huddled over coffee in the hospital cafeteria.

"He cares. He really cares. He sees each case as a separate battle and he's some kind of galactic warrior, throwing everything he's got against the damn tumor. But I wouldn't want to be near him when he loses his cool because an intern doesn't move fast enough or a nurse screws up on medication."

Anne understood their wonder at Charles's approach. Most oncologists grew hard and pessimistic as the years passed, as patient after patient suffered and died. Wearily they made their rounds. They lifted wrists through which luminescent bones jutted; they struggled to find veins in limbs from which all flesh had withered. They grew used to answering questions asked in a whisper because there was no strength remaining to emit a voice. Often they felt defeated before they had begun to fight.

But Charles was different. He vested each case with all his energy, his knowledge, his caring. When his beeper sounded he sprinted to the phone. Anne had been suffused with pride as she listened to the residents, although it had occurred to her that she had never seen Charles angry. Still listening to the conversation, she wondered idly what form his rage might take. Decisive rejection, she decided. She had kept her eyes riveted to her hematology text, but she had wanted to tell the young men that Charles Bingham was her lover. That he was wonderful. That they had not been mistaken in their assessment of him. That above all things he valued life.

"Don't answer the phone," she cautioned him as she left that morning. "You're not on call. Finish that damn paper. I don't want it hanging over our heads during winter break."

"All right. All right. Don't nag. Nagging is not the role of a lover. If you want to nag, you'll have to marry me."

"Another year," she retorted. "Not even a year." Smiling, she hummed the wedding march. He was newly moved by her beauty. Because she worked so often on the wards during this last year of medical school, she wore her thick fair hair in intricately plaited chignons that nestled softly at the nape of her neck. Her classmates, he knew, admired her competence and control. They did not know the Anne who teased him as he worked, biting at his ear, sliding her hands across his body. She dashed away and he chased her through the apartment, laughingly following the trail of clothing she left behind until at last she stretched out across the bed, submissive and seductive in her victory, in her nakedness.

"This is Dr. Bingham," he said as he answered the phone.

"My name is Helene Miles," the caller said. "I'm Anne Richardson's sister. I'm calling from Pennsylvania. Our mother died this morning. Hope said that you worked closely with Anne and you'd know how to reach her."

"I'm sorry. Very sorry."

His words were sincere. He could not grieve for a woman he had never met, but he anticipated Anne's sorrow.

"Was it sudden?" he asked.

"No. She was sick for the last few months. But she didn't want Anne to know. She thought Anne wouldn't be able to concentrate on her studies if she knew. That was how she was, our mother. That was how she was." Helene Miles was crying. Her voice grew fainter.

"I'll get in touch with Anne at once. And please accept my condolences."

"Thank you, Dr. Bingham."

He wondered that Anne's sister addressed him so formally and then he wondered if she knew about him at all, if Anne had ever spoken of him. It occurred to him for the first time that when he thought of Anne's family it was her friends who came to mind — Rutti, Merle, and Nancy — the "playground sisters," Sarah called them, and she was right. A sisterhood had been formed that day in November when they first met, a surrogate family free of the constraints and complexities of childhood memories and rivalries.

He hurried to the hospital and elbowed his way through the crowded lobby. Anne was on her obstetrics rotation and the elevator he took up to the maternity floor was crowded with visitors carrying odorless bouquets of hothouse flowers, the awkward bundles of laundry that he knew contained fresh pajamas and nightgowns. The hospital gowns repelled patients and their families. He observed once that only those of his patients who had abandoned all hope wore the flimsy blue-and-white-checked uniforms of illness. Chet always wore gay pajamas — green and white trains speeding up red seersucker mountains, baseball players in purple and blue uniforms dashing across gold flannel home plates.

190

Anne was not in the delivery room, the harried, acerbic charge nurse told him. She was somewhere on the floor, but it was hard to know where these young women medical students were.

"I think she's in the nursery," a student nurse said softly to him, and he flashed her a grin of complicity.

Anne stood at the glass window of the nursery, her face pressed against it. She curled her fingers and played inky dinky spider as though the purblind newborns, wrapped in their cocoons of receiving blankets, nestled in their cardboard cribs, could follow the movements of her fingers, as though she might coax smiles from the tiny mouths.

"Hey," she said very softly. "Hey there, you cuties."

He watched her for a moment and then moved forward.

"Anne."

Startled, she whirled around.

"Charles — has something happened?"

"It's your mother," he said. The words sufficed. Her face collapsed, assumed the sagging expression of incredulity peculiar to those who cannot yet assimilate or comprehend a loss. "Your sister called. It happened only a short while ago."

"But I spoke to her just last week. On Wednesday. No, Thursday."

"Your sister said she'd been sick for a while. Since the summer. She didn't want you to know. She was afraid it would interfere with your studies."

"Damn," she said. "God damn it."

"Easy. It's all right." He put his arms about her shoulders, steadied her head; she leaned on him as they walked to the elevator.

He went with her to the medical school office and waited as she explained the situation to the administrator and accepted condolences, and reassurances that arrangements would be made for her to make up the work and examinations she would miss.

"It's almost winter break," the administrative secretary said comfortingly. "And after all this is your last year."

Charles went with her to Hope and Ted's apartment and called the airline as she packed. There was a flight in the late afternoon. He booked two seats. Anne called Merle who in turn would call Rutti and Nancy.

They went to his apartment where he packed an overnight case and left instructions for his nurse. Chet was stabilized. His other patients presented no immediate problems. He would be back in a day or two. A family emergency, he explained. He looked at Anne; her emergency had become his own. She was his family. His only family.

Her sisters met them at the airport. Helene and Edna were older than Anne and closely resembled her in feature and coloring, but they lacked her energy, her determination. They were wan, exhausted from the long ordeal of nursing their mother while they coped with their husbands, their children, their homes. They spoke rapidly on the drive home, so conversant with each other's thoughts and moods that they finished each other's sentences.

"Mama didn't want you to know she was sick," Helene said.

"Because she was afraid you'd lose time from your studies . . . ," Edna continued.

"And you know she wanted you to finish your degree. You were . . . "

"Her daughter, the doctor."

Charles smiled, but neither Anne nor her sisters saw anything strange in the way they communicated. Their mother and her sisters had had the same habit of completing each other's thoughts. It was common among women who shared their lives, their responsibilities.

"Dad still can't believe it happened but . . . "

"He's accepting it because . . . "

"What can he do?"

Her father, gray-haired and gray-faced, hugged Anne, shook Charles's hand.

"Your mother wanted to see you settled," he said and began to weep; tiny tears crept their way out of the corners of his faded eyes. "She hated to think of you alone."

"But I'm fine, Dad. Fine."

Charles waited. He wanted her to tell her father that they would be married, that she would be "settled" and no longer alone. But she said nothing.

There was no spare bedroom for him in the house and he stayed at the Holiday Inn nearby. But he sat beside Anne at the funeral parlor as they received friends and neighbors.

"A wonderful woman," everyone said. "She couldn't do enough for her friends, her family."

Anne pursed her lips and Charles, pressing her hand, thought he read her thoughts. What had Sophie Richardson done for herself except purchase lottery tickets that never won? Anne accepted their condolences, recognized their curiosity, heard their whispers. Was that balding, thin doctor who had come down from New York with Anne her fiancé? They hoped so. Sophie had worried about her Anne being single. They glanced at their own married daughters, relieved that they had homes to go to, husbands to care for them. This new women's lib business was dangerous, threatening. They saw the new priestesses on television talk shows. Betty Friedan, Gloria Steinem, Germaine Greer. All of them women without men. Well, at least Sophie's Anne had her doctor friend.

Charles sat beside Anne at the funeral. He listened to the eulogy, his hand covering hers.

"Sophie Richardson was a woman who committed herself to kindness," the minister said.

Those kindnesses had been tangible. Lynn Claymore, a heavyset young woman who had been Anne's classmate, told them that when she arrived home from the hospital after an illness she found a pot of lamb stew simmering on her stove.

"It was your mother's own recipe," she told Anne. "I remembered how we used to eat it at your house after Girl Scouts."

She and Anne looked at each other, remembering the distant days of their girlhoods before Anne had left this valley town of narrow streets to go across the world to Africa, before the laughter and demands of children filled Lynn's days and nights — she had three children, she told Anne, and love filled her voice as she said their names.

An elderly woman told Anne how her mother had knit a sweater for her the previous Christmas.

"I needed a warm sweater. She knew that. But she made it of periwinkle blue because she knew I loved that color."

Anne went back to the Holiday Inn with Charles that night. She wept as she lay in his arms.

"That was her legacy," she said bitterly. "A blue sweater. A recipe for lamb stew."

"More than that," Charles reminded her. He had listened closely to the tales of pies carried into the kitchens of the newly bereaved, of the thermoses of soup left on kitchen tables and long flannel nightgowns fashioned for small girls and old women, all of them with a distinctive crocheted frill at the neck. Anne had such a nightgown, in a blue and white flowered pattern, but he had not known that her mother had made it.

"All right," she said. "Lots of good deeds. But what did she have? What belonged to her?" Oh, there had to be more to life than that. She remembered Nancy, plaiting her long dark hair as she sat at the edge of the Egremont pool, saying, "I want my life to make a difference, to count for something." Her friend's words had articulated Anne's own feelings, all their feelings.

She pressed her face against Charles's chest. Her tears moistened his skin, silvered the tendrils of her fine hair. He held her close and made love to her, soothing her grief with his passion, comforting her with the generous force of his love.

He left for New York the next day, but she stayed on. She wanted to help her sisters sort through their mother's things and to keep her father company. Her father spoke hesitantly of selling the family house, showed her brochures of a retirement community in the South. His hands, covered with liver spots, trembled as he shuffled the glossy pages, pointing at the pictures of delicate, silver-haired men and women perched on pastel golf carts.

"Things aren't the way they used to be," he said. "Helene wants to go back to work. Edna, too. They won't have time for me." He did not even mention Anne and she understood that her life had taken her beyond the pale of both his imagination and his condemnation.

Her high school friends visited her. They wore pearls and wool dresses and carried cakes in white bakery boxes. Anne wondered that they dressed so carefully for these casual visits until she realized that the shared conversation and coffee constituted a social occasion for them, a break in the routine of child care and housework and the part-time jobs they mentioned with casual indifference.

One friend did bookkeeping at home for small businesses. Another sold toiletries. "Just to help out," they said. They spoke of their children who had been placed on the honor roll, who had won awards.

"I'm so proud of my kids," Lynn Claymore said and ate another cookie, although she had spoken ruefully of going on a diet.

And are you proud of yourself? Anne thought, but she allowed the words to wither unspoken.

With her sisters she went to a housewares party in one of the new suburbs that had sprung up on the outskirts of the town. Their young hostess was proud of her teakwood furniture, of her pale blue wall-to-wall carpeting, of her draperies with their modern geometric design. Winter sunlight flooded her kitchen, bounced off her laminated white cabinets, her shining countertops covered with plastic products that would be offered for sale that day. Her guests admired the furnishings, took note of the cleanliness of the house.

They perched on the living room couch in their miniskirts and pastel sweaters. They patted the shining lacquer swells of their bouffant hair, nibbled at nut-encrusted cookies, sipped coffee from cleverly shaped cups while the children were herded by the baby-sitter into the finished basement.

"I have so many great things to show you," their hostess promised. "But let's have some fun first." Her voice was high and sweet and she spoke as though she had memorized a prepared script. Of course, Anne realized, that was precisely what she had done.

Newly sharpened pencils and pads with the company insignia were distributed. Their hostess explained the game. She would mention a word and they would write down their immediate association. Anne remembered how they had played Abstractions at Merle's dinner party. She thought of Werner's angry outburst. She left the room hurriedly and went into the bathroom where she cried for several minutes and then vomited up much of what she had eaten that day. She washed her face carefully, reapplied her makeup, and was relieved when she returned that the games were over and the products were being shown.

Edna bought a lettuce keeper guaranteed to keep lettuce fresh for weeks. Why would anybody want to keep lettuce that long? Anne wondered. She grew bored as they exclaimed over the see-through bread containers, nesting plastic tumblers, a green shredder. Reluctantly she bought a plastic ball for Helene's son and a bird feeder for Edna's yard.

She wanted to go, but the other guests lingered, reluctant to depart. They did not want to return to chores and dinner preparations. Anne suspected that they often opened cans in their wonderfully designed kitchens, that they relied heavily on convenience foods, that they seldom made stews using fresh vegetables. It seemed likely to her that they would neglect to unwrap their purchases for several weeks and that perhaps when they did they would be unable to recall why they had bought the plastic tumblers, the miniature ice-cube trays.

"You look pale," Edna said as they drove home.

"I'm all right. Maybe just a touch of a virus," Anne replied.

"Well, you're the doctor."

"Almost," she said. "Almost."

She left for New York the next day feeling a great deal better. Winter break was over and gratefully she resumed her schedule. Three weeks later she was again assaulted by nausea in the late afternoon. She looked at the calendar and realized that she had missed a period. She knew without even the shadow of a doubt that she was pregnant.

15

"YOU'RE SURE?" Nancy asked. "Absolutely sure?" She pushed her half-eaten plate of spaghetti away from her, drained her glass of Chianti, and made no protest when the waiter refilled it.

"Absolutely sure," Anne said.

"But you know sometimes there can be other reasons. I missed two periods in a row when I had that crazy flu."

"Nancy. The rabbit died. A bunny gave his life so I could be absolutely sure."

"All right. I give in. You're pregnant. I'll pay for dinner."

"Suit yourself. Besides, I hardly ate anything. Unlike your average primagravida, I do not get morning sickness. I get evening sickness or late afternoon sickness."

Anne leaned back in her chair and Nancy noticed how tired she looked. Dark circles rimmed her eyes and her skin had a pale, doughy look. She remembered her own exhaustion during the first trimester of her pregnancy with Keren and how she had submitted to the delicious luxury of naps in the middle of the afternoon. Dov had been so solicitous then, sprinting to bring her glasses of chocolate milk and the gothic mysteries that she had read one after another. She wondered how he would react if she were pregnant now in this new season of their lives when they spoke to each other so cautiously, so politely, when each day of their marriage was acted out on a stage set so narrow and so fragile that they moved very cautiously lest they disturb the balance and jar the props that sustained them.

"How does Charles feel about it?" she asked Anne.

"I haven't told Charles."

"Oh?" Nancy waited. During her year in treatment with Mina Sieberg, she had grown accustomed to waiting. Silence no longer frightened her.

"I don't want him to know," Anne said at last.

"Why not?"

"He'd want to marry at once. And I don't want to get married. Not before I graduate."

"Pregnant women graduate from medical school. And from law school. Pregnant women even get doctorates in clinical psychology. They manage. And so could you."

"Maybe. If I could be absolutely sure that everything would work out. But there's no way I can know that everything will be swimmingly normal and that I'd sail down the aisle to take my degree, slightly resembling a whale in my academic gown with everyone smiling in admiration. What if I develop toxemia and I have to stay off my feet? What if I begin to stain and the doctor orders bed rest? There goes the year. I'm doing an obstetrics rotation now. It seems to me that every day I read another case history and begin to worry about another what if." She twirled strands of spaghetti about on her fork, but set it down uneaten.

"Anne, talk to Charles about it. He's been so accepting, so understanding. He made it so easy for you to take that year in Washington. No guilt trips. No complaints." They all envied Anne her Charles.

"Charles is wonderful," Anne agreed. "But it's my life and the decision is mine. You know how important that is." There was cruelty in her emphasis.

"But we're not talking about me now, Anne," Nancy said evenly. It was too easy for Anne to use the lesson of Nancy's own marriage to support her own position. It was true that Nancy had allowed Dov to make too many decisions, to exercise too much control over her life, that she had placed her own professional training on hold so that he could complete his residency. But she and Dov began the game playing by a different set of rules. The women in her graduating class didn't think of becoming doctors and lawyers. They thought only of marrying doctors and lawyers. Their fiancés sent out résumés and graduate school applications while they sent off for china and silver catalogs, polished their typing skills, took the requisite education courses. All that was changed now.

"What a difference a decade makes," Dov said when he touched his champagne glass to hers during the joyless celebration of their tenth anniversary.

"Yes. Especially when that decade is the sixties." She strove for levity, but there was no way to ease the sadness that hovered over them that night as they sat opposite each other in an expensive French restaurant, picking at the excellent steak au poivre neither of them had any desire to finish.

"All right. It is *me* we're talking about. Me, my body, my future. The choice is mine. I get to choose what I want to do with my life." But Anne was crying now, tears striping her cheeks, mottling and contorting her face. She lifted her napkin to her eyes, then dipped it into the water glass and pressed it to her face.

"It's the hormones, Anne," Nancy said soothingly. "They go haywire during the first trimester. I was either manic or sobbing."

"I alternate between being mad and sad. Mad at myself for being so damn stupid and sad because — oh, what the hell." She shrugged and took another sip of wine.

She would always be angry with herself for going to Charles's hotel room after her mother's funeral, for accepting — no — for almost demanding his love and passion, an affirmation of life in the face of the finality of her mother's death. She had claimed his comfort, fully aware that she was playing sexual roulette. She did not have the violet-colored plastic case that contained her birth control pills with her in Pennsylvania. She had packed too swiftly, or perhaps she had not wanted to take her pills to her father's house, had not thought she would sleep with her lover in the town of her girlhood. She had taken a chance and she had lost, but no irreparable damage had been done. She would terminate this accidental gestation. This was not life that grew within her now, this formless bit of tissue, no more than the egg that was obviated by the pill was life. Such reasoning soothed her, justified the decision that she knew she would take. She repeated it now to Nancy.

"Anne, you know that I'm pro-choice — if we ever get the right to that choice. But abortion isn't birth control. Why not at least talk to Charles about it?" Nancy crumbled a bit of bread, watched the snowy crumbs drift onto the red cloth, frowned.

"Oh let's not go through that again," Anne said angrily. "It's my decision — it's my life. I just can't risk everything I've worked for. I just can't take that chance of not finishing, not when I'm so close. I keep thinking about Jean Liebowitz."

Jean had dropped out of medical school the previous year. She had traveled to Washington to meet Anne for lunch. Her face was wan and drawn, her voice thin. She just couldn't manage the demands of her life any longer. She was torn between her husband, her children, her studies. She could not sleep. She had lost seventeen pounds since the beginning of the semester. Her husband predicted a nervous breakdown. She disagreed with him. She felt that she was already experiencing such a breakdown.

"But it's only five more months," Anne said, urging her friend to reconsider.

"It feels like five more years," Jean replied.

Anne offered no more arguments, but her own resolve hardened. She would place nothing at risk this final year. Now she stared at Nancy unflinchingly.

"All right then. Your mind is made up. What do we do now?" Nancy asked.

"We network. We get some names. Doctors. No back alley stuff."

"But Anne, you're at the medical school. You have contacts."

Anne laughed bitterly.

"Doctors are self-protective. Abortion's a crime. Sure, they know who's doing abortions, but they reserve the names for the select few — a senator's niece, a governor's daughter, a longtime patient. If I start saying things like 'A friend of mine has this problem . . .' I'll get a lot of raised eyebrows and it won't take long for the whispering to start. I thought maybe some of the women in your consciousness-raising group might have contacts. Or maybe Merle or Rutti."

"I'm sure Andrew must know someone. Or at least how to find someone," Nancy said dryly, and they both laughed.

"I'll call Merle," Anne said.

"And I'll speak to Rutti."

"Dov?" Anne asked cautiously.

"No." Nancy was definite. Her husband was no longer someone with whom she shared her secrets.

The friends they called were alternately hostile and helpful.

"Why would I know the name of an abortionist?" a woman who had lived on Nancy's corridor at college asked angrily. "Do you think a single woman keeps a roster handy in case sexual exploits backfire?" Sarcastically she added, "I thought perhaps you were calling because you wanted to invite me to dinner, to introduce me to one of your husband's single friends. But I should have known better."

Nancy hung up feeling ashamed.

Still, she was hardly in a position to play matchmaker. Her own marriage remained tentative. She and Dov bought no new furniture, no new appliances for the larger apartment. They no longer spoke of the future. Dov was away more frequently and often did not sleep at home. He spoke of conferences and meetings and she did not challenge him. They had achieved parity. He never mentioned her therapy sessions with Mina Sieberg, although he paid the bills promptly, uncomplainingly. They were giving each other space, she told her friends.

"And sometimes that space grows so vast you can't hear each other, you can't remember what you once were to each other," Rutti observed softly.

Rutti struggled to imagine David's voice, his buoyant laughter. He was in Europe now and had been gone for several months. Every few weeks she received a cautious letter from him. He described the Belgian countryside, Amsterdam and its canals where his sister, Alicia, was spending her sabbatical year. His last letter had been from the town of Céret in the French Pyrénées where Soutine had lived and painted. He planned to spend the winter there. "It is very beautiful," he wrote Rutti, and she wondered what she would say if he asked her to join him there. But he had not asked her. She had not answered that letter and now it was weeks since she had heard from him. She realized with a sinking heart that she might never hear from him again.

Still, her work was going well and Sarah was happy. She had money for the first time in her life. She bought a small car and thought of buying a home in a northern suburb. Yet at night she lay awake in the darkness, beset by sadness. She closed her eyes and thought of

David. She padded out of bed, opened her atlas to a map of France, and located the village of Céret. Shivering, she studied the map and wondered if he was spending the winter alone in the Pyrénées. It was not unlikely that he had met someone. She had asked him for freedom and she had asked him for time. He granted her both. He too, then, had time and freedom. He owed her no explanations.

Rutti asked Dan and Mark about doctors who performed abortions. They worked with dancers and actresses and their relationships were honest and intense. "The perfect friendship," Mark told Rutti one night when they had both drunk too much wine, "is between a homosexual dancer and a straight actress who is involved in an unhappy romance."

"No," Rutti had objected. "The perfect relationship is between women who are honest with each other, who care for each other, who support each other." In that she had been fortunate.

Nancy asked for a referral at the consciousness-raising group to which she had been introduced by Grace Davies, a middle-aged black woman in her doctoral program.

"We don't get into anything heavy," Grace told Nancy. "But it gives us a chance to vent, to say what we're thinking, to realize we're not alone. That there are lots of women thinking the way we are. It's nice to say these dangerous things out loud. 'I have a life independent of any man's life. Work and career are important to me. I am tired of coming second and third and fourth. I want to be first. Number one. At least one day of the week.' Revolutionary thoughts like that."

Nancy felt comfortable with the group and admired the courage and openness of the women who met once or twice a month in each other's apartments. Plants dominated windowsills and tabletops, woven pillows were scattered across the floor, bright afghans flung across the chairs and couches. Sometimes they passed a reefer around and inhaled deeply, sharing the benign and pleasant high as they shared their thoughts. "Hey," they said, "don't let them lay that on you." "It's OK," they said. "You've got a right to feel like that." They said their names proudly, clearly. "Grace." "Tina." "Nancy." They had too often been called "sweetie," "honey," "doll." "Your name defines you," they told each other. "You are not a toy, a pet. You are yourself and you have to ask for what you want. The raise. The promotion. Help in the house. No one is going to read your mind." They taught each other the lessons their brothers and fathers and husbands had accepted as birthrights.

"I need a doctor who performs abortions," Nancy told them. "Someone trustworthy. Someone safe."

They asked no questions. They riffled through address books, made phone calls. She was handed several slips of paper. There was an excellent clinic in Puerto Rico. Three of the women mentioned the same doctor in Pennsylvania. An old man, Grace said. Very competent. Very compassionate. But old.

They spent the rest of the evening talking about the indignity of women having to scavenge for the names of doctors who would perform a simple procedure rendered dangerous simply because it was illegal.

"Abortion will become legal when the first man becomes pregnant," one woman said, and they all laughed.

"Abortion will become legal when women win the fight to make it legal," Grace retorted. She was on the board of the National Organization for Women and she brought them news of the plans discussed in Betty Friedan's living room. A women's march on Washington. A women's parade down Fifth Avenue. The time of speaking softly in each other's living rooms was passing. Soon their voices would be raised in a mighty shout that would resonate throughout the nation.

Nancy shifted uneasily; she fanned out the pieces of paper on which the women had written the names of doctors and clinics as though they were tarot cards engraved with mysterious predictions. She and Anne met the next day and compared the names they had gleaned. Some they discarded immediately. A doctor in Brooklyn had been prosecuted and sent to prison. Another doctor on the West Side had been responsible for the hemorrhaging and near death of a dancer friend of Mark's. They agreed at last that their best options were the clinic in Puerto Rico and the elderly physician in Pennsylvania. Puerto Rico would be safer, but it was too far, too expensive, and would require too much time. Nancy called the Pennsylvania number.

"I have a friend who may need your services," she said cryptically as she had been instructed.

"When was your friend's last menstrual period?" he asked, and then added kindly, "It is possible that she is mistaken. Sometimes young women become frightened."

"She is absolutely certain."

He asked if they could come in a few days' time. "The sooner the better," he said. The nurse would give them the details.

The nurse set the time and gave Nancy driving instructions.

"The doctor's fee is eight hundred dollars," she said. "And you must pay before the procedure either in cash or with a certified check, made out to cash. And please do not park in front of the office. There is a municipal parking lot just up the street. Park there." She was apologetic in tone. It was embarrassing to all of them that they were breaking the law — that they were taking precautions to avoid apprehension as though they were criminals engaged in sociopathic acts. Nancy tiptoed into Keren's room that night and pulled a blanket over her sleeping daughter. She felt a flash of fear for Keren, for Sarah, for all sweetly sleeping daughters who might one day be alone and vulnerable, betrayed by their lovers, betrayed by their bodies.

Again the friends acted in concert. Rutti would take care of Keren while Nancy accompanied Anne. Merle went to her bank and produced a certified check.

Nancy and Anne spoke little during the drive to Pennsylvania. Theirs was the silence of intimacy, broken casually and without preamble.

"What did you tell Dov about today?" Anne asked as they drove past the desolate pine barrens of New Jersey.

"Nothing," Nancy replied. She no longer offered her husband an accounting of her days. "I said that I might be home late, that I might not be home at all. That Keren was staying over at Rutti's, in any case."

And Dov asked no questions. With each passing month the silence between them widened and deepened. They were mired in the quicksand of their marriage, yet neither of them was ready yet to kick free — to move forward separately — or to reach a determination to forge on together. They agreed only that in any decision their first concern was Keren and what would be best for her.

"I am me! Myself! Alone!" a woman in the consciousness-raising group shouted triumphantly one evening. "My life belongs to me."

"When a woman has a child, her life is shared," Nancy replied. She was Keren's mother and any decision she made affected Keren. She said that very quietly to the group of women who sat in a circle on the floor sipping white wine from plastic cups. She saw other mothers nod in recognition of her unpopular truth and she saw the stubborn disapproval of those who had no children.

"You're using your daughter as an excuse," Grace said.

"Do you think it's evasive to weigh what a split will mean to Keren?" Nancy had asked Mina Sieberg.

And her analyst, who seldom replied to direct questions, had said, "No. I think such consideration is responsible."

"What did you tell Charles?" Nancy, braking to allow a wood-chuck to drag itself across the sun-speckled highway, asked Anne.

"He wasn't home, wasn't reachable. Chet, this little boy he's been treating, had a rough night and Charles stayed at the hospital. I just left a note telling him that I'd be in touch tomorrow." She did not tell Nancy of her relief that Charles had been unavailable, of how she feared lying to him and doubly feared to tell him the truth.

They lapsed back into silence, breaking it now and again to speak of their friends. They were both worried about Rutti, about David's long absence.

"I understand how she felt," Nancy said. "I understand that she needed time to regain herself, to reclaim herself. But it's been more than a year. He won't wait forever. He may not even be waiting at all. It may take another year to realize that she made a mistake, a terrible mistake and by then it may be too late. There are things that can't be undone."

Anne stared out the window. What she was about to do could not be undone.

It was nine-thirty when they arrived in the small village south of Philadelphia. The day was harshly cold but the air was clear, charged with the electric energy that often precedes a fierce winter storm. Such a storm was predicted for that evening, but they had listened to the forecast without trepidation. They would be back in New York by then.

Women pushing carriages and strollers, clutching the hands of toddlers, hurried down the town's major avenue. This was the hour when mothers of young children shopped. They called pleasantly to each other, waved brightly mittened hands, tightened their long scarves about the collars of their rainbow-colored nylon parkas. One young mother pushed twins in a stroller. She wore a lemon-yellow jacket and a kelly-green beret and her small daughters were bundled into yellow snowsuits and tightly knit kelly-green caps. Heads turned as the trio passed and the mother smiled in acknowledgment — a suburban queen, a mother daffodil with her babies, joyous and complacent.

"Disgusting," Anne said and grinned at Nancy.

"Disgusting," Nancy agreed. "But awfully cute."

"Nancy, do you think I am being selfish in this decision?" Anne asked.

"I don't know," Nancy replied carefully. "But you know, it's not too late to change your mind."

"I know," Anne said, her voice thin with misery. "I know."

They were at the doctor's address, a white house, newly painted, its wide porch bare of furnishings. There were two bells and Anne pressed the one marked Office. A woman's voice came over the intercom.

"Yes?"

"Mrs. Edwards and her friend," Nancy said.

Anne's face was drained of color and she leaned heavily against the porch rail.

They waited. The buzzer sounded, but Anne did not move forward.

"Anne?" Nancy kept her voice gentle, questioning. It was possible that her friend had changed her mind. Oh please, Nancy thought. Please. Let her back out. Let her say no. And then we'll have a wonderful breakfast in town. We'll laugh and quote Eliot to each other. "In a minute there is time/For decisions and revisions which a minute will reverse."

"Anne, we don't have to go in. You don't have to go through with it," she said aloud, struggling to keep her voice nonjudgmental.

The buzzer sounded again, harsh and impatient.

"No, I'm all right. I'm fine," Anne said. She hurried forward and thrust the door open before the buzzer ceased.

The room they entered, so reminiscent of all doctors' waiting rooms, was oddly reassuring. It was furnished with the requisite leather couch, faded Oriental carpet, wicker chairs and worn chintz cushions, which doctors' wives inevitably transfer, at the appropriate point of decrepitude, from their sunrooms to their husbands' offices.

Magazines were neatly fanned out across the scarred mahogany table. *Parents. Gourmet. National Geographic.* On another day Nancy knew that she and Anne would have laughed at the message such magazines might send to waiting patients. *OK, woman — have your kids, cook your meals, and when it all becomes too much for you, fantasize about the South Sea Islands.* A nurse entered and smiled at them reassuringly. They had not expected her to be so young, so attractive.

"Only a few questions," she said pleasantly. "If you'll just fill out this form."

Nancy sat beside Anne as she checked off her medical history.

"You have the doctor's fee?" the nurse asked as Anne handed the completed form to her.

Anne placed the long white envelope on the desk.

"The doctor will be with you in a moment." The nurse flashed them yet another smile.

The doctor, a short man propped up on thick crepe-soled shoes, slid silently into the room. He was very old, his papery skin lined with wrinkles, his shaggy white brows overhanging his bright blue eyes. It comforted Nancy that his dark blue suit was well cut and his light blue shirt freshly laundered, that his long white coat rustled starchily as he moved. She approved of his carefully clipped nails, of his hands rosy as though freshly scrubbed. His appearance advertised his professionalism. He was no quack, no back room abortionist.

"Mrs. Edwards?" He looked inquiringly from Anne to Nancy and was not surprised that neither of them responded immediately. He was used to women who briefly forgot the pseudonyms they themselves had selected.

"I'm Mrs. Edwards," Anne said. "Joan Edwards."

"Joan." How swiftly gynecologists called women they had never met before by their first names, reducing them at once to the status of subordinates or dependents, rendering them dependent on arbitrary kindness, false intimacy. "You are absolutely certain that you are pregnant? You've missed only one period, which means there is a margin for error."

"I'm absolutely certain," Anne said. "As you see from the laboratory reports, I've had a rabbit test — an HCG hormone test. There is no doubt."

"You seem familiar with the terminology."

"I'm a medical student."

"I see. Mrs. Edwards, I must ask you the question that I ask every woman who comes to see me. You are certain of this decision? You are certain that this is what you want, that you will have no regrets?"

Soundlessly she nodded.

His kindness unnerved and unsettled her. She saw that he had no enthusiasm for the procedure he would perform. He would much prefer to deliver babies than to abort them. She wondered how it was that he had gotten involved in performing abortions and how he had obtained his underground fame. She imagined a beloved daughter dying as a result of a botched abortion, a sister forced to endure an unwanted pregnancy. Immediately she chided herself for sentimentalizing and romanticizing him. He probably did it for the money. She found that it strengthened her to think harshly of him.

"You're determined then. Very well. You are in such an early stage that I am going to do a vacuum suction. You understand what that is? If not, I will explain it to you." He spoke softly, slowly. He was used to questions, familiar with the fear of the young women who came to him with bent bodies and pale faces, their eyes reddened with grief and shame.

"I understand it," Anne said faintly.

She had studied her obstetrics textbook the previous evening, had traced her finger across the drawing of the narrow cervix, moving up to the triangular uterus where the embryo nestled. She thought she was perhaps five weeks pregnant. The bit of tissue within her uterus was the size of perhaps two grains of rice. It was undefined by limbs; only microscopic buds protruded from it, although it had the anatomical genesis of a heart. She closed her eyes and mind against the image, fought her own depression. She did not mourn the egg destroyed in the flow of menstrual blood each month. How then could she mourn this bit of ectoplasm, unwanted, unformed, inchoate?

"All right then. If your friend will wait here — it is not a long procedure, although you will have to rest for a while afterward. Perhaps you would like to go out, have some coffee, and come back in forty-five minutes, an hour?" He turned to Nancy and smiled at her, an old man's affectionate, avuncular smile.

208

"That's all right. I'll wait here. I'll be right outside if you need me," Nancy told Anne.

She wanted to be there if Anne should change her mind (*and there was still time — "In a minute there is time/For decisions and revisions"* . . .). She watched Anne disappear beyond the door and plucked up a magazine, turning the page swiftly so that she could not study the glossy photo of a beautiful blond young mother holding her equally beautiful blond newborn. She thought suddenly of a girl who had lived in her dorm, a quiet blond girl who had left school one Friday afternoon and never returned. It was rumored that she had died in a sparsely furnished rented room after an abortion performed by a woman who was supposedly a practical nurse. Some said that she had committed suicide. The only thing that was known for certain was that she was dead. Her name was Midge; it startled Nancy that she should remember that.

Anne undressed slowly in the discreetly curtained cubicle that adjoined the white room dominated by an examination table spread with thick, absorbent white paper sheeting. Although the room was well heated, she shivered and huddled into the flimsy, pale blue paper gown the nurse had handed her. Carefully she folded her own garments, her black slacks and peacock-blue turtleneck sweater, her undergarments, even her socks. There was a long mirror in the cubicle and she studied her reflection, slid her hands across the flatness of her stomach as she imagined it protuberant, stretched by pregnancy.

"Are we almost ready?" the nurse asked.

"Almost," Anne replied, although she could think of nothing else to do. Impulsively, she plaited her hair into a single braid. There was still time, she told herself, still time to get dressed and exit, smiling apologetically. She prepared her speech. "I'm sorry, but I thought about what you said and in fact I have reconsidered. But I would like to compensate you for your time and trouble even though I find I can't go through with it after all because — because. . . ." She struggled to punctuate her rambling thoughts, to break the sentence down into half-formed phrases, vague and charming.

"The doctor is ready," the nurse reminded her with an impatient edge in her voice.

209

Anne sat down on the wooden bench, unfolded her sweater, and fingered the soft wool. It had been a gift from Charles. A "because" gift — their own lovers' shorthand — "because" I love you.

A phone rang. The sound, shrill and invasive, frightened her, spurred her to action. She tossed the sweater aside, pushed her way through the curtain, walked over to the examining table, and lay down on it.

"If you would just slide down. That's right. Now lift your knees slightly; place your feet in the stirrups," he said gently.

The glinting metal of the stirrups was cold against her bare feet. She felt utterly powerless; she was shackled to this table by rings of steel, a prisoner of her own will and willfulness. "Easy now, relax." She could not fight the involuntary muscular tension. Her body resisted him even as she obediently followed his commands. She felt the familiar cramp so similar to the spasms that preceded her menstrual periods. Perhaps his hand would emerge covered with blood and they would laugh together at the foolishness of her error, at the incompetence of the laboratory. She was not pregnant at all. It had all been a mistake. But when he held his gloved hands out to the nurse, she saw that their surface was only translucently slick. There was no blood. There would be no reprieve.

"Everything seems to be all right," he said, and a wild hysteria welled up within her.

Yes, everything was all right. It was just the small problem of a bit of unwanted tissue in her uterus, the negligent residue of an afternoon of careless love. "Love, oh love, oh careless love — oh see what careless love has done to me." A boy on her Peace Corps team had played that song on his guitar and they had sung it as they sat on the floor in their small shared house in Lagos. Singing, they had smiled at the song's naïveté, at the power of their own youth, at the irrelevance of careless love to their own wonderful lives. They were so competent, so capable. They had passed muster and journeyed to Africa from the cities of America's Midwest, from small towns in Pennsylvania and the Carolinas. They were John Kennedy's kids, his own corps, the vanguard of the young who would change the world. And now, ten years later, John Kennedy was dead. And Robert Kennedy was dead. And so too was Martin Luther King, Jr. Violence had silenced their oratory of hope. Gunshots had stilled the tender ballads.

Their dreams were unrealized, the carelessness of their love repudiated.

The nurse approached with a hypodermic needle.

"Just a little Demerol to relax you," the doctor said. "Please turn on your side."

She moved very slowly, playing for time. She could still change her mind, leap off the table.

"Stop!" she would command and he would come no further. She mouthed the word silently. *Stop. Stop.*

"Are you ready?" How courtly he was, how considerate.

"Yes."

He lifted the robe and she felt the sharpness of the needle in her buttock. The drug coursed through her system, disarming her, releasing her. She floated above the white-sheeted table, above the stainless steel trays on which glittering, sharp instruments were arranged in artful design. Words danced through her mind, floated through her lips.

"Let us go then, you and I, when the evening is spread out against the sky like a patient etherised upon a table," she said loudly, clearly, and laughed. And then she wept.

The nurse moved forward. She placed slender, wiry rods, the flexible wands of a magician, in the doctor's hand. He bent forward, inserted them into her vagina, moved them upward into the cervix, applying pressure gently, tentatively.

"You may experience some discomfort," he said, but Anne had separated herself from him, from her own body. She drifted about the room, floated languidly above her own submissive form.

"Just another second," the doctor said. "And another. We're almost there. Yes. Good. Now."

He removed the rod and replaced it with the flexible tube that the nurse handed him. A soft, mechanical hum filled the room and the tug of a new and powerful cramp forced Anne down from her suspension, restored her to her body and her pain.

"That's just the suction machine," he said reassuringly, but she did not look at the mechanism attached to the tube, so noisily sucking the bit of unwanted tissue from her uterus, vacuuming the infinitesimal bit of spongy ectoplasm with its microscopic heart formation into the small plastic receptacle.

"Stop," she commanded him furiously. "Stop now."

"Of course I'll stop now. It's over. You see. It's all over."

He smiled at her, pleased because she had been such a good patient, so brave, so pliant, so responsive to the mild drug. He was startled, then, that she wept so bitterly that her body was racked with her sobs; she could not explain that she had plummeted too swiftly, that it had all happened too quickly. She was not to blame that the tears were hot upon her cheeks and filled her open mouth and coated her tongue with the salinity of her sorrow.

He spoke soothingly to her, urging her to swallow the pill he held out to her. She grew calmer as the nurse helped her to dress, gave her a sanitary pad, escorted her to the door and then into the waiting room. The doctor spoke to Nancy and gave her a small vial of pills and a box of pads. Anne slept as Nancy drove northward through the snow that fell gently, steadily, shrouding the road in albescence, obliterating the sounds of traffic so that the car was suffused with an impenetrable white silence.

Three days later Charles Bingham stood at Chet's bedside and pondered the small boy's chart. It was clear to him that the child's condition was precarious; the cancer had remained invincible against vigorous assaults of chemotherapy. Chet opened his eyes briefly and Charles leaned close to him, lifting the scant ribbon of flesh that was the child's wrist.

"Can I do anything for you, Chet?" he asked.

"Make me die, Dr. Charles. It hurts too much. Make me die. Please."

But he could not make Chet die. He was pledged to preserve life. He checked and rechecked the blood count readings. Could Chet tolerate adoptive immunotherapy? Would his parents countenance it? But even as he turned a page of the chart, he heard a faint rasp. He saw the child's eyes open wide with fear and close again, the long auburn lashes threads of fire on the diminished cachectic cheeks. Charles jabbed the crash cart button and then ripped open the child's pajama top. He pounded the skeletal chest with his balled fists and pressed his mouth against Chet's, desperately breathing in and out, relinquishing his place only when the residents who raced into the room with the cart gently led him away.

"I'm sorry, Dr. Bingham, we've lost him," a nurse said. Charles nodded.

He knew that Chet was dead, that he had surely been dead even while Charles had tried to pound his heart back into a reluctant beat. Defeated, he went into the hallway where Chet's parents stood, locked in each other's arms.

They would not be comforted, not now, not yet, he realized. It made no difference to them that they had two healthy children at home, that the mother was in her sixth month of pregnancy. They knew that one child did not replace another, that lives are not fungible. At this moment Chet was their only child and his death absorbed them, overwhelmed them, as the lives of their healthy children did not. They wept, and braced themselves for the moment when they would approach his bed and see his body robbed of life. Still, when Charles approached them, the father offered his hand, the mother twisted her face into a half-smile. They knew that he had cared, that he had tried his best and fought death until the last bitter moment.

"We want to thank you," Chet's father said.

"I'm so sorry. He was a wonderful boy, a brave boy."

Charles did not tell them that he had believed against all odds that Chet would survive. That would offer them no comfort. Instead he said, "I should like to ask your permission to perform an autopsy. We may learn something that might help us, help other patients."

They nodded. Their long vigil was over, but Charles would face the same battle again and again. Other sick children would occupy the bed on which Chet had died, mobiles crafted of get-well cards would float above their heads, baseball caps would cover their bald scalps, and stuffed animals line their blood-flecked counterpanes. Charles would talk to these children softly, draw blood, fill IV tubes with the glistening drugs that might or might not counteract the merciless crab of cancer. He would speak to other parents of procedures and options; he would watch hope flicker and he would watch hope die. His hatred of the disease rankled within him; it filled him with fury and bitter determination.

"Yes. An autopsy. If it will help another child," Chet's mother replied. Her voice was barely a whisper and her hand rested on her abdomen as though to protect the life that would soon be born to her.

Charles left the hospital and walked slowly into the pale winter sunlight. Anne would be waiting for him at his apartment. He had not seen her for almost a week. Her rotations and his schedule conflicted, and then she had gone out of town with Nancy. He had been glad to see her take some time off. Her mother's death had unnerved her and she worked too hard.

It was almost dark when he reached his apartment building. He glanced up at the window, disappointed to see that it was unlit. Anne had had a lab that afternoon, he knew, a pathology lab, and it was possible that her work had detained her. Pathology was one of the few subjects at which she did not excel. It was life, genetic beginnings, that excited and intrigued her. She was impatient with the mysteries of death.

The apartment was dark when he entered, but his heart soared. He knew she was there. He smelled her perfume — the subtle scent of wild flowers — his Christmas gift to her. The fragrance of chicken stewing in herbs and wine told him that she had cooked them dinner. Her book bag was on the floor, her long black coat, handed down from Merle, and her plaid scarf draped a chair. He followed her trail into the bedroom. She was asleep on the king-size bed he had bought so that they would no longer have to make love on a sleeping bag spread open across the floor.

He bent over and kissed her cheek. She stirred, shifting position, and he saw that a streak of blood columned the pale blue sheets. Involuntarily he touched the crimson stain, felt its sticky moistness, heard his heart increase its beat.

Anne opened her eyes and smiled up at him.

"Hey," she said. "My lab was canceled. I got here early and made chicken in wine. The soupy kind. I thought we could eat it here. In bed. From bowls. I bought that good French bread too." Evening dusk shadowed the room but she did not switch on the light. "Charles. What's wrong, Charles? Is it Chet?"

"He died," Charles said. "This afternoon. About an hour and a half ago."

"Oh, I'm sorry, so sorry." She sat up then, pulled his head down toward her, kissed his face, the smoothness of his domed forehead. She knew how such deaths affected him.

"Anne." He pointed to the streak of blood, and she paled, and inched away from it. She wore only his striped pajama top and she fumbled to button it. She had been so careless, so stupid. And yet she could not have known. There had been only a light staining for a few hours immediately after the procedure. An aching cramp had disappeared within two days. She had thought herself done with it, had willed herself not to think about it. She had not anticipated this scarlet leakage; her body had betrayed her as she slept.

"Sorry about that," she said, struggling to keep her tone casual. "Stupid of me. I'll get a fresh sheet."

"Anne. Why are you bleeding?" He knew it was not menstrual blood that sullied the linen, although afterward he wondered how he could have known that.

"I want to get dressed, Charles. Wait for me in the kitchen. We'll talk. Maybe you'd better turn the flame down on the chicken. And perhaps set the table."

He nodded. They would not eat the chicken in wine from soup plates, sitting up naked in the large bed. They would not pelt each other with bits of soft white bread or, laughing as warm droplets rained on their bodies, feed each other crusts stained with the winey sauce. He would not lick crumbs from the soft pink buds of her nipples as he had so often before.

He set the kitchen table and turned on the radio, switching it off as Anne entered. Her long fair hair, newly brushed, caped her shoulders. She wore a black skirt and black sweater, and she walked toward him barefoot, a radiant penitent. She stood beside him at the sink, filled a glass with water, looked out the window into the darkness.

"When I went with Nancy last week," she said, "it was to have an abortion. I had an abortion."

"An abortion?" He repeated the word as though it were foreign to him.

"Actually it was a vacuum suction. The doctor was able to do it that way because it was so early. Just a few weeks — five, six."

He counted back. Five weeks, six weeks. Her mother's funeral. They had made love in his hotel room as long shadows fell across the slag-veined mountains. Her pregnancy had resulted from love and tenderness at that moment of loss.

"But why? Why an abortion?" he asked, grieved and bewildered.

She stared at him uncomprehendingly, drank the water, filled the glass again. Her thirst would not be slaked. How could it be that he did not understand her choice?

"Charles, what if the pregnancy had been difficult, if there were complications — I wouldn't have been able to finish the year — I wouldn't graduate, get my degree." Her voice was calm, her body rigid.

He stared at her as though she were a stranger, and sat down at the table. At once she sat opposite him.

"So you would have taken another year off and graduated late. You took a year off for the NIH project, didn't you?"

"That was different. I chose to spend that year in Washington. I wanted it. I planned it."

"And this wasn't planned? This pregnancy you terminated?" His voice was hard.

"Was it planned? Did we plan it? Either of us? Did we want a child now? Be honest, damn it!"

"No. We didn't plan it. But lots of things happen in life without planning. You're a medical student. You know that. Chet didn't plan to die. His parents didn't plan to bury him before his ninth birthday. We don't plan for death and sometimes we don't plan for life. But when it happens we accept it, we deal with it."

"I dealt with it," she said. "I made a decision."

"You," he said. "You!" he repeated, his voice rising in a shout. She remembered now the residents who had spoken of his anger, of the vitriolic explosion of his rage, and she was frightened suddenly, her throat tight, her body clammy. She put her hands in front of her face, as though to shield herself from the onslaught of his fury. "What about me, Anne?" he continued harshly. "Didn't I get to be included in the decision? Didn't I get to even talk about it? After all I played a role. The baby you aborted was mine. Didn't I have any rights?"

His rage ignited her own. She stood, thrusting her chair back so that it crashed to the floor. Neither of them moved to lift it.

"A baby." She spat the words out, her cheeks aflame, her voice hoarse. "There was no baby. There was embryonic tissue. Nothing. And it was in my body and it would have continued to grow in my body and I control my body. Me. Myself. No one else. Not you. Not anyone. My life is mine — my own!" She was shouting now, shouting

216

and weeping. She felt a cramp and was sure that she was bleeding. She ran into the bathroom, but there was no blood. She washed her face, splashing it punishingly with cold water, staring at herself in the spattered mirror as though at a stranger.

He was still seated at the neatly set table when she returned, his shoulders hunched. She knew that his anger was faded; disappointment and sadness had replaced it.

"Let me ask you something," he said without turning. "Did you plan to tell me about it? If I had not confronted you, would you have told me?"

"I don't know."

She lifted the fallen chair, sat opposite him, and studied his ravished features, the beryl brightness of his eyes in which for so long she had read the surety of his love.

"Listen to me, Anne," he said, speaking very slowly as though to be sure she understood him. "There was life within you. The beginning of life. And you destroyed it — without my knowledge, without my permission."

His words seared her with pain and anger. It was a stranger that spoke them, a man she did not know. Hadn't he said again and again that antiabortion laws were archaic, outrageous?

"I don't understand you, Charles," she said. "You've always been pro-choice."

"I am pro-choice," he replied. "But that means I was supposed to get a choice, too, or at least know about the choice you were struggling to make. And I assume," he added, "that there was a struggle."

"Yes," she said softly. "There was a struggle." She thought of how she had stood shivering in her paper gown behind the thin curtain of the cubicle. *Love, oh love, oh careless love — oh see what careless love has done to me.* "I knew that there was no way I could carry this baby in peace, that I wasn't ready for it. I knew that I would worry that everything I had worked for was in jeopardy. I kept thinking about Jean Liebowitz, about my mother. Oh, I know other women go on with school when they're pregnant. But I am not other women. I did not want this pregnancy. And I know something about women who carry unwanted babies. Anger, resentment, acidity in the amniotic fluid. And so I made my decision. And you know why I didn't discuss it with you — I didn't discuss it with you because I knew what you would say."

"You knew." He lifted a glass to the light and set it down. "You know that I have this mania, this passion. I've shared it with you. You know that I do battle every day of my professional life with a particularly ugly kind of death. Cancer. The bitch disease. And I fight and work and fight again because of the way I feel about life, because in the spring azaleas bloom and in the summer kids run across soft grass and because I think life is so damn precious, so damn wonderful. So I fight death and I lose and just today I lost again. And then I come home to you. And I find out that you opted for death. That there was life within you and that it was life that I had created and it is gone, as surely as Chet's is gone. And I know it was not a fetus and it was not a baby. But it could have been, Anne, it could have been. You knew what I would say. Damn right you knew."

"We see it differently, Charles," she said quietly, miserably. "It may be that we have always seen it differently."

"It may be," he agreed. His misery matched her own.

"What happens now?" she asked.

"I don't know. I don't know if I can ever forgive you." She recognized the honesty of his answer, but it kindled a new fury within her.

"And I'm not asking your forgiveness. And I don't need your forgiveness. Yes — perhaps I should have discussed it with you. *Perhaps*. But Charles, it is my life, my body — it was my call."

Now it was she who felt disappointed, betrayed. They had been together for three years. Three years during which he had supported her every decision, understood her priorities and goals, accommodated himself to her. Her friends envied her. Charles was so accepting, so understanding. Charles hopped shuttles to Washington, worked around her rotations, her exam schedules. They would not envy her now. She was deceived. They were all deceived.

"Your decision. Your body. Some things are more important than your right to make your own decisions — your goddamn independence."

"What things? What things?" She shouted so that she would not weep. "I didn't have a hysterectomy. I had an abortion. There will be other pregnancies." She sank back in her chair, recoiling from the

218

harshness of her own words, the shrillness of her own voice. A swirl of blue smoke circled them. He had neglected to lower the flame on the chicken and it was burning. She sat immobile as he turned the jet off.

Wordlessly she went to the bedroom and put on her shoes and tights. She took her sweaters, a few undergarments, the flannel night-gown her mother had made for her, from the bottom drawer of his bureau. She plucked her collection of Nadine Gordimer short stories from the bedside table, her *Little Treasury of Modern Verse* from the desk. All this she put in a large shopping bag. She searched beneath the bed for scuffs and when she looked up she saw that he stood in the doorway, pale, his eyes dank with sadness. But he made no pro-test. Anne shrugged. She shook the light blue slippers, watched a dust burr float to the floor, and put them into the bag.

She walked past him, put on her long dark coat, wound her plaid scarf around her neck, took up her book bag and shopping bag. Bowed by her bundles, like a refugee, she went to the front door. Misery paralyzed her. She waited for him to say her name, to restrain her. But he neither moved nor spoke. He leaned against the wall, his pale-domed head shining and bowed, his eyes half closed.

She left without closing the door. He heard her slow progress down the hall, the ring of the elevator, its arrival and slow descent. He moved to the window and watched her exit the building. She set her bags down briefly and lifted her face to the newly falling snow. And then she walked on, almost hurrying across the street, and out of his field of vision.

16

THE VILLAGE of Céret, a quiet hamlet in the French Pyrénées, prepared for spring. The windows of the thatch roofed farmhouses, washed until they glistened, were thrown open and the cool mountain breezes threaded with the salt scent of the Costa Brava wafted through the whitewashed rooms. Bright hand-woven rugs dangled from the branches of the olive trees and the dark wood furnishings were carried into the gardens so that the hardwood floors could be vigorously scrubbed. The villagers went into their fields and groves, surveyed the damage wrought by the severe winter, and prepared for the months of planting and harvest. Mountain goats skittered through the coarse tall grass and leaped up to nibble at the lacy white buds of orange blossoms that dangled from low-hanging branches and the tiny clusters of mimosa that nestled among long dark leaves.

Mimi and André DuPrés readied their small inn, the only hostelry in Céret, for the approaching season. They were surprised then, as they sat on their slate terrace polishing the copper andirons, to see the Perpignan taxi pull up to their doorway. A petite blond woman counted out franc notes for the driver, who placed her suitcases and a large leather portfolio on the path, waved, and drove off.

André hurried up to her, Mimi trailing behind him.

"Madame. Can we be of assistance to you?"

The woman smiled at him.

"I hope so," she said. "I am Madame Weisenblatt, Rutti Weisenblatt. You have a communication from a Jerusalem travel agent reserving a room for me."

"No. We received no such communication, but that of course is no problem. Our inn is empty. It is still some weeks before the tourist season will begin in the Pyrénées."

He bent to take her bags, her portfolio, and noted the New York address.

"You are tired, Madame?" Mimi asked, falling into step beside their guest.

"Very tired," Rutti admitted.

She felt as though she had been traveling forever, although only two days had passed since she had hugged Chana and Dror at Lydda Airport and flown to Paris. The journey from Paris to Perpignan had been exhausting. With each kilometer her fatigue had grown heavier and her doubts had intensified. This was an impulsive and foolish thing she had done; it was absurd that she should be traveling into the Pyrénées in search of David Lorenzo who, most probably, was no longer in Céret.

"I have taken a cottage for the winter," he had written in his last letter, but the winter was over and she had not answered that letter nor had she written to him from Israel to tell him of her arrival in Céret. How could she? She had not planned the journey and even at the very last moment, as she waited in the Gare du Nord for the Perpignan train, she had been racked with uncertainty.

"We will give you our very best room," Mimi said companionably. "And I will bring you tea. And then you must have a long rest before dinner. We prepare an excellent dinner here. Even out of season we have many guests."

"That will be wonderful," Rutti said gratefully.

She followed Mimi into a large, wide-windowed room that overlooked the foothills of the mountains where conifers grew in wild profusion. Their outstretched, needled branches embraced each other in intricate entanglements, and shafts of sunlight darted across their slender trunks. Rutti stared at them wonderingly. She had seen those trees before, sun-streaked and wind-tossed, arching forward as though they were not rooted in earth, but could at will climb the sloping promontory and ascend the mountain crest. In his wild landscapes

Soutine had captured them, impaling them on his canvases with lay-ered impasto, in whirling sheaths of color.

"They are very beautiful, no? Our trees, our mountains," Mimi said.

"Very beautiful."

"Madame is an artist?" André asked, respectfully placing her portfolio on a low table.

"Yes." The answer came naturally.

"Many artists come to Céret. Some stay for the winter. Ah, our mountains are wonderful in the winter."

Mimi returned with the tea and a slice of apple tart. She removed a white duvet from the wicker chest at the foot of the bed.

"It grows very cold at night in the Pyrénées," she said. "The dinner hour is eight o'clock."

"Thank you," Rutti said. "Thank you for everything."

The door closed behind Mimi and André, and Rutti thought of how simple it would have been to ask them about David. They them-selves had volunteered that many artists came to Céret. She could have then asked after an American artist friend of hers, a tall man with a soft dark beard and a deep and joyous laugh. Did they by any chance know whether he was still in the village? As she carried her hot drink to the window, where she watched the trees grapple with each other, impelled by the force of the mountain wind, she realized that she had not asked the question because she was not yet ready for the answer.

She sat on the window seat and wondered what her friends would say if they knew of her journey to Céret. Merle, of course, would be skeptical because Merle still played by the ancient rules. *Don't call him. Wait for him to call you. Say what he wants to hear and do as you please.* They teased Merle about that often, taunting her during their Friday lunches with their humor, their candor. Merle was good-naturedly indifferent.

"All right. Suit yourselves. Call me manipulative, submissive. But in the end I get what I want. The times may have changed but the old rules still apply."

"Oh, there may yet emerge a breed of men strong enough to accept the honesty of women," Nancy had said blithely. "Homo un-afraidus."

"Homo steinemus." "Homo friedanus." "Homo strongus." They had all giggled then as they called out the nonsense names and plunged their spoons into a single carton of ice cream.

That was one thing Rutti did not have to worry about. David was certainly strong. It was that strength that had given her the courage to leave him. And it was that strength that had impelled her to take this strange, uncertain journey.

Still, she thought, as she watched two orioles sing to each other from the dark triangular crowns of neighboring trees, she was not sorry that she was here now with neither foreknowledge nor guarantee. She had undertaken so many other journeys in her life, in search of elusive safety, in search of an irretrievable past. One more would not devastate her. She finished her tea and still fully dressed, she lay down on the wonderfully soft feather bed and covered herself with the soft duvet.

It was dark when she awakened. Disoriented, she thought for a moment that she was on the narrow daybed in Chana and Dror's small sitting room. Always she would think of the small kibbutz bungalow as her home, her real home, the place to which she could return as Werner had returned. Chana and Dror had acted as parents to her during the years she lived on the kibbutz. They had led her to the wedding canopy when she married Werner, her brother-husband. And in turn they had buried Werner, placing his grave beside that of their own son, Noah, who had been killed during the Sinai campaign. It was to see Werner's grave that Rutti had journeyed to Israel. Chana had written asking her to attend a small ceremony at the Beit Yair cemetery, when a sculpture in memory of the sons of the kibbutz who had fallen in Israel's wars would be unveiled.

"We understood that you needed time to accept Werner's death," Chana had written. "But perhaps now you are ready."

She was ready, Rutti realized. She did not think of Werner for days at a time, and when she did think of him she was no longer suffused with sadness.

She met Nancy for lunch at a small café near Lincoln Center and asked her if Sarah could stay at her home for the two weeks of her absence.

"No problem," Nancy said as Rutti had known she would. Keren and Sarah were in the same grade at the Hunter Elementary School and were close friends. "Why don't you stop over in Europe — see David?"

"I'm not even sure where he is. It's been awhile since I heard from him."

"Did you answer his letters?"

"At first. And then I stopped. Because each time I thought to write him or call him — he sent me his phone number in Amsterdam when he was staying with his sister, Alicia — I realized that I just didn't have the strength." Her voice trailed sadly off.

"The strength for what?" Nancy asked. How skilled she was now at being the patient, persistent questioner, the ruthless prober. Questions were easy, she knew. It was the answers that were hard-earned and painful. She lay beside Dov at night, knowing that he lay wakeful beside her, and pondered the questions she wrestled with in her sessions with Mina Sieberg. *Why did you marry him? Do you love him still? Why do you stay with him?*

"The strength to resist him," Rutti replied.

"But why should you resist him?"

"Because I wanted the chance to prove what I could do on my own — to be responsible only for myself and Sarah — to see what I could make of my life."

"And you've done that, you've accomplished that," Nancy said. She leaned forward — as Mina Sieberg did when she had something important to say, an insight to share — "Look, Rutti, when we first met you were doing that stupid clerical job. You barely made enough money to feed yourself and Sarah properly. Sarah talked baby talk and you couldn't bear to let her out of your sight. And now you're a recognized artist with more commissions than you can handle. You're supporting yourself and Sarah easily and well. And you did it all yourself. If you marry David now, you'd be coming to him with your independence proven. But Rutti, independence doesn't mean you have to go it alone. And it definitely doesn't mean that you walk away from someone who loves you — someone you love. The way Anne did."

They were both silent then. Anne had been selected for a coveted internship at the Mayo Clinic. They had taken her to lunch at The

Four Seasons on a Friday afternoon, toasted her with champagne, presented her with a monogrammed physician's bag.

"To Dr. Anne Richardson," Merle said, raising her glass. "You've come a long way, baby."

"We've all come a long way, babies," Anne replied and they thought of all the Friday afternoons — months and years of Fridays with simulated picnics on living room floors, hasty sandwiches at kitchen tables covered with books and drawings and notebooks, the children's merriment and quarrels as the women pinned up hems, exchanged hand-me-downs, traded dreams and laughter.

Anne laughed a great deal during that celebratory lunch, a ringing, nervous laughter that made Nancy strangely uncomfortable. The hour grew late, but Anne was reluctant to leave.

"Oh, one more cup of coffee," she pleaded, but they could not stay. The children would be coming home from school. There was marketing to be done, meals to be cooked. They left Anne alone at last. Elegant in her new lilac-colored suit and the tailored silk blouse that had been Hope and Ted's graduation gift to her, she sipped tepid coffee and stared across the room at a couple who sat with their heads bent close, their hands clasped.

"I think that my situation differed from Anne's," Rutti said softly.

"I'm not comparing them. I don't think you would do what Anne did."

"It wasn't Anne's fault, Nancy. It was Charles who ended it. You don't think Anne should have carried a child she didn't want?"

"I've thought about it, Rutti, and I don't think it was that Anne didn't want the child — she had the abortion because she didn't want Charles. Look, Rutti, why didn't she even tell Charles she was pregnant? She says that it was because he would have pressured her to marry him at once. But she knew that he would have heard her out, that he had always accommodated himself to her. And even if they disagreed in the end, at least he would have had the chance to argue for what he wanted. And if she really wanted to keep the truth from him, why didn't she do just that? Other women have." Nancy spoke slowly, reasonably, a teacher explaining the solution to a puzzle or an elusive syllogism.

"He saw the blood," Rutti protested.

"She allowed him to see it. I think she wanted him to know what had happened because deep within herself, she did not want to marry him — not then and not even when she had her degree. If they were married she couldn't have accepted the appointment at the Mayo. Charles was prepared to play house during the year she spent in Washington, a shuttle ride away, passionate weekend love with a view of the Lincoln Memorial. But he would not want a wife in Rochester, Minnesota."

"Nancy, she didn't even know about the Mayo offer then," Rutti argued, although she acknowledged that Nancy's words had the ring of truth, that she herself harbored similar, unarticulated thoughts.

"Rutti, I'm not making any judgments. Probably what Anne did was right for her. She had a choice and whether she was conscious of that choice or not, she made a decision. You have a choice too and you're going to have to think about what you want, what you really want now." Nancy took her friend's hand in her own and playfully traced the lines on her palm. "Long lifeline, long heart line. Don't waste either of them, Rutti."

Nancy's words followed Rutti to Israel. She thought about them as she stood in the Beit Yair cemetery and studied the memorial sculpture. The artist had crafted a bronze statue of a boy, his beautiful face turned eastward, his arms uplifted, a flute grasped in one hand and a microscope in the other. Werner would have approved of such a monument, Rutti knew, and she gripped Chana's hand hard as they joined the small gathering in singing "Hatikva."

She and Chana returned to the cemetery the next day. Small stones glinted on the grave markers, calling cards to the dead. Rutti picked up a pebble polished smooth by the winds that swept across the Judaean Hills. She put it on the slab of pale pink Jerusalem marble inscribed with Werner's name. She placed her hand on the carved letters and was pleased to find that the sun had warmed the stone. How Werner had hated the cold, how he had sought warmth all his life. Warmth and truth and a rationale that would help him accept the enormity of his losses, the cruelty of his times.

She wept; her tears darkened the pink marble so that it assumed a rose-colored cast. "I'm sorry," she said, her voice broken with grief. "Ah, Werner, I am so sorry." Chana, who had been plucking weeds from the shrubs beside Noah's grave, turned to her and took Rutti's hands in her own.

"Listen to me, Rutti. It is terrible that Werner is dead. But you are no more responsible for his death than I was responsible for the death of my Noah. Oh, how I blamed myself. As you blame yourself. We are so arrogant, we women. We are the nurturers, the protectors, and we begin to think that we can control the destiny of those we nurture and protect. We give life — should we not be able to prevent death? After Noah died, I lay awake thinking, 'Ah, if only we had not come to Israel. If only I had gone with my brother to Australia, then my Noah would still be alive.' One year later my brother's son crossed a street in Melbourne and was killed by a speeding driver and my sister-in-law wrote to me: 'Ah, if only we had come to Israel, then my Peter would be alive.' You did your best for Werner. And now you must seek your own happiness. For your sake. For Sarah's sake. And yes, even for Werner's sake. Because he wanted you to be happy."

And Rutti, kneeling and weeping, acknowledged at last what David had always known. She had spoken of the casting away of a cloak of shadows and he had perceived the real shadow. She admitted now that he was right as Chana was right. Her guilt had been misplaced, her sorrow punitive. She had substituted one cloak of shadows for another.

She and Chana walked through the herb garden, and as they stood amid the fragrant beds Rutti told her adoptive mother about David Lorenzo.

"What must I do now?" she asked, in the fragile voice of a small girl asking for advice. She had stepped backward in time and reclaimed the privilege of childhood.

"You must go to him," Chana said.

"But I don't even know if he's still in Céret," she protested.

"And you will not know unless you go there."

It was Chana who called the travel agent and made arrangements for the flight to Paris, the overland connections to the Pyrénées, the reservation at the small inn only kilometers from the Spanish border.

"Even if you do not find him," Chana told her at Lydda, "you will know and he will know that you sought him out. But you will find him. I am certain of it."

Rutti thought of Chana's words as she dressed for dinner, selecting a pale green dress David had always liked, brushing her hair so that it framed her delicate face like an aureole of wispy gold. She was aware that for the first time in months she was ravenously hungry. That hunger seemed an omen to her and she hurried downstairs, toward the scent of fragrant cooking and the sound of talk and laughter.

A fire blazed in the huge brick fireplace that dominated the dining room. The tables were set with snow-white napery, heavy cutlery, and thick stoneware dishes in the traditional blue Basque design. Several of the tables were already occupied and Mimi hurried through the room, balancing a tureen of soup and pausing to tell the young waitress to place bread on one table, wine on another.

The dinner patrons were, for the most part, well-dressed young couples who spoke rapidly, vivaciously, in a potpourri of languages. Rutti heard smatterings of French, Spanish, German, and English, as André guided her to a table near a large window that overlooked a windbreak of slender birch trees. Rutti studied the room. David was not there.

She ordered an aperitif and told André that she would rely on him to select her dinner. As she sipped her sherry, she watched the latecomers arrive and played the game of the solitary traveler, creating imaginary lives for these strangers she would never see again. The man and the woman, both silver-haired and elegant, she in a black dress, he in a dark suit, had once been married and still they met each year on the anniversary of the death of their only son, in this restaurant he had favored. The two laughing young couples were celebrating their engagements, their declarations of love. The two stylishly dressed women were sisters who ran a gift shop on the Spanish border.

Mimi approached with a plate of pâté surrounded by young green asparaguses. She coughed lightly as she set it down and Rutti realized she had been staring so intently at the doorway that she had been unaware of Mimi's approach.

"Madame is waiting for someone?" Mimi asked.

"No. Not really. Although I do have a friend who planned to spend the winter in Céret. But he has probably left. He is an artist, an American. A tall man, dark haired with a dark beard. David Lorenzo, he is called." She spoke rapidly, fearful that her courage might desert her if she hesitated. But Mimi smiled, nodded in recognition.

"Ah, M. David. Yes. He has come here often. He rents a cottage on the road to Port-Vendres, a beautiful place between the mountains and the sea. No, he has not left Céret. I am certain of that. They would not leave without saying good-bye to André and myself. We have promised them our recipe for cassoulet."

"He is not here alone then?" Rutti asked.

"No. He is here with Madame Lorenzo. A nice woman. Très gentille."

Rutti's heart sank. She should have known better. She should have realized that David would not come alone to spend long months in an isolated mountain village. It was too much to expect that he would remain constant in the face of her continued silence. She thought of his letters, all unanswered, although she had read them over and over and carried them with her to Israel and read them yet again on the journey to Céret. He had not betrayed her. She had betrayed herself.

"They will not come tonight. It is too late. But perhaps tomorrow. And I will tell him that you are here," Mimi said. She smiled amiably and filled Rutti's wine glass.

"Bien," Rutti said automatically, but already her mind was racing. She would leave Céret the next day she decided as she spread the pâté on the warm bread. She had gambled and she had lost. It astonished her now that she had expected to win, that she had allowed Chana's optimism to persuade her. All right. She had lost but she would recover. As she always did. She ate, her chair turned to the window so that she could watch the ghostly birches, the long silver leaves shivering against the impact of the night wind.

André placed another log on the fire. Mimi brought her a plate of beef soaked in wine, encircled by tiny, separate dishes of baby vegetables. She ate slowly, surprised that she could eat at all. The two young couples rose to leave and looked benignly at her. Did they wonder about her as she had wondered about them? She smiled so that she would not engage their sympathy or incur their pity. She needed neither. She had emerged from beneath her cloak of shadows.

Tongues of flame licked at the newly laid log, igniting the loose dry bark so that it crackled sharply. Suddenly a swirling ribbon of flame catapulted onto the hearth, dangerously close to the woven rug. Rutti rushed forward, took up the copper-handled broom, and pounded at the fiery debris until it disintegrated into cinders. Head bent, absorbed in the small task, she swept the ashes back onto the grate. A long shadow fell on the hearth rug and she turned slowly, her face aglow with the heat of the flames, her heart pounding.

"Rutti?' Her name was a question. He asked it in disbelief. "Rutti." The question was a statement — so gentle, so sad.

She looked at him and saw that the silver strands that threaded their way through his soft dark beard were more numerous, that he had grown thinner; his dark green corduroy shirt and his worn jeans looked as though they had been bought for a larger man. But his color was high, his cheeks so ruddy that she knew he had spent much of the winter working outside, sketching swiftly in fingerless gloves. Standing just behind him was a slender, pleasant-looking woman, dark-haired, olive-complected, with large golden hoops in her tiny earlobes.

"David." Rutti looked at him gravely, steadily although she leaned against the stone facade of the fireplace, fearful that without support she would succumb to the weakness that overcame her and fall at his feet. She struggled wildly to invent an excuse to explain her presence in Céret. *It never occurred to me that you would still be here. I wanted to see Soutine's landscapes.* The words tumbled about in her mind, her heart beat rapidly, her hand trembled as she blindly sought to replace the copper-handled broom.

But he did not give her time to speak. He rushed toward her, lifted her in his arms, lifted her high, kissed her forehead, her cheeks, her mouth, said her name again and again. "Rutti. Rutti. Rutti." Laughing, he whirled her about and pressed her close to him. She was no mirage; she was his love unlost.

His laughter engaged her own. She called his name in turn, pressed her fingers into the muscular strength of his arms as though to assure herself that he was real — real and full of love for her.

"Alicia, it's Rutti. My Rutti. Can you believe it. Rutti is here. In Céret."

Alicia. It was his sister who was sharing his mountain cottage.

Rutti smiled shyly at the dark-haired woman and gently pressed her extended hand.

Mimi hurried to bring champagne goblets to their table and André produced a bottle of rare vintage. The other patrons smiled and lifted their own glasses as André proposed a toast.

"*A l'amour et l'amitié,*" the innkeeper said.

"To love and friendship," David repeated, and he lifted his own glass to Rutti's lips.

They gathered at the Egremont house the last week in December. Their exuberance and their laughter trilled through the wide-windowed rooms. The children dashed in and out, wild with holiday joy, with the excitement of the season, with anticipation of the wedding. The four friends marveled at their good fortune, that all of them had been able to arrange for a week's vacation that would encompass Christmas and the New Year. They had juggled schedules, rearranged appointments, traded favors, coaxed and cajoled colleagues. It was an unusual holiday, they had explained, culminating in a New Year's Eve wedding. It helped that the bride and groom were not unknown. David's new book, *A Mountain Winter,* had won an international prize and Rutti's drawings of rooms had appeared as a two-page spread in the *New Yorker*. In the end appeals to romance and whimsy had prevailed and they were all together, locked contentedly in the rhythms of their friendship, their breathless confidences, their laughter.

Anne was the last to arrive, hurtling through the door on Christmas Eve when they had all but given up hope. Her plane from Minnesota had been delayed in Chicago, but she had pressed and pleaded, balanced power and powerlessness, until she was given the last seat on a departing flight.

"I told them I was on my way to perform a heart transplant and flashed my Mayo Clinic ID," she told her friends. "And when that didn't work I went to another ticket counter and cried and cried because I didn't want to miss my best friend's wedding."

They all laughed appreciatively. They had a new consciousness of their own power, a hard-gained recognition of their capabilities.

They knew themselves to be attractive women who, energized by their own competence, moved knowingly through the world. They prevailed in the small battles their mothers never would have entered. They were heroines of ticket counters and conference rooms; they knew how to ask favors and grant favors. Each small triumph ignited their pride, affirmed their hope.

They rushed into the kitchen to bring Anne the dinner that Lottie had cheerfully reheated; watching her as she ate, they filled her in on the news and the holiday plans. They laughed and clapped when Eric ran to Anne, kissed and embraced her, and immediately blushed beet-red.

The children had scampered across the generational boundaries and wandered now in the wilderness of prepubescence. Keren's budding breasts protruded sweetly and sharply against her yellow angora sweater. Nancy looked at her daughter in bewilderment. Was this the child she had wheeled through the park on the day of John Kennedy's assassination? The rush of life mystified her.

She looked across the room and saw that Dov was no longer sitting with Andrew, David, and Ted, who had spent much of the evening discussing Nixon's Vietnam policies.

"Nixon's not ending the war, he's withdrawing from it," Andrew said bitterly. Dov came out of the study, his face pale, his lips set, his pocket address book still in his hand. He had called someone in a distant city, Nancy realized, and she realized too that she did not care who it was he had phoned.

At the midnight hour they all followed Andrew as he led them to the sun-room. The door had been taped shut since their arrival, the doorknob adorned with a huge red ribbon.

"Happy Christmas, darling," Andrew said. He kissed Merle, pulled the tape free, and threw open the cream-colored, beribboned door.

They gasped with surprise and delight. The sun-room had been transformed into a studio. Only the glass doors leading to the garden had been left intact. The dark polished wood of the molding offset the pale green and white flocked wallpaper, which gave the room the air of a delicate fairyland. A new piano, a Steinway baby grand, stood welcomingly in the curve of the bay window, flanked by dark wood music stands. And in the heart of the room was a sea-green chaise longue and three white velvet armchairs.

Andrew bowed from the waist to Merle and led her, laughing and blushing, to the chaise, motioning Rutti, Anne, and Nancy to follow.

"My queen and her ladies," he said as they took their places in the white chairs.

"If Merle is queen, Andrew, then you must be king," Anne quipped.

He did not reply. He was a man who ignored comments that displeased him. His business associates often recognized, too late, that his silence was a powerful weapon. Issues that were not addressed died quickly.

He ignored Anne's comment now as he proudly displayed the small bath and shower and the large closet in which he had placed a minirefrigerator, a tiny pantry stocked with snacks and juices.

They marveled that he had even thought to buy a robe of soft white cashmere and dark green velvet slippers.

"It's a marvelous room, Andrew," David said. "No place here for a ghost to hide."

"What ghost?" Merle asked.

"Oh, village gossip. It all happened long before I bought my cottage. The story is that there was a suicide in this room. The young wife of the elderly Mr. Mayhew. She wanted to be an actress, or perhaps a dancer. He forbade it. He came home one day and found her dead in this room."

"How?" Merle asked. "How did she do it — pills?"

"Oh, I don't know. The rumors vary," David replied, laughing uneasily. "The story's probably not even true."

"Probably not," Andrew said smoothly.

He led them to the glass doors and they looked out at the garden, up at the dark sky across which gray clouds drifted.

"No snow," Greg complained.

"Oh, it will snow before the end of the holiday," Andrew assured them.

"Can you make that happen?" Anne asked softly. "Now that would really impress us, Andrew."

Nancy glanced at her warningly, but again Andrew ignored her. Merle was kissing his cheek, murmuring her thanks into his ear.

It did snow, two nights later. Andrew, Dov, and David piled the boys into the car and drove through the gentle windswept flurries to the Lenox movie house to see *Butch Cassidy and the Sundance Kid.* Rutti, Merle, Nancy, and the girls had seen it together on a Friday afternoon, guiltily substituting the film for the luncheon meeting because they all adored Paul Newman. He was, they all agreed, number one on each of their lists of ideal lovers.

"Definitely Homo unafraidus," Nancy said. "Lucky Joanne. Unlucky us."

"I'll have to catch it," Anne said, although she had not seen a movie for months. Her clinic work was so consuming that she slept only a few hours a night, ate cold meals, used her rare days off to work on her own research. "But I'm not complaining," she said when her friends worried about her. "It's marvelous. I love it. The work. The feeling of accomplishment. The excitement of learning. I've never been happier."

The four friends sat in Merle's beautiful new studio and looked out at the slowly falling snow. The tall briar bushes were laced with crystal fringes of ice and soft cushions of white settled on the low boughs of the apple tree. They wore faded jeans and the bulky pastel sweaters Merle had given each of them for Christmas — blue for Anne, lemon-yellow for Nancy, pink for Rutti. Merle had gifted herself with the same sweater in lime-green.

"The queen and her court in costume," Nancy said, and they laughed as they settled themselves according to Andrew's design.

"This room needs a fireplace," Merle said. "Then it would be perfect."

"Just tell Andrew and he'll arrange it," Anne suggested.

"Anne." Merle's voice was soft, monitory. "Don't."

"Andrew doesn't need your protection," Anne responded sharply.

"It's not Andrew I'm worried about. It's you."

"Don't worry." Anne grinned. "I haven't become a harsh attacker of men. Although 'harsh' is the wrong word, isn't it? 'Shrill' is what they call women if we make the mistake of disagreeing, or asserting ourselves. But I don't think I'm shrill either."

"No, you're not," Nancy agreed. "But you sure as hell are angry."

"I won't deny that," Anne said. "I wasn't angry with Charles at first but it grew on me. Yes. I am angry that he punished me for making a decision that really, truly, had to be my own."

"It affected him as well," Nancy said wearily.

"All right. It affected him. But it was my life. It's always the woman's life. For men it's only an aspect. For women it is the whole."

They all nodded their agreement. They needed no words.

"We are lucky," Merle said. "To have each other. To understand each other." She sat in this room her husband had created for her and understood herself to be a prisoner of his tenderness, his generosity. It was her friends she vested with her honesty, her friends who understood. "I want . . . , I want . . . " she might say tremulously, leaving the sentence unfinished, the thought unspoken. Andrew would not hear her or, hearing, would not question her. But her friends would hear her and, hearing, would have no need of questions.

The snow thickened and the vagrant wind tossed it through the darkness in wild swirls. Anne leaned forward. She spoke softly. She proposed a pact, a solemn pledge, a definition of the friendship that had been theirs through the years of the dying decade. They agreed and, smiling and grave, placed their hands on the low fruitwood table. Unembarrassed they made their pledges, swore their pact of sisterhood. "We will be there for each other, always."

Their own words moved and hypnotized them. They did not hear stifled laughter. They were startled to see Andrew's car, ghostly in its carapace of whiteness, move slowly and silently up the snow-covered drive, to hear men's voices and the children's shouts. They watched from the window as the boys tossed snowballs at the men, as Keren and Sarah dashed outside and threw themselves, arms spread out, across the lawn to create angel outlines that would soon be blanketed by fresh drifts. They turned to each other, smiled, and hurried to find their own winter jackets, eager now for the anonymity of cold and joyous vigor.

Rutti and David were married at the twilight hour on the last day of the year. Together they stood beneath the white marriage canopy that the pleasant young rabbi from Pittsfield brought with him. The happiness in the room was palpable as David placed the gold ring on Rutti's finger.

"Behold you are consecrated unto me according to the laws of Moses and of Israel." His voice broke as he said the words. She had been consecrated unto him from the very first day when he had come upon her in the garden.

She stared at him from behind the delicate lace veil Chana had sent from Israel, light-headed with joy that she had not lost him, that she would never lose him. And then the napkin-covered glass was on the floor and he crushed it, with a powerful and joyous stamp, and lifted her in his arms as their friends shouted with joy.

"I'm sorry, Dov," Nancy said softly. He heard her through the din and, not asking what she meant, he moved to the other side of the room.

Andrew lifted a glass of champagne. "To Rutti and David," he shouted just as Merle began to play the lovely klezmer tune she had learned to honor her friends.

And David and Rutti, with Sarah between them, began a hora, a wild dancing circle that snaked its way through the dining room and the living room, ending at last in the studio where they stood in a circle and clapped as Keren and Sarah whirled about like wind-driven flowers.

The Seventies

17

SHE SAT on a bleached and splintered bench in the sun-spattered park and gently rocked the high coach carriage so that it moved in rhythm with the vagrant wind. Contentedly, she looked across at the field where Greg played with a Frisbee. She watched as, bright haired and graceful, he vaulted forward, tossed the yellow plastic sphere skyward, and then raced after it. His green sweater almost exactly matched the tender young grass. Andrew sat beside her and, although the day was warm, he wore his heavy camel-colored cashmere coat, a high fur hat that was unfamiliar to her, and thick leather gloves. He did not remove his gloves even though they did make it difficult for him to turn the pages of the report that engrossed him, nor did he look up as the sky slowly darkened and the low but threatening rumble of thunder pierced the afternoon quiet.

Merle shivered against the sudden violent wind that jostled the carriage and tossed fallen twigs and branches so that they pelted and bruised her bare arms. Andrew's papers rustled noisily and were scattered, swirling through the newly dark sky like white paper flags of surrender. Frightened she turned to her husband, but he thrust her aside and plucked the sleeping infant from the carriage. He sprinted across the field, and as he ran he dismembered the child. One by one he pulled off the tiny limbs, tossing a small pink leg, a dimpled arm, an infinitesimal thumb, into the whirling wind.

"Stop!" Her voice was shrill with horror but he did not turn. She raced after him, but a heavy rain had begun and the huge black droplets unnerved her.

"Greg!" she shouted, but her son too had disappeared from her field of vision. She was alone and bereft. "Greg! Andrew!" Terror strangled her and her face was streaked by her burning tears and the icy pellets of the falling rain.

"Merle. Merle. It's all right. I'm here."

Andrew's arms were about her in familiar embrace. He held her close, smoothed her hair, calmed and comforted her.

"You had that dream again. That's all. Another bad dream."

"Yes. A dream. It was only a dream."

Exhausted, disoriented, she retreated into the sheltering cave of his tenderness, allowed him to dry her eyes, to whisper softly to her, to bring her the small white pill and the tall glass of warm milk.

"I wish you had never given that damn concert," he said. "I never should have let you go."

"I would have seen it anyway. It was on television — in the newspapers."

"But you were there. You saw it happen."

"I was there, but I didn't see it happen."

In fact, she had been at a reasonable remove from the milling crowd of students waving their placards, shouting their slogans, and the uniformed Ohio National Guardsmen who advanced toward them. She and Emanuel Klein, wearied by the concert they had given the previous evening, had been on the steps of the Kent State University Creative Arts Center awaiting the car that would take them to the airport. The chairman of the music department, who had arranged for their performance, apologized for the sparse attendance.

"These Sunday evening concerts are usually quite popular," he said. "But there's a great deal of unrest on our campus just now. In fact, one reason we wanted Mrs. Cunningham to play *A Child's Prayer* was because we thought it would be an affirmative, optimistic message. In view of what's been happening."

What had been happening, Merle knew, was a spate of virulent protests against the invasion of Cambodia. She had watched the news in her motel room after the concert and seen the footage of students torching a ramshackle ROTC building.

"Hell no! We won't go!" they chanted.

Still, she was unprepared that bright May morning for the

shrilling of sirens and the cacophony of terror that drowned out the music professor's cultivated voice. "Another disturbance," he said with some embarrassment, and Emanuel Klein, who had taught for so many years, who had weathered so many student disturbances, nodded understandingly.

But these disturbances were different, Merle thought. The mood of the sixties was shattered. Bullets destroyed the dreamers and the dreams became nightmares. Janis Joplin's desperate voice replaced the bell-like tones of Joan Baez and the Beatles were no longer content to let it be, but sang of Lucy in the Sky with Diamonds. Too many promises were being broken. Statesmen spoke in marble halls while young men died in distant jungles. Bewildered, the students organized "be-ins," "love-ins," "teach-ins," their lives turned inward as though they had despaired of the world outside. Merle saw fear in the faces of the students who had passed her on campus that morning. She knew that she was looking at a generation haunted by the fear that its very future was in jeopardy.

Still, she was unprepared for the shots that rang out, silencing the shouts of the students and the barking commands of the guardsmen. Shocked, she watched the speeding ambulances, smelled the acrid scent of cordite, heard the keening of the young, the terrible gasping sobs.

"Dead." "Shot." "Four." "No. Five." "More than that." The words ricocheted toward Merle and Emanuel in muffled whispers, in shocked and awed explication. They trembled, following the chairman of the music department to the gate. Their car would be waiting there, he assured them, his voice breaking with grief. Merle walked between the two men, thrusting her way through the crowd, her eyes downcast. Yet she could not avoid seeing the four bodies, surrounded by uniformed men and weeping students, sprawled on the ground. The wounded were placed on stretchers and the air was permeated with their screams of pain.

"Oh no. Oh no. Oh no," a girl said weakly again and again. Her words became a chorus of denial, of disbelief.

"Oh no. Oh no. Oh no," dozens of students repeated after her.

Streams of blood stained concrete and grass, trickled in scarlet rivulets across the concourse. Hurrying, Merle stepped into a carmine puddle and felt the sticky moistness against her leg. She lurched forward, sickened and faint. Emanuel Klein took her violin and the professor of music supported her until they reached the car.

She slept throughout the flight East, a light and fitful sleep. For the first time in many years, she dreamed of Tran, gentle Tran, asleep forever on a sea of her own blood.

Andrew was right. The recurrent nightmares that haunted her sleep had begun then. Night after night she awoke, her body damp with her own perspiration, the bilious aftertaste of fear souring her mouth.

"Nerves," their family doctor said. "You've had a terrible experience. Try not to think of what you saw that day."

She did not tell him that it was not the dead students she saw in her dreams, nor was it the uniformed guardsmen who filled her with terror. Repeatedly, she dreamed of an infant, newly born, her own baby — and each time it was Andrew who threatened the fragile life.

She never described her dreams to Andrew.

"A nightmare," she told him after each terrified awakening, and he did not press her.

She watched him now as he dressed. As always the pill left her dispirited, yet unable to get back to sleep. "It's so early," she said. The green numerals of the digital clock shimmered in the half light of dawn. 5:00 A.M. She watched with insomniac fascination as time moved forward. 5:01. 5:02. Nancy had told her that she advised patients who had difficulty sleeping to remove such clocks from their bedrooms.

"I have an early flight to Atlanta. A meeting about the mall." He knotted his tie, placed one clean handkerchief in his breast pocket, another in his attaché case. He was a careful man.

"Come back to bed," she said teasingly. She smiled, licked her lips, raised her arms so that the straps of her pale blue nightgown fell about her faintly freckled shoulders. Deftly she employed the sexual shorthand of their marriage.

"Merle." He laughed, pleased but unwilling. Still, he sat beside her and held her briefly in his arms.

"Catch a later plane." She pressed herself against him, whispered into his ear.

"I can't. You know I can't. There's an important deal going down. I told you about it."

"Come on. I have a more important deal. I want us to have another baby."

"Sure," he said, but he was already straightening his tie, glancing at his watch. "We will. One day."

"Not one day. Now. Now is exactly the right time," she persisted. "Greg will go off to Taft in the fall."

"Don't you think we deserve some time alone then?" he asked patiently, reasonably.

"We'll have time. Look at Rutti and David." But Andrew was no longer listening.

"Tonight," he promised. "We'll talk tonight."

He closed the door softly and she fell back into a heavy dreamless sleep, awaking just in time to dress for her lunch date with Nancy.

Seated opposite her friend in the small health food restaurant they favored, Merle picked bits of anchovy out of her salade Niçoise and desultorily recounted her dream.

"What do you think it means?" she asked.

"First rule of my profession: Never try to psychoanalyze your friends," Nancy said cheerfully. "Or your ex-husband. Dov insisted on telling me a dream when he picked Keren up the other day."

"Interesting?"

"Passably. He was lost in a desert, but when he looked to the West he could see the spires of a city and when he looked to the East he saw fertile plains. He felt paralyzed. He couldn't decide which way to go. I thought it was pretty obvious. The city is New York and the green expanse is his family's farm. He got annoyed when I pointed out to him that he was not paralyzed and he knew exactly which way he would go." Nancy shrugged. It still saddened her to talk about Dov, although their divorce had been final for months.

"Break your rule. Analyze my dream." Merle sipped her coffee and smiled coaxingly at Nancy.

"All right then," Nancy said. "Let me give it a go. But promise not to be angry if you disagree with my interpretation."

"I promise." Merle leaned back.

"I think you desperately want another child, which requires no great insight or perception on my part. And you feel that Andrew is actively, and maybe even viciously, trying to kill your opportunity to have another baby. In the dream your arms are bare — you're wearing a summer dress — and you're at peace with your children. You rock the carriage, you watch Greg toss a Frisbee. But Andrew doesn't recognize the season of warmth and he isn't interested in the children. He is absorbed in business papers and he wears the heavy clothing of winter. He takes advantage of your distraction when the storm breaks to seize the baby and dismember it the way he dismembers your arguments for having a child — always running off before you can finish a discussion." Nancy paused. Merle frowned, leaned forward.

"But you know that Andrew's not cruel or indifferent, Nancy. He's always been so supportive, so generous to all of us." She willed Nancy to remember how Andrew had helped and encouraged each of them.

"He's a wonderful man, Merle," Nancy agreed. "He's even more wonderful than you allow him to be. It's not his fault that you often prefer to manipulate rather than to confront — like that crazy summer when we furnished the Egremont house." She giggled mischievously and so did Merle. "But I think that there is truth in the dream. His resistance to your having another child is very real." Now her tone was serious.

"What about Greg? Why did he disappear in the dream?"

"Greg will be going off to school in the fall. Maybe you're afraid that he will begin to disappear from your life then."

Merle nodded. Nancy's words had endowed the recurring nightmares with a new clarity. The code had been broken, but she felt no relief.

"Andrew doesn't want another baby, Nancy. I know that. Not now. Not ever. That's not what he says but it's what he means. I'm not even sure he recognizes it himself. He was so frightened during my pregnancy with Greg. I remember. I remember." Melancholy rather than anger tinged her words. Still, it was good to have said them at last, to have acknowledged the truth.

"But why should the decision be his? Can't you act on what you feel, what you want?" Nancy asked.

"How would I do that?"

"Merle, you're on the pill."

"You mean I conveniently forget to take one pill — or several pills?"

"Not such a horrendous thing to do on a purely pragmatic level," Nancy said. "You've tried to reason with Andrew, to be open with him. Years ago you might not have had a choice, but now we have our own lovely little violet cases and we control our own lives."

"It's a thought," Merle said. Ravenously hungry now, she ate her salad, chomped at her croutons, reached across to Nancy's plate to pluck up the tangy black olives Nancy disliked. "I wonder though, why did I begin having these dreams just after the Kent State shootings?"

"You'll have to figure that out for yourself," Nancy said, gathering up her bag, her briefcase. "I have a patient at two. And at the risk of sounding terribly materialistic for someone in the helping profession, every patient hour means dollars in the bank and every dollar means I'm that much closer to earning our ticket for Israel." Since the divorce her resolve was even firmer. She and Keren would go to Israel. She was not escaping, Mina Sieberg agreed. She was acting out a healthy and adventurous impulse. Nancy had expected Dov to object when her lawyer asked that her right to take Keren to live in Israel be included in their agreement, but he had been silent. Later she realized that he saw Keren as a surrogate. He himself would not return to Israel but he would send his daughter in his place. Keren would walk with Dov's father through the fields of the moshav; she would eat his mother's cooking and be proudly introduced to the neighbors. Poor Dov. Nancy thought of him now with a commingling of contempt and pity. Her anger had dissipated. She could not blame Dov because they had married too young and had misread each other's dreams.

Merle watched her friend leave the restaurant. She noticed how the other patrons stared briefly, admiringly at Nancy, so purposeful and attractive in her sensible khaki poplin suit, her short dark hair curling softly about her face. She ordered a fresh cup of coffee and drank it slowly.

She remembered now her first thought at Kent State, as the two men hurried her past the scene of death, as she saw the blood and glimpsed the bodies. *Waste*. The word had darted through her mind.

Such a waste of youth and hope. *Waste*. The word revolted her, plucked painfully at the cords of buried memory. *Waste,* she had thought when Tran died in that tiny room where they had slept side by side. Three days after her return from Kent State, Merle's menstrual period had begun and the initial heavy flow had caused her to weep in sudden recognition. The blood that flowed from her body symbolized yet another child who would not be born to her. *Waste.*

She knew, as she stirred her coffee, tepid now and bitter, that there was only one way to end the torturous dreams. A new calm suffused her. She asked for the check and left a large tip. She walked to Bloomingdale's and bought herself a lime-green negligee and a matching peignoir. Three weeks later she knew she was pregnant, but she did not tell Andrew. Patiently she waited for the right moment. It came, of course, at Egremont.

Rutti and David had joined them for dinner and afterward Rutti had shown them her completed drawings for a new feminist calendar. She spread her work across the rosewood table in Merle's studio and Merle and Andrew studied them carefully. It was the first time they had seen "Hands of Four Women" and Merle recognized her own splayed fingers and thought of the pact they had made that winter evening. The subjects varied. Rutti had drawn an empty kitchen, the appliances shadowed, the counters overflowing, and she had sketched two women seated together in a park and walking together through a market. There was a drawing of a woman hunched over a typewriter and a profile of a slender, serious woman playing the violin. Startled, embarrassed, Merle recognized herself, and she passed the drawing to Andrew, turning quickly to the series of sketches Rutti had dashed off at the Women's Strike for Equality parade the previous August.

She marveled at the accuracy with which Rutti captured the mood of that day, the pervasive humor and optimism, the rhythm of hope that propelled them as they laughed and sang down Fifth Avenue, thousands strong, carrying placards and flowers, banners and babies.

The four friends had marched together, turning the day into a minireunion. Anne flew in from Rochester and she wore her white lab coat; a stethoscope dangled from her neck. Nancy carried a sign produced by Hope and Ted's graphics department: Don't Iron While the Strike Is Hot, it read, and the crowds of women who lined the avenue laughed and applauded when they saw it. At Forty-ninth Street they opened their arms wide to embrace Keren and Sarah, who darted away from Lottie to join them.

"Lottie, come on," Merle shouted and the smiling black woman hesitated for a split second and then walked and sang beside them. Rutti sketched Lottie, capturing her in full stride, in full smile. The final drawing was a tender sketch of Keren and Sarah sitting side by side on a window seat watching the falling snow and smiling confidently.

"They're marvelous, Rutti," Merle said. Rutti leaned happily against David, who placed his hand upon the swell of her abdomen as though to caress the small life nurtured within it.

"Rutti looks radiant," Andrew said when they left. "Maybe it's the pregnancy. Don't they say that pregnant women get a special glow?"

"I don't know," Merle replied. "Do I have a special glow?" She smiled teasingly at him.

"Merle — what do you mean?" His tone was puzzled, his gaze searching and serious. He moved toward her. His large hands slid across her body as though to confirm that her figure was newly full, her waistline disappearing, her breasts heavy, tender to his touch.

"I'm pregnant, Andrew. Three months pregnant," she said shyly, softly. "Isn't it wonderful?"

She saw the lie form on his lips, felt it in the tension of his swift embrace.

"Yes, darling," he said. "It's wonderful."

He asked her no questions and she volunteered none of the answers she had rehearsed as she reveled in her secret. "The pill is not infallible," she might have said. "It's possible I might have forgotten to take one. Remember the night I had the upset stomach — I might have vomited it up."

But he asked no questions and together, artfully, they acted out the scenario that had created itself. The lie became a truth so convincing they all but believed it themselves. They had planned this pregnancy to coincide with Greg's departure for prep school, they told their friends. Wasn't it wonderful that it had all worked out? Greg himself, vaguely embarrassed, confided to Eric that he was glad he would be away at school when the baby was born.

247

"Not bad timing," he said wryly and Eric nodded disinterestedly. The boy who had been too often left alone had grown into a moody and introverted adolescent who coveted his solitude. His parents' agency was one of the most successful small agencies in the city. A woman's magazine ran a profile of Hope, "A Woman Ahead of Her Time," and he looked listlessly at the photographs of his parents working together, their desks side by side, their heads bent over a drawing board, each with a pencil raised in judgment. There was even a picture of the three of them having dinner together. His mother had phoned twice that day to remind him to be home when the photographer arrived at dinnertime. She had preceded the photographer by five minutes, carrying with her the meal ordered from a gourmet take-out place.

"Was it difficult to be a mother and have a career?" the interviewer had asked Hope.

"What do you think?" Hope thought that the question, asked by one woman of another, was patently ridiculous.

Merle read that magazine as she read so many magazines during the months of her pregnancy. She lay on her chaise longue and contentedly turned the pages of *McCall's, Redbook, Ladies' Home Journal, Vogue*. She read gothic novels obsessively, reveling in her own indolence. She stayed at Egremont throughout her pregnancy. Sometimes she thought of the mythic Mrs. Mayhew, who had slept in her bedroom, walked through her garden. How could a woman who lived in this graceful and beautiful house, who was surrounded by the miracle of mountains and meadows, have been so unhappy as to take her own life? Merle's own contentment denied and confounded such misery.

Emanuel Klein phoned occasionally to ask her about taking a class or playing with a small chamber group. Automatically she declined.

"I'm nesting," she said.

"But are you practicing?" he asked impatiently.

"Of course I'm practicing."

And she did practice, sometimes for hours at a time. The music came easily. She played for her baby. It seemed to her that the fetus moved with luxuriant slowness within her when she played a Brahms étude, a Schubert lullaby.

248

Andrew arrived home one afternoon and watched from the shadow of the doorway as she played her violin. Her hair was the color of burnished copper and she smiled with serene secrecy as she played. Her body, majestic in its amplitude, swayed to the sweetness of the music. Mendelssohn. She had been playing Mendelssohn the first time he saw her.

"I think perhaps you did the right thing, Merle," he said softly and she set her instrument down and turned to him. She understood then that he knew what she had done, that he had known it from the beginning. She smiled at him gratefully.

Rutti's twins were born early in the autumn. Adam and Liora were strong and beautiful babies and Sarah cuddled them and paraded through the house holding them both, one propped against each shoulder.

"Careful, Sarah," Rutti said, but her admonishment was hesitant.

"I don't want Sarah to feel left out," she said worriedly to Nancy.

"She won't feel it if it's not true," Nancy assured her. "Truth is an absolute defense against neurosis." It occurred to her later that she was making such comments too glibly, that there was a dry, judgmental edge to her observations that she disliked.

"I think I'm jealous of Merle and Rutti," she confessed to Anne during their weekly phone conversation. "Aren't you?" It comforted her that she could speak so honestly of that jealousy.

There was a brief silence as Anne thought. Nancy knew that Anne would never reply to such a question without thinking about it carefully.

"No, I'm not jealous," she said at last. "I'm happy with my work. I know that I'm doing exactly what I want to be doing. I could never duplicate the Mayo experience."

She did not tell Nancy that when a colleague told her that Charles Bingham had married, she smiled politely, expressed her best wishes for his happiness, and then retreated into her bedroom where she spent hours weeping softly into the darkness. The next day she wrote him a note of congratulations, which she ripped into long strips that evening. Still, her reply to Nancy was honest. She was precisely where she wanted to be — doing important, valuable work.

"What's wrong, Nancy?" Anne asked softly.

"I think it's time for me to get on with my life," Nancy replied.

"I think it's time for me to be exactly where I want to be, doing exactly what I want to be doing." She would earn her doctorate in less than a year, just as Keren was ready to enter high school. They would move to Israel then, she decided, and the thought immediately lightened her mood.

"Amen, sister," Anne said.

"Don't you mean awomen?" Nancy asked, and they both laughed.

Greg came to Egremont for Thanksgiving. He came alone, although Merle and Andrew had encouraged him to bring a friend. It occurred to Merle that her pregnancy embarrassed him. He hovered uncertainly about her, alternately sullen and solicitous. She was startled when he asked if the baby would be a boy or a girl.

"We don't know that, Greg," she said.

"But don't they have some sort of test for that? A guy in my class — his dad's an obstetrician — he told me that they can do an amnio something."

"Amniocentesis," she said. "I didn't have it."

Her doctor had suggested it. He was a conservative obstetrician. He had attended her when Greg was born, and observed Andrew Cunningham's tension and fear. But she had resisted the test. It was true that she was in her thirties, but this was not her first pregnancy and there had been no problems so far. Indeed she had never felt better or stronger. "Just very lazy," she confessed, although she was not too lazy to cuddle Rutti's twins, to sing softly to Liora, to press Adam against her shoulder.

"Hey, Dad, don't you think Mom should have had that amnio thing?" Greg persisted.

"It's your mother's decision," Andrew replied. He had said as much when she told him of the doctor's suggestion. His message was clear. She had decided to have this baby and she would make all decisions about it. Still, it did not matter. The only thing that mattered was the child growing within her, the child who moved and shifted and who once, as she sat on her chaise studying sheet music, kicked so fiercely that the notated sheets were scattered about the floor.

"Sounds like a boy," Anne said when Merle told her during a phone conversation about the fetal activity.

"Don't be such a chauvinist," Merle said indignantly. "This baby is definitely a girl. A powerful female infant."

"How do you know?" Anne asked.

"Intuition," Merle replied.

She had dreamed the previous evening that she walked through a field bright with star-shaped pink blossoms, holding the hand of a small girl. Her daughter. Kate, she would call her, for her mother, who had died when she was so very young.

The baby was a girl. Merle went into labor on a clear November morning and Kate was born before noon. The doctor marveled that this second delivery should have been so much easier, so very swift. By the time Andrew arrived at the hospital, the baby was in the nursery.

"She's beautiful," Nancy said when she greeted him at the elevator.

"Gorgeous," Rutti happily agreed.

"She has just a wisp of auburn hair," Nancy told him but Andrew did not care. All that mattered was that Merle was all right, that she was delivered of danger. He wept when he looked at Kate in the nursery.

"Isn't she beautiful?" Merle asked drowsily.

"No more beautiful than her mother." He kissed her forehead, pulled the blanket about her, watched as her eyes closed. Her lashes fell across her high, sculpted cheekbones like thin copper needles. Again he was overwhelmed by her beauty, her fragility.

He phoned Greg at school. "You have a sister," he said. "A gorgeous sister. And Mommy's fine," he added quickly, assuming that his son's anxiety matched his own.

He sent his secretary to the infant-wear department at Saks and arrived at the hospital that evening laden with boxes. Merle sat up in bed and opened each parcel. She exclaimed extravagantly over each small flannel nightgown, over tiny shirts spattered with pink butterflies, over delicate pink sweaters and lace-edged dresses. She marveled at a jade-green snowsuit. She saw herself walking though the park on a wintry afternoon, Kate sweetly sleeping in the carriage, encased in a cocoon the color of springtime. Happily she piled the boxes into a small pyramid. She remembered suddenly how Keren and Sarah had marched beside Rutti and Nancy at the Women's Strike for

251

Equality parade. Oh, Kate would march beside her, sit next to her at concerts, kneel beside her in the Egremont garden and thrust silken bulbs into soft and yielding earth. Mother and daughter. Friends.

Twice she got up in the night and went to the nursery window to watch her daughter, who slept so sweetly, so peacefully. That night she slept with her fingers curled about a tiny pink sweater, soft as a cloud to her touch. Her sleep was dreamless. She had not erred. The nightmares were over. She awoke refreshed, renewed. Emanuel Klein called to congratulate her.

"Soon you will be back at work," he said.

She glanced down at the composition pad on her lap where that morning she had scribbled a few notes. The idea had come to her in the night — a sweet musical dialogue between flute and oboe. Mother and daughter. She was a mother and she had a daughter. The miracle of it caused her to smile.

"I'm working already," she told her teacher.

She fell back asleep and awoke to the sound of carts being wheeled down the corridor. Infants were being brought to their mothers to be nursed or bottle-fed. The phone rang. It was Nancy calling between patients.

"I can't talk now, Nancy," she said gaily. "My daughter's on her way. I have to make myself beautiful. I don't want Kate to be ashamed of her mom."

She tied her hair back with a white ribbon and put on the new bed jacket Andrew had brought her, a garment of thin white wool, threaded with strips of satin. "It looks bridal, not maternal," she had protested. "But you are my bride. You will always be my bride," he had replied.

She dabbed a few drops of perfume on her neck. She had read that infants had highly developed olfactory responses. She wanted her daughter to associate her with the scent of wild flowers. Her daughter. "Kate."

She said the name aloud, stretched languidly, and felt the swell of milk at her breasts. The carts continued their progress down the corridor. She listened as the student nurses tapped lightly at the doors. "Here's Baby Lisa." "Here's your handsome hungry son." Lusty infant cries trickled down the hall.

Merle waited expectantly, confidently. The carts passed her doorway. She was not worried. Perhaps Kate had had to have a diaper change. Perhaps they had missed her room and would come back. She did not lift her phone or press the nurse's call button. A few minutes more or less did not matter. It was only when the corridor was quiet that she felt the first stirring of unease. She got out of bed and put on her slippers. She had felt well enough the previous night to go down the hall to the nursery twice, but now weakness overtook her and she sat trembling on the bed. She reached for the phone, but before she could lift it her door opened and the nurse entered. She was a plump, middle-aged woman whose wide smile seemed to be an accessory to her starched uniform.

"Where is my baby?" Merle asked fearfully. "Has something happened?"

"Don't upset yourself, Mrs. Cunningham." The smile did not relax. "The doctor wanted to run some tests so we've taken Kate to the neonatal floor."

"What tests?"

"She just didn't seem to be responding properly," the nurse said guardedly. "The doctor will be in to explain it to you."

"Explain what to me? What are you talking about?" It seemed important to her that she get the nurse to stop smiling. "I don't know what you're talking about." But the smile remained fixed firmly in place as the nurse left the room, closing the door softly behind her.

Merle called Andrew's office but his secretary told her that he had not come in that morning.

"Why not?" she asked warily.

"I don't know." Merle heard the misery in the woman's voice, noted that she did not engage in congratulatory small talk. She dialed her own home but Lottie was out. She reached Nancy's office but Nancy was with a patient.

"Is it an emergency?" the clinic secretary asked.

"No." She hung up. Of course it was not an emergency. Just some tests, the nurse had said. Desperately she flipped through her address book. She would call Anne in Minnesota. Anne would know what to do. But she slammed the receiver down as her door opened.

Andrew and her doctor, both dark suited, both grave, advanced to her bedside.

"What's wrong? What happened?" The shrillness of her own voice shocked her.

"The doctors are concerned about Kate," Andrew said quietly. He sat beside her and gently wiped her tears with his large white handkerchief.

"Why? Why are they worried?"

"She wasn't sucking properly. The nurses couldn't get her to take the bottle. We had to start an IV glucose to nourish her. We want to run some tests," the doctor said.

"Tests for what?"

"We're really not sure. There could be any number of explanations. Perhaps some developmental immaturity. Some minimal retardation. Or the problem may be transitory and quite minor," he replied cautiously, but she noticed that he avoided her gaze.

She felt the tension in Andrew's arms and manipulated herself free of his embrace. *Retardation.* She knew how the word repelled him. Everything that surrounded him had to be perfect, beautiful. His home, his properties, his wife, his son. She turned her eyes from him, from the frown of fear that creased his face, from the fists he clenched and unclenched in acknowledgment of his own impotence. He could make no deals, write no checks. He was powerless.

"I want to see my baby," Merle said.

"It may upset you," the doctor replied.

"But you said it was just an IV hookup for the glucose."

"There are other tubes involved," he admitted uncomfortably. "We have to monitor her carefully. It's sometimes hard for mothers to see their newborns like that."

"Nevertheless," she said firmly.

The doctor glanced at Andrew, who nodded wearily.

They brought Merle a wheelchair and silently they made their way to the neonatal floor where the walls were painted a soft blue and masked nurses wore smocks the colors of wild flowers.

Kate's condition did upset her. The beautiful infant girl whom she had held to her breast at the moment of birth, whom she had watched sleep so peacefully only hours earlier, was pale, all color drained from her waxen skin. Her tiny limbs were flaccid and she was curled into the fetal position as though struggling to reclaim the peaceful protection of the womb. Delicate wires, thin tubes, were attached to every extremity. Jade-green plastic ovoids jeweled her heart and beamed their message onto the small screen above her isolette. Only Kate's mouth, the mouth that refused to suck properly, retained a vestige of color. It looked, as Merle described it to Greg on the phone, like an infinitesimal rosebud.

The doctor studied the screen, read the chart, consulted with a nurse.

"What is it, doctor? What's happening?" she asked anxiously.

"There is some distress," he replied, and she understood that her daughter was dying, that life was draining from her slowly, limb by limb. Her dream was vested at last with reality.

But Kate did not die that day. It took a week for the spectral patterns of light to stop flashing across the small screen — a week during which Merle held vigil, sometimes with Andrew, occasionally with Nancy or Rutti or Lottie but often alone. She was alone when Kate died at last and she would always remember that there had been no expression of pain on her child's face, that there had been no expression at all. The tiny visage that had so briefly known life was frozen into a miniature death mask.

"A blessing," she heard one nurse say softly to another as they drew a screen about the isolette, as they efficiently removed the tubes, the valves, the monitor, from the cruelly diminished infant corpse. Merle knew it was a blessing. Specialists had been called in and a diagnosis offered, couched in tentative terms. She and Andrew had met with the pediatrician, the neonatologist. It had been explained to them that Kate had been born profoundly retarded. She might never have walked. She might never have spoken.

"But what caused it?" she asked, desperate for answers, although Andrew sat silent, studying his clasped hands.

"I believe the retardation was only symptomatic," the pediatrician said cautiously. "There was severe developmental abnormality, a variety of birth defects."

"But what caused them?" she asked again, determined, persistent.

"It might have been any number of factors. Or a combination of factors," he replied uneasily. "Genetic defects, perhaps. Possibly your age."

"My age?" Her throat was constricted, her palms damp.

"Kate's case was quite rare and the body of research is limited. But such conditions do seem to present principally in infants born to older mothers — women in their mid-thirties, their forties. That's why your obstetrician suggested amniocentesis, if you recall." He had ascertained that at once.

Merle said nothing. She held a pad on her lap on which she copied a single bar of music again and again. The first chords of the piece she would have called "Mother and Daughter," the composition for flute and oboe that she would never write. She bit her lip, clutched her pencil.

"You can have other children," the doctor said comfortingly. "We would monitor your pregnancies more carefully. We could employ amniocentesis."

"Merle." Andrew's hand rested on her shoulder. "The doctor is right. We could have another child."

She did not answer, but rose to leave. The neonatologist walked them to the door.

"It is terrible for you now, I know," he said. "But it is all for the best. Such infants have a difficult existence."

"Kate," Merle said. "She had a name. Kate."

"I'm sorry." He held out his hand but she did not take it. She did not blame him but she did not want to take his hand.

"It wasn't the doctor's fault," Andrew said the evening of Kate's death.

"I know."

They sat side by side, staring into the fire. They had made decisions, agreed to an autopsy. Merle had spoken to her family in Michigan, to Rutti who, in turn, would call Nancy and Anne. They had agreed to tell Greg that the baby had died of a virus. There was no need to frighten him. They would bury Kate in the Egremont cemetery and ask only Rutti and David to be with them. Nancy would take the layette to the Women's Center. Merle kept only the small pink sweater, which she wrapped in tissue paper and placed in her bottom drawer next to a faded silk blouse that had belonged to her mother and the tortoiseshell barrette that had been Tran's.

"It wasn't anyone's fault," he added and took her hand, pressing her fingers to his lips. Abruptly, almost angrily, she pulled away.

"It was our fault," she countered harshly. "Yours and mine."

"Merle, what are you saying? Don't be foolish."

He put another log on the fire and bent to sweep away the ashes that had escaped the grate. He did not want to look at her. He could not bear to look at her. Like their infant daughter who had died that morning, her eyes were closed and her face was expressionless.

"We waited too long to have this baby. I should have become pregnant years ago, but I listened to you. I will never forgive myself for listening to you." She spoke very softly but her voice curdled with bitterness, with an anger she could not restrain.

"And yet you did become pregnant with Kate. You didn't listen to me then," he said. He pitied her, but he would not absolve her.

"No. But I had the right. I wanted a baby. I wanted Kate." Her voice broke.

"I accepted it."

"No. You weren't against me but you weren't with me, Andrew. I felt your separation. We didn't speak about the amnio."

"And would it have made a difference if we had? You wanted the baby. It was your baby, your decision." Again he studied his clasped hands, saw how the ashes dusted his knuckles; he did not wipe them clean.

"I don't know if it would have made any difference. But it might have. I've grown so used to listening to you, to giving you control, to allowing you to make decisions. . . . " Her voice drifted off. She leaned forward so that she would be closer to the heat of the flames, and still she shivered, although her face was bright in the glow of the firelight. The phone rang, and Lottie came in.

"It's Anne calling from Rochester," she said.

"Please tell her I'll call her tomorrow," Merle said. "I just can't talk to anyone now, Lottie." She particularly could not talk to Anne who had chosen not to have a child.

"Do you ever wonder whether the baby you aborted was a boy or a girl?" Nancy had asked Anne once, on a Friday afternoon, when they had all had too much wine.

"Never," Anne replied and they had not challenged her, although they noticed that she refilled her glass too quickly and her hand trembled as she lifted it. Rutti looked at Nancy reprovingly. There were questions that should not be asked even among the most honest of friends.

"All that I ever wanted was for you to be happy, Merle," Andrew said quietly. "All I ever wanted was to take care of you, to please you, to keep you safe."

"I know that, Andrew. I should have told you, long ago, that you couldn't will my happiness, that I didn't need to be kept safe. I'm not a hothouse plant. I'm not a child. I'm a grown woman. I should have told you what I wanted, insisted on what was important to me."

"I knew what you wanted," he said miserably. "But I was frightened. I remembered Greg's delivery — the danger, the pain."

"*My* danger. *My* pain."

He recoiled from the harshness of her tone. "We'll have another child, Merle. A baby that we both want."

"You didn't want Kate.'

"Not until I saw her, that first day. She was so beautiful, so tiny. She was ours." He remembered the wisp of auburn hair, rising from her pale head like a small and fragile flame. He buried his face in his hands and tears trickled between his fingers.

Merle stared at him. She had never seen him cry before, and she wondered that his tears did not move her now. Nothing moved her. She feared that nothing would move her ever again.

"We'll have another baby," he repeated in a muffled voice, but she did not answer him.

She slept that night with her back to him, reversing the habit of years. She did not want his protection. She did not want him to run interference against nocturnal terror. But she did not have a nightmare that night. Nor did they recur.

Some weeks later she told him that she had accepted two private students at Juilliard and increased her own program of study. She accepted Emanuel Klein's invitation to join a chamber music ensemble. Hours of rehearsal were required. She thought it best that she rent a studio near the school. She might find it more convenient to stay over several nights a week if rehearsals ran late.

"Of course. If that's what you want," Andrew said.

They spoke to each other with gentle courtesy. When they made love, he was cautious, restrained, as though fearful of tipping the delicate balance that sustained their marriage. They lived in intimacy as tender strangers. They were happiest at Egremont when Greg came home for vacation, although his visits home grew more infrequent. He was a popular boy and had many invitations. It did not occur to them that he could not bear the constraint of their silence, the correctness of their civility.

Merle and Andrew gave a large party at Egremont for Nancy and Keren before they left for Israel. Greg moved happily through the crowds of friends, took charge of the music that played on the stereo.

"You don't know what it's like here usually," he told Eric. "I feel as though I'm coming home to a morgue."

"I've always come home to a morgue," Eric replied gloomily. He still turned the television on as soon as he entered his parents' apartment because he could not bear the silence. He stuffed himself with potato chips and listened disinterestedly to the discussion of the Nixon White House, the growing power of the silent majority.

"Yeah, well, like your mom said in that interview, it's a trade-off."

"The only question is — what did we get in the trade?" Eric asked, and he passed Greg the bottle of beer they had filched from the kitchen when Lottie's back was turned. They both laughed. Beer, they knew, was supposed to induce a raucous gaiety.

It was at that party that Emanuel Klein invited Merle to join him on a European tour. She told Andrew of his invitation as they prepared for bed.

"Will you go?" he asked.

"Not yet. I'm not ready."

"I see."

He was silent. Still, he held her close that night and wakened twice to say her name aloud in the darkness. Her answering murmur reassured him. She was not gone from him yet. Not yet. Perhaps not ever. Thus comforted, he slept deeply at last, his face buried in the fiery cape of her hair.

18

LONG PURPLE shadows streaked the Valley of Hinnom and the slowly sinking sun stained the low stone wall a rose red. The wind, blowing westward from the Dead Sea, carried with it the mingled scents of sea salt and pomegranate blossom. Nancy leaned forward in her chair, stirred the tall glass of cold coffee she had carried out to the terrace, and waved to Shoshanna who lived across the road from them in the Yemin Moshe quarter of Jerusalem. She spread the daily mail across the table, automatically organizing it into piles but making no move to open any of it. This was her favorite time of the day, these brief moments that she claimed for herself, after her last appointment and before Ari arrived home from the Foreign Office and Keren dashed in, either bursting with excitement or bristling with indignation.

Keren, who had always been such a placid, malleable child, was now a passionate adolescent whose mood swings were unpredictable. Like an emotional acrobat, she tumbled from ecstasy to misery. But of course today she would be reasonably calm as she always was during Sarah's summer visits. Both girls delighted in Seth, and Nancy was pleased that they played with her son with such generous exuberance. Ari's sons were awkward and constrained with the toddler, as though uncertain how to react to the child of their father's second marriage. It did not help, Nancy realized, that Seth had been temperamental from infancy, either weeping passionately or chortling with hilarity. Even now he babbled excitedly to Margalit, the Hebrew University student who baby-sat him during the hours that Nancy taught and saw patients.

"Oh, Margalit is your Anne," Hope said breezily during her brief visit to Jerusalem to scout for locations for commercial shoots.

Nancy at once understood and disliked the comparison. Hope and Ted were recently divorced — her choice, Hope was always careful to emphasize. They were still partners in the successful agency they had built together and *very* good friends. Hope, who had not lost her southern accent, always emphasized the *very* when she discussed their relationship.

"Well, I hope she'll be as successful as Anne," Nancy replied defensively.

There was a letter from Anne today and Nancy set it aside to be read last, as a prize, a reward, for dealing with the more troublesome correspondence. Her phone rang and, although there was an extension on the terrace, she waited for her answering machine to pick up. As always she was surprised by her own message, delivered in the flawless but American-accented Hebrew that she had mastered since her arrival in the country four years earlier.

"Dr. Yallon cannot come to the phone. Please leave a message and your call will be returned as soon as possible."

The caller was a colleague in the psychology department at the Hebrew University who wanted to reschedule a meeting. Nancy did not pick up the phone. Instead she listened absently as Margalit cajoled Seth into a walk to Liberty Park. She waited until the front door closed behind them before turning back to the mail, which she now attacked in earnest.

There was the usual batch of invitations. Ari's position as cultural attaché at the Foreign Office placed them on every list and she glanced at invitations to an exhibition of paintings by Soviet immigrants at the Jerusalem Artists' House, the screening of a new film from Czechoslovakia at the Cinémathèque to be followed by a reception for the producer at the home of the mayor, three different chamber music recitals, and a tour of the sculpture garden at the Israel Museum. She set aside the invitation to the screening. Sarah and Keren would surely enjoy that. And of course they would go to the recital of the Juilliard Pro Musica Ensemble at the Islamic Museum. Emanuel

Klein was the conductor and she was eager to see Merle's mentor, especially since Merle had not written for several months.

She quickly discarded the mail from publishers and professional organizations, although she guiltily read the letter from the editor of a Swedish psychology journal who was awaiting her abstract on the impact of war and violence on the imagination of children. He had, he advised her, already received manuscripts from therapists in Ireland, India, and Liberia. He was awaiting her contribution as well as that of Fatima Nashif, an Arabic psychologist who practiced in Bethlehem.

I should call Fatima, Nancy thought. She had met Fatima Nashif several times at conferences and once at a party in east Jerusalem. It would be helpful if they could compare notes, perhaps even set up a control experiment with Arab and Jewish children. She placed the letter from Stockholm in the folder she would take to the university the next day and picked up the familiar envelope, a communication from Dov's secretary.

The competent young woman who administered Dov's successful practice in a Long Island suburb had sent Dov's vacation itinerary. He and his wife, Lisa, would be traveling through western Canada and Dov wanted to be sure that Keren knew where to reach him. Dov had not, in the end, married Nina Alcott. Lisa was a pretty young woman who taught nursery school. She listened, motionless and attentive, when Dov spoke. She dutifully joined him on his annual visits to Israel to visit Keren and his family on the moshav and she invariably brought Nancy a carefully selected, appropriately impersonal gift — a short story anthology, an ascot from Liberty of London, an address book from the Metropolitan Museum of Art. Nancy noticed that Lisa always nodded vigorously in agreement when Dov ventured an opinion during their very brief and awkward meetings. She too had nodded vigorously, all those years ago, when she had been bewitched by Dov's accent and his authority, when she had often slept through the night with her lips pressed against the butterfly-shaped scar at his neck and awoke imagining that they had shared the same dream. She set the itinerary aside to show to Keren and wished that Dov had taken the time to scrawl a note to his daughter. But doubtless there would be presents from Canada — a tartan skirt, a mohair sweater. Lisa had excellent taste and, as Dov often said proudly, she loved to shop.

She glanced at the bills, placed them in a separate envelope, and at last, pleased at its thickness, opened Anne's letter. Snapshots tumbled out and she studied them one by one, experiencing a familiar twinge of longing and homesickness. She stared at the shot of Anne, Rutti, and Merle, standing together beneath the apple tree at the Egremont house. They stood with their chins lifted because surely David had told them to look upward to the branches when he posed them. They smiled determinedly, and held hands. Rutti had grown a bit plump, Nancy thought, but then she had never regained her figure after the birth of the twins. The added weight, however, became her. She no longer had that waiflike look and her smile, once so nervous and hesitant, was generous with natural merriment, careless joy.

Merle's smile, in sharp contrast, was vague, her gaze distant as she stared toward her bedroom balcony. Was it a transitory mood, Nancy wondered, or had Merle still not recovered from the sadness that had haunted her since Kate's death? *Kate.* How odd it was that they always referred to that newborn infant, whose life had been so very brief, by name. Perhaps because Merle had not allowed the brevity of her daughter's life to mitigate the pain of her death or the reality of her birth. *Kate.* The very name inspired their sadness.

Her fair hair twisted into a chignon, Anne stood between her two friends, slender and stylish in pale blue slacks and a matching sweater, a string of softly shimmering pearls about her neck. It occurred to Nancy that the pearls were real. She wondered who had bought them for Anne and realized that it was not unlikely that Anne had bought them for herself. "I like giving myself presents," she had once written proudly to Nancy.

She sighed and shuffled swiftly through the other snapshots. Merle and Andrew stood side by side, their hands lightly touching, but their eyes averted. Merle and Andrew with Greg between them. How tall he was; he played varsity basketball for Dartmouth, the only freshman on the first string, Merle had written in her last letter. There was a candid shot of Rutti and David and one of Rutti holding Adam and David holding Liora. It was strange that Sarah spoke so seldom of the twins, although she dutifully answered Nancy's probing questions.

Yes, they were awfully cute. No, she didn't mind baby-sitting for them. Yes, she missed them here in Israel. Just as she missed David and her mother. It troubled Nancy that Sarah called David by his first name and it troubled her even more that she had begun to ask questions about Werner.

"What was my father like when you knew him?" she asked Ari. Ari, with his natural gentleness and diplomat's skill, phrased his answer carefully. "He was very brilliant, always studying — reading and writing. We always knew that his ideas were important, that he would be a great man."

And Werner's reputation, both in Israel and abroad, had grown through the passing years. His treatise on the cyclical nature of history had been published in many languages and his monographs appeared in sourcebooks. The story of his death, like many such stories, had been embellished and translated into a tale of mythical heroism. The cemetery at Beit Yair had become a requisite stop for tourists because of the beautiful sculpture of the child that stood sentinel over the graves, and the tourist guides waxed eloquent when they spoke of Werner. Nancy had been in that cemetery, listening to such a tour guide, the very first time she met Ari.

She and Keren had arrived in Israel at the start of the school year and Nancy had been overwhelmed by the demands of her own work, her intensive study of Hebrew, and the inordinate amount of time consumed by small tasks.

"I grow expert in confounding the bureaucracy," Nancy wrote proudly to Rutti, who alone among the friends, having lived in Israel, could understand the complexity involved in obtaining a telephone, installing a television set, registering a car.

Each small achievement had filled her with a perverse pleasure that balanced her frustration. She was, against all odds, managing alone. Her independence excited and energized her. She baffled Dov's family and watched their incredulity change to grudging respect when she drove Keren down to the Negev to visit them.

"You drove through the Negev by yourself?" his eldest sister asked. "But what if the auto had broken down in the territories?"

"It did," Keren replied, grinning mischievously. "We had to fight off the Arab boys who wanted to help us fix it. Although we let one of them help us change the tire. He was so cute."

"You changed the tire?" Dov's mother stared at her son's ex-wife through narrowed eyes and then her leathery face creased into a forgiving smile. She did not understand this American woman who lived so independently and worked so hard. Dov had made it clear in his letters that it was Nancy who had wanted the divorce. He was honest. He had given his wife cause to be unhappy, he told his mother, but it had been her decision that they separate. The old woman was bewildered. Dov's was the first divorce in their family. Still, she admired his wife who had so much courage and who had brought Dov's daughter to Israel. Her grandmother watched Keren dash through the fields with her cousin and felt renewed gratitude to Nancy.

"You will return here to pick Keren up?" Shulamit asked.

"Oh, Keren will manage on the bus," Nancy replied with more confidence than she felt. She was determined that Keren would not have to fight for her independence; she would be trained for it.

And Keren managed wonderfully well during those first months. She missed her father and her friends in New York, but her daily Hebrew lessons, her schoolwork, and her involvement in a drama group engulfed her in an unceasing whirlwind of activity.

"It's hard to be lonely when you're so busy," Keren wrote to Sarah.

Nancy's schedule was so hectic that she often found it difficult to scavenge the time to write to her friends and family. But with the arrival of summer her university program ended, her intensive Hebrew course took a recess, and many of her private patients went on vacation. For the first time since her arrival in Israel, she had an expanse of time to call her own and for the first time she recognized her own loneliness, her need for friends and companionship. She thought longingly of the summer days at the Egremont house, the lazy talk and laughter she exchanged with Merle, Rutti, and Anne.

On the Friday that Keren left to spend two weeks with her grandparents, Nancy placed an overseas call to Rutti. It did not assuage her loneliness to learn that Rutti was just clearing up after an afternoon spent with Merle and Anne, who had come to New York to present a paper.

"We talked about you," Rutti said cheerfully.

"Thanks. Thanks a lot," Nancy said. "But what I'm looking for is pity."

"Call Chana at Beit Yair. Go there for the weekend. You'll get pity and great cakes. A terrific combination," Rutti suggested. She kept her voice light, although she heard the loneliness in Nancy's voice.

Nancy did call and Chana was enthused to hear from her. She had met and liked Nancy when she and Dov had visited the kibbutz years earlier. Nancy recalled that when Chana had shown her the herb garden she cultivated, she had said softly, "This gives me my greatest pleasure. It is something that I myself have created, that I myself have accomplished."

"It must be wonderful," Nancy said, "to feel that your life has made a difference, that you have accomplished something important."

The two women exchanged occasional New Year's cards and Rutti wrote Chana about Nancy's divorce and her decision to immigrate to Israel with her daughter.

"It's strange that the Israeli-born husband chooses to remain in the United States and the American-born wife comes to Israel," Dror commented wryly.

"Come and stay with us at Beit Yair," Chana told Nancy, who accepted at once.

She found the quiet settlement, nestled amid the Judaean Hills, oddly unchanged since she and Dov had walked through the fields, Keren between them, and watched a spectacular rainbow arch its way across the cerulean sky. Dov had taught them the Hebrew word for each color of the spectrum and even now when she saw a prism, she heard his deep voice, peculiarly musical when he spoke his native language, repeating the colors. She knew Dov would always be a part of her life, invisibly trailing beside her along paths they had once walked together. It was as it should be. Mina Sieberg had, in the end, taught her to acknowledge loss, to recognize joy.

"Every death means mourning and memories," the white-haired analyst had said calmly. "Your love for Dov is dead and you have mourned it, but do not discount your memories."

Nancy said as much to a young patient only two days before. The young woman, a South African student at the Hebrew University, was suffering in the aftermath of a love affair with a fellow student who had left her and left the country.

"How will I live with this pain?" she asked Nancy, her voice anguished.

"Try to allow your memories to comfort you," Nancy advised.

She took her own advice. She walked alone through the fields and orchards of Beit Yair and summoned the comfort of her memories. She would never forget lying with Dov in the meadow thick with the overgrowth of sweet woodruff or the times they shared with their friends in New York and in Egremont. She remembered the evenings she and Dov spent with Rutti and Werner at the Thalia Theater and how they passed a single container of popcorn from hand to hand as Bette Davis and Joan Crawford drifted across the screen in chiffon gowns and bouffant hairdos. They did not, during those years of their young womanhood, bargain for death and divorce.

It occurred to her that she had never seen Werner's grave. She turned and walked to the small glen at the foot of a gentle hillside on which marjoram and rosemary grew wild. There the kibbutz children nurtured a rose garden at a slight remove from the serried graves. The mingled fragrance of herbs and flowers filled the air. White roses of Sharon were in full bloom, and Nancy plucked a flower.

Carrying the white rose, Nancy made her way to the grave and paused before the slab of polished pink Jerusalem marble onto which Werner's Hebrew name was carved. Its base was fringed with clusters of bright green parsley. Chana had told her that she scattered the seeds each spring so that the gravestones of Werner and of her son, Noah, would be bordered by the flowering herb. Throughout the summer and fall, she came to the graves and harvested sprigs of green that she used in salads and in soups.

"Perhaps you find that strange," Chana said apologetically to Nancy.

"No. I find it wonderful," Nancy replied earnestly. With Chana's action, life defeated death. In fact, she thought of writing to Merle to tell her of Chana's gesture. Perhaps Merle could plant herbs or tender leafage about the small alabaster ovoid that marked the grave of her infant daughter.

She placed the white rose on the gravestone.

"Poor Werner," she said aloud.

"He was, in so many ways, a wonderful man, a remarkable person."

She turned. It was then that she saw Ari for the first time, although she recognized him at once from the photo that stood on Chana's bureau.

"You must be Nancy, Rutti's American friend," he said. "My mother told me you were here."

"Ari." She held her hand out. She liked his name. Its simplicity implied strength and courage. She knew it meant "lion," and it struck her that he did indeed have a majestic, catlike quality. His thick, amber-colored hair was shot through with streaks of silver; he moved toward her with feline grace, encasing her hand in his own, enclosing his large fingers about hers so that she felt herself in the grip of a soft and protective paw.

"I came to visit my brother's grave," he said.

He placed a smooth pebble on Noah's headstone and his lips moved soundlessly.

"I am not a religious man," he said, turning back to her. "But when I come here, I pray. I pray that my brother did not die without reason. I pray that peace will come to our land and that my sons will not go to war."

"A good prayer," she replied. "An important prayer."

They looked at each other, their eyes locked in a stare of recognition so powerful that her heart hammered loudly. They turned then and ascended the hill, following the footpath carved between the wild carob trees and the gaunt almond saplings whose nuts glowed golden in the sunlight. The herb-threaded grass was soft beneath their feet and they spoke, as they walked, with a magical spontaneous intimacy. They marveled later that from that very first day, it seemed that there was nothing they could not say to each other, no question that would not be answered, no revelation that would not be accepted or understood.

"How many sons do you have, Ari?" Nancy asked.

"Two. Asher and Giddi. They live here on the kibbutz with Yaffa, their mother. You will meet them this afternoon. My mother has invited them to come for tea, as she always does when I visit."

"You don't live on the kibbutz then?" Nancy realized that she knew very little about Ari. Chana had told her only that he was a high-ranking officer in the reserves, that he had been a hero of the Six-Day War. "He did not have to serve," she said proudly. "If a family has lost a son and there is one surviving son, he is exempt from military service. But Ari insisted on serving and we would not stop him." Nancy looked up at the man walking beside her and knew that once he was decided on a course of action, no plea or argument would divert him.

He told her that he and Yaffa were divorced. They had grown up together on the kibbutz and had married while Yaffa was a nursing student at Hadassah Hospital and he was an undergraduate at the Hebrew University.

"We were too young," Ari told her. "We did not realize that we wanted different things from life. It was not her fault and it was not my fault. As we grew up, we grew apart. Yaffa loved life on the kibbutz. I wanted to work for the Foreign Office and live in Jerusalem. I tried it her way and I was not happy. She tried it my way and she was not happy. Finally, it seemed to each of us that we were most alone when we were together. We sat in the same room, prisoners of our own silence. Can you understand that?"

"I can understand perfectly," Nancy said.

And she in turn told him how she and Dov had met as students and how she had assumed that their marriage would be a partnership based on their love. They had each heard words that were never spoken and each had misread the other's dreams.

"We changed. And the world around us changed. My friends and I began to see our lives differently. Dov had difficulty with that. Oh, he said all the right things but he didn't believe them. And finally, it didn't matter whether he said them or whether he believed them. It was too late." Sadness tinged her words. Ari moved closer to her. He did not touch her, but his very presence comforted her.

They walked on, their shadows merging as they descended the hill. Now and again he held out his hand so that she would not miss a step and fall among the tangled roots and matted nettles.

They rested on a large rock spangled with mica and laughed as a lizard stared at them indignantly through beady black eyes, then slithered away. They had missed lunch and he picked figs and almonds. He peeled the fruit and she shelled the nuts. They ate very slowly, relishing the sun-warmed morsels they fed to each other.

She met his sons that afternoon. Asher was ten and Giddi was eight. The dark-haired boys were polite but subdued. Their eyes were the color of Ari's, dark gold — cat's eyes that glinted in the early darkness.

Nancy and Ari became lovers within weeks of that first meeting.

They anticipated each other's thoughts and words. He knew how to make Keren laugh. Nancy understood that his sons were shy with her and arranged it so that their early meetings always included a film, a trip to the zoo, or an archaeological site — anything that afforded them a neutral springboard for discussion.

"You are so wise," he said. "Do I love you for your wisdom?"

"Do you love me at all?" she teased.

"Of course. I love you and I want to marry you."

It was August and they lay side by side on her bed, blanketed by the heat and the sabbath stillness of Jerusalem. They luxuriated in the sweet calm that followed their passion. They had known each other for two months and they had known each other forever.

"I love you too," she said. "But I don't want to be married again. Not yet. Perhaps not ever."

He did not press her and she kissed him on each of his eyes in gratitude for his silence.

Their lives were frenetic. Ari's work at the Foreign Office involved conferences and meetings, frequent trips abroad to organize cultural exchange programs. Nancy had her patient load, her classes at the university, and Keren, who was increasingly self-reliant. Her Hebrew was excellent and their flat on French Hill was filled with her friends. She was active in a youth movement, her school's student council, a drama group.

"It is interesting," Nancy wrote to Rutti in one of the long letters that replaced their intense exchanges on Friday afternoons, "that Keren is now able to do what it took me so long to learn. She organizes her own life, makes her own plans, her own decisions. It never occurs to her or to her friends that anyone will say no to them, deny them the opportunity to do something they feel they should do. I think her generation of young women will have a much easier time than we did. They are collecting the dividends of our investments."

It occurred to her, as she reread her own words, that her sentiments were not uncolored by envy. It was natural, she supposed, that a pioneering generation should feel a certain subliminal envy for those who were the beneficiaries of their hardships, their innovations. "Ah, how easy this generation has it," veteran members of the kibbutz murmured as they watched children dive into the communal pool or sail down concrete paths on skateboards. It was they who had slept in tents, carted water from Jerusalem, and cleared the land of boulders. Anne wrote that the entering class of the medical school where she taught was forty percent female. *Forty percent*. She underlined the words. "They can't imagine what it was like for women when I began medical school. How many of us were there — ten — fifteen?" Reading Anne's letter, Nancy listened to Keren and her friends discuss the future and marveled at the insouciance with which her daughter's generation accepted a legacy so painfully garnered. They would do their army service and they would go to law school, medical school, travel in China, camp out in the mountains of South America. Nothing was beyond their aspiration, nothing would elude their reach.

Keren and a friend stayed alone at the flat when she accompanied Ari on a swift trip to Greece and another to Paris. They discovered that they shared a passion for small museums, that they were happiest wandering without destination through the ancient quarters of Athens and Paris, that they both delighted in hiking through the countryside and stopping to picnic on the bread, cheese, and fruit crammed into their rucksacks.

"We are perfect together," Ari said happily one afternoon in Paris. She waited, but he did not speak of marriage. Relief and disappointment commingled. When they returned to Jerusalem she invited Asher and Giddi for Shabbat dinner. For the first time they sat about the table as a family, she and Keren, Ari and his sons.

"Are you going to marry Ari?" Keren asked her the next day.

"No. I don't know. Do you think I should?"

The conversation both troubled and amused her. She and her daughter had graduated into friendship.

"I think marriage is stupid," Keren replied. "Why can't people just live together without ceremonies or licenses if they love each other? Then it's easier to split when it's over." Keren tossed her long dark hair and walked barefoot through the flat. How beautiful she is, Nancy thought, and marveled at her daughter's adolescent arrogance, at her youthful certainty.

She wrote her friends about Ari; she wished that they could know him and could speak of him as they had all spoken so lazily, so indulgently, about David Lorenzo and Charles Bingham, about Dov and Andrew and Werner — women who trusted each other, evaluating their men.

"Ari and I love each other," she wrote to Anne. "We're wonderfully comfortable with each other. Will it sound odd if I say that I feel as close to Ari as I do to you — that I feel I can tell him anything? No, I don't think it's odd. Ideally, the perfect lover should also be the perfect best friend — a man who is not afraid of intimacy and honesty, of emotional revelation and just plain silliness. And Ari is like that. Still, I'm not sure I want to marry again. What would marriage offer me at this point? I don't think I want another child. I love my independence. I love owning my own life and not having to discuss my decisions. What to do? I would like to do nothing and Ari has not issued any ultimatums. He is not the sort of man who would do that."

Anne's letters overflowed with news of her own life and work. She had published a scientific paper that brought her significant recognition and a promotion. She had bought a small house and discovered that she loved to cook and entertain. She had also become active in a political awareness group. "This business with Nixon and Watergate blew my naive scientific mind," she wrote. Men had drifted in and out of her life but there had been no one special for a long time. Which was a pity, she added without self-consciousness, because her biological clock was running and she definitely wanted to have a child. Rutti and David were wondrously happy with their twins. There had been a reunion of sorts at Egremont when Anne came east to deliver a paper. Merle seemed pensive and removed. And Andrew was strangely reticent. "Almost as though he's constantly afraid of saying the wrong thing. He walks on eggshells. Egremont is still beautiful but there is definitely trouble in Paradise." It was at the end of that letter that Anne referred to Nancy's hesitation about Ari. "Nancy, it may be presumptuous for a never married lady doctor to give advice to a divorced psychoanalyst, but here goes. I think you must remember that not all marriages are alike. Ari is not Dov and this decade has made a difference in attitudes and expectations. Most important, it sounds as though he loves you madly — loves you perhaps more than you love him — and I think this is an essential ingredient for a happy marriage from the point of view of women like ourselves. It came to me in the darkness of a particularly long night (I seem to endure a lot of particularly long nights) that if Charles had loved me more, he never would have allowed me to walk out that day. And your Ari sounds to me like a man who will never, ever let you walk out. I imagine him to be something like David — a man strong enough himself to be able to love a woman who claims her own life."

Although Nancy occasionally shared her friends' letters with Ari, she carefully placed this letter from Anne in the bottom drawer of her desk, among papers she had cause to refer to more than once.

It was decided that Nancy and Keren would spend the Rosh Hashanah holiday at Beit Yair and that Ari would come to Jerusalem for Yom Kippur. The kibbutz celebration of the Jewish New Year was relaxed and festive. Apples plucked from the orchards formed rosy pyramids on a table spread with white cloth. Small dishes of golden honey gathered from the communal apiary were placed beside each plate. Nancy met Yaffa, Ari's ex-wife, and the tall Australian she had recently married. She was surprised at how relaxed she was with Yaffa whereas she still felt awkward with Lisa, Dov's wife.

"Perhaps it's because relationships on a kibbutz are so much more natural," Nancy told Ari. "Maybe, because there's a natural equality between men and women, women feel less threatened, more at ease with each other."

Ari laughed.

"My mother and Yaffa would both disagree with you. Women have to fight very hard for recognition on the kibbutz. There's a tendency to assign them the conventional so-called women's jobs — the laundry, the kitchen, the children's house. There is a mythology about Israeli women — you know, they work beside the men in the fields, they serve with them in the army. But women do not go into combat. The so-called equality is illusory."

Nancy sighed and then laughed.

"Shot down again," she said. "I'll just have to organize a consciousness-raising group in Jerusalem."

"Let me raise your consciousness," he said, pulling her to him. "In honor of the New Year."

"In honor of the New Year," she repeated and watched as he drew the curtains, leaving enough of an opening so that later, when he lay beside her, she saw a crescent of stars, luminescent against the darkness of the sky.

"I love you," he murmured.

"And I love you," she replied. She watched the stars glint and glitter and then vanish behind a smoky gray cloud.

"Enough? Do you love me enough?" he asked drowsily and slept before she could answer his question.

On Yom Kippur they went together to a small synagogue near French Hill. Ari had been given the honor of reading the first prayer during the Torah service. Nancy watched as he kissed the fringes of his prayer shawl, held them to the Torah, and sang the blessing.

My lion, she thought.

His mane of golden hair, shot through with silver, was thick and radiant in the sunlight that poured through the narrow, arched windows. His voice, as he chanted the prayer, was a proud and muted roar of faith, of continuity. Head bent, he followed the reading of the scripture so intently that he seemed unaware of the man who tapped him on the shoulder, then whispered into his ear. There was no pause in the reading. Ari waited until the passage was completed and again he pressed the fringes of his prayer shawl to the unfurled scroll, sang the closing benediction, and walked briskly to Nancy's pew as he removed his prayer shawl. Other men in the synagogue also folded their prayer shawls and placed them in small velvet bags. Ari handed his to Nancy, briefly pressing the fringes to her cheek. It seemed to her that the satin tendrils were electric with faith and love.

"What's happening, Ari?" she asked.

"I've been called up. Israel is at war, Nancy." His voice was steady, his touch upon her arm gentle, comforting. He would comfort her against the danger that he faced. "Do you love me, Nancy?"

"Enough and more than enough."

Like the other women in that synagogue, she stood and walked beside him to the door. She remained for a moment in the warmth of his embrace, felt his lips light and tender against her own. And then she watched as he joined the parade of men, the worshipers who became soldiers, who marched down the streets of Jerusalem on the day of judgment. Only a few looked back at the women and children who stood in the doorway of the synagogue. The women returned to the service, which remained uninterrupted throughout the day, as more and more men left, until only the voices of women, children, and the elderly filled the small sanctuary.

"Our God is a God of judgment, merciful and forgiving," they sang, and Nancy prayed that His judgment of Ari would be tempered with mercy.

"He is a God of compassion." She repeated the chant. *Be compassionate to Ari,* she prayed, clutching Keren's hand; she was weak because she was fasting and because fear and regret weighted her, debilitated her.

She did not leave the synagogue until the sky darkened and the voice of the cantor intoned the Havdala, the prayer of thankfulness to God for separating the holy from the profane and for creating peace in the firmament. She thought of the crescent of stars she had watched the night Ari asked her if she loved him — *if she loved him enough.* She had withheld her answer then, the answer that was so clear to her now. She would marry him. Of course she would marry him. She loved him enough and he was strong enough; they were both strong enough.

"Oh, God," she prayed. "Bring him back to me so that he may hear what I have to say."

He was in the north. She learned that the next day from Chana, who spoke in the lowered voice, the monotonic cadence, of a mother who has already buried one son and now feared for the life of another.

"How do you know?" Nancy asked.

"I know his unit and I know where they are fighting," Chana replied cryptically. "Come to Beit Yair."

"I can't," Nancy said.

Her patients needed her. Young women whose husbands and lovers had gone to war. The fear of abandonment was in their voices, the fear of death choked off the words they could not utter. A middle-aged man who could not control the recurrent nightmare that had haunted him since his boyhood in Bergen-Belsen scheduled an emergency appointment. In recurrent dreams, he chased the shadows of his parents who had vanished from his life during his internment. Now he was afraid to sleep because his son and his son-in-law had been called up and he feared that he would pursue their shadows as well.

"Help me, Dr. Yallon," he pleaded.

Nancy increased her appointment load, conferred with colleagues. She volunteered to join a team of psychologists who went from school to school to speak with children about the anxieties the war provoked.

"What do you fear more than anything in the world?" she asked

275

the children and listened intently as they spoke of their fears that their fathers and brothers might be killed, that their homes might be destroyed, that they themselves, one day, might have to kill or be killed.

She herself feared that Ari would be killed, that he would not return from the north.

"I love you enough," she shouted fiercely into the darkness of the night. She was grateful that Keren was not at home, but working with her high school class at the post office. The life of the country was sustained by the women and children and those men who were either too old or too ill to fight. Like the other women, Nancy carried garbage to a communal dumping ground and ferried children to school, the elderly to appointments with doctors and dentists. She prepared a meal for the pretty young bride who lived in a neighboring flat and who had already been told that her husband had been killed on the Golan.

She listened to the news, to the ominous reports of fighting in the north. The Syrians attacked with might, using tanks and artillery. The Israelis were using old Super Shermans against Soviet T62s. Losses on both sides were heavy. Golda Meir's voice was grainy with grief. Her maternal visage did not reassure the nation. They did not want a mother. They wanted a leader. They did not reject her because she was a woman. They rejected her because she had not prepared for this war, had not protected them from it.

Nancy jumped when the phone rang. Twice she was awakened by calls from the States. Merle called and then Rutti.

"Are you all right?" Their voices trembled with compassion and concern. Nancy held the phone tightly and reassured them. She was fine. There was no fighting in Jerusalem. And Keren? Keren was caught up in the excitement, the drama. For her the war was an adventure.

"But Ari is in the north. Somewhere in the north," she told Rutti in the tight, controlled tone in which the women of Israel spoke of their soldiers.

"He will be all right, Nancy," Rutti said.

On the third day of the war an officer appeared at Beit Yair. He was directed to Chana and Dror's bungalow. Both of them welcomed him but only Dror watched him leave. Minutes later Yaffa arrived with Giddi and Asher. It was Yaffa who drove to Jerusalem to tell Nancy that Ari was missing in action.

Nancy did not weep. She asked about Chana and the boys. She brewed a pot of tea and filled two cups. They each took a few sips.

"He will be all right," Yaffa said. "I feel it in my heart."

"I hope so."

The phone rang. Both women lurched toward it. It was Dov, calling from New York. He wanted to speak to Keren, who was not at home.

"Make sure she stays in Jerusalem," he said. "Just make sure of that."

She hated him at that moment for the insouciant authority in his voice, for the guilt he imposed when he should have offered concern.

"Go to hell, Dov," she said and hung up.

Her tears came afterward; she did not know how she survived the days that followed. She adhered to her work schedule, her communal obligations. She and Keren drove to Beit Yair to see Chana and Dror. Together they listened to Golda Meir offer to negotiate a cease-fire with the Arabs. They heard Henry Kissinger promise Israel speedy delivery of arms. They applauded when Mount Hermon was re-claimed. Chana was pale, her face drawn, but like Nancy, she continued to work. They were women who refused to be subverted by grief and fear.

Keren's friends came and went at all hours of the day and night. Nancy opened the door to boys and girls carrying grease-stained bags of falafel and pizza. She answered the hesitant knocks of her neighbors who wanted to use the phone, to borrow a cup of sugar, cooking oil, an egg. It seemed odd to her that people continued to do their laundry and bake their cakes. Colleagues and friends came with books and records that might distract her. She grew irritated at their attention. The kindness of others did not negate the cruelty of her own premonitions. She was annoyed when the doorbell rang late in the evening as she was drifting into a hard-won sleep. Barefoot, in her white terry cloth robe, she opened the door, and her heart stopped.

Ari stood before her, his golden eyes glinting in the darkness. He took her face into his hands and kissed her gently on the lips. She collapsed into his arms and wept as he led her to the sofa, as he told her how his unit had been isolated from their division on the Golan, how they had lost radio contact and so were assumed missing. He ran his fingers through her hair and told her how they had moved through the mountain passes stealthily in the dead of night, inflicting what damage they could, eating wild grass and herbs.

"But you are alive," she said wonderingly. She touched his mane of amber hair, kissed the sinewy muscle of his arms, bit at his earlobes.

"I knew you were waiting," he said and then, preposterously, he fell asleep right there on the couch.

A month later they were married at Beit Yair and the week they celebrated their first anniversary, Seth was born.

Seth was two and a half years old now. They had moved into this house in Yemin Moshe on his first birthday and Ari himself had built the terrace where Nancy now sat, her lap littered with the photographs that Anne had sent. It frightened Nancy to think of the happiness that at last was hers. Her fear, she knew, was born of superstition. It was Dov's mother who had told her that she never counted her grandchildren. If asked how many she had, she replied, "Not ten, not eleven, not twelve," but would not give the exact number. "It would tempt the evil eye," she claimed.

Nancy did not argue with her. She herself hesitated to tabulate the sources of her joy; she would not tally the fulfillment of her work, Ari's love, the health and happiness of her children, the beautiful home in which their family lived in such contentment. There was peril in keeping such close watch on fortune's ledger. It occurred to her that only women handled good fortune with such vigilant circumspection. Perhaps it was because women were so familiar with loss, with the vagaries of their own bodies — or because they had so long perceived themselves to be vulnerable, at the mercy of men and of the fates. Now at last they were liberated. They claimed education and careers and fought for their right to control their own bodies, yet their mothers' fears and superstitions lingered and would not be dispelled. They did not count their children; they did not codify their joys.

The idea intrigued and perplexed her. She thought of how she and her friends might discuss and develop it during their traditional Friday afternoon meetings — how Anne and Rutti and Merle would argue it, each in turn, and how in the end they would abandon the intense discussion in favor of a giggling nonsense game or Rutti's ingenious mimicry.

Nancy acknowledged that she missed her friends intensely as she unfolded Anne's letter; she was pleased that there were three closely written pages. She read the letter slowly. There was the usual re-counting of news. Anne had traveled to New York in July to see the tall ships sail up the Hudson River in celebration of the bicentennial. Andrew, of course, was on the regatta committee and there was a wonderful party at his corporate offices, which overlooked the river. Merle looked fabulous but ethereal. There was talk of a bicentennial parade of women, but it had been difficult to generate any excitement over organizing one. "I thought that strange when I remembered how we marched in such strength only six years ago," Anne wrote, "but then the young women on my staff consider the battle won. *Roe v. Wade* is in place. Women are flocking to law schools and med schools. They really think we can have it all. I wish they were right."

"I wish they were right, too," Nancy said aloud.

She had listened to Keren and Sarah the previous evening as they discussed their futures. Keren planned to serve in the Israeli army and then to travel for a year or two. She spoke of China and India, of Nepal and Afghanistan. Like so many young Israelis, oppressed by the smallness of their country, the hostility of their neighbors, she longed to break free, to travel across mysterious continents, to climb mountains. She might study abroad or she might study at the Hebrew University. She wrote short stories that her teachers said showed talent.

Sarah wanted to be an actress and a singer. Her voice had a bell-like quality, a tender sweetness that some said was reminiscent of Piaf. She wanted to study with an accomplished teacher and perform at small clubs. She had heard that many singers got their start that way. She seemed wistful.

Nancy smiled, remembering how Rutti would not let Sarah out of her sight, how she took her everywhere. Yet the cosseted child had become a daring, adventurous young woman, struggling against an elusive sadness. Despite her mother. Or perhaps because of her. She marveled that neither Keren nor Sarah saw any barrier to success, any obstacle to ambition.

"Don't either of you want to marry or have children?" she asked casually.

"Maybe. After I've done everything I want to do," Keren said.

279

"Sure, I'll get married. When my career is set," Sarah replied.

"You can't have it all," Nancy warned.

Keren and Sarah looked at each other and giggled.

"But you do," Keren said. "And so does Rutti. Maybe we'll get lucky on our second go-arounds."

Their laughter was conspiratorial, their words edged with cruelty. They were their mothers' daughters. They had lain awake through nocturnal quarrels; they had listened to tense exchanges at breakfast that led to tears in the mid-afternoon. They had been rushed from after-school activities to baby-sitters and had eaten too many pizza dinners to consider pizza a treat. They knew themselves to be bereft. Werner was dead. Dov had a new wife. Their mothers had new husbands. They did not blame Nancy and Rutti, but they did not exonerate them either. They loved their mothers and admired them, but that love and admiration melded with anger.

"I don't have it all," Nancy retorted sharply. "No one has it all."

Keren did not understand the conflict that assailed her mother each day as she juggled hours and appointments. She could reschedule a patient who had an appointment the hour of Keren's piano recital, but she could not have known that Seth would take his first step the day she gave a paper at the Tel Aviv Psychoanalytic Institute. Everything was a trade-off as Keren, Sarah, and the young women on Anne's staff would discover for themselves. As a colleague had said with wry humor only the week before when rushing from a meeting with her child's teacher to a professional conference, "We thought women were achieving liberation. We didn't know we were just opting for a new form of indenture."

Nancy turned to the last page of the letter. Anne had saved the best for last. She was pregnant and delighted about it. The baby would be born in January. "I hope your Ari will not frown at the idea of your friend being an unwed mother," Anne wrote. "Ain't we lucky to live in an age when we use the term 'single parent'? Sounds so much more civilized. And aren't I lucky to be able to do this all on my own! I hope you're as pleased for me as Rutti and Merle are. Merle actually offered to come to Minnesota for a while when the baby is born. Now, I call taking midnight feedings an act of friendship!"

Although Nancy seldom answered letters immediately, she wrote to Anne that night. She recognized the plea for acceptance concealed in Anne's sarcastic bravado. She wondered who the father was. Anne had mentioned, in a previous letter, running into Charles Bingham at a medical conference. That would be truly ironic, Nancy thought. Keren and Sarah accepted the news with equanimity.

"So Anne is pregnant," Keren said. "Good for her. What's the big deal?"

"I wonder who the father is," Sarah mused. "I mean, the kid will want to know that one day. It might get to be a hassle to go through life saying, 'Mirror, mirror, on the wall — who's my papa once and for all?' " The girls collapsed with laughter, and Nancy, in spite of herself, laughed too.

She told Ari about Anne's pregnancy that night. The stories of her friends always intrigued him. He knew Rutti, of course, but Anne and Merle remained exotic and mysterious personalities.

"What do you think about her getting pregnant?" Nancy asked.

"It will be a high-risk pregnancy," he said cautiously. "Given her age."

"She'll have amnio. The way I did with Seth. The way I will again this time."

In this way she told him that she herself was pregnant again. She smiled at his roar of pleasure, surrendered to the crush of his ecstatic embrace. Still, she would not leave the question unanswered and when she pressed him yet again, he said thoughtfully, "Anne must be a courageous woman. But that will not be enough. Her child, too, will have to be brave."

"I suppose."

She would consider his answer later. For now, they sorted through the mail that she had so efficiently organized and decided that they would, of course, attend Emanuel Klein's recital.

19

EMANUEL KLEIN was overjoyed to be in Jerusalem once again. He had last visited the city in 1936 when Arturo Toscanini had conducted the Palestine Orchestra in the amphitheater of the Hebrew University at Mount Scopus. The members of the orchestra, most of them refugees from the land of Bach and Beethoven, had played beneath the stars, their eyes riveted to the dynamic conductor who dressed all in black.

"Music gave lie to the hatred that was Nazism," Emanuel Klein said when he spoke of that night, of those years.

It was music that had sustained him through his own ordeal of survival, as he wandered from continent to continent, settling at last in New York. There, for almost four decades, he found solace in his work, the rhythm of his days vigilantly protected by his wife who screened his calls, ordered his calendar, carried his meals to his studio at precisely the right hour. Of all the young musicians whose careers he guided through the years, Merle Cunningham was his favorite. He had not been surprised when she won the competition with *A Child's Prayer* all those years ago nor was he surprised that her more recent work revealed a depth of feeling, a new maturity. After the death of her infant daughter she wrote "Eve's Dream," an étude for strings, which a leading critic called "a musical polemic that expresses the ambivalence that haunts the modern woman — the yearning to nurture, the yearning to achieve." It was the melding of instruments that impressed Emanuel Klein. Poignantly and ardently, the cello argued with the violin and then both instruments were silenced by the surprising and tender plea of the harpsichord.

Merle was a disciplined musician, seldom missing a lesson, never failing to practice. Although he asked her to join his chamber music group several times through the years, she accepted his invitation only after her daughter's death. Before, her excuses were valid. She could not commit herself to a heavy rehearsal schedule or to the travel that membership in a performing group required. Her husband needed her. Her son needed her. Emanuel Klein had no difficulty accepting her reasons. As a musician he sympathized with Merle, but as a man he sympathized with Andrew, who had made quiet contributions to recitals and production costs through the years.

The death of Merle's infant daughter altered that pattern. She intensified her schedule at Juilliard. She rented her own studio and joined the chamber music orchestra. Greg was away at school, she explained. She did not have to be available to him. And Andrew, of course, was so busy. He had invented an essential component for videocassette recordings and used the profits from the sale of that patent to expand his real estate holdings. His photograph appeared with increasing frequency in business and financial publications. He traveled more than ever before, and as always he phoned home at regular intervals.

"Where is Merle?" he would ask Lottie, and if Lottie did not know he occasionally called Emanuel Klein. It was not that he wanted to speak to Merle; he wanted only to know where she was and that she was safe. There was a tacit understanding between the men that Emanuel Klein would serve as a silent accomplice to Andrew's admittedly obsessive surveillance.

Her teacher noted that Merle had acquired a new strength since Kate's death. Determinedly, she forged a new independence. Even her voice was no longer deferential, but clear and forceful. She no longer claimed that she had to discuss each decision with Andrew. Two years ago she declined to accompany the chamber music orchestra on a tour of eastern Europe.

"No," she said. "Not now. I am not ready."

"But perhaps you will discuss it with Andrew."

"I make my own decisions."

When he asked her to accompany him to Israel, she accepted without hesitation. "Yes. I would love to come." She was pleased to have been asked, pleased to accept. He had not suggested that she consult her husband.

On the plane, he asked her if she had written to her friend, Nancy, of her arrival.

"No, I want to surprise her."

That, too, was a new attitude. Merle had always favored the predictable, always opted for the conventional.

Merle spent her first afternoon in Jerusalem wandering through the city. She recognized at once that Nancy and Rutti had not exaggerated when they spoke of its beauty, of the palpable sense of history inspired by its landscape and its buildings, its encircling hills. She was fascinated by the convergence of East and West. Arabs in djellabas and kaffiyehs walked through the streets along with Israelis in shorts and open-necked shirts. She went to east Jerusalem and saw veiled Arab women in long, black, embroidered gowns standing beside Israeli women in sundresses and sandals. On one street corner, an Arab girl in a school uniform chatted easily with an Israeli woman soldier. The Israeli removed a book from her knapsack and they stood together in the hot Jerusalem sunlight and studied a text. They were probably classmates, Merle thought, and she considered how simple it would be if all past history could be negated and a new generation could begin life unhampered by ancient hatreds. She smiled at her own naïveté. The sixties were over. Bombs exploded at airports and in marketplaces. No one sang "We Shall Overcome" anymore. The Carter White House did not pretend to be Camelot. Still, against all odds, her own optimism lingered. Still, she felt the stirring of faith and hope when she played *A Child's Prayer*.

She paused at a stall and admired a display of chess sets in enameled boxes, each chess piece delicately carved. "The very best chess sets in Jerusalem — no — in all of the Middle East," the gold-toothed merchant assured her. "Each piece hand carved, hand polished."

She smiled and fingered the different pieces he offered for her inspection. A proud horse. A bishop who wore the mitre of the Greek Orthodox church, a veiled queen. "How much?" she asked. She had been told that she should bargain but when he quoted twenty American dollars, she found she did not want to bicker with him. The price was reasonable enough.

She would give the set to Andrew. He and Greg often played chess when Greg was home from Dartmouth and could spare the time. Her son was an athlete, a star basketball player and so handsome that her own heart often stopped when she saw him. The aggressiveness that frightened her when he was a boy had translated itself into a breezy self-confidence. He was a player who ran across the court to slam a ball away from an opponent in the midst of a dribble, a player who was always prepared to try for a basket from an improbable angle. And like many men suffused with their own confidence, he was not afraid to display a gentler side. He inherited a love of music and played piano in the Dartmouth orchestra. Girls phoned him in New York and at Egremont. They had tickets for a show or a concert, they had the use of a beach house for a weekend. Or they just wanted to hang out with him. *How about it, Greg?*

Merle remembered how the young women of her generation had hesitated to call a man. They invented excuses. *Did you find my gloves in your car? Gee, could I borrow that book you mentioned?* Her son's friends were forthright and direct. She admired them, and listened to her son accept or decline, invariably with gentleness and grace. He was at ease with girls and she wondered if that was because of his own friendship with Keren and Sarah.

She asked him about it once.

"Yeah. Maybe." He shrugged. The question did not interest him. He wrote to Keren occasionally, and when he and Sarah were both at Egremont, they were often together.

Sarah and Keren were both in Jerusalem now; Merle regretted that Greg had not joined her. The young people would have had an exciting reunion. She had suggested it to Andrew, but he reminded her that Greg and Eric had long-standing plans to spend the summer backpacking through the Northwest.

"Of course, I could probably get away and join you," he added, without looking up from the spreadsheets that covered his desk. She did not reply and Andrew did not mention it again. Like a cautious chess player, her husband made his moves with great deliberation, aware that the slightest error might result in a perilous endgame.

Andrew would love the chess set, she thought, as she counted out the dollar bills and watched the merchant wrap the box in a cocoon of Hebrew, Arabic, and English-language newspapers.

She wandered on through the market, pausing to touch the colorful fabric of the Druze weavers, to finger long strands of olive-wood beads, delicate mother-of-pearl pins. She had always traveled with Andrew and paced herself to accommodate him. Now she relished the leisurely freedom of the solitary traveler. She bought a glass of freshly squeezed grapefruit juice from a street vendor, a bag of shelled almonds from a barefoot boy. In the past, she had relied on Andrew to negotiate the logistics of travel, to manage their passports and tickets, their traveler's checks and reservations as he had managed all the practical aspects of their lives. Now she discovered that everything she had thought so complicated was in fact quite simple. She could easily handle her own affairs, read maps, convert currency. She had marveled at Anne's ability to make her way through airports, at Rutti's courage in traveling alone to Israel and Europe, at Nancy's daring to begin a new life in a new land. She saw now that she was capable of doing the same. Confidence replaced her initial trepidation.

That confidence energized her as she walked through the spice market to the end of David Street, pausing in front of a shop that sold ancient instruments. A large harp dominated the window, surrounded by Miriam drums and delicately crafted recorders. She toyed with a pair of olive-wood castanets and listened to the clear, sweet notes of a reed pipe from within the shop. She recognized the music as Milhaud's adaptation of the "Song of Songs." Emanuel Klein had thought of including it in his Jerusalem repertoire, and the orchestra had practiced it briefly before he abandoned the idea. The musician who played it now had mastered the melody and she herself kept rhythm with the castanets.

"Come with me from Lebanon," the pipe implored, "Come with me, my bride."

She decided to buy the castanets. They would remind her of this moment, of the sweetness of the piper's music, of the long shadows that carpeted David Street. She entered the shop. The proprietor rushed forward and the musician, his song concluded, turned to face her.

"Dennis," she said, and he grinned and bowed.

She clapped softly.

"I should have known," she said.

Dennis Montgomery had joined their ensemble only a few months earlier, although Merle had known him for several years. He had come to Juilliard in 1970. She remembered the first time she had seen him was when she returned from Rutti and David's wedding. Lean, in a faded Berkeley sweatshirt, he wore his long blond hair flowing about his shoulders; a soft fair beard covered his sharply jutting chin. It was said that he had lived for a time in Haight-Ashbury and then in a commune in the Northwest, where he had met the beautiful pianist with whom he shared an apartment on 117th Street. Merle had often seen him in the supermarket as he made his way down the aisle, his lover's child riding in the shopping cart. Once, while shopping, he had called to her across the produce counter. "Hey, Merle, I heard your Debussy this afternoon. Great. Really great."

She was grateful for his praise. She marveled at how easily he managed the child, the shopping, and his own flute case, which always weighted his canvas shoulder bag. She envied the pianist whose name, she had learned, was Andrea. She envied all the young women whose husbands and lovers walked so competently down the aisles of supermarkets, sat so patiently in front of whirring washing machines in Laundromats, played so easily with toddlers. Lucky Andrea, she had thought, and was surprised to learn some months later that Andrea had left for Denver.

"A good opportunity for her," Merle's informant, an oboist who lived with a choreographer, said. "Tenure track at the Southwest Academy of Music."

"It must have been," Merle responded dryly. Were relationships so easily dissolved because a good opportunity presented itself? she wondered. She mentioned it at the consciousness-raising group she attended occasionally.

"It depends on the relationship," Grace ventured. "And on their priorities, the guy's and the girl's. Sure, there are women who will prioritize career. Why the hell not?" Grace herself prioritized career. Her father had deserted her mother, leaving the family in abject poverty. "A woman's got to know how to earn her bread," Grace had said more than once.

Rutti was more analytic.

"I think women now may be reacting to the past. A sort of

antithesis stage, as Werner would have said. Almost Hegelian. We've had thesis and antithesis. I suppose we'll have to wait until women are more comfortable with their gains to arrive at synthesis."

Dennis and Andrea, then, were a casualty of the transition period. Dennis himself seemed to recover with a mercurial resilience. Within a few weeks of Andrea's departure, he cut his hair, shaved his beard, and joined Emanuel Klein's ensemble.

It was generally acknowledged he was an organizer and a catalyst. It was Dennis who had bought the right guidebooks and histories of Israel, which he then shared with the group. He even mastered key Hebrew phrases. His energy matched his enthusiasm; he plunged into new experiences with all the ardor of the dedicated initiate. Merle imagined that during his Haight-Ashbury period, when he had served as a cook in the Diggers' kitchen, he had mastered nutrition tips and recipes; and while a part of the Oregon commune, he had probably learned the rudiments of agronomy.

He stood beside her as she paid for the castanets. He did not purchase the shepherd's pipe he had played so effortlessly.

"There's another instrument store near the Damascus Gate," he said. "I want to see what they have."

"How do you know about it?" she asked.

"I asked around," he replied easily. "There's supposed to be a great café in the Straw Market. Let me see how we get there." He pulled out his guidebook and studied the street map. "OK. I've got it," he said, and she followed him through the narrow streets to a tiny café threaded between a shop that sold huge woven baskets and another shop that displayed low tables and stools fashioned of golden reeds.

The café was dim and cool, fragrant with the scent of coffee and the sweetness of newly baked cakes. They sat opposite each other at a triangular table and Merle realized that she was famished.

"You know, I forgot to eat lunch," she confessed.

"OK if I order for both of us?" Dennis asked. "I've got the food here psyched out, I think." He was neither protecting her nor preempting her. She was certain that in a restaurant that was more familiar to her, he would defer to her judgment.

She nodded and he ordered a platter of hummus and another of cucumber and tomato salad with a yogurt dressing. As they ate, he recounted his adventures in Jerusalem. Within a relatively short time, he had hovered at the edge of the City of David dig, discovered the orthodox convent of Saint Mark tucked away in a narrow lane on the outskirts of the Christian quarter, and examined, in two different instrument shops, shepherd's pipes of the kind he was determined to buy.

"How did you manage it all?" she asked.

"I'm a quick study," he replied. "I always have been. Maybe it's because I never had anyone to teach me the things I wanted to know."

He told her he had grown up in a small midwestern town at a remove from any center of culture. "It wasn't so bad that we were far away from cities with museums and theaters and concert halls," he said. "But it never occurred to my family that they were missing something important. My dad owned a hardware store. It was a good business and it gave our family a good life. Hey, I don't put that life down. Hard work during the day, ease in the evening — a couple of hours of television, maybe turn the pages of a book sent by a book club. Movies on the weekends. Sports in season. We were about as middle as Middle America gets. My sisters both had big church weddings. My brothers-in-law are named Clem and Mike. When I found a book of Norman Rockwell drawings in the library, I wondered how it was he didn't get to our house to do a couple of covers."

"And then there was you," Merle said.

"Yeah. Then there was me. Me and my music. Me and my books. My dad started me on sax lessons because he wanted me to play in the marching band. But the sax teacher had a flute and when I heard it for the first time I never wanted to put it down again. I was seven years old and I felt my soul turn."

He did not have to explain to her what he meant. She remembered, still, standing in her violin teacher's living room in Michigan and listening to the music that would change her life forever. How old had she been? Seven or eight perhaps, her red hair in braids and tied with pale blue ribbons. She remembered that very clearly. The ribbons the color of the sky and her heart turning.

"And I went to the library," he continued. "And I read and I read and I read. I read myself right out of Otisville, Ohio. Hey, I was in Paris with Jean Valjean and I went searching for the battlefield with Stendhal's boy in *Charterhouse of Parma*. War. I thought about war all the time. War and murder. Vietnam was just beginning and the guys in my graduating class were talking army, air force. Hey, I thought. Not to worry. We've got a breezy, with-it President. JFK will settle this and we'll all join the Peace Corps instead of the army. And then JFK was murdered."

"Where were you?" Merle asked. When would people stop asking each other where they were when Kennedy was shot? she wondered. And why did they ask? Why had she asked?

"I was in study hall. Filling out my application to the University of California at Berkeley. I was reading the essay choice and I had just settled on 'Write two hundred words about an event that changed your life' when some kid ran in and yelled, 'The President's been shot.' I wrote the essay three days later while we were watching the funeral on television. I remember how I began: 'The day John Kennedy was shot my life and the life of my generation was changed forever.' I don't know if I believed it but I wrote it. Where were you?"

"In a park on New York's West Side. Watching my son play in the sandbox. I was sitting with three women. I didn't know their names that day but now we're best friends. One of them, Nancy, lives here in Jerusalem. She doesn't even know I'm here."

In those few words she had established both the commonality and the distance between them. Like Dennis, she had been influenced by the death of the young President; his death had altered the course of her life. On that fateful November day when he had been a boy, not yet graduated from high school, she was already a wife and mother. She was perhaps ten years his senior. The decade between them was a vast divide.

"But you did go to Berkeley?"

"I went to Berkeley. My mother cried. California was another country, she said, and she was right. My father shook my hand and told me to study hard and stay away from weirdo radicals. I did study hard but it was hard to stay away from the radicals because they were only as weird as I was. They thought the way I did. They didn't want the war and they didn't want to fight it. Neither did I. But it turned out I didn't have to worry about that. I had a slight heart murmur and before I could become a draft resister I was 4F. I got caught up in the whole civil rights thing. Martin Luther King, Jr., came to Berkeley and I played in the orchestra at the concert that opened for him when he spoke. And then he was killed, too. I heard about it when I was sitting on the steps of Sproul Hall, making a poster. I was holding a magenta psychedelic-type Magic Marker and when I heard the news I began jabbing at the oaktag with it. I ended up with this big white sheet covered with what looked like magenta teardrops. Where were you?"

"My husband and I were in the emergency room at Saint Luke's Hospital," she said. "Greg, our son, had hurt his wrist that afternoon but he didn't complain about it till that night, and we couldn't get hold of a doctor. The television set was on in the waiting room and they interrupted the program to announce that King had been shot. I don't know if you've ever been in an emergency waiting room in a Manhattan hospital but the din is terrific. Within seconds that room was absolutely silent, still as death. I remember that there were two babies there, a white baby and a black baby and they had been fussing on their mothers' laps, but the quiet must have scared them because suddenly they stopped and stared at each other, stared at all of us. And then an old white woman who had her arm in a sling began to cry very quietly and we all began to cry. And those two babies began to bawl."

She did not tell him how she and Andrew had arrived home after Greg's wrist was examined to find Lottie, Rutti, and Sarah sitting in the dark huddled over a memorial candle that Rutti had brought with her. Rutti had called when she heard the news and Lottie had wept into the phone. "I'm alone and he's dead," she had cried. Rutti had dressed Sarah, thrust the candle into her bag, and hurried downtown to be with Lottie. That was Rutti. How strange, Merle thought, that eight years later she should remember the details of that night so clearly.

"I guess you could say King's death radicalized me," Dennis continued. "I gave up my plans to do graduate work — I had a fellowship at Juilliard and I just blew it off. I got into the Haight-Ashbury scene. Some pot but by some miracle no hard stuff. I think that was because of my music. I was always frightened of doing anything that would jeopardize that. I took off for a commune in Oregon and I met Andrea there. She had just split with her husband and she had this kid and she was getting her head together. She's a great pianist."

Merle nodded. "I heard her play. She's very good."

"Anyway, the commune began to go sour. People kind of forgot why it was they had come there. The rules were breaking down and you never knew who would be around when you woke up in the morning. And then one winter day it was so damn cold that the water in the toilet froze into solid ice. Andrea had to wear gloves to practice. Andrea looked at me and said, 'Hey Dennis, the sixties are over. Let's get our act together and take it on the road.' I was ready. I wrote to Juilliard and they offered me my fellowship back. She worked out a deal with the Mannes School. So we hit New York together — together but without any strings. No commitment."

"And then she went back west," Merle said. "With her child."

"With Chris. He's a great kid. Yeah. She left. She had a good offer. Her life was back on track. I was glad for her." Dennis drained his espresso cup and the mustachioed Arab proprietor hurried over with a copper *feenjan* and refilled it.

"But sad for you."

"For a while. But New York was where I had to be. I couldn't do the work I'm doing there anywhere else. And I had this offer to play with the ensemble. If I had followed Andrea, I wouldn't be sitting here with you telling you my life story and wanting to hear yours." He grinned. His smile was a confession and an invitation.

She looked up at the ceiling fan that whirled about their table. The moving blades hypnotized her. For the moment she forgot that she was the mother of a college-aged youngster, the wife of a distinguished financier. She knew only that she sat opposite an attractive and interesting young man in a small café in a city far from home. She knew that when she rose from her chair and left this café, she would go to the tiny stall on David Street that she had passed earlier and buy the unguents she had seen on display — a cream of balsam and myrrh for her skin, kohl to outline her eyes, a shampoo of henna to turn her long hair the color of firelight. And she knew too that Dennis Montgomery would come with her and hold her woven bag as she studied her face in the smoky mirror and made her selections.

"My life story is very boring," she said. "I grew up in a small Michigan town. I came to New York to study with Emanuel Klein.

I married and had a son and now I am in Jerusalem and I want to buy some kohl for my eyes and some henna for my hair."

"All right. I know just the place," he said.

"And so do I," she replied, and they both laughed as though they had just shared a wondrously funny secret joke.

He held her bag as she chose the cosmetics. She extended her finger and he sniffed the aromatic powders and oils, advised her to buy the small cakes of sandalwood soap, the talcum powder ground in Yemen and named for the Queen of Sheba.

"You're very beautiful," he said, as they walked back to their hotel.

"And you're very young," she replied.

"Don't."

"Don't what?"

"Don't put barriers into place," he said. "We're together in this beautiful, wonderful city. All of history is whispering to us. And we're going to make beautiful music together."

"Yes," she answered, smiling. "I suppose we are." She took the woven bag from him.

She missed the cocktail party that Emanuel Klein gave for the ensemble. She chose instead to luxuriate in a hot bath perfumed with fragrant oils. She dressed carefully for dinner, selecting a pale green dress of a gossamer fabric with wide gauzy sleeves that dangled like butterfly wings about her arms. She plaited her hair into a single braid, as she had worn it the night she and Andrew had met. She phoned New York before she went down to dinner, but Andrew was not at home.

"He's away. Somewhere in the West," Lottie said. "But he'll be glad you called."

"All right." Merle was glad to hear Lottie's deep, rich voice, glad to have reestablished contact with her own life, with her beautiful home, its soft carpets and paintings and lovely polished silver and woods bearing testimony to Andrew's success, his power. Her home was the citadel of his protection.

She selected a seat at the table reserved for the ensemble, far from Dennis Montgomery, and when they broke into small groups for an after-dinner stroll through the city, she chose to accompany

Emanuel Klein and his group to the Khan Theater while Dennis and his companions made their way to the Western Wall. They smiled at each other as they separated. She thought that he looked very handsome in his pale blue shirt and dark jacket; briefly, she wished that he had not cut his hair.

He was waiting for her the next morning when she came down to breakfast, and without discussion they decided to spend the day together. They boarded a bus for Jericho and ate lunch at a sidewalk café there. They hired a tourist guide who drove them to the excavations at Na'aran and who plucked dates for them from a low-hanging palm branch. The heat of the sun permeated the taste of the dark gold fruit. They passed a flower vendor and she admired the clusters of tiny white and pink roses.

"Jericho roses," their guide told them. "The blossom of lovers."

He sat very close to her on the bus back to Jerusalem. The bus swerved and she was thrust against him. He put his arm about her, protectively, and he did not remove it when they were again traveling smoothly.

"You used the sandalwood soap," he said.

"Did I?" She smiled secretly, flirtatiously, her heart pounding, her body electrified by his touch. They walked to their hotel in silence, fearful that the utterance of a single word would shatter the mood of the day. She hurried to her room. She would have to dress quickly. That night they would give their first concert for a select audience in the small auditorium of the Islamic Museum on Palmach Street.

She was already wearing the white sheath she always wore when she played *A Child's Prayer* when there was a knock at the door. A bellboy handed her a florist's box. A wrist corsage woven of small pink and white Jericho roses. There was no note nor was there any need for one. *The blossom of lovers.* She placed the corsage in water. It was beautiful but she would not wear it. *He had been a boy writing his college application the day John Kennedy was shot. She had been a young mother sitting in a park, watching her son at play.* She waited in her room until the last minute, hoping that Andrew would call as he often did before a concert, but the phone did not ring.

"You look very beautiful," Dennis whispered as she walked by him to take her place on the stage.

She smiled, touched his hand lightly, and looked out into the audience. Nancy sat in the third row, waving wildly, her face beaming, smilingly mouthing inaudible threats. And Merle smiled back at her friend, rose at Emanuel Klein's nod, lifted her bow, and began to play.

Nancy and Ari invited the entire ensemble back to their home after the concert.

"Not an official reception," Nancy apologized to Emanuel Klein. "But you can blame that on Merle. Imagine never telling me she would be in Jerusalem. You deceitful witch." She grinned at her friend, held her hand tightly, and guided her through her home. Merle looked around the master bedroom that faced the Valley of Hinnom.

"What a beautiful view," she said.

"Almost as beautiful as the view from your bedroom in Egremont," Nancy replied.

Merle looked out at the incline of the valley, studded with rock tombs and the strangely sculpted outcroppings of stone where once child sacrifices had been offered to Moloch, the Canaanite god.

"Ah, but your view has no ghosts sailing across it," she said playfully, and Nancy, who knew her so well, heard the sadness in her voice. She wondered whether Merle was thinking of the ghost of the woman who was said to have killed herself in the Egremont house or of the infant Kate, buried in the Egremont cemetery.

"Happy thoughts now, only happy thoughts," Nancy commanded with mock sternness. "So many great things happening. Rutti and David and their twins. The pregnancy bug is catching. I too am having a child — at least I hope it's a child and not children."

She was uncertain how Merle would accept her news, but her friend's smile and swift hug reassured her.

"Oh, Nancy, I'm so happy for you."

"And our Anne writes that she is soon to be a mother. Any idea who the father is?"

"I haven't dared to ask," Merle said. "And Anne hasn't said. I assume he's pretty much out of the picture."

"That would be my guess," Nancy agreed. "And it doesn't really matter unless it matters to Anne. Lucky baby to have Anne for a mother."

"She is woman — hear her roar," Merle sang, and they both laughed.

The murmur of voices drifted up the stairwell. Ari discussing the musical exchange program with Emanuel Klein. Lena Andreas, the cellist, asking Dennis Montgomery where she could buy a Miriam drum.

"We should go down," Nancy said. "I must do my diplomatic duty. But I must ask you something. Andrew won't mind your going to Minnesota?"

"I won't ask him," Merle replied. "And he won't tell me if he does mind. That's how it is, you see. And that's how it's been for a while now."

"Since Kate's death."

"Since Kate's death."

They stared hard at each other. Honesty had always been the touchstone of their friendship. They would not deceive each other now. But before they could speak the door burst open and Keren and Sarah hurtled into the room.

"Merle, Merle, it's really you. You're really here. Oh, how cool, how absolutely cool."

They hugged and kissed her, admired her dress, her shoes. Nancy watched them without envy. Merle had always been a favorite of the girls. She was always so soft-spoken, so unhurried, so generous with her time and her tenderness.

"I don't want a mother like you, always hurrying and yelling. I want a mother like Merle," Keren had once shouted at Nancy in a fit of anger.

"Then tell your father to make a million dollars and we'll hire a maid," Nancy had shouted back.

That had been during the bad times with Dov, the dark and angry times. She forgave herself for her anger. Her new happiness made such forgiveness possible.

"Hey, Merle, who's the gorgeous blond guy in your group?" Keren asked.

"Dennis Montgomery. Too old for you, Keren," Merle replied. And too young for me, she thought. She recalled the distant Friday afternoons when the friends had indulged in lazy fantasy.

"If you could sleep with anyone in the world, whom would you choose?" one of them — usually Anne as she remembered — would ask.

They would pass a single reefer around, because then they considered marijuana to be daring, a symbol of their nascent independence. They watched the gentle swirl of blue smoke, listened to the chatter and laughter of the playing children and laughingly made their choices. Anne opted for Christian Bernard, Cary Grant, Sargent Shriver. Once Rutti had offered Leslie Howard's name. "But he's dead," they had protested. "This is fantasy," she reminded them sternly. Nancy had chosen Moshe Dayan and Laurence Olivier. But Merle had always begged off. The fantasy game was edged with danger. Andrew had been the first man in her life, the only man in her life. To imagine making love to another man was to open a forbidden door, to acknowledge the narrowness of her experience.

"Andrew. I can't imagine ever sleeping with anyone else," she would maintain steadfastly, ignoring her friends' gentle jeers, their raunchy coaxing. Such sexual speculation was a new dimension of their emerging consciousness; the freedom to articulate their imaginings excited them. But Merle was never drawn into their game.

She went downstairs with Keren and Sarah and saw Dennis Montgomery deep in conversation with Lena, the dark-haired cellist. She sat on the couch and he moved to stand beside her. He smiled. He held a pale blue glass in which a golden liqueur shone like sunlight. He had an elegant grace, Merle thought. He put the glass down and tapped lightly on the table. He was demonstrating a drumming technique to Lena. Merle imagined his fingers moving across her skin, tapping lightly on each vertebra — she the instrument and he the musician. A light sweat coated her skin. Her throat was dry. She thought that when she and Nancy met for lunch the next day, she would say to her friend: "If I could sleep with anyone in the world, I would sleep with Dennis Montgomery."

Ari discussed the contemporary music scene in Israel with Emanuel Klein. There was a great deal of interesting work being done by both Jews and Arabs. In fact, an Arab named Abdul Nashif was giving a recital of original pieces for strings and woodwinds sometime that week. Perhaps he could arrange for tickets.

"I'd like that very much," Dennis interjected. "Would you be interested, Merle?"

He smiled at her but she shrugged indifferently. His assumption of connection at once intrigued and frightened her.

"Maybe," she said.

He walked beside her as the group strolled back to the hotel. The night was cool and the air was fragrant with the scent of pomegranates.

"You didn't wear my flowers," Dennis said softly.

"No. But thank you. They were lovely. I put them in water in my room."

"Ah." He smiled. He would not press her. He had not, after all, pressed the beautiful Andrea to remain in New York. He was of a generation of young men who prided themselves on their sensitivity. They understood a woman's need for space, for privacy. He walked her to her room and said good night to her at the door.

"It was a wonderful evening," he said. "And a wonderful afternoon."

"Yes. I thought we played well," she replied. She went into the room and closed the door softly behind her. Another fraction of a second passed before she heard him continue on down the corridor.

There was a message from Andrew. He had called to wish her good luck at the concert. She glanced at her watch and thought to call him back, but she realized she did not know where to reach him. It was after midnight in Jerusalem, which meant that it was early evening in the States. Andrew was somewhere in the Midwest. They were in different countries, in different time zones. The thought saddened her. She thought of all the mornings when Andrew had left their room at dawn to catch a plane for a distant city. He had always closed the door very softly behind him. If ever she left him, she had once thought, she would slam the door so hard that it would reverberate with finality and defiance. Surely Ibsen had meant Nora to slam the door when she left the doll's house.

Where had Nora gone? Merle wondered as she slipped the white sheath off and brushed her hair. And where would she herself go if ever she left the doll's house in Egremont, the house that Andrew had bought for her and that she and her friends had furnished like mischievous small girls. Alternatives raced through her mind. She could seek refuge with Rutti or Nancy or Anne. She could go back to Michigan and bring disappointment to her brothers' eyes. She could become a bag lady and carry her violin in a frayed Lord & Taylor shopping bag sprigged with red roses. Greg, coming down the street with his friends, would see her, grow embarrassed, and change direction.

She smiled at the ludicrousness of her imaginings as she undressed. Holding the corsage, she stood for a long time at the window. At last she slipped it on her wrist. She slept that night with her cheek pressed against the soft white and pink blossoms; their sweetness permeated the dream she could not remember when the first light of dawn awoke her.

She and Nancy met for lunch the next day at the Anna Ticho Museum. The room in which Anna Ticho had painted had been converted into a charming restaurant. Nancy and Merle sat at a window table and looked out at the beautiful flower garden.

"It's all so peaceful," Merle said. "You know, when you listen to the news at home you expect to come to Israel and see active hostilities. Terrorist bombs going off in the street. Standoffs between Palestinians and Israelis."

"It is peaceful now," Nancy agreed. "But there is a lot of tension in the country. I sometimes think it's like a simmering pressure cooker. Any minute the top is going to blow."

Merle picked moodily at her salade Niçoise. It occurred to her that they were eating the exact same lunch they had shared the day she had told Nancy of her yearning for another child, the day Nancy had advised her to deceive Andrew. She had done exactly that and Kate had been born. Deception plus conception had equaled death. A dangerous equation. And now again they sat opposite each other, but it was Nancy who was the mother of a toddler. Conceived without deception. Merle felt the pricking of anger, of an irrational jealousy. She bit down on an anchovy and allowed the salty fish to burn her throat before reaching for the goblet of water.

"What sort of tensions?" she asked.

"I suppose I'd call them 'seventies' tensions," Nancy replied thoughtfully. "It's funny how the situations in America and in Israel almost parallel each other in some ways. Remember what a national high we were on at the beginning of the sixties? It was our decade

— the decade of youth and hope, the decade when we'd turn the world around. John Kennedy walked around without a coat or a hat and he spoke our language. We were on our way. The Peace Corps kids took off for Central America and Asia and Africa and the freedom buses rode into the South. We thought we could do anything. All the walls were going to come tumbling down. We'd blow the horn and yell 'amen' and there'd be no more segregation. We'd wave our banners and sing our songs and there'd be an end to war. We'd call each other sister and open day-care centers and sexism would melt away. Oh, Merle, there was nothing we thought we couldn't do. And then we sat in the playground that November day and listened to your radio. . . ."

"News instead of Bach," Merle said. "They interrupted a piano composition — was it a Goldberg Variation?" She furrowed her brow. It had become strangely important that she remember the music that had been playing when they heard the news of John Kennedy's assassination.

"I think all our hopes died that day. Or began to die. The March on Washington was history; we had Watts and Detroit. And the war got uglier and the body counts went higher and we knew one thing for sure. Joan Baez wasn't going to sing us into peace. The answer, whatever it was, wasn't blowing in the wind. We'd been riding high in our beautiful balloon and suddenly we were grounded and we didn't even bother looking up again." Nancy's voice was bitter.

"But Israel was different, it must have been," Merle protested.

"Different and still the same, from what I hear from Ari and his friends," Nancy said. "The late sixties were boom time in Israel too — the Years of Euphoria, they call it. The Six-Day War had been fought and won and there wasn't anything Israel couldn't do. The war gave Israel trading chips. We'd hold onto the strategic spots if we had to, but everything else would go back just for a signature on a peace treaty. I have patients who talk about those days. Sixty-seven, sixty-eight, sixty-nine. The best of all possible worlds was going to be theirs. Remember, Merle, how we sat around Grace's living room and talked about alternative child-care programs, interracial play groups, support systems for women? They say that Arab and Jewish women met in living rooms in Rehavia, in villas in east Jerusalem, and talked about setting up Arab-Jewish play groups. They asked each other questions — they even waited for the answers. Someone said it was as though Israel felt itself poised at the edge of a messianic era without even needing a messiah. And then the bubble burst. Seventy-three. The Yom Kippur War. The invincible became the vulnerable. The idols of the sixties had clay feet. The myths exploded. The Bar Lev line was a matchstick defense. Golda Meir had played politics with the lives of Israeli soldiers." Nancy's voice was sad. She remembered Ari folding his prayer shawl, holding the satin fringes to her cheek. She remembered her fear, her near certainty that he would not return.

"Seventy-three," Merle said, thinking back across the three-year span. "Vietnam over once and for all. I remember the first time I heard a commentator — maybe it was David Brinkley — say that Kennedy had gotten us into Vietnam. I thought, 'How ridiculous — not *our* Kennedy, not our bright-haired President, the one who played touch football in the surf at Hyannisport. And then the boys who were never going to play touch football again came home and we began to hear about the anger and the despair and the drugs. I played a benefit at a VA hospital the year I was pregnant with Kate — the fury, the desperation in that room was real; the music seemed to bounce off it. And then the truth began to leak out; the silver sixties were tarnished. Martin Luther King, Jr., had been a womanizer. And Marilyn Monroe was dead too, and the rumor was that both John and Bobby Kennedy had slept with her. And the rhetoric was wearing thin. We were tired, burned out. I don't think Watergate even surprised us. Oh, sure, we accomplished some good things. Anyone who sits at a Woolworth lunch counter gets served and Lottie can pee in any rest room she wants to, in any state of the union."

Nancy smiled and lifted her coffee cup.

"I salute Lottie's right to pee. How is she anyway?"

"She's great. Her consciousness is raised. One night I forgot to tell her we weren't going to be home for dinner and she had already cooked. She let me have it. 'You know, Merle,' she said, 'Women like you can have the lives you want because of women like me. But don't push it.' And let me tell you, I haven't."

Nancy clapped softly.

"Good for Lottie."

"Good for Lottie. Right. But I don't think this decade is good for anyone, Nancy. It's not great for America — not great for Israel. It's probably not great anywhere."

"Not a bad decade for the sisters though. We got *Roe v. Wade* through. We did that."

"Just when Anne doesn't need it any more," Merle said slyly, and they laughed with the intimate malice of women who have shared too many secrets.

"Hey, do you think Jonas Salk could be the father of Anne's baby?" Nancy asked. "I think she picked him once when we played that great Friday afternoon fantasy game — remember — if you could sleep with anyone in the world, who would it be? If I remember correctly you never played, Merle. You were such a cop-out."

"I'll play it now. But you go first."

"Okay. Ari. Then Paul Newman. Then Pierre Trudeau, even though he's getting paunchy. What about you?"

"Dennis Montgomery."

"Ah," Nancy said serenely. "So that's the way it is."

"No," Merle said. "But that's the way it might possibly be. If. Maybe."

"And Andrew?"

"Andrew's in another country, another time zone."

"How long is it since Kate died?"

"Four years." She spoke in a whisper.

"Four years is a long time to punish someone," Nancy said quietly.

"I'm not your patient, Nancy."

"No. But you're my friend. And friends tell each other the truth."

"Enough." Merle lifted her hand warningly. Keren and Sarah were approaching the table and Merle realized that her friends' daughters — Keren so tall and dark, Sarah petite, her finely shaped head covered with curls of spun gold — were so beautiful that they caused patrons of the café to look at them and smile.

"We came to kidnap you," Keren said mischievously.

"And we are badly in need of kidnapping," Merle said.

She looked at Nancy and they smiled at each other, the surrendering smile of close friends who know when a conversation edges dangerously close to argument.

They spent the afternoon shopping and sight-seeing. Merle returned to the hotel late that afternoon to find a message from Dennis Montgomery. Ari had, in fact, arranged for them to attend a recital that evening of the music of the Arab composer, Abdul Nashif. Dennis thought it a good idea that he and Merle have an early dinner at a fish restaurant he had discovered in east Jerusalem and then go on together to the concert. He would meet her in the lobby at five-thirty. She was relieved that he had taken her consent for granted, that he had left her no room for indecision. She dressed carefully, selecting a white dress, high-necked yet barebacked, and twisted her hair into a loose knot. Just before she left the room she plucked a single blossom from the corsage of Jericho roses and pinned it to her collar.

Dennis wore white slacks and a white jacket, the snowy shirt usually reserved for performances. Already the relentless sunlight of the Middle East had gilded his hair to a golden sheen. He sprang to his feet when he saw her.

"I wasn't sure you'd come," he said. This first evidence of his uncertainty pleased her.

"Why wouldn't I come?" She smiled, and he leaned forward and lightly touched the rose.

They ate in the garden of a small restaurant not far from the Golden Gate.

Dennis ordered for both of them with the competent confidence of a longtime companion, familiar with taste and mood.

"Saint Peters fish," he told the waiter. "Broiled, the skin slightly crisp. Rice with raisins and almonds. A green salad. No dressing. White wine."

"How did you know?" she asked. It seemed to her a small miracle that he had so accurately anticipated her taste.

"I guessed," he replied, grinning. Like a small boy, he preened himself on this small triumph. He had known how to please her. She saw the glint of victory in his eyes, the sensual curl of his lips.

He had journeyed to Jaffa that day and found the shepherd's pipe for which he had searched. It was wonderfully carved and had a perfect tone.

"I'll play it for you tonight," he promised.

She told him of her conversation with Nancy as they ate the excellent fish and sipped the chilled white wine.

"I guess the situations are parallel — Israel and America going

303

through the euphoria of the sixties, the disillusionment of the seventies. But it's not only Israel and America. It's as though there's an international ideological virus. When I was in the thick of it at Berkeley we'd get messages from student groups in Germany, in France, in England. A cyclical reaction, one of the professors who led a teach-in called it."

"I had a friend who believed in a cyclical philosophy of history. My friend Rutti's first husband, Werner. He was Sarah's father."

"Oh, yes. The girl with the golden hair. Where is her father now?"

"Dead. He was killed here in Israel during the Six-Day War." She looked at Dennis Montgomery as though challenging him. She was of a generation that was already familiar with death. It was important that he know this. As though he had anticipated her intent, he reached across the table and took her hand in his own.

"When you told me what you called your boring life story, you didn't tell me that you had lost a child," he said. "Emanuel Klein told me about it this afternoon."

"She was an infant," Merle said. "She lived for only a few days. I cannot imagine why Emanuel discussed it with you." Grief constricted her throat, rolled heavily across her heart.

"He was warning me, I think. He's very protective of you."

Merle did not answer. There was no reply she could offer the young man who sat opposite her. She could not tell him that she was weary of being protected.

"He needn't have worried," she said, and she saw the shadow of hurt in Dennis's eyes.

He called for the check with an uncharacteristic peremptoriness and they walked to the concert hall in silence. They slid into the seats beside Nancy and Ari. Nancy raised an eyebrow. Merle shook her head imperceptibly and they both giggled.

Merle leaned forward to listen as the conductor lifted his baton. The concert was interesting; the music both confused and intrigued her. Abdul Nashif flirted with atonality yet there was a subtle, longing theme in his music. Merle felt Dennis Montgomery's hand on her bare back. His touch was an apology of a kind. She turned to him, smiled, and felt the increased pressure of his fingers on her vertebrae. One by one he pressed down, as gently and expertly as he manipulated the keys of his flute. Pleasure rippled through her. He would use her body as though it were a delicate instrument; he would coax forth reactions she had not thought herself capable of. She smiled into the darkness, turned her attention back to the music.

Gradually, she recognized that Nashif's music was intricately layered, each melody supported by a countertheme and then yet another augmented passage. The heterophonic result was almost hypnotic, totally involving her. She recognized, too, that Nashif's composition was very different from her own. *A Child's Prayer* made audiences weep. This music made the audience think.

The composer himself acknowledged this to be true when they met after the concert in a garden café. Abdul Nashif poured thick Turkish coffee from the large copper feenjan into the delicate ceramic cups and passed them to Nancy and Ari, to his sister, Fatima, to Merle and Dennis and Emanuel Klein who had joined them.

"It is the chromatic relationships which you are hearing and which perplex you," the handsome Arab said. "These are the *maqamot* of Arab music and are not well known in the West. I have mingled them with the influences of Western music as I have come to know them. The effect is complex and, I believe, not without interest." He was a pleasant young man, his narrow face dominated by a thick, darkly silken mustache, his dark hair tumbling about his forehead. Merle thought that Fatima was a beautiful woman. She too had glossy dark hair, cut and fashioned to frame her face like the wings of a raven.

"It is certainly interesting," Merle agreed. "I think American audiences would be quite excited by your music. What do you think, Emanuel?"

"I do not doubt it." As always, Emanuel Klein was courteous. He himself was baffled by Nashif's music, but then he was an old man and he acknowledged that it was increasingly difficult for him to assimilate new ideas, to accept new concepts. It was time for him to think about working less, perhaps even retiring. There were many candidates who could easily take his place. Merle, of course, was the most talented of his protégés. Perhaps she could take over, at least in part. The work was difficult and he was grateful that his wife understood that and did so much to ease his day — monitoring his phone calls, seeing to the running of the household, bringing snacks to his practice sessions. But then Andrew made the same services available to Merle. A rich husband was not, after all, unlike a devoted wife. The thought amused him. He smiled as he turned his attention to Dennis Montgomery, who was speaking of the possibility of arranging an American tour for Nashif.

"Perhaps you could organize an Arab-Jewish ensemble from Israel, and tour college campuses. That could serve a double purpose. There would be the music and the demonstration that it is possible for Arabs and Jews to live side by side, to work together, to make music together," Dennis said enthusiastically, turning to Ari.

Emanuel Klein noticed that Merle's attention was riveted to the flutist, that she moved imperceptibly closer to him as he spoke. He was not surprised. He had toured with many ensembles through the years. He understood the almost symbiotic closeness that could develop between performing artists who traveled together for a length of time in foreign countries and exotic cities. The lingering scent of unfamiliar flowers, the loneliness of empty hotel rooms, and the long solitary hours promoted a desperate intimacy that was too often mistaken for love. He wondered if he should say something to Merle, but he was after all her teacher and mentor, not her chaperon. It was enough that he had spoken to young Montgomery, that he had made him aware of Merle's vulnerability.

"In order to do that — to undertake such a venture — one would have to believe that such utopian cooperation was possible," Nashif interjected.

"But I thought you did believe that, Abdul," Ari said. "After all you've studied here at the Rubin in Jerusalem, at the Tel Aviv University. You've performed in Israeli cities and I am sure you have played in as many kibbutzim as Arab townships."

"Such a tour might be possible, eventually and under certain circumstances," Abdul conceded.

"I think that my brother means that he does not want to be your show Arab," Fatima Nashif said.

"If he made such a tour, with my ministry's support, it would be because he is a good musician, not because he is an Arab," Ari replied stiffly.

"Come now," Fatima countered. "Let us be honest and acknowledge that we live in the media age. Artists and intellectuals are public relations pawns. Nancy and I have each been asked to contribute monographs to a Scandinavian journal on the impact of violence on the imaginations of children. Do you think for a moment that we were selected on the basis of our unique talent? Or was it because we are both women — one Arab, one Jewish, working in Israel? The editor is not stupid. He knows that we will attract interest, surely a mention in *Time* or *Newsweek,* perhaps even a television sound bite."

Nancy sighed, and turned the conversation to a discussion of a group of children she met with in a day-care center.

"They're the kids I really want to write about," she said. "They're mainly from underprivileged, emotionally barren backgrounds. Very hostile, with an undercurrent of violence. I don't think it has a damn thing to do with living in so-called beleaguered Jerusalem. I think it has a lot to do with the fact that they come from families where both parents work and there's a lack of nurturing."

"We are finding the same problem in our community," Fatima agreed. "Even in rural areas. The mother of too many children works in the fields and leaves a daughter who is barely a teenager to care for the children. You see a lot of anger, externalized and internalized."

"Perhaps a compassionate child care program is the solution to the Middle East problem," Ari suggested wryly.

"No. More funding for artists and musicians — that will solve the Arab-Israeli conflict," Abdul said and they all laughed, the tension broken at last.

The smiling proprietor set a plate of pastries on the table, removed used cups, and replaced them with clean ones. It was good for his café to be filled with laughter. Passersby looked in and thought his patrons' joy was contagious. Already the tables near them were occupied. He placed a bottle of anisette next to the feenjan. "Please," he said. "Accept our hospitality."

"Why not?"

Dennis circled the table and splashed the milky liqueur into each cup. When he filled Merle's, his hand brushed her arm and she smiled sleepily at him.

"Perhaps we should go. I'll walk you back to the hotel. No need for everyone to leave," Dennis said.

Nancy lifted an eyebrow and Merle shrugged and smiled, the teasing, intimate smile of their Friday afternoon exchanges.

Again, Merle and Dennis made their way down the dark and silent street. A cool breeze brushed their cheeks and when Merle shivered slightly, Dennis took off his white jacket and draped it over her shoulders.

"Thank you," she said softly.

In reply, he brushed her lips with his own, his face so close to hers that he could feel her lashes against his cheeks. He touched his finger to them, felt the tickle of their flutter.

"Butterfly kisses. That's what the children used to call them," she said.

The children. He understood that she spoke of her son, a college student now, backpacking across the Northwest, and of the two beautiful young girls, Keren and Sarah, her friends' daughters.

"There is something to be said for butterfly kisses," he murmured, but now he pulled her close to him and kissed her. Her hands reached up to touch his hair, to caress the nape of his neck. And then, slowly, gracefully, she pulled away so that again they stood side by side, her white dress caped by his jacket, her red-gold hair radiant against the night's darkness.

"Come Snow White — let's hurry — let's run. I'll show you my shepherd's pipe. I'll play it for you in the moonlight."

She laughed and then without warning, she broke into a run and sprinted on ahead of him, down the broad avenue. He vaulted after her, laughing, calling her name.

"Merle! Merle!"

A group of Israeli youngsters stared after them, laughed too, and echoed him.

"Merle! Merle!"

She ran faster and faster, and he matched her pace. They arrived at the hotel together, laughing and breathless, their faces aglow. They fell into each other's arms and holding hands walked into the lobby.

"Mrs. Cunningham?" The desk clerk was embarrassed, hesitant. "A message for you."

Still laughing, she approached the desk and took the pale green message memo. "Mr. Cunningham called. Please call him back. *Urgntly.*" The word was misspelled, she noted, with that odd attention to detail that often overtakes those confronted with emergencies. The number was not a familiar one. Even the area code eluded her.

"My husband," she told Dennis. "I must call."

"Must you call tonight?" he asked. "Couldn't it wait until morning?"

She heard the plea in his voice, saw the desire in his eyes. How young he was to think that such a call could wait until morning. He was not a parent. He did not yet live in fear of ringing phones, distant sirens.

"It will take just a few minutes," she said.

"I'll come with you."

She did not object. He stood in the doorway of her room as she placed the call. She kicked her white pumps off and her feet were rosy beneath her sheer stockings.

"These shoes were not made for midnight sprints through Jerusalem," she said.

He wanted to kneel beside her and massage her heels, but he could not do that, not while she spoke to her husband across so many miles.

She tapped her foot and waited impatiently, obsessed by dark and ominous thoughts.

Never had Andrew used the word "urgently" in a phone message. He was afraid to frighten her, sought to protect her from anxiety. Something must have happened. Something terrible. Greg was backpacking through Canyonlands National Park in southern Utah. She had objected mildly. The park had no sleeping accommodations and Eric and Greg had been warned that the terrain was difficult and inhospitable, the climate unpredictable.

"Look, Mom, this is an adventure. I may never have another chance to do this and even if I do, who knows whether places like Canyonlands will still be preserved with the way the environment is going to pot."

She smiled. Her generation had campaigned for civil rights, for women's rights. They had marched on Washington and waved their banners for peace and brotherhood. "Make love, not war!" they had shouted at Vietnam protest rallies. But Greg and Eric, Sarah and Keren, worried about the forests and the oceans. They worked for Greenpeace and signed petitions against Styrofoam and aerosol. It was as though they had taken lessons from their parents' generation. They despaired of people. It was the environment that claimed their passion. She had not argued with Greg. She would not allow fear to constrain him as Andrew's fear had constrained her.

"All right, Greg. Have a terrific time, but be careful," she had said.

But he had not been careful and now she sat in a hotel room in a distant city and awaited Andrew's voice, waited to learn the consequence of his carelessness, of their permissiveness. Had Greg fallen from a cliff? Had he lost his footing on an embankment? Masochistic nightmare images overtook her. She saw Greg lying motionless at the bottom of a precipice. She saw the pallor of her son's pain-twisted face, his jade-green eyes, the exact color of her own, filled with tears. She balled her fingers into a fist, bit her lips.

"Merle." Dennis's voice was soft, pleading, but she waved him away.

"Operator, operator, are you getting through?" she shouted angrily into the phone. "One minute. One minute. We have your party. Go ahead, please."

"Andrew. Andrew! What happened?" she screamed.

But it was Greg who answered her, his tone troubled yet controlled.

"Mom. Listen carefully. Everything is all right. Really. Dad had a mild heart attack. It's not serious, the doctor said. Honestly. And he's doing fine. It was like a warning, they say."

Relief and disbelief, in concurrent waves, suffused her.

"No, no, it can't be," she protested, her voice quavering. "Not Andrew. He's so healthy. Greg, Greg, what happened? What really happened?"

She struggled to assimilate his words. They rattled through her mind like isolated pieces of a puzzle that she was powerless to join together. *Heart attack. Doctor. Serious.* But Andrew had hardly been sick for a day throughout their marriage. Yes, he tired more easily now, but his body retained a lean, muscular resilience. He could play two sets of tennis, cycle for miles. The weekends he and Greg were at Egremont together they hiked mountain trails and Andrew always returned still energetic, his craggy features ruddy with health. She remembered the morning she left for Israel. She had watched him dress and had marveled at the beauty of his body, the straightness of his back, the rippling strength of his arms. No. It was not possible. He could not have had a heart attack.

"He was somewhere in Minnesota when he began to have chest pains. He was checking out some property or something. Anyway, he called Anne, hired a private plane, and flew to Rochester. Anne took over. She had a bed ready, a top cardiologist. And she knew I was hiking in Canyonlands so she placed a call to the ranger station there and got word to me. She was terrific, Mom." Greg's voice was admiring.

"Thank God. Thank God." Tears burned her eyes. Her heart swelled with gratitude to Anne for helping Andrew, with gratitude to Andrew for not dying.

"I thought it was you, Greg," she whispered. "I thought something had happened to you in Canyonlands."

"Oh, Mom, cut it out. What could happen to me?" He spoke with the arrogant certainty of the young and the strong. And now he claimed new authority. Suddenly, overnight, he who had always been protected by his parents had become their protector. Roles had been reversed: he stood beside his father and reassured him; he spoke to his mother across an expanse of continents and seas. He made arrangements with doctors and nurses. He had been catapulted into manhood.

"I'll come," Merle said. "I'll come at once."

"Listen, Mom, Dad has your concert schedule. He knows that you're supposed to play one more concert in Tel Aviv tomorrow. If you come careening up here without doing that he's going to think that he's worse than we've told him — even though we've been telling him the truth. He even said that he'll understand if you go on and tour Israel the way you planned. He's going to be fine, really."

How like Andrew Greg sounded — so reasonable, so persuasive. Andrew had always thought of her first — of her needs, her safety, her comfort. Even when he had dissuaded her from having another child, he had never closed the door to her challenge. But it was she who had refused to challenge him, to oppose him. It was her own cowardice, the cowardice that had overtaken her the night of Tran's death, that had caused her to retreat into the safety of his protection. It was she who had chosen to dress in the clothing she thought he

311

favored, to engage in the playful subterfuge that had characterized that first summer at Egremont. The doll's house was of her own construction.

"Greg, I'll play the concert tomorrow, if you're sure he's all right. But I'm coming home right after that. Is Anne there? Can I speak to her?"

"I'll put her on. And hey, Mom — I'm glad you're coming."

"Merle, don't be frightened. It was a minor infarction and he's doing really well. We had a terrific cardiology team with him and he's in full recovery. Minimal damage. Minimal scarring. He'll be fine." Anne's tone blended professionalism and friendship.

"Oh, Anne, thank you," Merle said. Relief surged through her. "Can I talk to him?"

"No phone in his room. Old-fashioned ideas in this modern clinic. He'll be here for a few days and then go to Egremont for R and R. We want him to take a couple of months off. Lucky Andrew. You get more time off for an infarction than for a baby." Anne laughed.

"Stick to babies," Merle said. "I'll play the concert tomorrow and get myself straight to Egremont. You'll tell Andrew I'm coming?"

"Of course I'll tell him. You know, Merle, he kept on saying he didn't expect you to come home but I know how happy he'll be that you're doing just that."

"I know," Merle replied softly. "Of course I know."

"How's Nancy?" Anne asked. "Tell her to write. I need her blessing. I need everyone's blessing." She giggled.

"She's great but she has a pretty crazy schedule," Merle replied. "I'll tell you about it when I get home. Anne — Andrew's going to be all right, isn't he?"

"Absolutely all right," Anne said firmly, and Merle believed her because never had the friends lied to each other.

"Thank you," she whispered into the phone, and although the connection was broken, she stood for a moment longer, clutching the receiver and swaying from side to side. Dennis Montgomery moved swiftly toward her. He took the phone from her and led her to the easy chair that faced the window. He brought her a glass of water and watched as she sipped it gratefully. Her mouth was so dry, soured by fear. But there was no reason to be afraid. Anne had told her so.

"My husband, Andrew, had a mild heart attack," she told Dennis.

"And you're going back?" he asked, although he had heard the conversation and knew the answer.

"Yes. I'm going back. Right after the Tel Aviv concert. Dennis, I'm sorry. I wasn't playing games with you."

"I know that," he said, scowling. The scowl endeared him to her. He was so young. He had been so kind.

"You love him, it seems."

"So it seems," she replied gently. She leaned forward and took his hand in her own, lifted it to her lips. She kissed each knuckle, her lips as light as her lashes had been. Butterfly kisses.

"I loved our time together," she said. "I loved our talks. I loved your flowers. I wish I had heard your shepherd's pipe."

"I'll play it for you one day," he promised. He unpinned the single flower from the collar of her dress and placed it in her hair. "Good night, Merle. I'm glad he's going to be all right."

"And you'll be all right too," she said, fearful that she had been cruel and that her cruelty, her carelessness, had wounded him.

"Yes. I'll be all right," he replied. He bent and kissed her on the forehead. He closed the door very softly behind him as he left, as all the doors in her life had always been closed.

Nancy and Ari drove her to Ben-Gurion Airport after the Tel Aviv concert. They remained with her as she waited to board the midnight flight.

"It was very good to share this time with you," Ari said in his correct, formal English.

"Come and visit us in the States." She hugged Nancy and kissed Ari on the cheek.

"That's always a possibility," Ari said. "Diplomats do get posted out of the country." He smiled at Nancy. There were whispers in the office, but he could not share them with her. Not yet. He pulled her close, felt the swell of her pregnancy, the wonder of his child growing.

Merle slept for most of the flight. She slept and dreamed of Andrew. He smiled at her across a candlelit room. She saw him moving toward her, awoke briefly, and slept again. He would come to her, she knew. As he had always come to her. He was not to blame for loving her too much. And now, she was going to him. Flying through the night, across Greece and Italy, France and England. She was flying to him.

His driver was waiting for her at Kennedy.

"He's all right, Mrs. Cunningham. He's fine," he said in answer to the question she had not asked.

He stood on the porch of the Egremont house and she watched him lean against the rail as they drove up. They had not lied. He was all right. He moved toward her with strength and purpose, but she saw the new lines that had carved their way across his brow, she saw the new fear in his eyes.

"Merle?" Her name was a question, his smile a plea.

She answered both. She ran toward him, into his outstretched arms, and wept against his chest.

"I love you," she said. "Oh, Andrew, I love you."

The Eighties

20

It WAS a year when the seasons converged and crowded upon each other. Driving home to Oak Park, after a long day at Chicago's Michael Reese Hospital, Anne noticed that the early blossoms of fall — the orange and russet chrysanthemums, the tall purple asters — neighbored the last pink roses of summer. The fallen foliage, scarlet and gold, danced in the wake of the wind across lush stretches of suburban lawn.

She braked for a light and watched a mother and a small girl, each wearing a white shirt and a denim skirt, cross the street. The child sneezed and briefly the mother held up traffic as she ferreted in her purse for a tissue. The freakish nature of the weather had caused a great many summer colds, Anne knew. Tommy had been listless and sneezing for days and, as usual when he was ill, he grew irritable and perverse. Still, his cold would run its course and the unseasonable warmth of this early autumn would vanish. The days would grow shorter and she and Tommy would have to forgo their long, slow walks along the twilit streets of their quiet neighborhood.

Anne loved the unhurried pace of that hour when Maureen, their live-in baby-sitter, was off to her classes at the University of Chicago and Anne's own work was done. Tommy's hand rested firm within her own; the air was fragrant with the sweetness of the season. "What's that?" Tommy asked, pointing to a flower, a dangling leaf, an anthill inhabited by diligent laboring insects. Patiently, she plucked a blossom, offered it to him to touch, to smell, told him its color. She lifted him so that he might touch the low-hanging branches of a tree and study its leaves.

"Maple," she informed him, showing him how the shape of the leaf was different in size and color from that of the oak tree that shaded their neighbor's gazebo.

One summer evening she had knelt beside him and together they had watched a colony of ants labor to build a small hill in the crack of the pavement. He watched two glistening insects push a grain of earth toward the small mound.

"They're friends," he said. "Friends work together." His preschool teacher was an energetic Bank Street graduate who peppered her instructions with assorted aphorisms.

"Yes, friends do help each other," she agreed. "Like my friends. Like Merle and Rutti and Nancy."

"And like me and Ved," Tommy answered proudly.

Ved Singh, who lived next door, was Tommy's best friend. Neighbors smiled when the two small boys hurtled down the street together on their Big Wheels. Ved was dark haired and dark-eyed, his skin the color of almonds; Tommy had a ruddy complexion and thick blond hair always in need of cutting. Ved was a constant visitor and Maureen, kindly and casual, cared for both boys, an agreement welcomed by sari-clad Padma Singh who had two children younger than Ved and was pregnant again. The Indian woman reciprocated by inviting Anne, Maureen, and Tommy to family dinners. She wove a garland of flowers for Anne on her birthday. Never, during the three years that they had been neighbors, had she asked a single question about Tommy's father. Professor Singh, who taught anthropology at Roosevelt University, bowed deeply whenever he saw Anne. Her relationship with the Singh family validated Anne's decision to move, shortly after Tommy's birth, from Minnesota to the Chicago suburb favored by academics and professionals. A single woman physician with a young son was not an anomaly in such a community. There would be no awkward questions, no invasion of her prized privacy.

"It's not that I want to be deceptive," Anne said with uncharacteristic defensiveness when she explained her decision to leave Minnesota to Merle, "but I'm not naive. I know my having a baby and raising it is going to make waves. The times have changed, but not that much."

She supposed that Mrs. Singh and her other neighbors assumed

318

that she was widowed or divorced. Once a cluster of mothers in the playground had fallen into an awkward silence when she and Tommy had approached and then, too swiftly, had begun to talk in a shrill and uneven chorus. She realized that in all probability they had been speculating about her. She remembered how she and Merle, Rutti and Nancy, would build fantasies about the other women in the park.

She smiled at her Oak Park neighbors, sent Tommy off to join the other children on the swings, and drifted into casual conversation with the other mothers. She answered their questions about the efficacy of mumps shots, the impact of diet on growth. They respected her for her knowledge, her achievement. She offered her recipes for rice salad and zucchini soup. They liked her because she was down-to-earth, her life well organized, her child well behaved. They did not envy her because, after all, in spite of her beauty and her accomplishments, she was alone.

Slowly, fragile friendships were formed. She was invited to dinner parties and seated next to single men from their husbands' firms, cousins who were newly divorced, widowers still shocked by their loss and their loneliness. Anne accepted invitations to dinner, to a concert, to the theater from such men. Some she saw for several weeks, or even several months, before she began inventing evasive excuses. She was tired, she was busy, she was working late. The words were familiar. She had repeated them often enough since her break with Charles Bingham.

She had had lovers, of course. There had been the brilliant English geneticist who had been her constant companion during her first year at the Mayo Clinic. He was on an exchange fellowship and it was only after he and Anne were deeply involved that she learned that he was married. His wife, he explained, was in a convalescent home in Nottingham. She was a depressive and his own connection to her was purely a legal and religious formality, which was why he had never discussed her with Anne. Besides, what difference could his marriage make to a woman like Anne who so proudly advertised her independence and was uninterested in conventional ties? "All the difference in the world!" Anne shouted at him. She had not wanted to marry him, but she had assumed that his honesty matched her own. She felt herself betrayed and she wondered that he could have so deceived her, deceived himself, and deceived the woman who wandered through the formal gardens of the Nottingham sanatorium.

She was more cautious after that. She monitored the revelations of the men she met at medical conferences — men who sat at the edge of beds in Holiday Inns in their underwear and spoke bitterly of wives who did not understand them, of indifferent children, of homes in which they felt themselves to be itinerant guests. Some of them roused Anne's sympathy, some her contempt.

Jeffrey, a tall, tow-headed psychiatrist who had also been in the Peace Corps in the early sixties, shared her passion for English detective stories and country music and the grade B movies that flickered weakly across the television screen at three in the morning. They watched such movies in the drowsy aftermath of lovemaking, her head resting on his chest. He was a divorced man. Photographs of his children stared at them from his cluttered bureau. His daughter had long thin braids and smiled shyly. His son was gap toothed, and looked angry. It had not been an amicable divorce.

"My wife wanted too much," Jeffrey said enigmatically and Anne did not ask him to explain. Charles Bingham had also wanted too much. She understood.

He told her that he loved her and she thought, for a while, that she loved him too, that they could have a good life together. She cooked him dinner for his birthday, poured champagne from a chilled bottle, gave him a cashmere robe.

"To the future," she said.

Abruptly, he stopped calling her, and when at last she phoned him, he said in a voice quivering with fright that they were growing too close, that he needed his space, that he was afraid to commit.

"All right," she said tonelessly, although she had already begun to cry.

She remained pleasant to him when she saw him at the hospital or in town. It bewildered her that she had thought seriously of marrying a man whose language she did not understand. What did "too close" mean? "Space," she suspected, was the craving of the claustrophobe who feared the encirclement of love, who feared even to say the word and instead restricted himself to an utterance like "commit." Not a word she would ever use.

Jeffrey left Rochester some months later and for a long time

Anne stopped going out at all. The small talk on casual dates wearied and bored her. She had her work, which was all-engrossing, and her colleagues and friends. She was lonely but not alone. She spent holidays at Egremont, staying with Merle and Andrew, cuddling Rutti's twins. Her friends visited Minnesota.

One Christmas she traveled to Pennsylvania and visited her sisters and their families. They spoke about their mother.

"She was always so tired," Anne said. She thought again of her mother scrubbing pots late at night, staring through a narrow window at a pale crescent moon.

"Tiredness comes with the territory," Helene said lazily.

What territory? Anne wondered. The special province of women, bounded by cheerful clutter, noisy with the laughter and quarrels of children, permeated with the fragrance of cooking and the odors of a household always in flux? Helene worked in a bank, cooked enormous casseroles for her husband and children, prepared lunches at the first light of dawn. But unlike their mother, she did not wash pots late into the night. Her sink overflowed with dirty dishes and cutlery, grease-stained pans sat on her stove, waiting for her husband, her sons.

"I am an emancipated woman," she said, and the sisters laughed.

Edna gave Anne the blue and white afghan their mother had made.

"She crocheted it the winter Grandma was sick. The last winter. She sat next to the bed and I was convinced that when she had finished the last square Grandma would die," Edna said. Sadly Anne thought about women who believed that their own stitches held lives together, that their battles for domestic order held a chaotic world at bay. Rutti had washed linens when Werner died.

Helene made the lamb stew for which their mother had been famous. Anne copied down the recipe. Onions, carrots, dill. The secret of the stew was in the dill. She remembered how the sprigs of green had clung to their mother's fingers, already fragrant with vegetables and spices. She carried the recipe and the blanket back to Minnesota. A sweet legacy. What would she be remembered for, she wondered — a few footnotes in medical textbooks, her monographs in the *International Journal of Genetic Research*?

She cooked a large pot of the stew, but the friends she invited to dinner canceled at the last minute. She ate some of the stew herself and thrust the casserole back into the refrigerator. A breakthrough in her research kept her at the laboratory late several nights that week and she did not eat at home. Weeks later, she pulled the casserole out and retched to see the viscous green mold that had settled over the meat and vegetables. She wept that night, surrendering at last to self-pity.

She had lunch the next day with her old classmate, Peggy Andrews, who was newly arrived at the clinic. Peggy had divorced her husband after ten years of marriage and two children.

"A boring 'General Hospital' type story," she told Anne wryly. "He was sleeping with his nurse. Actually, with his nurses. He's not just an internist. He's a PC — two offices, two nurses. He didn't think it would bother me. After all, I had my career. Women should have liberated themselves from feelings of jealousy, the bastard said. I almost liberated him from his masculinity. And so here I am in the wilds of Minnesota — a bachelor girl with two kids — now and probably forever."

"Oh, you'll marry again." Anne was consoling.

"Probably not. Statistically, it's not in the cards. The pool of eligible men shrinks when you hit your mid-thirties. And the ones who are around are gay or once-burned-twice-shy or misogynist or mother-fixated, or they're impotent and it's your fault — they could get it up only if you weren't such a castrating overachieving bitch — or . . ."

"Or they need their space or they're not ready for commitment or they have a wife hidden away in another country and their religion frowns on divorce. As do their accountants and their suicidal children."

"Exactly," Peggy said. "Exactly." She ordered another bottle of wine and they both grew pleasantly drunk. "At least I have my kids," she added. "At least I'm not alone." She was not an insensitive woman, but she had drunk too much wine to see the hurt in Anne's eyes.

That day Anne left work early, finished a solitary dinner, and called her friends. She wanted company, but she would compromise and accept conversation. There were busy signals and unanswered rings. She listened to messages on answering machines. "We cannot come to the phone just now. Please leave a message at the sound of the beep and your call will be returned."

She did not leave a message. When her friends returned her calls, she herself would be unavailable. There were all trapped on a treadmill of busyness, playing endless games of telephone tag. She brewed a pot of coffee and drank cup after cup, thinking hard, thinking carefully.

Peggy was right. The odds were against her marrying, but that did not mean she had to be alone. She too could have a child. A child with whom she could walk down the street at the end of a long summer day. A child who would be part of her, who would belong to her, loving and beloved. She was suffused suddenly with longing for such a child, a longing she had repressed since the wintry day in a small Pennsylvania town. Now desperation and hope coalesced. She would have to be very careful, her choices considered, her decision well thought through. In the end, the responsibility would be hers and hers alone. She lay awake that night and listened to the too-loud ticking of her bedroom clock. She smiled into the darkness. The passage of time had ceased to frighten her.

Two months later she was pregnant. Her colleagues at the clinic were outwardly supportive.

"How brave of you," said Cal, with whom she worked on a DNA research project. His face was red and she knew that he was congratulating himself on his own open-mindedness.

"Why brave?" she laughed. "I'm not going off to war. I'm not Sally Ride preparing for a ride into space. I'm not Gloria Steinem about to address an NRA convention. I'm just doing what women have always done. I'm having a baby."

"But you're doing it on your own." His blush faded. He would not allow her to elude the snare of his grudging admiration.

"All women do it on their own," she retorted teasingly. "Even the staunchest feminist can't offer an alternative to that. Childbirth is definitely woman's work."

"Oh, you know what I mean." He was tight-lipped, embarrassed.

"Yes. You mean I'm not married and I'm going to raise the child on my own," she said more gently. "But that will be all right, Cal. I'm lucky. I can afford it. I can afford a home. I can afford help. I'll be all right. Really."

The women on her staff were strangely ambivalent. Natalie, a research assistant, asked to be assigned to another project. She was ten years younger than Anne and single. Within weeks she announced her engagement to a hospital administrator who had long pursued Anne and whom she had ruefully dismissed as boring.

Linda Cummings, a hematologist, the wife of an immunologist and the mother of twins, encountered Anne in the women's room.

"May I speak with you frankly?" she asked.

"About what?" They had known each other for ten years and had never had an intimate conversation.

"About your situation. I think what you are doing is very selfish," Linda said sternly. She washed her hands carefully after removing her wedding band so that soap would not collect in the intricate engraving. She was a woman who took excellent care of her possessions; her house was immaculate, her research papers impeccably footnoted, her husband well tailored, her children kept clean and well nourished by an expensive household staff. She polished the ring with a paper towel before slipping it back on her finger.

"Not that it's any of your business — but why selfish?" Anne said. She looked in the mirror and studied herself with clinical detachment. Pregnancy suited her, she decided complacently. Her color was high, her eyes bright, her white-gold hair was thick and lustrous. She wore a navy blue shift patterned with dancing dolphins that Merle had sent her from New York. It came from a shop called Great Expectations that, Merle reported, specialized in maternity clothing for the professional woman. She added that she had told the store manager there ought to be separate sections for pregnant lawyers, pregnant doctors, pregnant engineers. The manager had not been amused.

"Who will take care of your baby? Who will nurture it?" Linda Cummings persisted.

"Who takes care of your children? Who nurtures them?" Anne retorted.

"My situation is quite different. A child needs two parents."

"And some hardly get to see even one parent — if there's a conference in an interesting city," Anne replied. She applied eyeliner with a steady hand.

Linda Cummings blushed. She and her husband had just returned from a pharmaceutical company junket to Rio. Their children had not accompanied them.

"See you around the day-care center," Anne said, slamming the door to the women's room behind her.

Eric called every several weeks to check on her. He had left college and was working for an environmental protection group in San Francisco. He moved so often that Anne kept a separate page in her address book to record his frequently changing phone numbers.

"Why doesn't he let us know where he is?" Hope asked plaintively when she phoned from New York.

Anne did not remind Hope that too often Eric had not known where his parents were. Ted had remarried. His wife was only a few years older than Eric, a sweetly smiling blonde who spoke with a slow drawl not unlike Hope's Kentucky accent. Hope herself traveled constantly. There were print shows in Sweden, shoots on the Riviera, video productions in Jerusalem. Designer clothes replaced the thrift shop evening gowns with their tarnished spangles. Shortly after the divorce Hope had disappeared to Mexico and returned with her equine nose newly straight-bridged and tight-nostriled.

"What does my mom think about your having this kid?" Eric asked.

"I think she's glad for me because I'm happy about it," Anne said carefully. Hope, after all, had always been generous. She had been generous during her years of struggle and she was generous now in her prosperity. She had supported Anne during Anne's recovery from the abortion and she supported her during this pregnancy. Hope was not to blame because she was a better businesswoman than she had been a mother. She had tried, she had really tried, although Eric could not see that, although he could not forgive her for the long, silent afternoons of his boyhood. It was Anne who had sustained him then and who sustained him now. He called her when he came down from a high, when girls left him and when he left girls, when friends disappointed and jobs petered out. Anne's strength reassured him. He viewed her pregnancy with quiet pride. She could do anything.

Merle came to Minnesota shortly before the birth — a radiant Merle who smiled often and whose laughter rang with a new warmth. She spoke to Andrew each evening; their soft, loving exchanges were sparked with a new spontaneity.

"Don't work too hard," Merle commanded her husband. "Don't forget to work out on the exercycle."

The protected had become the protector. Her new vigilance was born of love. She and Andrew spoke of adopting a child, a little girl, but Merle was honest about her ambivalence. She was working closely with Emanuel Klein and seriously considering the suggestion that she succeed him as director of an innovative music program.

"I'm really thinking about it," she told Anne. "The influence of the yuppie code. It's my turn now. I want to see what I can do — with my music, with the orchestra. I don't want to be torn again the way I was when Greg was growing up."

"I know what you mean," Anne said. Complacently, she patted the great swell of her pregnancy. She would not be torn as Merle had been torn. Unlike Hope, she would know how to manage. She had always known how to organize her life, how to arrange her priorities. She had earned the confidence that had led her to this decision.

Tommy's birth was uncomplicated. Anne cradled the newborn infant in her arms, marveled at the wrinkling of his raspberry-colored face and the luminous nails that crowned each tiny finger and toe. Her son bawled with hunger and she lifted him and kissed his face. She placed him on her breast and he sucked vigorously. She laughed at the tug of his mouth. Her body sustained him. She was connected to him, bonded by blood and love, and by choice.

"Mine," she whispered into the delicate shell of his ear. "All mine." She felt a surge of triumph. There would be no sharing of this child. Her love, her care, would be sufficient.

Merle stayed with her for three weeks and Rutti flew out for several days. The three friends played with the infant with all the absorption and intensity of young girls who, as they drift out of childhood, become strangely obsessive about their dolls. They fed Tommy and changed his clothes. Rutti sketched him asleep, sketched him yet again in his prenursing fury, and then again with his face peacefully resting against the rise of Anne's breast, his eyes closed and his long silken lashes sweeping his cheeks. One night they phoned Nancy in Jerusalem and giggled and chatted for ten long expensive minutes.

"Oh, Nancy, he's the most wonderful baby," Anne said.

"I think Nancy will be coming to the States sometime soon," Rutti said when they hung up. "David had lunch with the Israeli consul and he said there was talk of Ari coming here to organize cultural exchange programs throughout the country."

"How would Nancy feel about that, I wonder?" Merle mused. "She's pregnant again. Keren is happy at school and Nancy has her practice, her courses at the university. Now she'll have to uproot herself again."

"You see?" Anne said bitterly. "The script has been rewritten, but the story line is the same. Daddy gets a new job and the wife and children dutifully pack their bags and follow him."

"Not exactly," Rutti said. "Things have changed. David's sister, Alicia, got married last year. She had tenure at the University of Massachusetts and Bruce had a law practice in New Jersey. A good practice, too. He gave it up and started over in Amherst. A new scenario."

"Lucky Alicia," Anne said dryly. "One small step for woman. One giant step for womankind."

"Don't be sexist," Merle protested and tossed a pillow at her.

Anne tossed it back and Tommy cried angrily, imperiously. Laughing, the friends raced for him. Anne's newborn son was their soft-skinned toy. His lusty cry, his tears, reawakened in them the sensuous carnality of new motherhood. When Tommy cried in the night, Merle felt her own breasts swell and ache. Rutti phoned home to check on the twins.

"They're sleeping, David?" she said. "But it's so early." She was disappointed that they slept so happily in her absence, that they managed so well without her. But of course David was as wonderful a father as he was a husband. Strong and competent, tender and firm. The twins played in his studio as he worked, called to him from the garden.

"Daddy, we want you."

"You'll have to wait. Daddy's busy." His words were unmarred by guilt or ambivalence.

Anne told her friends that she planned to leave the Mayo Clinic. Her DNA research had attracted international attention. Research centers knew that Anne would bring grant money with her. She had already had tentative offers from Chicago and Los Angeles.

"But why not come east — to Boston or New York?" Merle suggested. "You'd be near us."

"It's just not a good idea. Too many complications." Anne's reply was brusque and they assumed it had something to do with Tommy's father. They asked no more questions. Despite the intensity of their intimacy, they had always carefully observed the parameters of privacy; they waited for information to be volunteered, seldom offering unsolicited advice.

In the end Anne accepted the offer from the Michael Reese Hospital in Chicago. There was an energy in Chicago that excited her after the quiet years in Rochester. The pleasant suburb of Oak Park offered a painless commute. She and Tommy settled in smoothly. It had, of course, helped considerably that Tommy was an easy baby, an attractive, happy child. Freckles spangled his turned-up nose and his strawberry-blond hair was thick and curling. He laughed readily, the hearty, untroubled laugh of an adored child who assumes that the world has been created for his pleasure. He made friends easily and was a welcome addition to play groups. He was the child who shared his loot bag at birthday parties and comforted the playmate who suffered a fall or wept over losing a game. And his friends responded in kind.

"Wait for Tommy," Ved admonished other children who wanted to start a game before Tommy could join them.

"Tommy, Tommy, ride with me," children called when he pushed his bright blue Big Wheels onto the pavement.

The children on Anne's street rode in a convoy each afternoon, but Tommy was not among the small boys who waved to Anne as she drove up. When she phoned from the hospital earlier in the day Maureen had told her that Tommy seemed out of sorts.

"Nothing serious, but he's tired and listless and he does have the sniffles. I'm just feeding him juice and letting him watch 'Sesame Street.'"

"It's probably the weather," Anne assured her.

A friend on pediatrics had told her that the unseasonable warmth of the fall had precipitated a strange flu epidemic. Late summer colds lingered and the children's weakened resistance made them vulnerable to infection. "If I were you, Anne, I'd give up DNA research. The Nobel Prize is going to go to whoever cures the common cold," her friend said.

"Tommy," Anne called cheerfully as she entered the house.

He sat on the couch, curled up in the cocoon of the blue and white afghan and sucking at a corner of it. Anne gently removed the corner damp with his saliva, the rich blue faded to a milky hue.

"How's my big man today?" she asked and ruffled his hair.

"I'm not a big man, silly," he said petulantly. "And I hate Mr. Rogers. He's silly."

"You don't have to watch," Maureen said placidly. She pressed the remote control and the screen went blank. She shrugged and smiled at Anne.

The bright daughter of a Kansas City electrician, she was a pleasant, serious girl who wore rimless glasses and whose brown hair hugged her head in a neat Dutch-boy cut. An economics major at the University of Chicago, she planned to go on for an MBA.

"Why an MBA?" Anne asked at their first interview.

"Because that's where the money is," Maureen replied without embarrassment.

Maureen shared her generation's candid, cheerful greed, their tenacious pursuit of the good life made better by the flash of plastic credit cards. Theirs was a validated narcissism. They drank large glasses of carrot juice at health food bars, studied their bodies in the long mirrors that faced their exercise machines at indoor gyms, spread mousse made only with natural ingredients on their well-styled hair. Anne's younger colleagues at the hospital, the new crop of interns and residents, traded notes on their condos and health clubs, their skiing vacations in Aspen and Vermont. They spoke lovingly of brand-name products, popular restaurants. Cuisinart. Godiva. Nautilus. Reeboks. Perrier.

"What makes Maureen's ambition so different from our own, when we were younger?" Rutti asked when Anne discussed it with her. Rutti remembered herself as a young mother clutching Sarah's hand, walking long blocks to save bus fare, laundering the blouse she had worn that day so that she could wear it again the next day. She too had wanted a better life. They had been ambitious, all of them.

"We wanted to achieve," Anne replied. "They want to acquire." Her assessment was harsh, she knew, but not inaccurate.

Still, she liked Maureen, admired her determination, her easy humor. And Maureen was good with Tommy, as Anne had been good with Eric.

"Turn the set on," Tommy commanded Maureen fiercely. He snatched the blanket away from Anne and continued to suck on the frayed and faded corner.

Maureen switched it back on.

"He's been that way most of the day," she told Anne. "The cold is getting to him. Mrs. Singh says that a lot of the kids at the nursery school have it."

"Kindergarten," Tommy said. "I'm in kindergarten."

"All right, kindergarten," Maureen agreed pleasantly. She gathered up her notebooks and texts and left.

Anne pressed her lips against her son's forehead. He pulled away, but she tackled him in an embrace and tickled him until he sprawled in giggling surrender across the sofa.

"No fever," she said. "But if you're still feeling sick by the weekend, I'll make an appointment with Dr. Irwin."

"You're silly," Tommy said. "The weekend isn't until the day after tomorrow. I'll be better."

Anne called twice from her laboratory the next day. The phone was in an open area and as she spoke she saw Sally and Philip, the two residents who assisted her, glance at each other knowingly.

"Give him some orange juice, Maureen," she said when Maureen told her that Tommy's appetite seemed to be returning. "And I don't think marshmallow fluff and peanut butter can hurt him if that's what he wants."

Anne smiled at Sally and Philip, inviting their amused complicity, but Sally did not smile back. She was openly disapproving and intolerant. She would never consume valuable laboratory time with personal problems. She and her friends vowed that when they had children, they would manage differently. They would arrange for adequate child care and be psychologically able to separate. They were confident that they would be able to do so, having discussed it in the assertiveness-training courses most of them attended.

But Sally was conciliatory when she left.

"I hope your son feels better over the weekend," she told Anne. She was flying to New York to spend two days with the corporate attorney who was her current lover. He, in turn, would come to

Chicago in a few weeks' time. Sally loved the tense ride to O'Hare, the swift flight, her lover's welcoming smile. She was at once emancipated and beloved, independent and attached.

"Oh, he'll be fine. It's this strange weather. A lot of kids have summer colds," Anne replied.

"Indian summer," Philip observed glumly. "There'll be a cold snap soon."

"Oh, I hope not," she protested amiably. "I love Indian summer evenings. Tommy and I take long walks then. When he's feeling well."

"Oh, kids are resilient," Philip assured her. He thought Anne Richardson was a brilliant doctor and a beautiful woman. He wondered if she was widowed or divorced or even if she had ever been married at all. He wondered what it would be like to touch her white-gold hair and he felt a new misery at his own encroaching baldness. He hoped that she was widowed rather than divorced. It occurred to him that Tommy might be adopted. That idea pleased him. It was not uncommon now for single women to adopt children. He knew a nurse who had adopted an infant abandoned by an addicted mother. And a friend of his sister's, a high school English teacher, had flown to Brazil and returned with an onyx-eyed little boy.

"Yes. Children do have marvelous powers of recovery," Anne agreed eagerly.

And Tommy did feel better during the weekend. He played with Ved on Saturday afternoon, but when the other children took their Big Wheels out, he returned home.

"I want to watch 'Sesame Street,' " he said, taking up his blanket and pressing the tortured corner into his mouth.

"It's not on over the weekend," Anne said. "You know that, Tommy. Let's take a walk instead."

But Tommy would only walk as far as the corner to the giant oak where they always paused to see how a long young branch had forked itself against a tattered and discolored strip of yellow ribbon. The ribbon intrigued Tommy, and Anne had tried to explain to him that it had been tied to the tree because Americans were imprisoned in a distant country called Iran.

"But now all the Americans are free," Tommy affirmed each time she finished the story.

"Yes. They're all free," Anne invariably replied as she lifted him to the tree so that he might touch the disintegrating bit of yellow satin. Had so many months really passed since the television screen had been free of the footage of the blind-folded, humiliated hostages, since Ronald Reagan, the President whom she could not dissociate from the Sunday matinee films of her childhood, had told the nation that the hostage nightmare was over? Anne had phoned Merle that night and asked her how Paris Mitchell of *Kings Row* had managed to appease the Ayatollah and Merle had laughed softly. Life moved so swiftly. They were caught in its vortex, in the whirlwind of their times, in the mist of their dreams.

Once, Anne reflected, she had willed the years to pass quickly. She had been in such a hurry to graduate from medical school, to be launched on her career, to gain independence, recognition. Now she cherished each passing day; she savored the long sweet seasons of her golden-haired son's childhood, the continuity of the life she had crafted and that she alone sustained.

"Time for the story of the ribbon," she said when they reached the oak tree. Usually he listened eagerly, pleased with the ritual. When she said the word *Iran,* it was Tommy's habit to giggle wildly and shout "I ran — you ran — he ran — we all ran — far far away!" But tonight he was fretful. He pulled at her skirt.

"Home. Let's go home," he said, and he did not wave to Ved who honked his horn noisily as he pedaled past them.

Rutti called that night with the news that Ari had been posted to New York and that he and Nancy and the children would be living not far from Merle and Andrew on Riverside Drive.

"Well, it took them long enough to offer him the assignment," Anne said. "Weren't they talking about it four years ago, when Tommy was born?"

"Oh, he was offered it then but the timing was bad. Nancy didn't want to leave Israel then. She had just set up her clinic and her tenure at the university wasn't assured. And she was pregnant with Noah and Keren was facing army service. But now Keren is finished with the army and the clinic is well established. And Noah and Seth are at the right age for an easy adjustment." It upset Rutti that Anne was so disagreeable, so critical. Was she jealous of Nancy, she wondered, and immediately she chastised herself for her disloyalty. There was no need for beautiful, accomplished Anne Richardson to be jealous of anyone.

"What's wrong, Anne?" she asked softly.

"Tommy's so irritable. It's just a summer cold, I know, but he's so tired. I'm worried."

"Autumn blahs," Rutti offered consolingly. "The twins have them too. It's this crazy weather. Sarah came down with something every September."

"How is Sarah?" Anne asked.

"She's OK, really. At least I think so. She doesn't come to Egremont very often. She takes classes with Uta Hagen, waits tables at some Village eatery, and runs around to auditions. She and Keren will probably take an apartment together this fall."

"Sarah. Keren. An apartment," Anne said wonderingly and they both laughed. They were remembering the two small girls in a sand-box, the two small girls who had perched on the bed each Friday afternoon and sang along with *The Magic Garden* while their mothers cupped their hands around lukewarm cups of coffee and talked and talked and talked. And now, with mysterious swiftness, those two small girls were young women. Anne had seen Keren on her infre-quent visits to the States. Like Nancy, she was tall and dark-haired. She spoke slowly, carefully, as though conditioned to caution. Anne did not know her well, but she sensed a secret, almost a reticent strength. Sarah, however, had a fragile beauty. She was as tiny as her mother and her blond hair was closely cut, helmeting her finely shaped head. She wore intricately shaped hanging earrings and brace-lets ringed her slender wrists so that when she moved she created a teasing, lilting music. Her gestures were swift and graceful, her laugh-ter contagious. When Anne walked with her or sat opposite her in a restaurant, men turned to look at her and then swiftly averted their eyes as though the innocence of Sarah's large-eyed gaze confounded their thoughts and feelings. Yet Rutti's daughter seemed to be haunted by sadness, her wry humor masking cynicism.

"We'll have to get them a housewarming gift. Like a dead bolt for their door," Anne continued. "I'll call you back when Tommy is his own sweet placid self again. Like his mom."

"Tell me another, oh placid one," Rutti countered and hung up.

Anne imagined how Rutti would go into David's studio, repeat her conversation with Anne, discuss plans with him for the rest of the weekend. Should they take the twins into Lenox or perhaps drive deeper into the Berkshires and hike a minitrail with them? Perhaps they should invite Merle and Andrew for dinner. Anne thought of her own weekend, of amusing Tommy, of worrying about Tommy without anyone to share either the amusing or the worrying. Briefly, she allowed self-pity to wash over her. Damn it — it was hard sometimes, so damn hard. She slammed a copper ashtray down, kicked over her ottoman. She did not begrudge herself these brief, irrational explosions of rage. She had, after all, opted for single parenthood, not sainthood.

She went upstairs and looked in on Tommy, fast asleep in his red-and-white striped ballplayer pajamas. She removed the blanket corner from his mouth and drew the comforter closer about him. His face seemed very pale, but when she touched his brow she was satisfied that he was not feverish and that he breathed lightly, evenly.

"You are being a neurotic, obsessive woman," she told herself and went downstairs to listen to the recording Merle had sent her. The familiar movements of *A Child's Prayer* comforted her and she closed her eyes and imagined Merle playing.

Tommy was more energetic by Sunday night and on Monday morning Maureen and Anne agreed that he was well enough to go to school. Maureen walked Tommy and Ved to the large red brick building and Anne, driving by on her way to the city, waved to them. They all grinned and waved back. You see, she told herself, everything is all right.

She spent a great deal of time that morning working with Sally. The lab phone rang and she waved Philip to answer it.

"If it's for me, take a message," she said tersely. She read Sally's notes carefully. The younger woman had done some impressive chromosome isolation, perhaps stumbling onto something. A single chromosome, dormant for generations, might trigger a genetic predisposition to a disease of nervous degeneration. Sally's findings were exciting and exhilarating. They would have to lease time on a sophisticated computer and arrange to view the slides through the lens of a high-powered electronic microscope.

"Anne." Philip stood beside her. "The call is for you."

"Just take a message." She did not look up.

"It's Maureen. It's about Tommy."

She took the call at once.

"What's happening, Maureen?" she asked, struggling to keep her voice casual. Maureen called her at work only in case of emergency.

"It's Tommy. The school nurse called. She said he had a fever and that he should be seen by a doctor. Today."

"All right. I'll call Dr. Irwin and arrange for an appointment. Pick Tommy up and I'll meet you at home."

Manny Irwin had been a year behind her at the same medical school. For the first time, she asked him to give her a priority appointment.

"Sure, I'll fit you in, Anne," Manny said easily. "But I'm sure it's just another one of what I'm calling Indian summer flus. I've been seeing them all day."

Anne did not contradict him. She hung up and turned to Sally.

"I'm sorry to run out on you like this," she said. "But Tommy is sick. Run the rest of the experiment and we'll work together tomorrow."

"I understand," Sally replied, but her tone was cool, disapproving. "I suppose your sitter doesn't drive."

"As a matter of fact, she does," Anne said and stared hard at her.

She had long been aware of the fact that the younger women in her profession were oddly critical. When the competent woman who chaired the pathology department had been forced to take a leave the previous winter because both her elderly mother and her adolescent daughter were ill, Anne had overheard two young women on her staff complain.

"She could have made other arrangements."

"There are plenty of home health care services."

Their criticisms were self-protective. The actions and decisions of other women made them professionally vulnerable. They were unforgiving, judgmental. As Sally was unforgiving, judgmental. But then Sally had not yet stood nocturnal vigil at the bedside of an ailing child. She had yet to feel the clutch of fear, the knot of maternal desperation.

Damn it, I'm doing what I have to do, Anne thought as she drove to Oak Park. I don't owe that little bitch any explanation.

But she forgot about Sally when she reached home. Tommy's skin was chalk-white and tiny fever patches burned on his cheeks. His blue eyes, usually agate-bright, were dull and he lay listlessly on the bed. Anne knelt beside him, kissed him, passed her hands across his neck. His glands were swollen and she noticed that purplish spots dotted his ankles and shins.

"Hey, Tommy-O, we're going to Dr. Irwin and he's going to make you all better." She pressed her fingers against the spots. No protrusion, she noted with relief. They were probably just a local irritation or an allergy that would soon disappear.

Maureen offered to go to the doctor with her and Anne declined.

"Take the day off," she said. "I may even stay home tomorrow." Sally could go to hell, she decided. Wait until she has a sick kid.

Tommy was Manny Irwin's last patient that morning.

"Hey there, Thomas, looks like you've shot up another inch or so since June. Keep it up and I'll have to stand on tiptoe to examine you," Manny said cheerfully. He was a short, rotund man whose hair had thinned in medical school and who had the self-disparaging, compensatory humor peculiar to men who have always felt themselves to be unattractive. Anne liked him and she had been pleased to learn that he had bought a pediatric practice in Oak Park.

"Are you married, Anne?" he had asked her when she first brought Tommy to him for an examination almost four years ago. "Divorced? Widowed?"

"None of the above," she replied, staring at him defiantly.

"Hey. Don't bite my head off. I'm not asking you for Class Notes or on behalf of the Moral Majority. I promise not to report you to Jerry Falwell," he protested, aware of the nervous tapping of her foot, the anger in her eyes. "I just want to get some medical history here. And I assume that Tommy had a father. Superwoman that you are, immaculate conception is still a bit beyond you. I hope."

She relaxed, smiled, and told him what she knew of Tommy's father's history. No diabetes. No history of other hereditary diseases. No mental illness. Normal parental longevity. "Naturally, I checked all that out," she said, grinning mischievously.

"Naturally." He patted her head. Manny Irwin was the only man who had ever patted her head.

He even patted it now as he lifted Tommy out of her arms.

"You don't mind waiting out here, do you, Anne?" he said. "Make believe you're a normal mom. Read the *Ladies' Home Journal.* Knit an afghan."

"Shut up, creep. I do read the *Ladies' Home Journal* every month and I am knitting an afghan." She kissed Tommy and watched as the nurse followed Manny into the examining room and closed the door behind her.

She turned the pages of a magazine, but she could not concentrate on the words. She glanced at the pictures. Pert young women in business suits and running shoes grinned up at her from the glossy pages. She studied a collage of photos of Nancy Reagan in a red suit, a red gown, a red shirt-waist dress. Red was a big color. She might buy herself a bright red suit, a bright red dress. She might even cut her hair. She glanced at her watch. *What was taking Manny so damn long?* But then he had always worked slowly, methodically. She remembered doing a biochemistry project with him back in medical school. She suggested that he come to Charles Bingham's apartment and they spread their lab sheets across the floor. Charles returned home unexpectedly and Manny Irwin was embarrassed and told too many jokes. Charles was kind. But then he had never been unkind, Anne acknowledged, until that last day, that very last day.

She flinched at the memory, stood up, and walked about the room. A mesh playpen stood in the corner, filled with toys for the small patients. Anne knelt beside it, fingered a Big Bird puppet, a set of Fisher-Price circus animals, a bright red fire engine. Tommy had each of these toys. Only a week ago she sprawled across the bed as he stalked her with Big Bird.

"Big Bird is angry with Mommy," he proclaimed threateningly. He was angry with Anne because she had insisted that he put his toys away.

"Oh, no. Help me, Oscar. Ernie, Bert, help me," Anne shouted and giggled as Tommy tickled her with the puppet's furry wing. Together they tossed the toys onto the shelves. Tommy crammed the circus animals into the fire engine. "My father's a clown. In the circus," he announced.

"Yes. With a big red nose," Anne agreed amiably.

"What are you going to tell Tommy about his father?" Merle asked her once.

"I'm thinking about it." Anne's answer was evasive but accurate. She was thinking about it still, but hadn't reached a decision.

"Where's your daddy?" Ved Singh asked Tommy one afternoon.

"I don't need a daddy," Tommy replied calmly. "I have my mom. She drives. She works."

"OK," Ved agreed. "You're right."

Poor Mrs. Singh, Anne had thought. She did not drive and she did not work. Hence, the need for Dr. Singh. She had giggled softly. But she envied Padma Singh now. If Ved were ill, her husband would sit beside her. A polite and protective presence, he always accompanied her to the doctor.

The door opened. The nurse, a pretty, blond young woman who wore a pink uniform with a large Miss Piggy pin on the pocket, smiled at her.

"Dr. Irwin would like to see you."

"Of course." She took encouragement from the nurse's smile. Tommy was all right. Tommy was fine. She followed her into Manny's book-lined office and watched as the nurse took Tommy by the hand and led him out.

"Tommy and I are going to have some apple juice," she announced cheerfully.

Anne smiled at Manny.

"So what do we have?" she asked. "A late summer cold, a change of season flu?"

"What do you think, Anne?"

"Ah, the Socratic method. All right. I think it's probably a flu aggravated by a possible allergic reaction."

"Why an allergic reaction?" He did not look up from his notes. He did not meet her eyes.

"I saw a purplish rash on his ankles and shins."

"Also on his buttocks."

"So? An allergy. Right?"

"Anne, has he had a sore throat recently?"

"Oh, just a minor inflammation. Maybe two weeks ago. Similar to the one he had at the end of last summer. He's climate sensitive, I think. It went away. It was nothing, really."

"But this year it was followed by the cold and now the rash?"

"Yes. Why? What's on your mind, Manny?"

"I'm almost certain that the rash is purpura," he said gravely. "I tried the glass test."

"The glass test," Anne repeated. She recalled learning the technique during her rotation in pediatrics. It was not complicated. If a child presented with purplish, irregularly shaped dots, a glass was pressed against the rash. A rash that remained visible under the pressure was almost certainly caused by purpura. She had not thought to try the glass test on Tommy. "Then it is a virus, after all."

Her voice was calm even as she struggled to remember the casebook implications of allergic purpura. The rash, of course, was caused by an abnormal reaction between the antibodies that normally protect against infection and blood vessels. She recalled it was sometimes caused by a reaction to a food, a drug, or a virus. It was also possible that the antibodies were produced to combat a streptococcus bacteria.

"If I remember correctly, Manny," she said carefully, "there's usually a spontaneous recovery from allergic purpura."

"Usually." He countered her calm with his own but the worried expression did not leave his face. "If it is allergy or infection related."

"What else could it be?"

"Anne, I just have a hunch, but I want to be certain and follow it through. I've taken blood from Tommy and it's already en route to the lab. You may be right that it's simply allergic purpura. But there is a possibility, given Tommy's other symptoms, that it could be thrombocytopenia purpura." He looked at her kindly, sadly. He had three sons and the youngest, she knew, had been born with a congenital heart defect. He was no stranger to parental agony.

"No!" Angrily she rejected his sadness, his kindness, the preposterousness of his hunch. Her fingers curled into a fist and flashed to her mouth. Her throat rasped and she found it difficult to breathe. She did not recognize her own voice when at last she spoke.

"You're talking about a leukemic symptom."

"It's just a possibility," he repeated. "I want to be certain that we've covered all bases."

"I understand," she said. "But I think you're wrong."

"I probably am." She heard the misery in his voice. He yearned to be wrong. "Meanwhile, keep Tommy warm. Watch out for dehydration. I've prescribed something to bring the fever down."

"You'll call me?"

"I put a rush on the tests. And I'll be in touch as soon as I get the readouts. But it may take a while. They'll need cultures. All that stuff."

"Yes," she said. "Of course. All that stuff. But you'll call me when you have some news."

"The very minute."

"Remember I lent you my biochem notes."

"I am forever in your debt. I never would have finished medical school without you. No Jewish girl would have married me. Stay calm. Get some rest and if Tommy's feeling better perhaps you'd join us for dinner Saturday night. Just a small group of friends. An interesting attorney who works with Lynn."

"Thanks, Manny. I'll let you know." She wondered if the "interesting attorney" was widowed or divorced. Probably divorced, she decided. He would talk endlessly and bitterly of his ex-wife's insensitivity. If Tommy was better, she'd take him and Ved out for pizza on Saturday night.

Tommy's fever subsided that night. Padma Singh sent over a sweet coconut custard, which he ate with a good appetite. He plastered the television set with Colorforms. He wore his Mets shirt and his most faded jeans. He was pale, but appeared to be regaining his energy. On Saturday night Anne made spaghetti for dinner and he rewarded her with a series of what he called "pasghetti kisses." He pressed the sauce-soaked strands against his lips and then onto her cheek.

"Disgusting," she said, slapping him lightly. "Crazy child. Idiot boy."

"Crazy Mommy. Idiot lady," he countered mischievously, giggling.

The rash had not faded.

"Tommy has a rash — some sort of allergy," Anne told Rutti who phoned on Saturday to tell her that Merle was planning a party for Nancy and her family.

"Oh, a rash. The twins are always covered with rashes," Rutti said nonchalantly and Anne felt better immediately. Manny Irwin was being overly pessimistic and overly cautious, she decided.

"When's Nancy coming?"

"Early November. Merle's thinking about Thanksgiving. An Egremont house party."

"This is September," Anne said dryly.

"But you know Merle. She has to have everything organized."

"Andrew's influence. The sins of the husband are visited upon the wife. You see the advantages of being a single lady, Rutti?"

"No," Rutti replied cheerfully. "Get married, Anne. Make an honest child of Tommy."

"Don't be a Jewish mother," Anne retorted, smiling. "Sarah will leave home."

"You don't think I'd dare to mention marriage to Sarah," Rutti said. "She'll remind me that she's only twenty-two." Rutti did not add that Sarah might not answer at all. Intimacy frightened her, Rutti knew, although she did not know why.

"And she'll be all right. Go paint a picture, Rutti. Or maybe do some line drawings or something creative. Stop meddling in the lives of contented singles."

"Good-bye, Anne. Give Tommy a kiss for me. He'll be fine. Really."

Anne hung up. She had not fooled Rutti. Her friend had heard the worry in her voice. She tiptoed into Tommy's room. As always, he slept clutching the afghan. Tomato sauce rimmed his mouth. He had resisted washing his face before bed and she had not pressed him. She kissed him, licking lightly at the scab of sauce that dotted his cheek. He smiled in his sleep.

"No tickling. Crazy Mommy."

She thought him wondrously beautiful. Joy rippled through her because he was her son, because she had dared to bear him.

On Monday morning she called Manny's office.

"Nothing definite. Some half-assed technician screwed up one of the tests. Tomorrow."

"Sure. I'm not worried. Tommy's really doing better."

"Good."

Still, Anne called Maureen twice that afternoon and each time Maureen reassured her. Relieved, she conferred with Sally about her research. She had arranged for Sally to use a sophisticated electronic microscope at the University of Chicago.

"I hope Tommy's feeling better," Sally said when she left. It was, Anne recognized, an expression of gratitude and apology.

"He'll be fine, Sally."

But he was not fine. The fever had returned and he was once more listless and without appetite. She called Manny at home.

"I was just going to call you, Anne. The results of the blood work came in late today."

She surprised both him and herself by not asking him to discuss them over the phone.

"I'll come to your office in the morning," she said. "Eight-thirty?"

"Eight o'clock would be better."

"Eight o'clock."

That night she read two chapters in a textbook she had not opened since medical school. She also went through several back copies of a medical journal looking for a specific article. She read with great concentration, and at last she took a very long hot shower and put on a fresh nightgown. She lay awake in the silent darkness of her bedroom and said aloud the word she had avoided using since the onset of Tommy's illness. She whispered it at first and then uttered it slowly, clearly. It was an obscenity upon her tongue and she erased it by repeating her son's name again and again. *Tommy. Tommy. Tommy.* She did not weep, but her eyes were seared by grief.

She sat opposite him once again in the book-lined office. Wordlessly Manny passed the folder containing the lab reports to her. She put on her half-glasses and read them carefully. There was, she saw at once, an alarming increase in the number of white blood cells in Tommy's body. There was an indication of abnormality in the leukocytes. There was also an indication of increased lymphocyte production. That would account for the swollen glands. She returned the reports to Manny, removed her glasses, replaced them in their case, and put the case back into her large leather bag. Each gesture was a small victory in her battle for control.

"Your hunch appears to have been correct, Manny," she said evenly.

"We won't know anything for certain until we do a bone marrow biopsy," he said miserably. "There's still an outside chance that we may be dealing with a virulent infection — that Tommy's body is battling it in an irregular way."

"Of course. A bone marrow biopsy. Manny, you won't be offended if I see someone else on this?"

"I won't be offended. You'll need a good pediatric oncologist. I can give you the names of a couple of good people in Chicago."

"I don't want good," Anne said. "I want the best. I want Charles Bingham."

"Yes. He is the best. I just read his article in the *Journal of Hematology*. No one can touch his research or his methods."

"I reread it myself last night," Anne said. She had fallen asleep with the last words of Charles's article whirring through her mind:

> "There is now cause for cautious optimism in cases of juveniles afflicted with acute lymphatic leukemia. Drug therapy, marrow transplants, remissions as a result of radiation and diet give hope to those whose prognosis might once have been deemed hopeless."

"You know, of course, that he does not see patients — he's no longer on attending staff."

"He'll see me, Manny. Could you send him Tommy's records, the lab reports?"

"Will do." Of course Charles Bingham would see Anne Richardson. They had been lovers, an enchanted couple who had walked through the corridors of the medical school so absorbed in each other that their colleagues, embarrassed by their intimacy, rushed by them, envious. Manny wondered briefly about Tommy's father. An idea skittered through his mind and he dropped it at once. Blue-gray eyes were not uncommon. His own son, the boy wasted and wearied by heart disease, had eyes of just that color.

He walked Anne to the door.

"Anne, I'm sorry," he said.

"No need for condolences, Manny. Tommy is not going to die."

"You'll be in touch." He proffered neither contradiction nor reassurance.

"As soon as I talk to Charles."

She phoned Charles Bingham's office as soon as she reached her laboratory, but he was unavailable.

"He's on vacation until the end of September," his secretary said.

"Can you give me his phone number at home or at his vacation house? I am Dr. Anne Richardson, a close personal friend." She was not lying. She supposed that she and Charles were friends. Over the years they had greeted each other pleasantly when they met at professional gatherings. They had even had coffee together and shared meals on occasion. And there had been an evening of serendipitous intimacy only a few years ago when both of them had been stranded by a sudden snowstorm after a seminar in the Rockies. Anne seldom thought about those hours when pellets of snow had pounded against the wide windows of a hotel built to celebrate the vast expanse of mountain peaks. She had even met Nicole, Charles's wife, a sweet, fair-haired woman who wore tortoiseshell glasses and limped very slightly. Perhaps it was the limp that had attracted Charles, Anne thought unpleasantiy when she first met Nicole Bingham. A woman who limped could not run away. Banished, she would walk slowly, haltingly, and he would have time to hurry after her, to forgive her and take her home. As Anne had not allowed him to hurry after her, as she had made no effort to return to him.

"I cannot release Dr. Bingham's number." The secretary was shocked at her request. It was her duty to protect her doctor. She was a cadet in the vast army of nurses, administrators, secretaries, whose sacred role in life was to run interference for the men they served. But Anne was not defenseless against such women. She had learned how to counterattack.

"Please take my name and number and make certain that you ask him to call me today. He will be extremely upset if he does not receive this message," she said with more authority than she felt.

Her phone rang within the hour.

"Anne. Charles. What's the problem?" He did not pause for formalities. If she called him after all these years, there was a good reason. She told him about Tommy, struggling to keep her tone free of fear.

"Manny is right," he said when she fell silent. "I wouldn't jump to conclusions, but the symptoms would indicate the need for further tests. Definitely a bone marrow biopsy. The procedure is relatively simple, as you know, Anne."

"I know. But I would still feel more comfortable if you would do it. I understand that you're on vacation — that it's an imposition —"

"Stop," he said firmly. "Nothing you ask of me could ever be an imposition. I'd like to see you at the office I maintain at my home. I don't want to go to the hospital because I'd be besieged. Can you make it on Thursday — let's say at three. No. Four. I'd schedule it earlier but our younger son is competing in a swim meet upstate and we had planned a sort of mini–family holiday." He was apologetic, but there was a hint of pride in his voice. He who had grown up in the Oklahoma heartland, indentured to farm chores and an unarticulated ambition, had a son who competed in swim meets.

"That's fine. I think I'll call Merle Cunningham and see whether we can spend the weekend at Egremont."

He was silent and in that silence she sensed reproach. She should not have mentioned Egremont where they had spent so many happy hours together. Or perhaps she was being hypersensitive. It might well be that after all these years, happy in his marriage, the memory of his years with Anne had faded. As her memories of the years with him had not. But then women nurtured such memories, keeping them safe in a secret corner of their consciousness. A woman remembered the moist sweetness of her first kiss, the tender caress in a darkened hallway. Anne had not forgotten that she was wearing a pink sweater the night a boy's lips first pressed against her own. Nor had she forgotten the scent of the azaleas, the softness of their petals on that first afternoon when she and Charles Bingham had stood side by side in the Botanical Garden.

"I see Merle and Andrew occasionally at hospital functions. He's on the board, you know," Charles said at last. "All right then, Thursday."

"Yes. Thursday. And Charles — thank you."

"I'll be spending several days in New York," she told Sally and Philip. She did not offer them any explanations nor did they ask for any.

"We're going to New York," she told Tommy that night. "We're going to visit an old friend of Mommy's — Dr. Bingham. And then we'll go to Egremont and visit Aunt Merle and Uncle Andrew and Aunt Rutti and Uncle David. And you'll play with the twins. Won't that be fun?"

He shrugged. His eyes glittered like pale blue sea glass. His skin was chalky and a suppurating sore had erupted at the corner of his mouth.

"Hello, Tommy." Charles Bingham smiled down at the child and shook his hand. "I'm pleased to meet you." He smiled at Anne. "How are you?" It was not a pro forma question. She realized he did want to know.

"I'm holding up. Tommy and I had a fun flight from Chicago. You're looking well, Charles."

He was looking well. He belonged to the rare group of men who grow more attractive with age. The fringe of hair that rimmed his bald pate was pure silver now and its luxuriant thickness was matched by the new carefully trimmed silver mustache that sprouted above his lip. His features still had an avian cast, but he had gained weight and there was an authoritative sensuality in the fleshiness of his face and form. Nicole had done her work well. Charles, who had always dressed with casual indifference, wore well-tailored blue slacks, a striped open-necked shirt, and leather sandals that had surely been crafted in the workshop of an expensive Florentine craftsman.

"You, too, Anne. Beautiful as always. Your mother is a beautiful woman," he told Tommy gravely.

Anne blushed, although she had dressed carefully for this visit, selecting a white linen suit because she remembered that Charles favored white, brushing her hair so that it fell in smooth silken folds to her shoulders and then tying it back with a gossamer blue scarf that matched her blouse. She had not remembered, until she and Tommy were in a taxi speeding to Charles's home, that the scarf had been a gift from him. He himself had tied her hair back with it the night he gave it to her, but the knot had been loose and the scarf had slipped and caped her naked shoulders. Would he remember that? Probably not. She hoped not.

"Yeah. She's pretty. And she's a good driver too," Tommy said and they both laughed.

"A wonderful house, Charles," Anne said admiringly.

The three-story brownstone was not unlike the houses she had most admired when she lived in New York; it was, in fact, the sort of house she had always imagined she might live in one day. She vaguely recalled bringing Charles's attention to such houses during their long wandering walks through the city. She followed him now down the long hallway, carpeted with a thick Oriental runner and lined with golden oak bookcases, a scrivener's stand on which an exquisite ormolu clock rested — all pieces she might have chosen.

"Nicole is into antiques," Charles said. Anne did not tell him that she too was "into antiques."

"Yes. I see."

She heard the sound of footsteps on the floor above them and then a small boy's shout, a girl's trilling laughter. She wondered how many children Charles and Nicole had.

"Three," he told her, as though reading her thoughts. "Two boys and a girl. Twelve. Ten. Eight."

"Terrific spacing," she said. The child she had aborted would be fourteen now. She wondered if Charles still mourned that loss. Each year, on the date of the abortion, she herself was assaulted by an oppressive melancholy. Once she had had a crying jag. Only last year she had had a headache so severe that she could not work. She was exasperated by the unreasonableness of that amorphous sadness. She had no regrets, she told herself. She had done what she had to do. Still she could not stanch that unbidden grief.

"They're nice kids," he said proudly. "Perhaps you'll meet them later. We'd like it if you could stay for dinner."

"I'm sorry. Merle and Andrew expect us for dinner and Tommy may be tired. . . . But perhaps a drink." She smiled at her son, lifted him into her arms, pressed her cheek against his golden hair.

He examined Tommy. She glanced at his desk, saw Tommy's records, the lab reports. He was a meticulous diagnostician. A page of notes and questions was clipped to Manny's report.

Gently he probed Tommy's body, applied pressure to the glands, studied the rash. He administered the glass test, then frowned.

"Dr. Irwin did that already," Tommy said.

"Yes. I know. What's your favorite food, Tommy?"

"Spaghetti."

"Do you like ice cream?"

"Yeah. Chocolate."

"How about a big plate of chocolate ice cream?"

"I'm not hungry."

"OK. But I'll owe you a chocolate sundae when you *are* hungry."

He grinned at Tommy and Tommy smiled back. Anne had forgotten how wonderful Charles was with children. He had what Manny Irwin called "pediatric charisma." Sick children sat up in bed and called him when he passed through the wards. "Dr. Bingham, tell me a joke." "Dr. Bingham, tell me a story." "Hey, Dr. Bingham, examine me." "No. Me first." Charles always had a story or a joke and took the time to pause at a child's bedside, to administer a swift and playful tickle; the pockets of his long white coat bulged with lollipops and peppermint sticks.

A peppermint stick emerged from his shirt pocket now.

"Have a smoke, Tommy," he said, and Tommy giggled and popped it into his mouth. "OK, get dressed. You and I have a date tomorrow morning at my hospital. I bet it's bigger than your mom's hospital in Chicago."

"I don't know. I've never been there," Tommy said.

Charles glanced questioningly at Anne and she nodded. It was true. She had never taken Tommy to Michael Reese Hospital, not even for the staff Christmas party. She had, in fact, been obsessive about keeping him away; she wanted to keep him safe from exposure to illness, to ambient bacteria, to her life away from him.

He sat behind his desk, made notes, and did not look at her as he said, "I'm going to admit Tommy so we can get the marrow biopsy out of the way."

"You're thinking the same thing as Manny."

"Manny was very careful, very thorough. We're all thinking the same thing. Otherwise you would never have come to me."

"What are you all thinking?" Tommy asked. He knelt to tie his shoes, a skill he had recently mastered and of which he was very proud.

"We're all thinking that you're a pretty terrific boy and that we've got to do something to figure out what's making you feel so sick. We're like detectives and we're looking for clues."

"Like Fargo, North Dakota."

"Ah, you're an 'Electric Company' fan. Come upstairs. You can watch with my son Jed while your mother and I have coffee."

"Charles. Please."

She did not want to go upstairs. She did not want to see his wife, be introduced to his children. She wanted to rush back to Merle's house and have Lottie make her a cup of herb tea, and hover over her while she drank it. She wanted to lie down in the cool dimness of Merle's guest room and take a long nap. And she wanted to awake with the nightmare of the past several days over. She imagined Lottie's laughing voice. "You just had a dream, Annie girl. Your baby's not sick. He's fine. He's a strong, healthy, beautiful boy."

"Just for a bit, Anne, a little while." She recognized the nervous plea in his voice. Nicole knew she was here. It was necessary that he establish the normalcy of their new relationship. It was necessary that his wife be reassured.

"All right," she said.

She followed him up the carpeted stairwell into the large room where splotches of sunlight danced across the fat cushions of the chintz-covered sofa and chairs, where his sons, Joey and Jed, played chess on a bright blue carpet, and where Emmy, his daughter, sat curled in a rocking chair reading *Charlotte's Web* as she sucked her long corn-colored braid.

"You catch our family at a moment of unusual peace," Charles said as he introduced them. "Yesterday at this time, Jed and Joey were at each other's throats."

He turned to relieve Nicole of the heavy tray she carried.

"It's good to see you again, Anne," Charles Bingham's wife said. She too was wearing white, a skirt and collared blouse, and for a fraction of a moment the two women smiled at each other and cast knowing glances at Charles. Each recognized that the other had dressed for him and each knew that he was unaware of their effort. She held her hand out to Tommy. "Hello, Tommy. It's nice to meet you. You know that your mother and Dr. Bingham are old friends."

How kind she was, how composed. She poured the coffee with a steady hand and sliced the cheesecake that she proudly said came from a terrific new bakery on Columbus Avenue. She was of a generation of women who took as much pride in a newly discovered bakery as their mothers had taken in the cakes of their own confection.

"The West Side is getting so gentrified that it's frightening," she said. "The yuppies are definitely taking over."

"Yuppies," Charles repeated. "You should hear the young doctors I interview. They ask me about vacation time before they ask me about the research. They want to know about deals with drug companies, research and royalty splits. Questions that never would have occurred to us." Their generation had asked about equipment, time for research and writing.

"They're Ronnie's babies," Anne observed wryly. "The Reagan generation. Doctors are mild compared to the Wall Street whiz kids — the venture capitalists who see themselves as the Peace Corps of the eighties. They think they're altruistic — after all, they're creating jobs, putting money into circulation. They're not going to waste their time sitting around a communal house in Lagos strumming guitars and teaching kids how to build septic systems."

Their coffee cups clinked companionably against the saucers. The Bingham children took Tommy upstairs to see their bedrooms and to watch "The Electric Company."

Nicole put on a record. Julian Bream. Anne, too, had developed a taste for the classical guitar. She leaned back in her chair and listened to the sounds of the life that had almost been hers. Like Alice, she had stepped into the looking glass and saw her world through a new perspective.

Charles placed a stool beneath Nicole's foot. The limp, Anne saw, was a congenital deformity. Nicole wore a corrective shoe. Charles was as solicitous of this wife as he had been solicitous of Anne. She imagined him lifting her own foot, his long fingers gentle about her ankle. She remembered the steaming cups of coffee he had brought her as she studied through the long winter nights. He had pulled the covers over her as she slept, left towels on the radiator so that they would be warm when she emerged from the shower. But she did not forget the price that had to be paid for such solicitude, such love. She had weighted the scales carefully fourteen years ago and taken correct measure. A web of sadness threatened and she rose swiftly while she could still extricate herself from its ensnarement.

"I'm afraid we'll have to leave," she said. "Merle and Andrew will be waiting."

"Merle and Andrew Cunningham," Charles explained to Nicole. "He's on the hospital board. You've met them."

"Oh, yes. We've been with them several times. She's the composer of *A Child's Prayer*."

"Yes. They're my very close friends," Anne said. She wondered why Merle had never mentioned meeting Nicole and spending evenings with the Binghams. But, of course, Merle was protecting her. Anne was the vulnerable single woman, vigilantly shielded by her conspiring friends.

"Tommy," she called. He came down, less lethargic now. He clutched two small plastic figurines Jed had given him.

"From *Star Wars*," he said excitedly.

"Bring them to the hospital tomorrow, Tommy," Charles said, patting his head.

"I'm so glad we had this visit, Anne." Nicole walked her to the door. "I hope everything will be all right."

"Thank you." Anne waited for Charles's lips to brush her cheek.

She took Tommy's hand and walked down the steps of the house that might have been hers. The windows were open. Nicole had changed the record. James Galway played "Annie's Song" on his silver flute. She wept softly in the taxi that carried her to Merle's house, and because Tommy was asleep, exhausted by the events of the day, he did not ask her why she was crying. She could not have explained to him that her tears were both tears of regret and tears of relief.

The removal of the marrow for the biopsy was routine and Anne was grateful that they had the weekend at Egremont to recuperate from the tension. Charles had spoken to the pathologist and asked that the biopsy be completed as swiftly as possible.

"Of course, I want to scan the tissue myself," he told Anne. "I will be as careful with Tommy as I would be with my own children." He paused.

"Because he's my son." It was not a question; it was a statement.

"Because he's your son," he repeated, hesitating briefly as though the sentence was unfinished but he dared not complete it.

"Thank you, Charles."

They stared at each other, mindful of the danger of further conversation.

Tommy was happy at Egremont. He played contentedly with the twins, trailed after David into the woodlands. Emulating their father, each twin carried a pad and crayon, and David gave Tommy his own drawing tablet and a set of chalks.

"To keep?" Tommy asked.

"To keep," David assured him.

Merle, Rutti, and Anne relaxed on chaise longues. Sarah and the bearded young actor who had accompanied her from the city had volunteered to cook lunch.

"Tommy may get tired," Anne warned David.

"I'll carry him back on my shoulders. In fact, I'll carry him there on my shoulders." David, his body thicker but still muscular, his beard flecked with gray, hoisted Tommy up. The child laughed and Anne was comforted to see that color had returned to his cheeks. *Perhaps they had been wrong. It was possible that they had been wrong. Oh, please, God, let us be wrong.*

She turned to Rutti. "David's a wonderful father."

"I've been very lucky," Rutti said. "So far." She exercised the cautious doubt of the survivor. Nothing could be taken for granted.

"And the harder you work the luckier you get," Merle said wryly, placing her hand on Rutti's.

Anne envied her friends for living in such close proximity to each other. She envied them the ease of their lives, the protectiveness of their husbands. She recognized that envy. It did not tarnish her love for them. She had made her own choices and she had few regrets. *She would regret nothing if only Tommy would get well.*

"Sometimes there's very little relationship between luck and work," Anne said.

They were silent. They acknowledged her worry and her pain and looked helplessly at each other.

"Did the tests go well, Anne?" Merle asked cautiously.

"The tests went. We have to wait for the results. But at least when we have them we'll know what we're up against," Anne said. Her tone was grim but determined.

"Anne, you know that we're with you," Rutti said.

"I know. Of course I know."

Their sadness was palpable. To disperse it, Merle reached for the green air letter on the table.

"From Nancy," she said. "An update. It seems that Ari's appointment is for five years, which means Nancy can do a postdoc at the Psychoanalytic Institute. The boys will get a solid foundation in En-

glish and Keren wants to take some writing courses. She's also instructed me to organize a Thanksgiving reunion here at Egremont.
Could you arrange that, Anne?"

"It will depend on Tommy's condition," she said.

"Of course." Merle and Rutti spoke in unison and they linked
hands, taking strength from touch.

David strode out of the woodlands with Tommy balanced on
his shoulders. Andrew, who had been reading on the patio, moved
forward to meet them. David transferred Tommy to Andrew and
lifted his own children, one on each shoulder. Together then, the men
and the children, laughing and talking, walked through rhomboids of
sunlight to the lawn where the women sat.

"I saw a rabbit," Tommy said excitedly.

"A chipmunk. It was a chipmunk. He can't tell a rabbit from a
chipmunk." Adam corrected him disdainfully.

"Don't pick on Tommy," Andrew said pleasantly, but Merle
recognized the rare monitory edge in his tone. She had not heard it
since Greg had grown up, had passed out of the province of their
protection. Why should Andrew be so protective of Tommy? she
wondered. It was true he had a special fondness for Anne. He had
always admired her, but he had come to know her well during the
months he spent in Minnesota working on a development project
right after Kate's death. And then, too, Anne had been at his side as
he recuperated from his heart attack.

"She was fantastic, Mom," Greg had told Merle. "She really
cared. One night she even slept in a chair next to his bed."

Merle remembered her son's words now and leaned forward.
She stared at Tommy as though the curve of his lip, the tilt of his
nose, might provide her with an elusive clue. The wild thought that
had come to her unbidden appalled her. It demeaned her marriage,
her love for Andrew, her love for Anne. She thrust it aside, but she
could not forget what Nancy had said in Jerusalem, all those years
ago, when they discussed Anne's pregnancy: "Whatever our Anne
wants, she gets. She doesn't allow anything to stand in her way."

Merle knew the thought was unkind, but it hurt no one. After
all, it was only a thought, irrational and unfounded.

It was David who answered Andrew.

"Tommy can take care of himself," he said reassuringly. "Can't you, Tommy?"

He spoke to Tommy with the same confident gentleness that always bolstered and comforted Adam and Liora.

Merle and Rutti glanced at each other and lowered their eyes as Anne gathered Tommy into her arms.

"It doesn't matter if it was a chipmunk or a rabbit. Was it cute, Tommy?" she asked.

"Its eyes were like big black diamonds," Tommy said and then, with his head resting on his mother's shoulder, he fell asleep. They watched in uneasy silence as she carried him into the house.

Unable to sleep that night, Rutti went into her studio. She took up a soft charcoal crayon and from memory she sketched David with Tommy astride his shoulders. She frowned as she worked and when she finished, she went to the cabinet that held the first editions of David's books. She pulled out *The Lovely Lakes of Minnesota*. He had done his sketching for that volume in the Superior National Forest and then journeyed south to visit Anne. Rutti had suggested the visit. She was worried about Anne, who always sounded calm but seldom sounded happy. What year would that have been? She turned to the title page and calculated the year of publication, accounting for the gap between the completion of the manuscript and the printing. About five years ago. She shook her head angrily. The thought was wild, her imaginings distorted. That was what happened when she allowed herself to become so fatigued. It had all been too much — getting ready for her New York exhibit in a few months' time, caring for the twins, worrying about Sarah, who seemed so rootless — and David too was exhausted. They were overextended. They needed a vacation.

The thought calmed her. She glanced at the newly completed charcoal drawing, and for the first time in many years, she destroyed her own work. She ripped the thick paper in half and then in half again as though shredding her own doubt, her own uncertainty.

Anne called Charles on Monday morning. He asked her to delay her return to Chicago for a few days. He was unhappy with the initial pathology report and had asked for a consult at Sloan Kettering.

"What are you unhappy about, Charles?" Anne asked. She did

not alter his language. In recent weeks she had come to understand the need for medical euphemisms.

"There are some inconsistencies I'd like explained."

She called Chicago and told Sally she would not be returning for several days. The younger woman did not mask her irritation.

"I don't think that's exactly fair," she said.

"Life isn't fair, Sally," Anne replied brusquely.

She marveled at the younger woman's temerity. During her own residency she herself had been deferential to senior staff, a demeanor shared by the other women in her class. They were a tiny minority then, a small group of women who slowly and hesitantly inched their way along the corridors of power and knowledge dominated by men. Now women interns and residents openly articulated their discontents; incidents of sexual harassment exploded into court cases. Today Peter Forbes would not receive a letter like the one Anne had written him. Subordinates spoke petulantly of "fairness." Grudgingly Anne admired Sally's honesty, but she did not forgive her.

She called Maureen and told her their return was delayed. "I can use the time to study," Maureen said. She was not indifferent to Tommy, but her own ambition and goal was dominant.

Anne placed one last call. It was a call she had never anticipated making. I will never have to rely on him for anything, she had thought when Tommy was born. I can do everything for a child. I can nurture. I can provide. She had soared high in the balloon of her own self-image, fired by her own independence, her own competence. She was triumphant, invulnerable. She, a physician, had not taken into account the vagaries of disease, the mysterious biological betrayal that turned her son's skin the color of chalk and drained him of his energy. She had neglected to factor that into her long-range calculations. She cursed herself for her own stupidity, her horrendous arrogance, as the phone rang again and again. He picked it up at last. She did not hesitate. Nor did she apologize. Tommy was more important than her pride. His discomfiture. He listened carefully. His voice was hoarse as he asked the questions she had anticipated. "But you can't be certain?" he said when he had heard her out.

"Not until we have a firm pathology opinion."

"Call me then." He hung up without saying good-bye. She was not surprised. She expected nothing more and nothing less. She had contracted for nothing more and nothing less. And he, in all fairness, had contracted for nothing at all. She marveled that his shock had not been more profound, his credulity and acceptance unstrained. But then he had always been an emotional acrobat, tumbling from the high wire of one relationship into the safety net of another.

Charles called in the morning and asked her to meet with him at his hospital office. He sat behind his desk, Tommy's folder and the various reports surrounding it open. She remembered that he had spread his materials that way so that he might read them as a geographer reads a map. Skillfully he navigated himself through the available data and established a course, the simplest and most direct of therapeutic routes.

"Anne, Tommy has acute lymphatic leukemia. I know that does not surprise you. But he's a lucky boy. It's been picked up at a very early stage. The cells are active and I'm almost certain they'll respond to chemotherapy. I think we have an excellent chance for a complete remission." He spoke firmly, directly.

She gripped the arms of her chair and tried desperately to control the weakness and nausea that overwhelmed her.

"You're not just saying that. . . ." Her voice faltered. Her medical training deserted her. She was a mother beset by terror, ambushed by love.

"You know me better than that." In his steady, unflinching gaze, she read the affection he would always have for her, the honesty he would never deny her.

"All right." She swallowed hard, felt her mind begin to work again. "Where do we go from here?"

"I want to admit Tommy and begin a protocol. I'll need a few days, perhaps a week. Then he can be transferred to Chicago, to your own hospital or another medical center. You'll have to be getting on with your own life."

"Yes. Of course." She had forgotten that she had any life at all that did not center around Tommy. But she knew that could not continue. There were realities to be faced, work to be completed, bills to be met.

He briefly described the drug therapy he favored. He predicted a swift remission. He did not discuss the side effects. He understood Anne's study habits and knew that she would go from his office to a medical library. He spoke softly, slowly as he watched the color return to her face and heard renewed strength in her voice. He reflected that she had changed little over the years. She was still beautiful, but her expression was gentler now. Achievement and recognition had blunted the hard edge of determination, the sharpness of ambition. But her strength, the strength that he had admired and loved and then loathed, was not diminished. He felt the electric energy of her maternal protectiveness. She would be more than her son's ally against this terrible illness. She would be his cowarrior.

"And then?" she asked. "After the course of chemo?"

"I've been involved in a team research project — the breeding of antibodies tailored for the individual patient's malignant cells. I think it may be a viable approach for Tommy. The protocol I'll set up can be implemented in Chicago. Of course I'll be in touch with your Chicago oncologist — there are some excellent pediatric people there — but I want you to come East from time to time so that I can monitor Tommy myself."

"I read about your antibody research," she said. "It sounded very promising."

"I'm optimistic," he said guardedly.

"OK." She sat up straighter. "Let's go to worst-case scenario. The chemo fails to cause remission, the antibodies don't work. What then?"

"Marrow transplant," he said flatly. "I don't think we'll go to your worst-case scenario, but still it would be prudent to be prepared. I'd suggest a compatibility test with blood relations — yourself, Tommy's father, cousins. There is often a good match with siblings, even half-siblings." He did not look up. He could not meet her eyes. He did not want to know who had fathered her child. Such uneasy emotional terrain frightened him. He glanced at the picture of his family, silver framed upon his desk — Nicole standing in a country garden with Jed, Joey, and Emmy. He was thankful for the loving simplicity and gentleness of his marriage. He knew now and had known for a long time that he had sent Anne away all those years ago not because of the abortion but because her power frightened him. The complexity of her ambition had conflicted with his own need for a simpler refuge, his longing for a pacific retreat.

She nodded in agreement.

"You'll speak to Manny Irwin and decide on a Chicago facility. I'll give you the names of some oncologists you might want to consider."

"Thank you. Tommy will be admitted this afternoon?"

"Yes. I would estimate that he'll be here for a week. But I'd like to see him again in November. Could you come back sometime around Thanksgiving? All things being equal."

"Yes. That would be good."

Nancy would be in from Israel. Tommy would be on his way to remission. September, October, November. Already she wished the months away. Already she longed for the cold breath of the new winter against her upturned face. She looked out the window and saw that the convergence of seasons had ended. The leaves of the tall tree that stood sentinel were sere and brittle; she shivered to hear them rattle in the autumn breeze.

21

"**Y**OU WILL be careful, Keren? New York is not as you remember it. These are different times."

Dov Yallon pulled his silver Jaguar over to the curb at the corner of Park Avenue and Seventieth Street and spoke to his daughter without looking at her. Since Keren's recent arrival from Israel, he had found it increasingly difficult to meet her eyes. It seemed to him that there was a watchfulness in her gaze, a mute judgment in the somber stare she too often turned on him.

"You're imagining it," Lisa, his wife, had told him. "Latent guilt. Although it's ridiculous for you to feel guilty, darling. Remember, it was Nancy who wanted the divorce and you're both so much happier in your new lives." She spoke with the certainty peculiar to those who have never doubted their own choices and are thus amazed at the ambivalence of others.

"Perhaps you're right." Dov found it easier to agree with Lisa than to argue with her. He had learned that much from Nancy. He remembered, with wrenching sadness, the anger and accusations that had resonated through the final days of his first marriage. Silence and acquiescence might well have eased the tension between them, but he knew that Nancy would never have accepted such simple palliatives. She was too honest, too intent on exposing the root of truth concealed by their superficial grievances.

"Of course I'm right. This move to America is a difficult adjustment for Keren, but she'll manage. She's marvelous — so stable, so well adjusted."

In that Lisa was accurate. During his annual visits with Keren, he had always been amazed at her cheerfulness, her receptivity. As she matured he noted that she was possessed of a competence and stability that both surprised and relieved him. The divorce, then, had not damaged her. Keren's equanimity proclaimed his own innocence and he absolved himself with practiced ease. If Nancy had prioritized their marriage rather than her career, he would never have sought intimacy and comfort elsewhere. He excused himself with equal facility for his decision to remain in the States. There were too damn many physicians in Israel. He could do more for his family by practicing on Long Island and sending them generous checks than he could if he had become an overworked practitioner in the government medical station of some desert town. And he had done his best for Keren. Not many men would have allowed her to go off to Israel with Nancy. Dov knew men who organized to claim custodial rights, who argued about alimony and child support. He was contemptuous of them, proud of himself. He had not made Keren a pawn in the marital game. And he had to admit that Nancy had been a wonderful mother. Lisa was right. Keren was a terrific girl, a beautiful girl. He kept a photograph of her in her army uniform on the desk in his consulting room and he was always pleased when patients asked about her.

"My daughter," he replied proudly. "She's an officer in the Israeli army. As I was." He allowed his voice to grow soft, his gaze to become distant. There was drama and mystery in his past. He knew that his patients, most of them middle-aged women who sat opposite him clutching their expensive leather handbags, were appropriately impressed, even moved. Occasionally as he spoke to them, he touched the pale butterfly-shaped scar at his neck and remembered how Keren had traced it with her fingers when she was a small girl.

Why, then, he wondered, as he impatiently tapped the leather steering wheel, was he haunted by such anxiety? He had, after all, been excited when Keren had decided to come to the States with Nancy and Ari and enroll at a university in New York. It would give him a chance to really know his daughter, to enjoy her without the knowledge that their time together was curtailed or defined.

But the reality of her presence had disturbed him. Perhaps it was because she so closely resembled Nancy now — the youthful, dark-haired Nancy whom he had first met on a college campus, who walked with him through a field fragrant with the scent of sweet woodruff. Keren was older now than Nancy had been when he first held her in his arms, and she too was tall and slender, her thick hair falling to her shoulders, her large, dark eyes flecked with amber. And she had Nancy's habit of inclining her head slightly forward when she listened to a conversation, of webbing her fingers into a small nest on which she rested her chin when she was reflecting or judging. Too often he glanced at her as he spoke and found her in just that pose; her expression unnerved him, and he felt an unfamiliar anxiety for which he forgave himself. This was, after all, an unsettling time for him. He had thought his life settled, but events had taken an unexpected turn. "You will be careful?" he asked Keren yet again.

"I'll be fine," Keren said, gathering her things, smiling reassuringly at him. "Remember, I was an officer in an intelligence unit."

"A knowledge of Arabic isn't going to be much help on the streets of New York," he retorted. "Do you have enough money?" He took out his wallet and peeled off several bills, which he pressed into her gloved hand. "Here. Take a cab to the gallery."

"I have plenty of money," Keren protested. "Don't worry." But she shoved the folded bills into her canvas purse. She had learned long ago that her father perceived any rejection of his gifts as a personal affront. Like many children of divorce, she had schooled herself to understand parental sensitivities, to soothe parental guilt. She leaned over and kissed him on the cheek. Briefly, lightly, her finger touched the scar at his neck and then the car door slammed behind her.

Dov watched her through the rearview mirror as she strode down the street. She walked with purposeful grace, her hair caping the bright red wool jacket that Lisa had helped her select. He smiled, pleased that he was the father of this beautiful young woman who walked with such confidence, such ease, down the crowded Manhattan street.

Keren did not take a cab. She decided to walk to the gallery where Rutti's exhibit was being held, and at once she felt a new vigor, a lifting of the nagging depression that had threatened her during the drive into Manhattan. It was, after all, only four-thirty, that oddly peaceful hour at the end of a workday when the city seemed to relax, when pedestrians slowed their pace and passersby exchanged wary

361

smiles as streetlights flickered on. Darkness came early in November and Keren moved through the gathering dusk wondering when she would stop feeling like a stranger in this city where she had spent her childhood.

But of course, she reflected, she had been too young to claim New York as her own then. She remembered herself as a small girl, frightened and anxious, clutching her mother's hand as they crossed a huge avenue, weaving their way between buses and taxi cabs. It seemed to her they had always been in a rush; they streaked across broad concourses to dash into convenience stores for a container of juice, a carton of eggs, a quart of milk. More often than not supper was just a TV dinner, thrust into the oven and eaten straight from the foil tray. She was dropped off at school, at music lessons, at homework centers in basements of churches. She and Sarah played tag in the corridors of the Art Students League as they waited for Rutti to finish a class. They played old maid in the waiting room of the clinic where Nancy saw patients, tossing the cards at each other with nervous giggles. Chasing each other and waiting, with increasing impatience, for their own lives to begin, they were the restless daughters of overextended, striving mothers.

It was understandable that she did not know New York as she knew Jerusalem. It was in Jerusalem that she emerged from the cocoon of childhood into the exhilarating freedom of adolescence. She walked its streets alone, discovering herself, her secret yearnings and sudden joys, as she discovered the byways and parapets, the secret passageways and low urban hills of the city her mother had chosen to make their own. Here, Nancy seriously and firmly told her, they would find new purpose, new meaning. Here they would build lives that mattered, *lives that made a difference.*

She came of age in Jerusalem. It was in Jerusalem that she learned a new language and made new friends and rushed, with those friends, to help fortify the city against the threat of war. There, too, like a spectator in a small and intimate theater, she watched her mother fall in love with Ari Raviv; she leapt from the audience onto the stage and joined them in the new pageant of their lives: their marriage, the move to Yemin Moshe, the birth of their sons, and now this assignment that brought them back to New York.

The theatrical simile pleased her. She might become a writer yet.

She smiled and allowed the simile to develop as she stood on the corner and waited for a light to change. Yes, she had long been watchful, attentive, an eager understudy anticipating her own turn to perform, listening for a cue.

"Will Keren come with us to New York?" She left her bedroom door ajar and listened to Nancy and Ari's worried nocturnal whispers. "Will Keren be happy? Is it fair to ask her to uproot herself yet again?"

"Lisa and I would be very happy if you chose to attend college in America, but of course, we want you to do whatever would make you happiest," Dov wrote from New York.

She did not doubt her parents' love, but she knew although both Nancy and Dov would deny it, that she was peripheral to their new lives, their new marriages. Only Sarah understood her feeling and articulated it with a perspicacity and accuracy that startled Keren.

"I figured it out," Sarah told her during her last visit to Jerusalem. "It came to me in an astronomy class. It's like my mother and David and the twins are a planet — you know, Venus maybe or Saturn — and I'm one of the moons circling them. There's a magnetic pull, an attraction, but in the end I'm not part of them. I'm only in their orbit, circling them. I'm separate, alone. Do you feel that way, Keren?"

"Sort of," Keren admitted.

Keren wondered now if that was why Sarah was not coming to the gallery for Rutti's opening. Her friend claimed that she had to rehearse for her own performance that night. "Hey, I've been to enough of my mother's openings," Sarah said. "You go and we'll all have dinner later — you and me, Greg and Eric — at Ballads and Blues — before my set." Perhaps her friend nurtured her own loneliness, her own isolation.

The light changed and she hurried across the street.

"Hey. Hey. Wait." A hand reached up and grabbed Keren's long black skirt. Unnerved, repelled, she stared down at the hand. The fingers that clutched the fabric were caked with dirt. She glimpsed a ragged blue sleeve exposing a wrist ringed with grime. But the voice was soft, pleading, a young girl's voice sibilant with sorrow.

"I need a dollar. Can you give me a dollar?"

Barefoot, she sat on the sidewalk. Ash-colored hair hung in lank strands about her pale, thin face. She wore a denim skirt and her skeletal torso was encased in layers of garments covered by a light blue sweatshirt. A sign that read I Am Eighteen Years Old and I Have No Home hung around her neck.

Keren stared at her in horror. Why? How was it that this girl had no home? A rose-colored light emanating from a boutique show window bathed the street in its glow. The air was heavy with the fragrance of mimosa plants displayed in front of a florist's shop. Did the girl see the light? Did she smell the sweetness of the blossoms?

The tug at Keren's skirt became violent.

"Please," the girl said, but there was no plea in her voice. She spat the word out in anger; her saliva frothed in a snowy spray onto Keren's skirt. Her anger turned Keren's pity into fear. Firmly, she pulled her skirt free of the grasping claw. She did not look at the girl and pulled out one of the bills Dov had given her. A five-dollar bill, she noted without regret. She thrust it into the outstretched hand and hurried on, impelled to run but moving instead at a measured pace. She moved more slowly as she waited for her nausea to ebb.

She was on Madison Avenue now. The shop windows were ablaze with light, each display revealing a small, enchanting world. A Victorian alcove glowed in the window of an antique shop. A richly brocaded love seat was covered with elaborately stitched cushions and a long burgundy throw. Memorabilia was arranged on a polished mahogany table; there were photographs of uniformed men and smiling women in gossamer evening gowns set in intricately crafted leather frames, a Dresden shepherdess, leather-bound books, one of which was open to reveal a page embossed with gold leaf. A thick Oriental rug patterned in red and blue was on the floor. A delicate china lamp, crowned by a fringed shade, cast a muted light.

Keren studied the charming scene. It was a home waiting for life to inhabit it. She imagined the girl on the street walking into the room, picking up a book, sitting down on the love seat. Inexplicably her eyes filled with tears and she hurried on. She passed a shop that sold only T-shirts — black and white T-shirts and T-shirts of every color of the rainbow spangled with flowers and stars, imprinted with reproductions of Manet and Seurat landscapes. A black sweatshirt provided the background for Rouault's grieving Christ, and as Keren watched, a salesman plucked it from the window and held it up so that his customer, a tall woman wearing jeans and a very long mink coat, could examine it.

She glanced into the window of a boutique that sold only socks. Chartreuse anklets that matched the sallow complexion of Rouault's Christ. Peppermint-striped socks. Knee socks across which Snoopy and Charlie Brown scampered. *The homeless girl had been barefoot. She should have bought her shoes, stockings, instead of giving her money. The girl would buy drugs with the money. She had already bought drugs with the money.*

Keren hurried on. She did not pause at the boutique that sold sweaters the colors of wild flowers, nor at the shop that displayed only gloves, nor at the jewelry store in whose window a single necklace of emeralds was imprisoned in nets of gold, dangling from a fir tree. It was not yet Thanksgiving, but many windows were decorated for Christmas.

She schooled herself to avert her eyes at street corners so that she would not see the women cocooned in too many garments and carrying plastic shopping bags that overflowed with cans and with oddly shaped parcels wrapped in brown paper. She distanced herself from the ragged and unshaven men who pushed shopping carts into intersections and screamed curses at the cars that swerved to avoid them. But she studied the windows of the food shops and was intrigued by the displays of desserts: strawberries afloat on waves of whipped cream, currants embedded like small rubies in golden pastries, kiwi slices smiling up from the faces of flat tarts. There were cheese shops and charcuteries, delicatessens and salad bars, shops that sold only pasta and shops that sold only sushi.

The food shops were crowded. Couples and men and women alone, small families, children shuffling their book bags and teenagers in tentlike sweaters, impatiently waited their turn. Up and down the avenue people rushed by, tenderly cradling the stiff white paper bags that contained their dinners.

Keren wondered if there had been such shops when she was a child. Their meals then had been the fast food of the time-obsessed, the budget-conscious. Pizza on soggy paper plates, Chinese food congealing in grease-scarred cartons. Her grandmother and aunt, visiting from Cleveland, frowned when they found such cartons in the rear of the refrigerator. Dov exploded with rage once because Nancy left him a hamburger in a McDonald's box for dinner. He threw the yellow plastic container across the room and the ovoid of meat burst free and landed on the window, adhering to the grimy glass.

Keren — how old was she then? — perhaps eleven or twelve, old enough to stay home alone while Nancy saw patients at the clinic — scrambled to clean it up, made her father an omelette, washed the dishes, and then pretended to do her homework as Dov sputtered his anger into the phone. His words echoed back to her.

"I get home from the hospital exhausted and where is she? At her damn clinic. Why the hell can't she wait until I finish my residency, get on my feet? Why can't she do her share?"

His accusations were unfair. Keren knew that. Nancy did cook and clean and it was Nancy who scurried with Keren from school to lessons to baby-sitters. It was Nancy who arranged the intricate schedules that involved Sarah, Greg, and Eric. And yet Keren understood her father's anger, his resentment. It was the price, she thought then — they all thought then, she and Sarah, Greg and Eric — that women had to pay if they were to claim their own lives and develop their own talents. Her father was often enraged. Sarah's father was melancholy. Merle was safe because Andrew was rich and she had Lottie, and Anne was safest of all because she was free. So the children reasoned. They accepted Dov's irritability, Werner's sadness, Andrew's complacent expectations, as absolutes. They were wrong, of course. Rutti's marriage to David, Nancy's marriage to Ari, taught them as much.

"You see," Sarah told Keren one evening as they shared a joint and looked at old photographs, "it wasn't so much that our mothers were liberated, as that our fathers were enslaved." They laughed, pleased at the sophistication of their insight, pleased that they were sufficiently removed from childhood dependency to judge their parents.

Keren watched now as a mother encouraged a small girl to select her own sushi. She wondered if children liked the Japanese delicacy, although she had no doubt that she and Sarah, Greg and Eric, would have relished the raw fish. They had been adventurous children, courageous and adaptable, leaping eagerly toward new challenges. It was wonderful that they were meeting for dinner that evening, the four of them together for the first time in years.

She hurried across the street. The Enrico Gallery was on the next corner. She bought a bouquet of yellow roses from a pale girl in an oversize black coat. Rutti loved yellow roses, Keren remembered. She ignored the religious literature that the girl tried to press on her, and with a sudden burst of energy, she sprinted down the street and into the brightly lit gallery.

"Keren!" Rutti, wearing a peacock-blue velvet dress richly embroidered in metallic threads which closely matched the silver-gold aureole of hair that framed her delicate face, hurried toward her across the crowded room. Laugh lines were etched into the corners of her eyes and about her mouth.

"For you," Keren said and offered her the flowers, stooping slightly to kiss her mother's friend on the cheek.

"Ah, Keren, you are my sweetness, my *ziessinke*." Rutti had not lost her charming Viennese accent. "Nancy, Merle, come see what Keren has brought me."

And Nancy and Merle, arm in arm, moved across the room to join them. Keren smiled to see that they too were wearing blue, Nancy in a tailored navy blue coatdress fashioned for her by a Rehavia dressmaker skilled at creating wardrobes for the wives of Israeli diplomats, and Merle in a cowl-necked light blue chemise of the softest cashmere.

"I guess Anne didn't come because her blue dress is at the cleaners," Keren said and they all laughed.

"Fresh. My daughter is very fresh," Nancy said, hugging Keren. "Did you have a good time at your father's? Would you be so flip with Lisa and her friends? It was all coincidence. You don't think we phoned each other and asked what color we'd be wearing, do you?"

"Well, I wouldn't be surprised," Keren retorted amiably and the three women giggled like young girls. Their friendship reignited their youth. They spoke in half-sentences, tossing the words to each other like team players in a familiar game. Nancy dropped a phrase and one or the other of the friends rushed the fractured thought to completion. "Do you think?" "Did you read?" "Oh, yes, that was what I thought." "That was how I felt. Exactly how I felt." Their faces were aglow with pleasure, their laughter trilled. Merle reached out and drew Rutti into an easy embrace and the three women, each in a different shade of blue, stood together and smiled at Keren.

Across the room Andrew, David, and Ari, stared up at one of Rutti's new oils.

"Come see Rutti's work," Merle said. "It's a wonderful exhibit. Such a pity that Anne couldn't be here for the opening. And it's a shame that Sarah had to work tonight. Well, they'll come another time."

"Yes. Yes, of course," Keren said. She shrugged out of her red coat and followed Merle and her mother, allowing Rutti to be claimed by a bearded critic who approached her with his pad open, his pen ready.

The stark white walls of the brightly lit gallery were covered with Rutti's drawings and etchings, subtle watercolors, and pastel chalk sketches that had all increased dramatically in value when she had switched to working in oils. The more recent canvases dominated the far wall.

Keren accepted a catalog from a gallery employee. *One Woman's World: The Work of Rutti Weisenblatt Lorenzo* read the title page. And it was Rutti's changing world that revealed itself on these walls, Keren realized, as she moved slowly across the polished floor, sipping champagne from a plastic fluted glass offered to her by a gallery employee. In tones of black and white, in shadows of gray, in pencil, in charcoal, and in pen and ink, Rutti had chronicled the lost, sad years of her childhood. A small girl stood at a train station, sought refuge beneath a leafless tree, climbed a rocky hillside. A small-breasted adolescent stood beneath an orange tree and offered fruit to a sad-eyed youth. Rutti and Werner reaching out to each other, companions in sorrow and loss.

"And there are Chana and Dror," Nancy whispered to Keren, pointing to the pen-and-ink sketches of the strong faces of Ari's parents, who had been foster mother and father to Rutti and Werner. Keren thought of the mysterious intertwinings of their lives, how one relationship had led to another. Because Rutti and Nancy, Merle and Anne, had met in that West Side playground, Nancy and Ari and Rutti and David came together and a new network of lives and loves evolved.

They moved on, pausing before the drawings that were familiar to them — the four friends seated on a bench in the playground, a swift drawing of small Keren asleep on the grass, all the children holding hands on the Egremont lawn. The last of the black-and-white drawings was that of the four hands outstretched, fingertips touching. Keren remembered that night; a fire was blazing in the fireplace and the voices of the women were soft as they pledged their friendship.

Sequentially arranged, the exhibit segued into pastel portraits: Merle in her pale green gown, her auburn hair loose as she bent over her violin; Anne in her white jacket, her silver stethoscope bright about her neck; Nancy seated in a deep leather chair, her eyes pensive. In these separate portraits the women who had sat together on the playground bench were no longer interdependent. They had graduated into their own lives.

Although a small crowd stood in front of the display of watercolors entitled "Empty Rooms," Keren and Nancy avoided it. They did not want to see the meagerly furnished room, the bare window, the unmade bed, that had been Werner's. Nor did they want to view Rutti's re-creation of the crowded bedroom, once shared by Nancy and Dov, in which every surface was littered with books and piles of unfolded laundry. They were familiar with the peaceful re-creation of Merle's elegant studio, but they both wondered why Rutti had chosen to drape with long shades the windows that looked out on the gardens when actually Merle had encased them in sheer curtains. They did not express their puzzlement, but moved on to study Rutti's most recent work, portraits and landscapes done in oil on large canvases — a medium of permanence. Using the impasto technique, Rutti had painted gamine-faced Sarah; David holding the twins, each of them grabbing at his soft dark beard; Andrew and Merle looking at each other, their exchanged stare vested with magnetism. The final portrait on the wall, done with a lighter hand, a gentler perception, was that of a golden-haired boy.

"That's Tommy. Anne's son," Nancy said. "Rutti sketched him during their last visit to Egremont when his illness was first diagnosed, Merle told me."

"But he's better now, isn't he?" Keren asked. "He and Anne are coming for Thanksgiving, Sarah said."

"Yes. Apparently, he's had a remarkably good response to the drug therapy. They're flying in from Chicago tonight. Our Thanksgiving reunion. Andrew and Merle are meeting them at La Guardia. Anne and I are having lunch tomorrow."

"Just Anne and you?" Keren was surprised. She would have expected all four of the friends to meet, to commandeer a corner table at a small restaurant where they would talk a great deal, eat a great deal, and peck at one another's desserts.

"Yes. That's what Anne wanted. I suppose because it's been so many years since she and I have been together."

"I suppose," Keren said.

"What do you suppose?" Ari, accompanied by an olive-skinned young man whose black hair fell in jet swatches across his high forehead, came up to them, smiling.

Nancy held her hand out to her husband's companion

"Hello, Abdul. I'm so glad you could come. Keren, do you remember Abdul Nashif?"

"Of course. I've been to your concerts in Jerusalem."

"Then perhaps you'll come to my concert in New York," the handsome Arab said. "It's part of this cultural exchange program that Ari has arranged."

"I'd love to," Keren said. She glanced at her watch. "Listen, I have to run. You know I'm meeting Greg, Eric, and Sarah at Ballads and Blues for dinner."

"Sarah really should have come tonight," Nancy said.

"She's singing later. She had to rehearse," Keren replied defensively and wondered why she was making excuses for her friend. Always she felt she had to protect Sarah, whose melancholy made her vulnerable.

She put her empty glass on a tray littered with other discarded flutes. Gallery patrons were preparing to leave. "Rutti Weisenblatt Lorenzo is a very hot artist," Keren heard a woman say in a shrill voice. "Hey, art is hot," her companion replied.

"Where does your friend sing?" Abdul Nashif's question was casual.

"At the same place we're having dinner. Ballads and Blues. It's sort of a supper club in Greenwich Village just off Bleecker Street," Keren replied. Suddenly she was impatient to be with her friends, to be gone from this brightly lit, white-walled room with its subtle revelations, its painful memories, its ambience of success and acquisition. Someone stepped on a plastic champagne glass, creating an explosion of sound that caused nervous giggles.

"Have a good time, darling. Take a cab home if it's really late." Nancy had never worried when Keren walked alone through Jerusalem or hiked in the Galilee, but the streets of Manhattan filled her with fear.

"All right. I'll give you a call."

"We'll be home later. We're having dinner with Abdul."

"Great." Keren smiled her good-bye to the tall Arab. She hadn't remembered how very handsome he was.

"Good-bye, Keren. I hope your friend sings well at this club." He smiled pleasantly and helped her into the bright red wool jacket that Ari had fetched for her.

Keren kissed a flushed Rutti and David, aglow with pride in the reception his wife's work had been given. She hugged Merle and Andrew, who both fussed over her and found her maturity, her beauty, hard to believe. They were still bewildered that their own son had grown to manhood. "Our love to Greg," Merle said. Her hand touched Andrew's cheek, moved up to brush the craggy slope of his forehead, to brush away a graying lock of hair. She wished that they could go straight home and have dinner on a tray in the den. Their weariness did not shame them. They lusted now after shared solitude just as they had once fled from it.

Keren closed the door of the gallery softly behind her. She walked only half a block before hailing a cab. She briefly pressed her face against the window and then settled back in the cracked leather seat and fell asleep. The driver wakened her when they reached Bleecker Street.

"You're here, Miss. Here you be." He was West Indian and spoke in the lilting accent of his island home.

"Where, oh where do I be?" she asked and they both began to laugh.

Keren gave him a large tip and slammed the door behind her. She moved carefully down the long stone stairwell that led into Ballads and Blues.

Although the cavernous brick room was dim, Keren saw her friends at once. They sat in a booth at the rear of the room, their faces softly lit by the flame of the tall candle on the center of the table. She waved to them and they called her name exuberantly; their shouts of welcome caused other diners to turn and smile. Greg and Eric ran toward her and each in turn embraced her. Tall, muscular Greg, his thick straight hair the color of firelight, his features blunt, lifted her easily off her feet and twirled her about in a small dance of gladness and affection. His sea-green eyes studied her approvingly.

"Keren grown gorgeous," he said.

"He said the same thing to me," Sarah told Keren as she slid into the booth. "He probably says the same thing to all the girls."

"Women," Greg corrected her. "I say the same thing to all the women. To all the gorgeous daughters of all the awesome, liberated dames."

"Let's drink to all the awesome, liberated dames," Eric said. He waved to the waitress, lifted his empty beer stein, and held up four fingers. She nodded and brought four glasses brimming with the frothy golden brew.

Keren, who disliked beer, lifted her glass and grimaced. Eric still assumed that everyone's tastes matched his own — the narcissistic egotism of the only child, Nancy had once called it, and although Keren disliked the jargon of her mother's profession, she had to admit its accuracy. She looked at Sarah and knew that Sarah shared her thought. They giggled and Greg and Eric laughed, too, the familiar, automatic response of their childhood so easily reactivated.

"To Merle and Rutti, Nancy and Anne — the playground sisters," Greg proclaimed solemnly.

They clicked their glasses together and drank deeply, solemnly, and then each put a hand on the table and allowed their fingers to touch. They grinned mischievously. Keren and Sarah remembered how they had crouched outside the door of Merle's studio and peered in as the pact of friendship was sworn.

"Forget it. I'm not going to swear my fealty," Greg said. "That was strictly sixties stuff."

"Hey, it's working for them into the eighties," Sarah reminded him. "Look at what's going on with Anne now."

"What's going on with Anne now?" Keren asked.

"Her son Tommy's been really sick — some form of leukemia — scary. Merle and my mom have been Anne's support system.

Anne came East and stayed with Merle in September when Tommy was first diagnosed. And they've both been out to Chicago to kind of prop Anne up. They say Tommy's doing pretty well. He's on this new treatment — a protocol they call it — that Charles Bingham set up. Do you remember him, Keren? He was Anne's main man when we were kids."

"Charles Bingham." Keren repeated the name. She remembered him well, although he had disappeared from their lives when he had disappeared from Anne's life. She had asked her mother why Charles no longer came to visit with Anne. *Doesn't he like her anymore?* She feared to ask that question because she feared that her own parents no longer liked each other. That was the year when divorce swept through her class at school like a dangerous epidemic. Classmates left to live in distant states or different neighborhoods because their mothers were going back to work, back to school, because fathers were driving across the country or checking out another life-style. Keren was worried that if Charles and Anne were no longer together, then it was possible that Nancy and Dov would also separate. The domino effect.

And she also remembered her mother's answer. "Of course Charles still likes Anne," Nancy said carefully. "But sometimes people outgrow each other." Her mother's words did not comfort Keren. She imagined Anne growing larger and larger, bursting free of Charles's constricting embrace, just as she herself, a tall, too swiftly growing child, strained the seams of her dresses and skirts. It was years before she grasped her mother's meaning and by then it no longer mattered.

"Everyone's pretty optimistic about Tommy," Greg said. He had inherited his father's considered, conservative manner. His calm reassured them, restoring the gaiety of their reunion.

"Hey, let's order," Sarah said. "You don't want me to faint from hunger during my set. The onion soup is great here. And the fish and chips. I don't know about the other stuff because it's out of my price range."

"Come on, Sarah. Poverty's out. Get with it," Greg responded, kissing her cheek. "Besides, I'll spring for it."

They ordered, Greg and Eric mockingly delivering their choice in pig Latin, which Eric translated into Spanish. Keren and Sarah clapped when the order was correctly read back to them. The waitress smiled and bent to whisper something in Eric's ear. He hesitated, and then answered her in Spanish.

"What did she say?" Sarah asked.

"She wanted to know if we were related."

"And what did you say?"

"I think I was pretty accurate — I said that we were like family to each other in a complicated way."

"What are we then? Cousins? Siblings? Ah, I know, surrogate siblings," Keren interjected.

"Maybe. We grew up together. We have a shared history. We're close enough to be related. Which means that if we had sex with each other, it would be sort of incestuous," Eric said. He smiled teasingly. "Might make it interesting."

"Uh oh. I don't want to sleep with either of you," Sarah retorted. "At least not now. Maybe later, much later, if I don't find anyone I want to marry and I decide to have a child, I'll ask one of you to do me the honor."

"Has Anne established a tradition then?" Greg asked wryly and Keren noticed that Eric's cheeks were blotched with the patches of angry red that had marked his childhood outbursts of temper.

"Shut up, Greg," he said harshly. "Leave it alone."

"But Anne must have made some sort of a choice. Who *is* Tommy's father?" Greg persisted.

"It could be anyone." Sarah's voice was flat. "It could be someone we know or someone we don't know. Maybe it was Charles Bingham and maybe it's someone we never heard of. It could be a stranger whose name she's forgotten or maybe it was you, Eric, or even you, Greg. You know — *Tea and Sympathy, Candida*. Anything is possible. But I think it's stupid to talk about it. The only one to whom it makes any difference is Anne. And Tommy." Her voice rose as she spoke, gathering intensity, betraying a subdued rage. She seldom mentioned her own father, although Keren knew that Sarah visited Werner's grave whenever she was in Israel.

"Sarah's right," Eric said.

They were relieved when the onion soup was served and when Keren, to change the subject, told them of her walk down Madison Avenue.

"Maybe I'm experiencing culture shock," she said, "but I felt as though I were in some sort of never-never land — a fairy-tale country with all those boutiques and food shops, with everyone dashing in and out of them, flashing their plastic credit cards as though they were waving magic wands."

"But they are magic wands," Greg said. "That's just the point. And we are living in a fairy-tale decade. Welcome to the eighties. We're obsessed with royalty and with enchanted lives." He spoke quickly, his voice resonant with a charismatic intensity. He taught English at an inner-city high school and Sarah had told Keren that he had been cited as a gifted teacher. His students listened when he spoke; Keren understood why. "We've got our kings and queens, our princes and princesses," he continued. "Nancy and Ronnie are sitting on their thrones. Diana and Charles are dancing cheek to cheek. The new billionaires build their own castles, create their own principalities. Donald Trump and Ivana, Jane Fonda and Tom Haydn for the more socially conscious. And we trail after them hoping that they'll live happily ever after because then maybe we'll have a chance to live happily ever after. Meanwhile we stockpile the ammunition of happiness. We buy what they have or as close to it as we can get. Cars. Television sets. Phones for our cars and phones for our bathrooms. We have important things to say, royal commands to issue when we're driving down a highway or taking a shit. The kids I teach may live in fleabags, but when they touch their gold chains or zip up their leather jackets, they've crossed the border into the magic kingdom."

"You've got it all wrong, Greg," Eric said moodily. "We're not living in fairy-tale times. We're in caveman country — the age of the predator. Everyone wants to grab a gold ring because they know that the carousel only goes around once and they know that if they don't move fast enough there won't be any rings left. That's one thing this city, with all its fancy boutiques and delis teaches you — there just isn't enough to go around. Ask the bag ladies and the bums sleeping in Penn Station, pushing their way to a heated grating on Park Avenue and they'll tell you that. Listen, I worked late last night and I walked home. I had to pass one of these huge appliance stores. It had like a hundred television sets in the window and they were all on; I guess they keep them playing all night so that in case you feel like buying a box, you can rush out at three in the morning and check the reception. And every damn set was tuned to 'Dynasty' —

twenty-one-inch screens and forty-inch screens — in living color, all showing the private jet landing and Linda Evans looking noble in ermine and Joan Collins swishing about in satin and diamonds. And guess who's watching it? Three bag ladies, leaning on their shopping carts. One of them is busy winding a filthy bandage over her ulcerated knee while Joan Collins throws a glass of champagne in a waiter's face. That's the eighties for you. The haves on the screen and the have-nots on the sidewalk, with a sheet of plate glass wired with burglar alarms separating them." His voice was bitter and he motioned to the waitress for another glass of beer.

"Hey, Eric. I never figured you for our resident cynic," Sarah said. She lifted her spoon, and arching her head backward, she allowed a long string of melted cheese to dribble into her open mouth. "After all, you've traded in Greenpeace for corporate raiding. You've switched uniforms. Good-bye jeans — hello three-piece suit. And yet you're the one gunning for poor Joan Collins."

Keren leaned forward to listen to Eric's answer. Eric had always intrigued and mystified her. He had been a moody playmate, a restless adolescent who dropped out of college in the East, transferred to a school in Oregon, and graduated with honors in record time. Sarah told her that he was deeply involved in the ecology movement. Then suddenly, he was working as an investment banker, and turning the pages of the international edition of *Time* in a Jerusalem café, she saw a photo of Eric captioned "Wall Street Whiz Kid Knows When to Merge and When to Acquire."

"Give me a break, Sarah," Eric said. "I'm just seeing it the way it is. No cynicism, just reality. OK, I was into saving the earth and saving the whales and saving the whole damn planet. I organized rallies and wrote stuff and I got myself arrested in some forest near Tacoma, protesting against a nuclear facility they were going to build too close to the trees. I was a fucking hero. A cop kicked me in the head and I got seven stitches. See?" He pointed to a pale scar at the corner of his left eye. "This scar was like a badge of honor — a real credential in the war for the greater good. 'Hey, you got wounded,' the cute groupies would say and they all wanted to hear my stories and because I was such a big brave hero, some of them even slept with me."

Keren bit into her hamburger. She thought of Dov's scar, of the way he left his shirt open at the neck so that it could be seen.

"I told my war stories," Eric continued. "And one night after I'd finished telling everyone about what I'd done and what the cop had said and what the judge had said, I listened to the other guys and I realized that no one cared all that much about the damn nuclear plant or the spotted owl or the timberline. What everyone felt really bad about was that they'd been born in the wrong decade — that they'd missed Woodstock and the sixties. We wanted to feel important and we wanted to feel needed and we all thought that maybe that would happen if we linked arms around a construction site and got our asses kicked in. Maybe, as a perk, we'd win one or two battles and the world would be a little better. Maybe we'd even get our thirty seconds of fame on the evening news. But they were building the nuclear plant near Tacoma anyway and I noticed that the guy who was telling about how he got arrested somewhere off San Francisco Bay in a Greenpeace demonstration was balding and had a gut and I thought, 'Who needs this crap?' There's a better way to save a plot of land. You get enough dough together and you buy it. Bingo! I felt like Newton when the apple fell on his head. So that's what I'm going to do, Sarah baby. Oh, I probably won't make enough to buy up a forest but I'll make enough to make a dent somewhere. And I'm going to make a difference. Watch me."

"You sound like a hippie in a three-piece suit," Greg said.

"The yuppies are the hippies of the eighties," Eric retorted. "Same profile. The same search for instant gratification, the same conviction that they're unique, special and unique, and special people deserve unique, special treatment. Hey, they're allowed to break the rules. The hippies put on their tie-dyed T-shirts and ran barefoot in the park, breaking the rules, grabbing what they wanted. The yuppies wear their Ralph Lauren jackets and float junk bonds and grab what they want. Reefer's out but coke is in. The hippies looked for action at Woodstock and the yuppies stalk it at Studio Fifty-Four. Strobe lights instead of campfires. It's all different and it's all the same. The dream lives on. We're going to make a difference." His mouth twisted bitterly. He undid the knot in his striped tie, took his jacket off, and rolled up his sleeves.

"That was my mother's credo," Keren said softly. "She wanted to make a difference. That's why she went to Israel."

"That's what they all wanted," Sarah said. "How many times did we hear it? They rewrote the nursery rhymes of our childhood. Why the hell should Miss Muffet sit on a tuffet — she had better things to do. And Jill was too busy to go up the hill with Jack. Who cared that Peter the pumpkin-eater had a wife and couldn't keep her. She could damn well keep herself. Merle, Anne, my mother — they didn't uproot themselves the way Nancy did, but they all wanted to achieve, to make their lives count for something." Her own intensity startled her.

"And they did achieve. And their lives do count for something." Greg's voice was steady, serious. Good teacher that he was, he invited them to look back across the years, to remember all that had been achieved, the odds that had been overcome.

He grinned and, as though embarrassed by his solemnity, waved to the waitress and called for another round of beer.

"None for me. I'm going to do my set soon," Sarah said. "And no deep philosophical discussions while I'm singing."

She busied herself with lipstick, blush, an eyeliner the color of the gentians that grew wild on the hillsides of the Galilee. She ran her fingers through the clusters of golden hair that hugged her head, took her guitar out of the case, and left the table.

The overhead lights were extinguished and the room grew quiet. The candle flames danced in the new darkness and Keren lifted her hands to the warmth of the taper that glowed on their table. A circle of blue light bathed the podium and Sarah stepped into it and smiled at them through the cerulean haze. In her simple black dress, her finely shaped head bent forward, she resembled the forest nymphs David Lorenzo had drawn with such tenderness and skill. Briefly, she closed her eyes. Her long lashes, the color of spun gold, brushed her cheeks; she lifted her guitar and began to sing. Her voice, now light and sweet, now tremulous with power, filled the quiet, candlelit room.

"Let it be," she sang and the sweet anthem of acceptance, the lyric of their adolescence, washed over them. She sang the same song in Hebrew and her audience hummed along. She sang of a house in New Orleans named for the rising sun and then segued skillfully into a Roberta Flack ballad. "You're breaking my heart with the pain."

Her voice throbbed; each wondrously held note was wrested from deep within her. She sang with her eyes closed, as though in a trance, swaying slightly and now and again moving out of the spheroid of liquid blue light; it seemed that her voice was disembodied, that it emanated from a vast darkness.

"She's wonderful, remarkable," a man said in Hebrew.

Keren turned. Abdul Nashif had slid into their booth. He leaned forward, mesmerized, his eyes fixed on Sarah.

"Abdul — I didn't think —" Keren began, but he lifted a finger to his lips and cautioned her to silence. She sat back and sipped the beer she neither liked nor wanted.

Sarah finished her set with a ballad of her own composition.

"I call it 'Choices,' " she said in a shy, brave voice that endeared her to her audience. But when she sang, her voice was strong. "Too many choices — how will I choose?"

Keren listened carefully. The words were simple, yet vested with poetry; the chords were complex and Sarah's fingering was deft. The song's message was familiar. She and Sarah had often discussed it, mocking themselves for their own uncertainties. So much had been offered to them. Arrows pointed in every direction but no road was clearly marked. Nothing was expected of them that they would not choose for themselves and that very freedom frightened them. They were both the beneficiaries and the victims of their mothers' long, exhausting battles. They could do anything they wanted. The onus was great and weighed heavily upon them. Their mothers had succeeded against all odds. It would be terrible if they were to fail when there were no impediments to their success.

"We want you to do whatever will make you happy," Nancy said simply and reasonably to Keren before they left for the States. She offered Keren the gift that she herself had been denied; she had been expected to go to college, to marry a doctor or a lawyer, teach for perhaps a year or two, and then devote herself to raising a family and running a home. Nancy imposed no such restrictions, no such limited expectations on her daughter, and she was disappointed by Keren's hesitancy. Perhaps, Keren thought, if Nancy heard Sarah's song, she would understand.

Sarah sang the last refrain and her hand drummed sharply against the polished wood of the guitar. Her heart-shaped face was white with exhaustion. The circlet of blue light became a sphere of roseate radiance that turned her golden ringlets the color of amber.

"She's beautiful, so very beautiful," Abdul said. "Like an angel."

"Yes. Yes, she is," Keren agreed. A melancholy angel, she thought, as she watched Sarah weave her way through the admirers who surrounded her.

The overhead lights came on and she introduced Abdul to Eric and Greg.

But Abdul's attention was riveted to Sarah, who joined them, her eyes feverishly bright with the question she could not bring herself to ask these friends: "How was I? Was I good? Really good?" She did not speak, but there was no silence because Abdul clapped and Keren, Eric, and Greg added their applause to his; the booth reverberated with the rhythmic beat of their admiration and approval.

Sarah blushed, and turned to the tall Arab.

"You remember Abdul Nashif?" Keren said by way of introduction. "We met him in Jerusalem, the summer Merle was there with Emanuel Klein's ensemble."

"Yes. Yes, of course," Sarah said. "We went to your recital. It was wonderful." She remembered the subtle atonality of Abdul Nashif's music, the tension as he blended Eastern and Western themes.

"I am flattered that you recall it," he said, making room for her in the booth.

He spoke to her softly. He himself was experimenting with lyrical ballads. He wondered if she ever sung accompanied only by the beat of a drum. She shook her head and turned to her friends to listen to their conversation. Should Keren study at NYU or Columbia? Where should she and Sarah look for an apartment? The East Village was cool and so was the West Side.

They ordered coffee, but when it arrived they found they did not want to drink it. The lights dimmed in readiness for the next singer.

"I don't want coffee and I don't want to hear any blues," Eric said. "What do you say we split?"

Keren and Greg nodded, but Sarah and Abdul looked at each other.

"I would like very much to hear the blues singer," Abdul said. "Perhaps you could stay and keep me company, Sarah?"

She nodded.

"You don't mind?" she asked her friends. "We'll have all of Thanksgiving weekend together at Egremont."

"Who minds? Who needs you?"

Their response was affectionate, their laughter spontaneous. Greg tousled her hair, Keren kissed her on the cheek.

"You were great," she said. "Speak to you tomorrow. I'll see you soon, Abdul."

"Yes," he said. "Soon."

They left, weaving their way through the smoke-filled room, newly crowded now with young people who had come late to drink, to listen, to be seen. At the door, Keren looked back and saw that Abdul and Sarah were deep in conversation, his head inclined toward her, his gaze intent. Sarah's face was bright and her hands fluttered as she spoke. Her lips were curved in a hesitant smile as though joy had taken her by surprise.

22

Like many people who move at regular intervals, Anne was always surprised by homes that remained virtually unchanged through the years. Holding Tommy's hand, she entered the Cunninghams' study and marveled at how little the room had altered since that distant November day when the four friends had first assembled there. Now, again, the harsh winds of November assaulted the tall evergreen that stood sentinel in the small urban garden. Today too a fire blazed in the brick fireplace and the copper bowl on the low rosewood table was filled with yellow roses. Of course, there were always additions: the olive-wood chess set that Merle had bought for Andrew in Jerusalem, and, hanging above the fireplace, Rutti's daring new oil, a stark wintry mountainscape bathed in the bright light of the morning sun.

Anne settled Tommy into the black leather chair and showed him how to operate the television set by pressing the switches on the panel built into the armrest. Andrew's invention. She smiled, remembering how embarrassed Merle had been when she first showed it to them. Wealth had been a stigma in the sixties. The children of the middle class demonstrated against segregation, against the war in Vietnam, wearing the costumes of the poor: faded and patched jeans, flannel shirts, sweaters that unraveled at a touch. Merle favored black slacks, black turtlenecks, and two-hundred-dollar Frye boots, although she had always changed into dresses of soft pastel wool before Andrew came home.

"Hey, that's cool," Tommy said. He switched channels, raised and lowered the volume.

"How'd you sleep, you guys?" Merle came into the room carrying the *Times*. "Did you eat?" She curled up on the tweed couch that faced the fire and, with the practiced ease of the veteran New Yorker, separated the newspaper into sections. She was looking for a review of Rutti's opening and tossed the paper aside when she did not find it. It would appear the next day.

"Lottie fed us, thanks," Anne said. "And we slept well, didn't we Tommy?"

She smiled, although the truth was that she had hardly slept at all. Attempting to conceal the dark circles beneath her eyes, she applied a pale layering of powder, a dusting of blush, a subtle application of jade shadow. In the end, she was satisfied with her reflection in the mirror. Her platinum hair was twisted into a loose coil tied with a velvet ribbon that exactly matched her long-sleeved, wide-skirted dress of forest-green silk. She and Tommy were to see Charles Bingham later in the day and she wanted his admiration, not his pity.

"I'm going to leave now, Tommy," she said. "You know I'm meeting Aunt Nancy downtown. Are you sure you're comfortable? Do you want a heavier sweater?"

"Oh, Mom, leave me alone." His voice rasped with irritation. He was tired. The trip from Chicago had been complicated by violent winds that buffeted their plane, causing the stewardesses to flash thin-lipped smiles as they adjured passengers to tighten their seat belts and the pilot to caution them not to leave their seats. Twice Tommy looked through the window and watched flashes of lightning ricochet off the silver wings of the plane.

"Look, Mom, look at that. Are we going to die?" He asked the question mischievously, teasingly. He knew that death did not come in a brightly lit plane, cutting its way through the dark night sky. No. Death came on tiptoe, stealing into small white hospital rooms, noxious with the odors of medicine and disinfectant. It was heralded by alarms that resonated through long corridors alerting nurses and interns in white uniforms who moved swiftly on crepe-soled shoes and hissed commands at each other. Tommy recognized those who accompanied death and assisted the dying. Stewardesses and pilots were the personnel of life.

Three times during his stay in the hospital, children died. Ellen, a freckle-faced girl, had played Chutes and Ladders on his bed one day and been dead the next. He heard the sounds of death in the night, the wail of the alarm, the screech of the crash cart careening down the corridor, the hurrying footsteps. "Where's Ellen?" he asked the next morning of the pleasant, chubby-cheeked woman who worked in the sunny playroom.

"Oh, her parents took her on vacation," the woman said and the pouches of flesh on her cheeks quivered. She smiled valiantly, but Tommy was not fooled.

"Ellen's dead," he told Anne when she visited that afternoon, bringing with her new library books and the comic strip that he and Ved were drawing together. He could not write yet, but he told his mother how to caption each drawing and she followed his instructions carefully and with great seriousness.

"Yes," Anne replied. She was reading his chart, as she did each day at the onset of her visit. "That's very sad, isn't it?"

He searched her face for signs of fear, but she betrayed none and her courage inspired his own. He relaxed against the pillows. His mother would know if he was in danger. She was a doctor. She understood the scribbling on his chart. She explained to him once that the clear liquid dripping through the long clear tube into the needle inserted into his vein consisted of chemicals that did battle against the disease which had so mysteriously invaded his body. He did not really understand.

"Are these chemicals, like, magical?" he asked at last. She did not think his question foolish. She never thought any of his questions foolish. "Sort of," she replied solemnly.

She bent over his comic strip and told him that next time he would have to leave more space because she had difficulty fitting the words into the balloons that Ved always drew too small.

He stopped thinking about Ellen then. Besides, Ellen did not even have leukemia. She died of liver cancer, which Sam, the small black boy who had briefly shared his room, told him was much more dangerous. Sam, too, had died. His death had been quiet, unfrightening. He smiled one night and told Tommy that he could play with his new Lego set the next day. Then he settled quietly into sleep.

"Sam's not moving," Tommy told the nurses in the morning and then he stayed still himself as a screen was swiftly drawn about Sam's bed, as the soft-soled shoes hurried across the floor and the voices murmured sadly. He allowed the fat-cheeked volunteer to take him to the playroom and when he returned all Sam's things were gone and his bed was newly made. Sam's parents came to see Tommy the next week and Sam's mother, a very thin woman whose eyes were like melting chocolate in their moist grief, gave him the Lego set.

"Sam liked you very much. He would have wanted you to have it, Tommy," she told him, and Tommy watched as his own mother leaned forward to take Sam's mother's hand in her own. It angered him that she was crying.

"Stop crying!" he shouted at her. "I'm not dead. I'm not going to die." He ripped the Lego box open and began to build with frenetic speed, snapping the bright red, blue, and yellow plastic pieces together, searching for wheels, for triangles. "I'm making a house. I'm making a car. I'm making a tractor," he shouted. No one who was going to die could do the things that he could do; no one who was going to die could work as fast as he could.

"Of course you're not going to die," Anne assured him calmly.

She walked Sam's parents to the door and shook hands with each of them. She stayed with Tommy much later than usual that night, played two games of Candy Land, and read him *Curious George Goes to the Hospital* yet again. She spoke to the night nurse and to the resident. Tommy did not know what she said to them, but he was pleased that they listened to her so attentively.

"Yes, Dr. Richardson."

The resident wrote something in his notebook. Anne told them something very important. She shared a secret with them. He would not die because his mother was a doctor. She understood hospitals and diseases. She would not let him die.

"Of course we're going to be all right," she told him calmly as the plane climbed above the storm, as the seat belt sign flickered off and the strewardess distributed packets of almonds, which he did not really like. "Silly Tommy. We're going to New York and Dr. Bingham is going to see how much better you are and we're going to have Thanksgiving with our friends — with Aunt Merle and Uncle Andrew."

"And Greg," he said at once because they had long played this game in which he named the children of his mother's friends.

"And Aunt Rutti and Uncle David."

"And Sarah. And Adam. And Liora."

"And Aunt Nancy and Uncle Ari."

"And Keren. And Seth. And Noah," he said automatically, although he did not know Nancy or her family. They lived in Israel, but he had seen the snapshots that his mother received regularly and he knew that Nancy was part of her life, as linked to her as Rutti and Merle who called all the time and visited when they could. And, of course, Nancy always sent him birthday cards and presents. The stuffed camel that he cuddled tightly during the plane ride, draping it with his pale blue blanket, was a gift from her and she had sent him the wonderfully carved puzzle — a family of goats crafted of olive wood — that he had placed in his valise.

And, of course, just as his mother promised, everything was all right. The plane landed only a little behind schedule and Aunt Merle and Uncle Andrew were waiting for them at the airport.

Tommy pressed another button on the TV and Bert and Ernie, both of whom he and Ved disliked intensely, flashed onto the screen.

"Oh, good, 'Sesame Street,'" Anne said brightly and he stared at her angrily because she had forgotten his aversion to the furry puppets.

"I hate 'Sesame Street,'" he retorted stridently. "And I don't want you to go out."

Merle glanced at Anne who was carefully tying the belt of her camel's hair coat.

"You know, you and Nancy will have the whole weekend at Egremont," she said hesitantly.

"Merle, please. Tommy will be fine. And you know it's been years since I've seen Nancy."

"All right then." Merle knew that it was difficult to dissuade Anne when she had reached a decision. She smiled in defeat and turned to her friend's son.

"I'll tell you what, Tommy. I'll teach you to play chess," she said. She was glad that she did not have to be at the conservatory today. Although she had assumed many of Emanuel Klein's responsibilities, she worked only three days a week.

"All right." He consented grudgingly. Any display of eagerness would be considered a triumph for his mother. "I know all the moves. Ved's father taught them to me."

"Have fun." Anne dropped a kiss on her son's golden head. She was relieved that the chemo had not caused him to lose his hair. She touched his cheek lightly. His skin was so smooth, so cool to her touch. Oh, he did look so much better, she assured herself, and her heart grew lighter. His color was restored, there was a new resilience in his step. And he had gained weight — the best sign of all, Dr. Perry, his oncologist, asserted. The protocol of treatment was wonderfully effective. Everyone on staff in Chicago agreed that the remission had been startlingly swift. They had been lucky, but she was too experienced a doctor to rely on luck. The human body was a vast labyrinth and treachery lurked in every organ, in each nerve and muscle. A single enzyme, infinitesimal and imperceptible, could unleash disaster. She had to be prepared.

She glanced at her watch.

"I'm going to dash now," she said. "Have fun."

But neither her friend nor her son answered her. They studied the chess board and Tommy made the first move. A pawn, thrust two spaces forward, releasing a bishop. It was, Merle thought, a daring move for a small boy, a novice player. But then again, from the moment of his birth, Tommy's life had been charted for challenge.

The twin towers of the World Trade Center scraped the silver-webbed sky. Tourists and vendors milled about the broad, sun-dappled concourse. Office workers hurried past them, swinging their attaché cases, glancing at their watches, some pausing to check the contents of a briefcase or portfolio. A siren shrilled and car horns blared angrily, but the clusters of Japanese students continued to click their cameras and smile beneficently at each other. Small children clutched colored helium balloons and jumped from the concrete benches, shouting excitedly to their parents. The aroma of roasting chestnuts mingled with the cloying sweetness of cotton candy. It was Thanksgiving Eve and the frantic greedy race for holiday pleasure was already under way. Anne wove her way through the dense crowd and entered the building.

She glanced into the windows of the shops that lined the lobby as she made her way to the elevator. Elegantly dressed young couples hurried past her, carrying shopping bags filled to overflowing. The women wore long fur coats and brightly colored silk scarves draped about their necks. They moved purposefully, their faces frozen into masks of anonymity. Anne imagined them converging at once on a single destination: a shimmering pleasure dome with the miraculous capacity to expand so that it might accommodate all those intense and eager young men and women.

She allowed herself to be propelled into the elevator that soared silently upward to reach the Windows on the World restaurant where she was to meet Nancy.

"Why Windows on the World?" she had asked Nancy.

"Oh, I just feel like being a tourist and going to an eighties kind of eatery," Nancy replied. "Indulge me. The tallest building in Jerusalem is maybe five stories."

"You've got it." She laughed into the phone. She was in no position to argue. They were meeting at her suggestion, almost at her insistence. "It's been so long since you and I have been alone together," she told Nancy.

There was, she thought, a saving grace in their meeting in an unfamiliar part of the city, in an ambience free of shared moments. Still, she felt a moment of unease as she stepped out of the elevator into the radiant expanse of the restaurant, ablaze with the light that poured in through the huge windows. The restaurant was true to its name. Its windows looked down on the world of New York and from its great height, the skyscrapers were diminished, the traffic appeared slowed; the urban turmoil was rendered mute and strangely peaceful.

She waited for Nancy in the reception area and wondered nervously if her friend had changed, if the five years of separation would impair the natural humor, the automatic intimacy, that had always existed between them.

It will be all right, she told herself as the elevator door opened and Nancy rushed toward her.

"Anne. Oh, Anne, you look marvelous."

They embraced, laughter and tears mingling. All uncertainty was dispelled and they were locked again in the unyielding, loving vise of their friendship.

"This is wonderful," they said in unison and burst into familiar laughter. They stepped back and studied each other with affection and approval.

Anne took note of the silver strands that threaded Nancy's dark hair, which she wore now in a shoulder-length, bluntly cut bob. There was a new, matronly solidity in her figure, a new darkness in her complexion, but her soft lips curled easily into the familiar generous smile.

"I love your dress," Anne said, touching the soft gold wool of the high-necked, loose-waisted chemise.

"A wonderful seamstress in Jerusalem. She understands the needs of professional women who have their babies when they are no longer young and pay the penalty of losing their waistlines. Which did not happen to you, Anne."

"Well," said Anne, "I only had one baby. Maybe the next time around."

"Are you planning another time around?" Nancy asked.

"Do I look as though I've gone completely mad?" Anne countered and again they collapsed into laughter.

Arms around each other's waist, their faces wreathed in smiles, they followed the solicitous headwaiter who led them to a table that overlooked the river. They looked down at the fairyland below them. The towers were silvered by sunlight and sailboats and launches skidded with elegant ease across the slate-colored waterway.

"Cocktails?" the waiter asked as he presented them with enormous leather menus.

"Of course," Anne said authoritatively. "This is a celebration, a reunion. Two vodka martinis."

When the drinks arrived, they toasted each other, invoking a ritual reminiscent of their shared Fridays, when they had celebrated each other's triumphs with glasses of white wine, their laughter rising above the children's chatter.

"To our Dr. Anne," Nancy said, repeating the toast she had made when Anne told them of her acceptance to medical school.

"To our Nancy, one courageous lady," Anne repeated the salute she had offered when Nancy told them of her decision to divorce Dov, to move to Israel.

"To Maestro Merle. To Maîtresse Rutti." They lifted their glasses, giggling, as the pet names, unused for years, sprang from the recesses of memory.

Laughter enveloped them. They were suffused with joy that they were together again after so many years, that their friendship was intact, that their thoughts and memories soared toward each other with such spontaneity, such ease. It was wonderful that the day was so bright, that the city spread out below them was so beautiful, so vibrant with promise and energy, that a holiday weekend stretched before them.

They ordered with uncharacteristic abandon, choosing unfamiliar foods, ignoring prices. And they laughed again at their daring when their food was served, their wine glasses filled.

"Salmon tartar?" Nancy said quizzically, looking down at her platter."I must have been mad. But look how beautiful it is — just like a painting. It's a shame to eat it." The raw strips of fish were intricately arranged, set in low inlets and surrounded by tiny islands of black caviar and shoals of baby potatoes peppered with parsley.

"Nouvelle cuisine," Anne told her. "If you don't eat it, the chef has an anxiety attack and has to arrange an emergency session with his analyst. Who could be you."

"Don't rush me. I'm just getting my office furnished. And I've never yet had a chef as a patient. How is your linguine *avec* morels?"

"Spaghetti is spaghetti," Anne replied. "Still, we've come a long way baby. Good-bye peanut butter and Campbell's soup. Anyway, tell me about Rutti's exhibition."

"It was terrific. She's doing some marvelous oils, and of course, her other work was wonderfully arranged. Lots of viewers, and sales were so brisk the gallery staff couldn't keep up with them. Ari and I were amazed that young people in this country seem to have so much money."

"Yuppies," Anne said. "And DINKs."

"Dinks?" Nancy repeated questioningly. She sipped her wine, spread caviar on a piece of potato.

"Double Income No Kids. This is the age of acronyms. We're too busy in this country to speak in actual words — some of which might have more than one syllable. Hey, we're in too big a hurry. Places to go, people to see, and so much to buy. It's all Betty Friedan's fault — DINKs are what you get when the feminine mystique is demystified."

"I don't think I'm following you," Nancy said.

"Sociologists say that as a result of women's lib we have all these terrific young women doctors and lawyers and MBAs who marry all these terrific young men doctors and attorneys and MBAs, and all of them are so intent on climbing the career ladder that there's no time for kids but there *are* all those wonderful salaries that can be used to buy all those great co-ops and condos with health clubs on the roof. And then, of course, all those rooms have to be filled with all sorts of wonderful things."

"Ah," said Nancy. "I see. The women's movement is to blame. This is what we got for going to consciousness-raising sessions. We're to blame for materialism gone wild, for conspicuous consumerism. Mea culpa. Mea maxima culpa." She grinned and lightly beat her breast.

"Consciousness-raising groups are out. No one knows about them. No one needs them. Everyone's consciousness is raised. Too high, I sometimes think," Anne retorted. She thought of Sally, her research assistant, who anticipated no obstacles to her ambition. She was certain she was in control of her life, the architect of her future.

"Never too high," Nancy said. "Although sometimes I wonder. I'm glad Keren won't have to swim upstream the way we did, but sometimes I think her own freedom overwhelms her, bewilders her. Maybe there was something to be said for fighting a negative current."

"No," Anne said flatly. "It was not good. It was draining. It exhausted us. And it broke our hearts." She drained her wine glass and did not refill it.

"I know." Nancy felt an encroaching depression. The exhilaration with which they had begun the meal was gone. They had come down off the high of laughter and exuberant exchange. The years, after all, had taken their toll.

"Was Sarah at the exhibit?" Anne asked.

"No. She was singing at some club in the Village. She's a wonderful girl, our Sarah, but she always seems — I don't know — sort of lost. I'm not sure she ever really came to terms with Werner's death."

"Perhaps that's part of it, and of course she's in a tough field. Every day a new audition, maybe a new decision. Do I dare? Do I dare not to dare? It's tricky. But you know what happens to most lost girls — they get found."

"Not always," Nancy said.

"Of course not always. Look at me, yours truly. Case in point."

"Not exactly," Nancy reminded her. "You made a choice. There's a difference between being lost and choosing to find your own way."

"I made a lot of choices." Anne refilled her wine glass, drank deeply. Nancy wondered if she often drank so much at lunch and immediately dismissed the thought. That was not Anne's style.

"Do you want to talk about Tommy now, Anne?" she asked gently.

"Yes," Anne replied. "I think it's time to talk about Tommy."

She waited until the table was cleared and a white carafe of coffee was set down. Carefully, Anne filled both of their cups. "You know that Tommy got very sick a few months ago. It was leukemia. We were very lucky, I think. We discovered it at an early stage and it does not appear to be a particularly tenacious or aggressive strain of the disease, although the name is frightening. Acute lymphatic leukemia. I won't get too technical, but it's being controlled by a protocol of therapy that Charles Bingham prescribed. He's been wonderful, by the way. He and his wife." She was careful to mention Nicole, who sent Tommy cards and small gifts, puzzles and workbooks. "Tommy appears to be in remission." Anne spoke slowly and deliberately, as though she had rehearsed each word, each inflection.

"Oh, Anne, you must be so relieved. It was very hard, I know. Rutti and Merle wrote me." Nancy looked at Anne with sympathy and admiration. She wondered whether she could be as strong if her own children were in danger. A patient in Jerusalem, a rabbi's wife unable to recover from depression after the loss of a son, had told her that the Talmud says that God weeps when parents bury a child.

"I'm relieved, of course I am. But I'm not sure we're out of the woods. I've read a lot about leukemia since Tommy became ill. It's unpredictable, especially with kids. The doctors are optimistic about Tommy. The remission may be permanent, there may never be another flare-up. Or it could be just a respite, a breathing spell before a renewal of the cancer, before the treadmill to death. It's unlikely but I want to have some backup, some insurance, in place in case that happens." She was quite pale now. Her makeup had faded and Nancy saw the circles of misery beneath her friend's eyes. She had spoken the two dread words, "cancer" and "death," and their very utterance had drained and exhausted her.

392

"I'm not a medical doctor, Anne. You'll have to explain. What would constitute backup? What insurance is possible?"

"The worst-case scenario is that if there is a recurrence of cancer — which everyone seems to think won't happen — and if all other chemo and drug therapy is ineffective, Tommy might be saved by a bone marrow transplant. His own marrow would have to be matched with that of a donor. It's a tricky and often an impossible process. I won't go into the details, but there would have to be six compatible antigens in the marrow transplant — and usually such donors are most likely to be found in the immediate family. The best possibilities are siblings, even half-siblings." She spoke in the clipped, pedantic tone of a teacher who will not welcome questions or discussion and added a great deal of milk to her coffee, although she usually drank it black.

"What about parents?" Nancy asked.

"I've been tested, of course. And his father's been tested. Neither of us has even three compatible antigens."

"Does Tommy have siblings — half-brothers, half-sisters?" Nancy asked hesitantly. She felt as though Anne had left a trail of clues and she would have to sort them out to arrive at the question her friend wanted her to ask.

"Yes." Anne's voice was very low. She lifted her coffee cup and set it down again. She stared down at the tablecloth, crumbled a piece of bread, assembled the crumbs in a pattern.

"Do they know about him?" The question was gentle. Oh, how hard this must be for Anne who had clearly wanted so badly to keep her secret, who had not thought that she would ever have to reveal it. Nancy's heart broke for her friend who had worked so hard, tried so hard. She recalled Anne's pallor as she sat beside her in the doctor's office in that small Pennsylvania town whose name she no longer remembered.

"Not they. She." Again Anne spoke so softly that the monosyllables of her reply were barely audible. "And no. She doesn't know about it."

"He has a half-sister," Nancy said. She spoke very quietly. Her fingertips were cold, her cheeks ablaze. "Who? Do I know her? Who is she, Anne?"

"Keren." She whispered the name, then said it aloud. "Keren."

"My Keren?" Nancy's throat was dry, her voice strangely unfamiliar to her own ears. Shock rippled through her. She sat erect, fearful that if she relaxed her posture she might collapse. She felt light-headed, and her heart beat with frightening rapidity.

"How can that be?" she asked, although she knew the answer.

"Dov is Tommy's father."

Anne said this clearly, as though the words were a release. Their utterance exposed a wound long hidden, a dormant emotional infection that had sapped her strength. She wept then and Nancy stared at her, her own eyes burning.

"Stop it," she said harshly. "Damn it. Stop crying."

Anne's tears were unfair weapons. It was Nancy who had been betrayed. Rage possessed her, swept over her like a storm. She gripped the table's edge. The cloth moved dangerously. She imagined glassware and silver crashing to the floor, food and wine sullying the napery, their clothing, splashing against their legs. Sourness rose from her throat and filled her mouth.

She sprinted across the deeply carpeted floor, through the bright, many-windowed room, to the women's lounge, and in the safety of the small white cubicle, she vomited the elegant lunch ordered with such gaiety, such laughter. The barely digested raw fish floated in coral fragments on the blue water. She retched again. She would expunge the affection and friendship she had felt for Anne, the love she had once had for Dov, the melancholy fondness she had retained for him after the dissolution of their marriage. She was betrayed and doubly betrayed. Friend and husband. Ex-husband and ex-friend. And now she was being asked for kindness, for sympathy. And now Keren was plunged into a new traumatic obligation, entrapped in a new emotional coil. She leaned toward the door of the cubicle and banged her forehead softly against the cool metal surface. She washed her face with cold water and carefully patted it dry. She combed her hair and smoothed her thick dark brows with a trembling finger. Then she left the lounge and slowly made her way across the huge room, back to the table where Anne waited for her, her head bowed like a penitent child.

"I'm sorry, Nancy," she said miserably. "I never meant for you to know."

"I'm sorry too. But now I know. And I'll have to know more." She schooled herself to professional silence. She was trained to forbearance. She would not allow her anger to obscure her judgment. She sat back prepared to listen, impervious to the annoyed stare of the waiter who clearly wanted their table vacated, to the curious gaze of the two women at the neighboring table who had watched her flight to the women's lounge.

"I want you to know that this was not Dov's fault. I take full responsibility."

"Anne." Nancy struggled to contain her fury. "This is not a court of law and I'm not meting out judgment. What's done is done. At this point it hardly matters who initiated the affair."

"It wasn't an affair," Anne protested weakly.

"No? All right, what would you call it? You tell me." Her voice was hard and she made no effort to soften it. She had a right to the resentment that bit at her.

Pain distorted Anne's features. Her eyes were lowered, her voice again so soft that Nancy had to strain to hear her.

"I don't know. I can't find a word for it. An encounter. A very brief encounter." She twisted a linen napkin into a clumsy knot. "Please, Nancy, hear me out. You know that I always thought that I would marry — have a husband, a home, children, after I had my degree. But then the years passed and one relationship ended and then another. The odds were getting slimmer and I began to wonder whether I really wanted to marry. What I did know was that I wanted a child. More than wanted. I was desperate to be a mother and time was running out. I decided that I'd have a child on my own. I thought about possible fathers. Remember that game we used to play — how we made lists of men we considered to be ideal lovers?"

"Yes." It was strange how that idle, mischievous game of their young womanhood still teased their memories. Merle referred to it in Jerusalem during her brief involvement with Dennis Montgomery. He was married now, Merle had told her, to a talented young cellist, a student whom Merle supervised.

"I even remember your choices," Nancy said, and despite her anger, she smiled. "I don't suppose you wrote to Jonas Salk or Christian Bernard and asked them to father your child?"

Anne shook her head ruefully. Even now the humor that had always been so intrinsic to their friendship asserted itself. Even now.

"Believe it or not, I thought about it," Anne said wryly.

"I'm sure you did." Nancy's voice was cold again, withering in its contempt.

"Nancy. Please. This is hard enough without sarcasm." Misery crept back into Anne's voice.

"I apologize. I shouldn't be sarcastic." Her voice was brittle; any moment it might crack and she would lose control. "I should ask you why you didn't choose artificial insemination, a sperm bank."

"Was it asking too much to want the father of my child to be someone I knew, someone with whom I had a relationship, a friendship? I wanted to know that my child had been conceived in warmth, affection — not through a medical procedure — that the father was someone I knew, someone I would always know. It's possible, although I never said it to myself or to anyone else, that maybe I was frightened of exactly what happened to Tommy. I'm a geneticist. How could I not have worried about heredity, organ transplants, gene pools?" Her words trailed off. She rested her elbows on the table. Her energy was depleted; she despaired of being able to continue and yet there was still so much to say.

"But why Dov?" The question was plaintive, almost pleading.

"I suppose because I always knew that Dov was attracted to me, felt something for me. From the very beginning. Something in the way he looked at me, came too close and then not close enough. I knew I had to be careful, to keep my distance. Your friendship — our friendship — was too important to me."

"I'm gratified to hear that," Nancy said coldly. She remembered Dov's harsh evaluation of Anne: she was too aggressive, too ambitious. That harshness had masked his attraction.

"Oh, Nancy, this is so hard. Please." Anne's eyes were lowered, her face flushed.

Nancy stared at her. It was hard and she would not make it easier. Anne had made nothing easier for her; she had violated their friendship and insulted their intimacy.

"And afterward? After we were divorced and you and Dov weren't in the same city?"

"We saw each other now and again at medical conferences," Anne continued slowly, hoarsely, each word dry with misery. "We always talked, had dinner or a drink. We shared a history, a connection. You. Keren."

"Me. Keren," Nancy repeated bitterly.

"Once or twice he sent me monographs he thought would interest me. DNA fascinated him, and so I'd send him reprints of my articles. There were Christmas cards, a wedding announcement when he married Lisa. I sent them a wedding present. A silver vase. It seemed appropriate. You were living in Israel. You had married Ari and had a new life. I think I forgot that you had ever been married to Dov. That happens, you know."

"I know," Nancy replied sadly. There were times when she, too, thought of her first marriage as a dream, when she could not imagine that Ari had ever been married to Yaffa. "And after his marriage to Lisa?"

"The same thing. The once or twice a year meetings. Maybe a playful flirtation over drinks. We knew each other so well." Her tone was puzzled as though even now she could not understand the gay and muted teasing, the knowledge of mutual arousal that would fade harmlessly when he returned to New York and she left for Minnesota. Such games were played at conventions in distant cities; they were harmless exercises, mischievous respites from tedium.

"And you, Anne? Were you attracted to him, to Dov?" The explosive question was softly asked.

"He's an attractive man. I was lonely. And I was searching." Her honesty was searingly painful. She spared neither Nancy nor herself. "There was a pediatric conference in Seattle. I was asked to present a paper. I saw that Dov was to be a panelist. I called him at his office and asked if Lisa would be coming. He said no. I suppose he saw my question as an invitation. Which it was. We became lovers in Seattle. A circumscribed affair. Three days. No scenes. Very civilized. We weren't in love. There was Lisa and I even told Dov that I was involved with someone in Rochester. Seattle was strictly extracurricular. He assumed that I was taking precautions. We were — in a way, almost like brother and sister." She fell silent, exhausted, almost relieved.

"You didn't think that you were committing incest — in a way?"

Nancy copied Anne's deadened monotone; her mimicry was harsh and pitiless.

"No. I thought only that I was trying to have a child. That if I became pregnant I would know the background of that child's father. That I would always be able to contact him."

"Oh, God, Anne. You weren't conducting an experiment. It wasn't a goddamn med school research project." Anger laced her words with shrillness. "You slept with the man I was once married to, with Keren's father." She closed her mind against the image of Anne and Dov making love, of Anne's long fingers tracing the pale butterfly-shaped scar at Dov's neck, of Dov's breath moist against Anne's breasts. She remembered, with luminous clarity, tenderness she had thought long forgotten. "Don't talk to me about scientific rationalization, gene pools, heredity. You did as you pleased to get what you wanted the way you've always done what you pleased to get what you wanted. Pregnancy wasn't going to stand in the way of your finishing medical school. And sleeping with your best friend's husband wasn't going to stand in the way of your becoming pregnant in exactly the way you wanted to become pregnant."

"Ex-husband." Tears coursed down Anne's cheeks. She had anticipated Nancy's anger, her feelings of betrayal, but she had not expected an explosion of hatred, an accusatory condemnation that reached back across the years. Her body shook. She did not think she would ever stop shaking.

"But not ex-father. Dov is Keren's father. And he is Lisa's husband. But, of course, Lisa didn't matter. Why should you worry about Lisa? *You* wanted to have a baby."

"It never hurt Lisa. Dov and I were never together again. I didn't see or hear from him for two years, and then it was at some pharmaceutical junket and Lisa was with him. We all had dinner together," Anne protested.

"Like you said. Very civilized. No scenes. Except that there was Tommy. Did Dov know about him?"

"He knew that I had a child," Anne said carefully. "The medical grapevine. Maybe he was suspicious, but he never contacted me. I called him when Tommy's leukemia was diagnosed. I wanted him to have his marrow tested for compatibility."

"He must have loved that," Nancy said bitterly. Self-protective, self-protecting Dov who had called her when the Yom Kippur War raged to caution her about Keren. *Go to hell,* she had told him. Had he told Anne to go to hell? It would not surprise her.

"He was furious. Frightened and furious," Anne said. She had reeled with shame at his fury, but understood his fear. She had neither exonerated him nor blamed him. "Still, he took the test. Negative. Like my own. Otherwise I would never have involved Keren. I never would have hurt you. You know that?" She looked pleadingly at her friend, willing her to understanding, to forgiveness.

"Know? I don't know anything. I'm so damn angry. I feel so betrayed. No. Used. No. Deceived." She summoned up words one by one, tested and discarded them. They did not suffice. Her mind was dark and shadowed by fear. What would they, what could they, say to Keren? *We want you to undergo these tests because you have a half-brother and he is ill. Your father, Dov Yallon, is also the father of your Aunt Anne's son, Tommy.* The situation was ludicrous, horrific; their alternatives, appalling.

"I know. And you have every right. But Nancy, I'm frightened, scared. Scared to death. For Tommy." Again her tears fell and again she ignored them. "He is all I have and oh, dear God, I love him. I want my child, my Tommy. You have so much, Nancy. What am I asking you for, after all?" Her voice broke. She could say no more. There was nothing left to reveal. She had scraped herself dry and offered Nancy the exposed wound of her terrible fear.

Nancy stood, surprised that she was steady on her feet.

"I can't talk anymore, Anne." She could not bear another moment, she would not listen to another word.

"Nancy, please." Anne's eyes were closed, her voice a whisper. "It's Tommy we must think about. Tommy." Her child's name was a benison, a magical incantation. It would soothe Nancy's hurt, invoke her compassion.

But Nancy was gone. She was halfway across the room, moving swiftly toward the bank of elevators. Anne's view of her was obscured by the phalanx of waiters already preparing the elaborate cocktail hour buffet.

A light rain had begun to fall, and Anne watched as rivulets streaked the huge windows. She sat motionless, as mourners often do, fearful their slightest movement will jeopardize the delicate balance that sustains them against the avalanche of grief. She knew she was bereft. Nancy had gone from her.

At last she poured herself another coffee, but the brew had turned tepid and bitter. Still, she sipped it slowly, willing herself to calm. She and Tommy would see Charles Bingham that afternoon. He would be pleased with Tommy's progress. He would offer her kindness and optimism and she would accept both gratefully.

Everything will be all right, she told herself. Everything has to be all right. Now, as always, she allowed herself little margin for failure.

Music and laughter filled the Cunninghams' Egremont home. A fire blazed in the living room fireplace and embers glowed on the hearth in Merle's studio. Lottie sang lustily in the kitchen as she attacked a mound of serving dishes. She moved more slowly now, but she had indignantly refused Merle's offer to hire someone to help her.

"I can manage," she said. "We don't want anyone who's not family here."

She defined them as they saw themselves, as they saw her. A family of friends. Merle did not quarrel with her. Instead, they all pitched in to help, retreating from the kitchen only when she banished them.

The younger children, Adam and Liora, and Seth and Noah, Nancy's sons, dashed up and down the stairs. Their after-dinner game of hide-and-seek had degenerated into a frantic chase and they tumbled about the landings, laughing loudly as they tagged each other.

"Out!" Seth shouted joyously. "You're out. He is out. Everyone is out!" He was proud to be speaking English, exuberant at being able to use the word newly learned in his American school.

"I'm not out!" Tommy shouted from his perch on the top step.

"How can you be out if you're not even playing?" Adam asked.

"I am so playing. I'm the referee," Tommy retorted. "Your father said so."

David, who had a knack for organizing children's games and then withdrawing from them, nodded and smiled at his son.

"You understand about referees, Adam," he said.

"Well, David, if you ever give up on art and illustrations, you can become a nursery school teacher," Anne said. She held her hands out to the flames and wondered if she would ever feel really warm again. It was nerves, she knew; she had not felt warm since her lunch with Nancy.

"Why not? The sexual stereotypes are breaking down. Greg tells me the kindergarten teacher at his school is a young man. There are worse fates. Milk and cookies at noon. Class trips to the zoo. No need to worry about editors or publishers or sales figures. It begins to sound more and more attractive." He laughed easily and stroked his beard.

"Anything sounds more attractive to me than medicine and hospitals at this point," Anne said. She leaned back in her chair and watched the group of young people gathered about the piano. Greg was playing and Abdul, Keren, Eric, and Sarah were singing the score from *Cats*. They were harmonizing "Old Mephistopheles" now and Anne hoped they would switch to another score before they reached "Memory."

"I imagine you've had your fill of hospitals these past months. Tommy's been in and out?"

"Mostly in," Anne said. "Charles set up a pretty aggressive protocol. I'm glad. It's been miraculously effective. Tommy looks so much better, doesn't he?"

"Yes. Yes, he does," David said honestly. "What does Charles think?"

"He won't know for certain until he gets all the lab results back. But he has seen the reports from Chicago and he's satisfied that Tommy's in remission," Anne replied. "My Tommy's a very lucky boy."

"Lucky to have you for a mother," David said; he was startled by the sudden expression of pain that flashed across Anne's face. "Did I say something wrong, Anne? Something stupid?" He reached out and took her hands in his own. Her fingers were ice-cold and he massaged them slowly, warming and comforting her as he so often warmed and comforted Rutti.

"No, David. It's just that I used to tell myself the very same thing. We were lucky to have each other, Tommy and I. I would congratulate him and myself because we were such a unique mother-and-son team. We were breaking all the rules, going it alone and doing so well. And then Tommy got sick. I'd lay awake at night and think maybe I was being punished for my hubris — for the arrogant pride of the new woman. I had been too self-sufficient, too independent. Crazy thoughts. Crazy feelings. I'm a doctor. I know better. Still, it forced me to recognize that it's hard. It's hard to be alone and raise a child alone. It seems that we may luck out after all, but we could have been a lot luckier." Sadness, rather than bitterness, weighted her words.

"Could have. Would have. Should have. All futile expressions, Anne. I gave up using them long ago. We make choices, or at least we think we do, and then life sets limits and fate socks it to us. Some things happen and some things don't. Everything in combination — choice and chance. I came to Egremont to begin a new life with Kathya. Choice. A driver came too quickly down a country road and she was killed. Chance. It was Rutti with whom I began that life. There was no could, would, or should about it. It was out of my control. Just as a lot of your life has been out of your control, Anne." David spoke softly, but fluently. He was that rare man who is at ease speaking intimately to women.

"That's where you and I are different," Anne said. "You're a fatalist. Maybe that's why you had the strength to give Rutti so much latitude after Werner died. But I always thought that I was in control, that I could write my own script. Act One. Act Two. A reasonable scenario, and it all seemed to work. Each scene was playing as I had written it. I had my medical degree, my career. And I had written my happy ending. My prince would come along. And so I waited and waited but he didn't come. I had to rewrite. And the new ending was all right — until Tommy got sick. Chance."

"Come on," David said. "You haven't reached your ending yet. And you're not alone. You're part of a family of friends. We've always been here for you. And now Nancy is back with us, for at least a few years."

"Nancy." Anne repeated the name sadly. David suddenly realized that Anne and Nancy had avoided each other throughout the day. There had been the usual excitement when the friends met, the usual

exchange of kisses and embraces, of hilarity and exuberant exclama-
tions, but Nancy and Anne had not embraced, had not exchanged
laughter or teased each other with loving affection. He remembered
now something that had particularly struck him. Nancy had brought
gifts from Israel. She gave Merle and Rutti similar pendants, a small
hand, crafted of filigreed silver, not unlike the one she wore. But she
gave Anne a woven scarf, turning away before Anne could thank her.

The hands, David knew, were symbolic of the pact they pledged
all those years ago, their fingers splayed, fingertips touching. Surely
that was what Nancy had in mind when she selected the pendants.
Had Nancy and Anne had a falling-out? He would ask Rutti. She
would surely know. He changed the topic, almost too swiftly.

"It's wonderful to see the young people having such a good time
together."

The group at the piano shifted position. Greg surrendered his
seat to Abdul and Sarah moved closer to the keyboard. She turned
the pages of the sheet music, discarding *Cats*. Good, Anne thought
with relief, they're going to skip "Memory."

Abdul pounded out the overture to *Fiddler on the Roof* and they
all laughed. She laughed, too. After all, it was funny that an Israeli
Arab was playing the score to a musical about a Jewish village in
eastern Europe. Funny and hopeful.

"He's very talented, Ari tells us. Ari's arranged for him to give
recitals in a number of cities across the country and then perhaps to
study at a conservatory here. He's been staying with us. Sarah invited
him to stay through the weekend," David said.

"I like him," Anne replied, as though she had sensed a question
in his statement. She had talked briefly to Abdul during the meal and
had been struck by his intelligence and intensity.

Sarah was singing now. Goldie's song, her indignant answer to
Tevye's question "Do you love me?" Sarah, who usually sang tender
ballads, belted out the vigorous lyrics, her hands on her narrow hips,
her golden-ringleted head nodding from side to side. Abdul's fingers
flew across the keys, but his eyes did not leave Sarah's face.

"He seems quite taken with her," Anne observed.

She noticed that Rutti, who sat across the room, looked now at
Abdul, now at Sarah — her glance darting from one to the other as

though she had been presented with disparate pieces of a puzzle and could not fit them into place.

"You know how musicians are," David replied. "They're not like writers or artists who need their solitude and work alone. Musicians need community. I'm glad Sarah has met someone who understands her work. She sometimes seems so — I don't know — adrift, I suppose. We worry about her."

"I think these are difficult times for young people," Anne said carefully. She wanted to comfort him as he had comforted her. "Too many barriers have been torn down and the new boundaries aren't in place yet. Give her time."

She did not tell David that she shared his concern about Sarah. The dreamy, frightened child was now a sad-eyed young woman who masked her loneliness with a brittle cynicism. It seemed to Anne, who had so long felt herself to be an outsider, that Sarah hovered at the edge of the life David and Rutti had built for themselves and resisted their efforts to pull her into its center. She loved the twins and was playful and gentle with them, but Anne knew that she did not feel integral to their lives. Perhaps she wasn't. Many families, after all, have a changeling child — a son or daughter who does not fit, who does not want to fit, who in every family photograph stands at an imperceptible remove from the group, the sole grave face amid smiling siblings. Anne had been such a child. Perhaps it was herself she saw in Sarah.

The song was over. Everyone clapped. Abdul rose and took Sarah's hand. He bowed, she curtsied, and Greg again took command of the piano. Abdul and Sarah darted toward the front closet, donning parkas, hats, gloves.

"I want to show him the woodland trail," Sarah whispered to Anne as they passed her, and Anne hoped that the youngsters were dressed warmly enough. She watched through the window and saw that they had broken into a run, that their faces were bright, and she knew they would not feel the cold.

The doorbell rang again and again. Merle had invited friends and neighbors and the room was suddenly reverberant with animated conversation. The children had disappeared and Anne went in search of them. They were in an upstairs den watching *King Kong*. Tommy sat cross-legged on the floor and he looked up angrily as she approached him, her hand extended.

"Go away," he said forbiddingly. "I don't have a temperature."

"Of course you don't," she agreed gladly and turned to leave. But Nancy stood in the doorway.

"Anne, can we talk?" How calm Nancy's tone. How steady her gaze.

"Yes, of course," she said, surprised that her own voice should be so controlled.

They went into a small guest room and sat side by side on the chintz-covered window seat that overlooked the garden, the sylvan landscape of their long friendship. The scene evoked so many shared memories. It was in the garden that they had all giggled together as they conspired mischievously with Merle to furnish the house. And beneath the apple tree, Anne and Charles, Nancy and Dov, had often spread a blanket and shared twilight picnics. They had studied together in companionable silence. Now they were no longer students, but accomplished professional women and their silence was no longer companionable.

Together they watched Sarah and Abdul emerge from the woodland trail, hand in hand. The two young people stood for a moment in the shelter of a long shadow. Abdul touched Sarah's face, traced the slope of her cheekbones, rested his fingers on her slender neck. Sarah smiled at him and they returned to the house, walking slowly, not touching.

Nancy's heart sank. Should she speak to Rutti, warn her? But warn her against what? Sarah's needs? Abdul's tenderness? The danger of a love affair between an Israeli Arab and the daughter of Werner Weisenblatt? There was nothing Rutti could do. Keren and Sarah were women now, in possession of their own lives. Their mothers' vigilance and concern was of small consequence. She looked at Anne, who shook her head sadly. They shared the same thoughts and feelings, but they could not talk about it. Anne's revelation had made such confidences forfeit.

"Everyone says that Tommy looks so much better," Nancy said. She did not look at Anne as she spoke but continued to stare out the window. The children were in the garden now, pelting each other with the fallen, unharvested apples.

"Yes. Charles was very pleased with his condition. He thinks that Tommy is in remission and the need for any extreme measure is unlikely. But he still thinks it would be wise to have the name of a possible marrow donor, just in case."

"Then Keren will be tested," she said softly.

"Oh, Nancy, thank you." Anne reached out and touched her friend's hand. It was as icy cold as her own.

"It's for Tommy." Nancy spoke swiftly, pulling her hand away.

"I know."

"I don't want Keren to know about you and Dov. I'm going to tell her that the child of a cousin of mine — some obscure Cleveland relation — is ill with a blood disease and the entire family is being tested. I spoke to Dov and he agrees."

Anne was silent. It had not occurred to her that Nancy would speak to Dov, but then so many obvious things failed to occur to her. She wondered if Dov had asked about Tommy. It pained her that he had not asked to see the child he had fathered, that he had expressed no interest in him. It was what she had wanted; she could not blame him and yet she did.

"We both feel that Keren's had a lot to adjust to — our divorce, my remarriage and Dov's, the move to Israel and now a new adjustment in America. There's no reason to compound all that with the knowledge that her father slept with her mother's closest friend and she has yet another half-brother. That's a bit much, don't you think?" There was a purposeful harshness in Nancy's tone.

Anne shivered, and hugged herself for warmth.

"As you put it, it is."

"And I don't want anyone else to know. Not Merle, not Rutti. For Keren's sake. For Tommy's sake."

"I didn't think it would be for my sake, Nancy," Anne said sadly. She waited with desperate hope for Nancy to soften, to offer a word of regret, of assurance.

The early darkness of late autumn shadowed the garden. Together they watched the children dash indoors. Then Nancy walked slowly from the room, leaving the door ajar.

The sounds of renewed holiday gaiety drifted up the stairwell. Merle played a medley of holiday songs on her violin. The children sang, Tommy's high sweet voice rising above the others. "Over the river and through the woods, to grandmother's house we go . . . " Laughter punctuated each new verse, the giggling merriment of long familiarity.

Anne looked toward the woodland trail. The tall evergreen stretched skyward, its feathery branches brushing the new and tender darkness.

23

THEY WERE their mothers' daughters. They had been bred to intimacy and honesty, initiated early into independence. Companions from childhood, observers of their mothers' friendships, sharers of secrets, Keren and Sarah were ideal roommates. Often they sat up late, perched cross-legged on the open sofa bed strewn with books and papers that dominated the living room of their West Side apartment. Wearing the oversize, long-sleeved, and high-necked white muslin nightgowns that they both favored — Merle's regular birthday gift to each of them — they talked and laughed, watched old movies on cable, and played tapes. Occasionally they fell asleep with the light still on, the television still blaring. It was usually Keren who awoke. Still half moored in sleep, pleasantly disoriented, she switched off the set and the lights and padded away to her bedroom. The apartment, in a brownstone owned by Andrew Cunningham, had been carefully and sensibly divided. Keren took the bedroom because Sarah often worked late at clubs and because she needed the privacy for her writing. Even when Sarah was not at home, she found it necessary to close the door to her room when she wrote.

Now and again she read her work aloud to Sarah, who listened with her eyes closed. Keren wrote vignettes about life as she observed it in New York, as she had observed it in Jerusalem. She wrote a long prose poem that Sarah set to music and sang at Ballads and Blues. Listeners lowered their heads when Sarah softly strummed her guitar and sang of young girls walking alone through moon-silvered streets.

They were not lonely, they assured themselves and each other. As Sarah wrote to Abdul Nashif in Jerusalem, they were too busy to be lonely. Keren had her writing courses at Columbia, her part-time job at Rizzoli, her meetings with a conservationist group chaired by Greg. Sarah dashed from her voice lessons to her waitressing jobs and then to her gigs at small clubs scattered throughout the city. On nights when they were both free, they dressed in their thrift shop finery, loose satin rainbow-colored shirts, long dark skirts, high boots, and long scarves shot through with threads of silver and gold. They went to discos and to dimly lit coffeehouses or to basement bars where musicians wearing dark glasses played jazz. Sometimes Greg or Eric or other friends joined them. Often they went alone. They were, after all, the daughters of women who had done a great many things alone.

Their phone rang often. Friends sought their advice, invited them to parties, shared confidences. Keren jogged each morning. Sarah rode her bicycle through Central Park. Riding and running, they waved casually to other young people also riding and running, anonymous companions easily recognizable by their sweatpants and headbands, their faded university T-shirts, their clean hair and earnest expressions. They were all young people in control of their bodies, in control of their lives.

Sarah and Keren went to brunches at the co-op apartment Eric had bought on East Seventy-seventh Street and ate gravlax on natural grain bread and baby vegetables organically grown and sculpted into long thin wands. Eric's friends were investment bankers, commodity traders, management trainees. They thought it interesting that Keren had lived in Israel and planned to return there. They questioned her about the Palestinians and she struggled to reply. "It's a pressure cooker over there," a young man said, and she shrugged.

There were pressure cookers everywhere, hissing and boiling, building up to explosions. Central America was a pressure cooker and eastern Europe was a pressure cooker and so was Afghanistan. Their generation was sitting atop a volcano. Their hearts hammered when the news came on. They talked quickly, ate and drank extravagantly, traveled on jet planes, and hurried down broad urban thoroughfares in leather sneakers because they knew themselves to be racing against time, seizing the moment. They were not fooled by their President's easy smile and drawling phrases. Someone in every group could do a Ronald Reagan imitation.

Rutti gave each of the young women a membership to the Museum of Modern Art, and they spent long weekend afternoons wandering through the galleries and watching vintage films. Often when they arrived home the phone would be ringing and they flashed each other looks of conspiratorial recognition. That was the hour when Rutti or Nancy, always circumspect about invading their daughters' lives, infringing on their privacy, chose to call and ask casual, carefully phrased questions about their week or their weekend. Despite Rutti's discreet silence and Nancy's unquestioning acquiescence, Keren and Sarah knew their mothers were greedy for information about their lives and dutifully they spoke of their work, of the parties they had been to, the films they had seen, Greg's girlfriend, a sweet, shy midwesterner who taught at the same school. They invited their mothers for lunch and Nancy and Rutti arrived with gifts: place mats and ceramic vases, coasters from the Metropolitan Museum of Art, a Marimekko cloth in shades of orange and brown to cover the battered Salvation Army table in the dining alcove. Their mothers were like small girls, deprived of dollhouses of their own, who delight in finding small treasures with which to furnish the play areas of more fortunate friends. Rutti and Nancy roamed the small apartment and smiled approvingly. They sent surprise gifts. A wok. An answering machine.

"It's because what we're doing is important to them," Keren told Sarah one night as they ate cold leftover spaghetti off of paper plates and watched "Cagney and Lacey." "We're living the life they never had."

"Give me a break," Sarah objected, half seriously, half jokingly. "I'm tired of making good for their lost opportunities. I'm tired of feeling guilty. I even feel guilty because they work so hard at making us not feel guilty."

"Poor us," Keren agreed sarcastically. "It's not easy to be the daughters of consciousness-raising-group graduates."

They laughed. Their friends had neither time nor need for such groups.

Young men drifted in and out of their lives. Sarah was vague, amused by and finally indifferent to those who pursued her. They, in turn, thought her elusive and mercurial, and grew discouraged quickly. Keren's relationships, too, were intense and brief. The freedom and impermanence of their lives both excited and frightened them. They were comforted that certain things remained stable: their parents' phone calls and invitations, their work and study, and for Sarah, the pale green air letters that arrived from Abdul Nashif each week, which she read sitting still as a statue on the cushioned seat of the bay window.

They went to dinner one night at Merle and Andrew's and were surprised to learn that it had been weeks since Merle had seen Nancy and Rutti. "I talk to them on the phone, of course," Merle said wistfully, "but we hardly see each other."

Contact between the friends had lessened considerably. They were all so busy, of course. Nancy was teaching, studying, seeing patients. Rutti was preparing for a London exhibition, her first international show, and Merle was chairing a development campaign for the conservatory, organizing luncheons, recitals, black-tie evenings. And Anne was in Chicago. The playground sisters' friendship had always weathered distance and crowded schedules, but this was different. Keren and Sarah understood that the emotional adhesive that for so long had cemented their intimacy had lost its power. They were puzzled, but pleased when Merle and Rutti flew to Chicago for Anne's wedding. Nancy did not go. Anne had given so little notice, she said. She could not reschedule patients and classes, juggle sitting arrangements for Seth and Noah.

Keren and Sarah speculated that there were other reasons for Nancy's decision. It gave them an odd, perverse enjoyment to judge their mothers, to analyze the friendships that had dominated their childhoods. It endowed them with a new maturity, vested them with a secret and sly superiority.

Anne's decision to marry had taken them all by surprise. Her groom was a nuclear physicist named Sanjit Prav, the widowed uncle of Tommy's best friend, Ved. He had two young sons, an adolescent daughter, and a huge extended family.

"He's a wonderful man," Anne told Merle when she called with her news. "Tommy loves him." It occurred to Merle later that Anne had not said that she loved him. Still, both Merle and Rutti reported that the wedding, performed in Anne's living room by a judge, was moving and dignified. The two dark-haired boys, the beautiful sari-clad daughter, and Tommy held hands as they stood beside the bride and groom, all affirming and celebrating the new relationship. Merle took a great many photographs and she invited Nancy, Rutti, Keren, and Sarah to lunch and passed them around. She had considered making a small album for Anne, but now she was uncertain.

"Anne was never really sentimental," she said worriedly.

"That's the understatement of the year," Nancy replied; they were all startled by the harshness of her tone.

Sanjit Prav was dark and fine-featured, his jet hair gently graying. In one photo he looked with grave-eyed love at a smiling Anne, who wore for her wedding a white silk suit with a long skirt and loose jacket. There was a picture of Tommy in a crowd of laughing children. He was surrounded by honey-skinned boys and girls with onyx eyes, his new siblings, his new cousins, his new playmates. In yet another photo, he stood with Anne, Sanjit Prav, and Sanjit Prav's children. The boys' arms were about each other's shoulders and they wore matching gray slacks and navy blue blazers.

"That's wonderful," Keren said. "Now Tommy has a real family."

Nancy looked hard at her daughter and then turned away. She understood why Anne had made this marriage. She had endowed Tommy with a family — with a father and brothers, a sister, an army of cousins and aunts and uncles. In a way, she had acknowledged defeat.

"Tommy looks great. He's really recovered then?" Sarah asked Rutti.

"The doctors are satisfied that he's in remission. No more chemo. No more medication. A small miracle. Anne says that Charles Bingham assured her that statistically Tommy's in a pretty safe category. If there's no recurrence in five years, they'll even stop monitoring him."

"That's terrific," Keren said.

"Wonderful," Nancy agreed. She wondered if Dov knew, if he had even bothered to find out. It made little difference now. Keren's antigens had after all not been compatible with Tommy's; she would never have been considered as a marrow donor. That was yet another irony in the strangling necklace of ironies that had all but choked the life from her friendship with Anne.

Nancy did not chip in for a wedding gift with Merle and Rutti who, after much discussion, sent a set of apple-shaped crystal dessert dishes.

"We don't want her to forget her connection with the Big Apple. And her friends here," Merle said.

Nancy sent a set of towels, which both Keren and Sarah agreed was a strangely impersonal choice. "I wouldn't want to get bath towels as a wedding gift from my closest friend," Keren said.

"Then I will never give you bath towels," Sarah promised. "Still, I wonder what happened between your mom and Anne."

Merle and Rutti also wondered about it. Saddened and troubled, they conferred. Always they had been direct, swift to ask and to act. The friendship they had all shared with such love and closeness, the support that they had offered each other through the years, was too precious to be surrendered without a battle.

"What could it be?" Merle asked Rutti.

They hazarded guesses. A slight? A misunderstanding? No. It would have to be something more than that to create the tensions, the distance, they could not overlook. They had dinner with Nancy and confronted her.

"Are you angry with Anne?" Rutti asked directly.

"Not angry. Disappointed," Nancy replied. She compressed her lips, passed her hand across her face as though to wipe away the memory of that disappointment.

"About what?" Merle leaned forward insistently. If they knew what had happened they could help, offer explanations, comfort.

"I don't want to talk about it." Nancy was firm, her voice steady, but they saw the pain in her eyes.

They spoke to Anne. The three of them were coincidentally in Chicago — Rutti for an opening at a new gallery, Merle for a recital at the Lake Shore Conservatory. They stayed at Anne's.

"I don't think we're too old for a slumber party," Merle said gaily. They were all in a good mood. Merle's audience had been enthusiastic and Rutti's new oil landscapes warmly received; Anne had just learned that she had been awarded a new grant for her DNA research. They wore flannel nightgowns, drank mugs of hot chocolate, and giggled excessively. Sanjit Prav smiled benignly at them and went upstairs to bed, leaving them in the den. They watched *Brief Encounter* until two in the morning and passed a box of Kleenex from hand to hand.

"If I could sleep with anyone in the world, it would be Trevor Howard," Rutti said.

"Oh, not that fantasy game again," Merle said, laughing. "Was it Nancy who picked Moshe Dayan?"

"I think so," Anne replied, stretching in exhaustion. They had tossed so many names about during those Friday afternoons of their young womanhood, throughout their years of dreams. "How is Nancy?" Her question was shy, hesitant.

"You're not in touch at all?" Rutti asked.

"Barely."

"What happened between you?" Merle asked.

"You'll have to ask Nancy." Like Nancy, Anne was firm, but misery settled upon her face like a mask.

Rutti and Nancy did not discuss their conversations with their daughters, but Keren and Sarah sensed the truth. Secrets existed where once there was candor, and now for the first time, there was awkward chatter, the viral symptoms of a weakened friendship.

"I guess nothing is forever. Things change," Keren noted. Correspondence with her friends in Israel had diminished. A former boyfriend had married, two of her Jerusalem friends were living in London. Melancholy encircled her like a gossamer shawl that, for all its lightness, she could not shake loose. Transience was familiar to her, but it still filled her with fear and sadness.

"But we won't change. We'll be friends forever," Sarah said fiercely.

"No pacts. I refuse to swear a pact." Keren tossed a pillow at her friend. Sarah retaliated and they laughed as they rolled about on the unmade sofa bed, entangling themselves in snares of blankets and linens, their faces flushed. Their laughter rang with defiance. They refused to surrender their childhoods, they were tenacious in their grasp on joy. Their mothers' friendships would not subvert them. At last, exhausted, they lay back amid the rumpled bedclothes.

"What do you want more than anything in the world?" Keren asked dreamily. It was the formula question of their girlhood sleepovers. They had always answered each other honestly.

"I want my father to come back. I don't want him to be dead,"

Sarah had said a month after Werner's funeral. "I don't want my parents to get a divorce," Keren had said a week after Dov moved out. They were children then, reliant on their parents to define their happiness, their deepest yearning.

"I want to be rooted. Rooted in love. I want to be at the center of someone's life, to have him rooted at the center of mine," Sarah answered now.

"But you and I both know that you already have that," Keren said. It was the first time in all the months since his departure that she had referred to Abdul Nashif. Almost in apology because she had trespassed over an invisible border within their friendship, she dropped a kiss on Sarah's head and went into the bedroom. As she closed the door behind her, she heard Sarah pad over to the small oak chest and open the bottom drawer. She knew that her friend was removing the olive-wood box that contained Abdul Nashif's letters.

By tacit agreement Keren and Sarah had not discussed Abdul even when he was in the States. He and Sarah had been constantly together. They juggled classes, jobs, practice hours, and rehearsal times to be together. Sarah listened as Abdul practiced in the stark Juilliard studio that Merle had arranged for him to use. Once, bringing him coffee and a sandwich in the afternoon, she met Merle in the corridor. Merle smiled warningly.

"That's exactly what Emanuel Klein's wife did every day. I didn't think women still did that for their men."

"Oh, it works both ways," Sarah replied. When she completed her set at Ballads and Blues, Abdul invariably had a cup of hot tea waiting for her with the sugar added and the lemon sliced thin, floating atop the steaming drink, just as she liked it. He protectively waved her fans away as she drank. He understood singers. He understood the exhaustion that followed a set, the need for soothing heat on vocal cords strained by effort and passion.

"Oh, yes. So Abdul's a New Age man. Good for you. Good for both of you." Merle smiled and hurried away. She thought that her friend's golden-haired daughter and the dark Arab whose skin was the color of almonds were an enchanting-looking couple, and she thought too that it was at once fortunate and terrible that they would be separated so soon.

The knowledge of that imminent separation gave their relationship a throbbing urgency. It was, they each thought secretly, a magical interlude in their lives, an enchanted island of time.

"My Sarah," Abdul said as they lay side by side in a nest fashioned of their own garments on the bare floor of the unfurnished apartment that she and Keren had just rented.

"My Abdul."

Love and sadness, truth and lie, commingled in their murmurs of possession. He was not hers and she was not his and yet they were pledged to each other.

On their last day together they agreed that they would write, that they would call. Secretly, each feared that soon the letters would fail to arrive and the calls would cease as the distance and the futility of the exchange exhausted them. They did not anticipate the urge to hear each other's voices, which spurred them to the telephone in the middle of the night nor were they prepared for the delicious trembling, the surge of joy that overtook them as they waited for a phone across the world to ring; they did not know that their voices would tumble over each other with gladness, eagerness. They had so much to say, so much to share.

Abdul told her that he was working hard, playing, composing, traveling through the country giving concerts at both Arab and Jewish schools, at kibbutzim and townships. He still believed that it was possible for Jew and Arab to live and work together. His sister, Fatima, shared his views, with reservations. "Fatima thinks we can live side by side, work side by side. Not together, but side by side." He did not argue with his sister. There was no time for arguments.

And Sarah too worked hard. Her voice teacher encouraged her to audition for off-Broadway shows. She laughed with Keren, danced with abandon at parties and clubs, smiled at young men who knew her name and wanted desperately for her to know theirs. She acknowledged that Abdul was part of her life, but he was not her life. From her mother she had learned that women could build independent lives, secure their own futures. Rutti had done that during Werner's life and again after his death.

"I'm proud of you, Sarah," Rutti said to her one afternoon.

"Why?" Sarah asked.

"You are living these wonderful years so well."

"Am I?" Sarah's smile was vague, her mind full of thoughts of the letter she would write to Abdul that night.

Keren watched as her friend wrote to her distant lover. She pitied Sarah and envied her. The confluence of emotions did not surprise her; elation and melancholy assaulted Keren at unexpected times. She understood that she and Sarah were living the best, the most exciting, years of their lives and wondered why it was that she was so often suffused with an inexplicable sadness, why she yearned for solitude when she was with her friends and yearned for companionship when she was alone. Her life was stimulating, her life was fun, but contentment eluded her. She thought she might return to Israel, but knew that she would not. Not yet.

She went to the window and looked down at the dogwood tree. She had watched each day, as the small furled buds swelled and the branches that sustained them bent beneath their weight. Now they were in blossom and glowed lustrously in the darkness.

That night she began a short story. She was not pleased with it in the end, but swiftly started another. She was finished with the vignettes, with the amorphous, symbol-strewn poems. Her serious work had begun.

The telegram informing Keren that she had won second prize in a short story contest sponsored by a prestigious literary journal was waiting for her when she arrived home from class one fall afternoon. She read it in disbelief and then laughed aloud. "Sarah!" she called, but Sarah was out. Keren remembered she was auditioning for a role with a repertory company. She reread the telegram and dialed her mother's office. Nancy was with a patient, Lynn, her secretary, said. But of course if it was an emergency, her voice trailed off questioningly.

"No. No emergency. It's just that my life is finally happening," Keren said.

She called her father but Dov was at the hospital. She did not want to call Lisa. Her father's wife regarded Keren's writing as a hobby, a harmless and acceptable time filler before the more serious business of marriage and motherhood. Lisa, Keren and Sarah agreed, remained firmly moored in the fifties.

"She's caught in a time warp," Sarah had decided and Keren did not disagree.

She did call Ari. He came to the phone at once and exulted with her.

"But I'm not surprised, Keren. We always knew you would succeed. We just didn't know it would happen so soon."

"So soon?" she squealed. "Ari, I've been working for months and months."

"As long as that?" He mocked her gently. He was proud of Keren, proud of the affection they felt for each other. "Keren, can you do me a favor? There's a cocktail reception that I am hosting this afternoon for a group of sculptors. I'm very short-staffed. Your mother was supposed to be here, but she had an emergency patient and my assistant is out with a cold. Do you think you could come around and serve as a surrogate hostess? And then I'll take you out to dinner to celebrate your triumph."

"I'll come and play hostess but I don't want you to take me out to dinner. I want to go home with you and spend some time with Seth and Noah. I hardly ever get to see them."

"Wonderful," Ari said gratefully. Keren was wonderful with the boys; she was, in fact, wonderful with all children. When they visited his parents on the kibbutz, she often volunteered at the children's house. "She will make a wonderful mother," he had said casually to Nancy one night. He was unprepared for the anger in Nancy's reply.

"Give her time," Nancy said harshly. "I don't want her pressured." She herself had not been given time. She had been thrust into a pattern by the expectations of others.

"I was only making an observation," Ari replied gently. He smiled, kissed her on the shoulder, on the neck. Nancy feared for her daughter, he knew, and he understood that fear. She had been so vulnerable to pressure from her family, from Dov, so frazzled with guilt after her divorce as she struggled to finish her degree and be a good mother to Keren. She wanted Keren to enjoy the freedom of her young womanhood. Early marriage had failed her, had failed Ari. She wanted Keren to be spared similar disappointment.

Ari had confidence in Keren. He had long recognized her resilience and persistence. He did not doubt that she would succeed, although it occurred to him that her perception of success might differ widely from the success her mother willed for her.

The reception room at the Consulate was already crowded when Keren arrived. She kissed Ari and pinned the blue and white hostess ribbon to her black dress.

"You look wonderful," Ari said.

"It's my disguise," she replied. "This is my diplomatic corps costume." She laughed, but she did take pleasure in creating disguises for herself.

She wore faded jeans, T-shirts, and bulky sweaters to her classes at Columbia and changed into tailored shirts and neat collared blouses for stints at Rizzoli. Evenings she might transform herself into a gypsy, draped with chains of gold and beaded necklaces, or she might wear the simple black dress she had chosen for this reception. As a child she was eager to please, to play any role to appease her mother's anxiety, her father's anger. She changed costumes and reinvented herself to reassure them; it was a talent that she had never lost.

She twirled about, her hands plunged deep into the pockets of her scoop-necked dress with its sweeping skirt. She pressed the telegram between her fingers and smiled at her own foolishness. She had taken it with her to this reception like a child, who, having excelled in an examination, carries his test paper to a family dinner.

"You don't need a disguise," Ari said. "You're eminently acceptable as Keren Yallon. But now make yourself useful. Circulate. Make people feel at home. And have some wine."

He offered her his own glass and moved off to greet the British cultural attaché, steering him over to the impressive Jerusalem marble statue of a mother tenderly cradling an infant. It was such work, Ari believed, that would eventually lead to peace and understanding.

"Culture breaks down all barriers," he had told Keren when he explained why his career meant so much to him. "There are no nationalist inhibitions to an appreciation of art, of music. Literature is translated into many languages. The same audience that responds to Merle's work will respond to the work of Abdul Nashif, to the composition and music of Israelis and Indians and artists from eastern Europe, from Asia. Understanding will not come on the battlefield, but in the library, the theater, the concert hall."

He had fought in two wars and his son was named for his brother killed in the Sinai. Each time he visited his parents' kibbutz home, he wandered sadly through the cemetery where he had first met Nancy and where so many of his friends were buried. War was the way of death. Art was the way of life. He knew that there were those who thought him naive, who argued against him in the committees of the Foreign Office, but he was determined.

"What is remarkable in this work," Keren heard him say to the Briton as they slowly circled the statue, "is its transcendence of location, its universality of expression. It was created by an Israeli sculptor, but the subject, the mother and infant, might easily be an Arab woman, a Frenchwoman, an American, cradling her baby, protecting it."

"Or an Englishwoman, or an Irish woman," his companion rejoined.

"Exactly. Exactly," Ari said and the two men moved on, pleased to find themselves intellectual allies during this tumultuous time when the halls of the United Nations were resonant with bellicose rhetoric, when small nations with famine problems experimented with nuclear energy, when religious wars flared and nationalism simmered on every continent.

Keren took up a small pile of catalogs and glided through the room, greeting new arrivals, making sure each guest had a catalog, a glass of Israeli wine. The gallery grew crowded. United Nations personnel mingled with art students. A woman in a sari spoke animatedly with a tall African wearing a brightly patterned dashiki. Their presence was a triumph for Ari, Keren knew. The Indian and African diplomatic corps seldom attended receptions sponsored by the Israelis.

Keren smiled, guided an overdressed woman to the rest room, answered questions. Yes, Israel was a small country to have produced so many talented artists, but there was a great emphasis on creativity and culture in the country. She showed the driftwood carvings of an Arab artist to an editor of *Art News* who was interested in doing a piece on the use of unorthodox materials. She guided a writer for *Ms.* to the work of a Negev sculptress and promised to send her material on the work of other Israeli women artists. At last, satisfied that she had earned a break, her mouth aching with the effort of a constant smile, she stepped out onto the terrace, reached into her pocket, and withdrew the carefully folded telegram. Again she read the magical words. She had won. Her story would be published.

"Not bad news, I hope." A tall, pleasant-looking man stood beside her. He held two glasses of wine, one of which he offered her. She took it gratefully and smiled at him.

"No, actually, it's very good news," she said, and still holding the telegram, she took a long sip of the wine. She hadn't realized how thirsty she was or how strained her throat had become from the constant chatter.

"Do you want to share it?" His question was hesitant. She saw that he was blushing, and embarrassed, he lifted his hand and thrust back the cowlick of sandy hair that had settled on his high forehead. She liked him for his shyness, his hesitancy, and impulsively, she held the telegram out to him.

"Hey, second place," he said. "That's terrific. Especially for the *Mountain Lakes Review.*"

"You know it?" Keren was surprised. The review was a rather obscure publication, although prestigious in the literary community because annual anthologies of short stories generally contained at least one work that had first appeared in its pages.

"I'm a writer myself," he said. "Or at least I think I am. Some days I'm surer than others."

"I know that feeling," she said. "It always makes me nervous when people ask what I do. If I say I'm a writer I feel like an imposter. I'm glad that I'm taking courses so I can say that I'm a student, and then I hope they don't ask what I'm studying."

"Ah, but now you'll be able to say that you are a writer with a story soon to appear in the *Mountain Lakes Review,*" he reminded her.

"Yes, that's true." She folded and put away the telegram, anticipating Nancy's pleasure when she read it. It sometimes seemed to Keren that her professional success was more important to her mother than it was to her. Nancy was fiercely intent that Keren develop her talent.

"I don't want you to repeat my mistakes," she had said more

than once. Keren thought her words were inadvertently cruel. Her mother's mistake had been her marriage to Dov, her too early motherhood, which meant that in a way Keren had been her mistake.

"I want to thank you for not asking me where I've been published," her companion said.

"Oh, I'm a deeply sensitive person," she retorted gaily and downed the rest of the wine. It occurred to her that she was getting pleasantly drunk. She had eaten very little that day and this was her third glass of Chablis.

"I think that's probably true, Keren."

"How did you know my name?"

"It was on the telegram," he reminded her.

"But that's not fair. I don't know your name."

"I have no telegram to share with you," he teased. "It's been weeks since I won a prize and my mother has framed that telegram and hung it on the living room wall."

"Then you'll have to tell me your name because I don't think I'll ever be in your mother's living room."

"Oh, but I'm quite sure you will be," he said seriously. "Still, fair is fair. I'm Alan Silberman."

"You're not."

She stared at him in doubt and wonderment. The name was familiar to her as it was to every student in her writing program. Alan Silberman's stories had been appearing for years in quality magazines like *Harper's* and the *Atlantic*. They were widely anthologized. He had written a prize-winning novel about a young boy coming of age in Brooklyn and a *People* magazine critic had compared him to J. D. Salinger. Keren remembered the exact words. "Alan Silberman has stormed Salinger's throne — a literary palace coup has been executed." She had loved the book and had spent hour after hour in the Columbia library reading the stories. But surely they had not been written by someone as young as the man who stood beside her now, blushing and smiling.

"Why? Why can't I be Alan Silberman?"

"You're too young." Alan Silberman had been publishing for almost a decade.

"I'm thirty. That's not so young. My mother thinks it's very old. She thinks anyone who is thirty should be married."

"Then she'll have to give your wife the framed telegram."

"Oh, she intends to. She will give her all the framed telegrams."

"Are there so many then?"

"A few. Perhaps more than a few. I took my first prize ten years ago. When I was in college."

"Wow." Her admiration was genuine. "Were you twenty?"

"Nineteen. A very lonely, unhappy nineteen. A commuter student at a dormitory school. A nerd traveling the subway, living in an overheated apartment with a widowed mother. Not a lot of money. Polyester sweaters. Few friends. Correction. No friends. I can't go on without violin accompaniment. Hearts and flowers. Something really poignant."

"It could have been worse," Keren said. "You could have had acne."

"I had acne. Name it, I had it. I wore glasses. I had scoliosis. Luckily I also had a typewriter. So while my classmates were pledging fraternities and joining crew, I was pecking away at my first stories and my mother was bringing me glasses of warm milk and telling me she never knew premed students had to type so many reports."

"Premed?"

"I was supposed to be premed. She wanted me to be a doctor. I didn't like not pleasing her so I told her I was premed."

"I can relate to that," Keren said. "I know how to be what my parents want me to be. All my parents."

"All your parents? How many are there?"

"One mother. One father. One stepmother. One stepfather. My mother's friends who think they are my mother. Oh, yes, two half-brothers, but I don't have to pretend with Seth and Noah. With them I can be me. Whoever that is."

"That is Keren. A very pretty, very charming young woman," he said, but now he did not blush as he looked at her. "I'm glad I came to this party. I almost didn't. I'm not too great at parties."

"How did you happen to get invited?" Keren asked.

"I wrote an article on the impact of war on Israeli literature. An overview. The Israeli cultural attaché, Ari Raviv, read it and invited me to lunch and put me on his list. At least I guess he did because I keep getting mail and invitations. He's a nice man and I'm a lonely guy. No longer nineteen, but still lonely. So sometimes I accept an invitation. And how did you get to be included in this swell international crowd?"

"Nepotism. Ari Raviv is one of my parents. My stepfather to be exact."

"It's a small world," he said and she laughed.

"Can't you write better dialogue than that? You do in your stories."

"I get better as the evening wears on. Have dinner with me and you'll see."

"I can't. I'm having dinner with Ari. I want to see my brothers. But you could come with us. That is, if your widowed mother isn't waiting for you."

"I'll call her and tell her I'm having dinner with a Jewish girl. She'll dance for joy and dust the frames of my telegrams. You are Jewish, aren't you?"

"I'm even a veteran of the Israeli army. How much more Jewish can you get?"

She was definitely drunk, she decided. She had never before spoken so easily, so flippantly, with anyone. She looked at Alan Silberman and thought that his face, pocked though it was with acne scars, was remarkably sympathetic. She tucked her arm through his.

"Call your mother, then," she said. "You can use the phone in Ari's office."

They spent that first evening at the Ravivs' apartment. Nancy was jubilant over the prize. She read the telegram aloud and then rushed to the phone to call Rutti and Merle. Ari opened a bottle of champagne.

"To Keren," he said.

"To Keren," they all replied. Even Seth and Noah tasted the frothy wine and giggled.

After dinner Alan talked to the boys, paying careful attention to Noah's collection of toy cars, to Seth's postcard collection. He sat cross-legged on the floor of their room while Keren read her brothers a chapter of *The Little Prince* in Hebrew, Seth snuggling against her. She rested her hand on Noah's head, knowing exactly when to pause in her reading and carry him to his bed because he had fallen asleep beneath the tender pressure of her touch.

"Are the boys asleep?" Nancy asked when they returned to the living room.

"Keren is marvelous with them," Alan said admiringly.

"They're great. I love reading *The Little Prince*. It was the first book I was able to read through in Hebrew." She remembered the thrill of that first reading, of the recognition that she had mastered the language of the country where her father had been born, where her mother had chosen to live.

"Yes," he said. "It must have been an escape from loneliness in a new country."

She was startled that he understood.

"Exactly," she replied softly.

"You must come and see us again," Ari said cordially. Although Nancy shook Alan's hand, she did not repeat her husband's invitation.

They went to her apartment where Keren found a note from Sarah on the kitchen table. She would not be coming home that evening. She was rehearsing for an audition with a friend in the Village and it was simpler to stay over there.

"I don't believe that," Alan said when she read him the note. "I believe it's a conspiracy. You called your roommate and told her that you and I needed to be alone here tonight and she split."

She laughed and he held her close and buried his face in her long dark hair.

"Why would I do that?" she asked.

"Because it is important that we have this time. Because I love you and I want to stay with you."

"Alan, this is ridiculous. We've known each other for a couple of hours."

"But we will know each other forever." He spoke with great seriousness and she looked into his gray eyes and believed him. He kissed her then, his lips gentle and sweet against her own.

They talked late into the night, each surprised at how easily the words came, because they were both private people, cautious in their friendships and their confidences. Alan explained how he struggled to protect his mother from pain, to compensate for her losses. Keren listened quietly. He spoke in word pictures and she saw his mother, the thin, anxious schoolteacher obsessed with her responsibility for the precocious, lonely child she raised alone.

"You might think that I'm a wimp — a weak mama's boy with an Oedipal thing," he said ruefully, his fingers tracing their way across

425

the contours of her face, resting on her closed eyes, following the generous line of her lips.

"No. I think you're gentle and grateful and caring," she said. "And you did what you wanted to do. You became a writer. It's not a symptom of psychological disability not to want to hurt your mother." She told him how she had spent much of her childhood trying desperately to please and placate both Dov and Nancy, making excuses for each to the other.

"Were you relieved when they divorced?" Alan asked.

"I don't know. Sarah and I used to play that we were orphans. If we were orphans, we told each other, we wouldn't have to worry about our fathers and mothers. And then, of course, we'd feel terribly guilty. What kind of kids were we, to want to be orphans? Although, as Sarah always pointed out, it wasn't that we wanted them dead — we just didn't want them around for a while. We felt too responsible for them." She giggled, mocking the child she had been, the fears and fantasies that had obsessed her.

"I can relate to that," he said.

"Are we being too honest too soon?" Keren asked, suddenly fearful.

"There is no such thing as too honest or too soon," he replied.

He listened as she described the first years in Israel, her mother's marriage to Ari, her term in the army.

"Would you want to return to Israel?" he asked.

"I think so," she said. "But I'm not sure. It begins to seem that I am not sure about anything."

"Are you sure about me?"

"Alan — really."

"I know. We've only known each other a few hours. All right." He laughed. "But soon you will be sure about me. I say it now. You'll say it soon."

It was late when he left. He would not stay over. His mother would worry, he said without embarrassment. But he called Keren early the next morning to tell her that she was a miracle, to ask her where they would meet that evening. The morning call, the evening meeting, the long nights of talk and laughter, became the pattern of her life. Sarah met him and liked him at once. Keren went to Brooklyn and had dinner with his mother. Nettie Silberman was plain but charming, even vivacious. She had long ago colored her hair to a gay rose-blond hue, and like Alan, she was pleasant and gentle in manner. She welcomed Keren warmly. As they did the dishes together, she told Keren she was the first young woman Alan had ever brought home.

They went to Egremont for a weekend. "Why not? The house is empty. Enjoy it," Merle said. She thought of Keren as the daughter she never had and welcomed her confidences. She no longer regarded the infant Kate as a daughter. The sick baby had become a ghost, a miniature penumbra remembered with tenderness.

Keren and Alan reveled in the privacy of the Cunningham house and in the morning, as they walked the woodland trail, he told her that he had something very important to say to her.

"But you always have something very important to say to me," she replied gaily, although she felt a shaft of fear.

"Keren, when you showed me your telegram that first night, I had a letter in my own pocket that I didn't show to you."

"Yes?" She waited. There was a familiar tightness at her throat. She braced herself for disappointment.

"The letter was from a foundation offering me a grant to finish my next book in Italy. It's an important grant, a generous one. I wouldn't have to worry about money for two years. It would unlock the doors of libraries and archives. It's extremely prestigious."

"I see."

"Only hours before I met you, I wired them. I accepted it, of course."

"Of course."

They walked on in silence. The dry leaves crackled beneath their feet. A small animal darted out of the underbrush, disappeared amid a tangle of roots.

"Was that a chipmunk?" he asked.

"I don't know." She wasn't able to see because her eyes were burning with tears.

"It's the crazy timing," he said.

"Such inauspicious timing," she agreed, her voice very flat. Or had the timing actually been auspicious? How simple to rush into an all-consuming love affair when he had the insurance of an easy, acceptable exit. She looked at him, at his open pleasant face and the thought seemed ludicrous. Not Alan. Of course not Alan. Yet what was he telling her? And why, during all their long hours of intimate revelations, had he never mentioned the grant?

"I'm supposed to leave for Italy in two weeks' time."

"Our anniversary," she said. They would have known each other a month. Oh, how foolish she had been, how ridiculous.

"We will make it our anniversary forever," he said. "We will be married exactly a month after our meeting and on our wedding night you can say to me, 'But Alan, we've only known each other for four weeks —' "

"Alan —" She felt faint with relief. She leaned against the copper beech, the hide-and-seek haven of her childhood. She knew now that she would not have had the strength to sustain losing him.

"Say yes." His arms were around her, pinning her to the tree. His breath was moist at her ear.

"Alan, really." Her voice caught in her throat.

"I know. I know. We've only known each other for two weeks. But such a two weeks!" He was exultant. He pulled her toward him, held her tight, defied her to escape his embrace. The leaves of the beech tree rustled. She looked up and saw that two huge crows were boldly perched on the branches, staring down at them with beady-eyed expectancy.

"We have witnesses," she said.

"Then your answer is doubly binding."

And now he did not wait for her to speak but kissed her, silencing any words she might have uttered, claiming her without argument or hesitancy.

Nancy was furious, her cheeks were mottled, her eyes bright with febrile anger. "This is ridiculous. You don't know what you're saying. You cannot understand what you're doing." Barefoot, like a woman in mourning, she paced the floor of her office, returned to her desk, buzzed her secretary. "Hold all my calls, Lynn. All of them." She sank into her high-backed leather chair, her professional throne of authority.

"I know what I'm saying. I know what I'm doing," Keren replied quietly. She sat opposite her mother and observed her fury. She was not frightened. She knew that Nancy took swift control of her own moods, that she understood how to harness fear and anger. "I'm saying that I love Alan Silberman, that I am going to marry him and go with him to Italy."

"You've known him for exactly two weeks."

"Two weeks and one day," Keren said. "We keep very careful track. I think Alan can actually give it to you in hours." She knew that if she could make Nancy laugh she would be on safe ground. Merle had said as much. Her mother's friend had become her coconspirator.

But Nancy did not laugh. "All right. Two weeks. Four weeks. Whatever. And on the basis of such an in-depth relationship you're going to give up your studies, your job, your apartment and follow him to Rome because he has a fellowship? Keren, for God's sake, haven't you learned anything, anything at all? That's exactly what I did. I gave up my studies to follow your father East so that he could do his residency. You can't seriously tell me that you're going to repeat my mistakes."

"No. Actually, I'm going to make my own mistakes. Live my own life. The way you always taught me to," Keren replied evenly. "I am not you and Alan is not Dov. This is 1982, not 1959. I'm not giving up my life, my career. I'll write in Rome. Alan wants me to — he wants to help me. He knows that my work is important to me."

"Your father made similar promises," Nancy said. Such words came easily in fields of sweet woodruff: *I want you to be all that you can be*. How soft Dov's voice had been, how charming his accent.

"But Alan is different."

"You don't know him. You don't know who he is," Nancy said harshly. "You've known him so short a time."

"And you knew my father for over a year before you married him and you didn't know him at all." Now it was Keren who was angry, Keren whose fury could not be contained. She stood before her mother, red-cheeked and fiery. "I'm way ahead of you, Mom. Way ahead of where you were when you married Dov. I've had the example of your life, and of Rutti's and Merle's and Anne's." Sarcasm seared her words so that each name was an epithet.

"I hope so. I hope you've learned from us. We tried to build a different world for you. All I ever wanted was for you to have the freedom I never had — freedom to work, to study, time to find out who you are, what you want."

Keren sank back into her chair.

"I'm grateful to you. I know you want me to have my chance. But I *will* have it. And Alan will help me. He wants me to continue my work. He'll never expect me to put my life on hold because of him. Mom, he would give up his grant if I wanted him to. All right. We haven't known each other long enough. I know that. But sometimes you have to take a risk, a gamble. Didn't you do that when you went to Israel? Didn't Rutti do that when she married David?"

"You use the examples of our lives when they prove your case," Nancy said. She sat opposite Keren and forced herself to weigh her daughter's words. "You don't want to be like us yet you do want to be like us. You can't have it both ways, Keren."

"I'm not trying to have it both ways," Keren replied, speaking slowly, deliberately. "I admire a lot that you did, you and Merle and Rutti and Anne. But there were — there are — things that bothered me. The way that Merle playacted with Andrew. The scramble for time. I would never want to have a child the way Anne had Tommy. . . ."

"Let's leave Anne out of this," Nancy said tightly.

"Why? Why must we leave Anne out of it? You talk about honesty, but you've never told me why you're angry with Anne."

"I'm not angry with her," Nancy said. "Not any more." That much was true. Her anger had faded. Only days earlier she had wakened from a dream, her face wreathed in a smile because she and Anne had been sitting beside the pool at Egremont talking and Anne had told her something confidential, amusing. She understood the dream: she missed Anne, and the humor and intimacy of their friendship. Her anger had dissipated, but she remained unforgiving.

"All right. Not angry. But removed. Cold. That's what frightens me."

"My feeling about Anne frightens you?" Nancy was puzzled. Yet she recognized that the fear in Keren's eyes was real. Her daughter's face was pale, her voice faint. And she had come into the office an hour earlier so buoyant with happiness, almost leaping across the room to hug Nancy to tell her the news — "We're going to be married. Alan and I. Isn't that wonderful? Isn't that marvelous?" She had anticipated Nancy's shock but not her anger.

"It frightens me that you can be so removed from someone you once cared for. That you can nurse a grievance for so long, with such coldness. I worry that if you can do it to Anne, you can do it to me. And I couldn't bear that, Mom. I couldn't bear that." Keren was crying softly now, the joy and buoyancy reduced to sorrow and anxiety.

Nancy's heart turned. She went to her daughter, knelt before her chair, smoothed her dark hair, wiped her eyes, lifted Keren's hand to her lips and kissed it, kissed each finger as she had when Keren was a frightened child.

"I couldn't do that. No matter what, I could never distance myself from you. I promise you. I love you. I just want to think more about this, to be absolutely certain that what you are doing is right for you. Talk to your father, to Ari. Will you do that?"

"Of course I will," Keren agreed.

She would talk to everyone. She and Dov would have lunch in an expensive restaurant, probably with Lisa, and together they would try to dissuade her. She anticipated their arguments. The brevity of her relationship with Alan. The upheaval in her own work and study. Alan had never visited Israel and Keren considered it her home. Oh, there was so much against such a hasty decision. Lisa would be earnest. Dov would be forceful, the angry, protective parent. And Keren would not disagree with any of their arguments. They would be right in all that they said.

Ari would be more pacific. He would surely advise her to wait, but when he understood that she would not, he would smile and wish her well. Because in the end she would not be dissuaded. She knew she was doing the right thing.

She rose to leave, embraced her mother.

"Try to understand," she said.

Nancy had said as much to her own mother, when she had married Dov and then when she had divorced him and again when she had decided to move to Israel. The generations imitated each other; daughters begged for understanding and mothers lay awake night after night, weighted with worry.

"I am trying," Nancy replied.

She watched Keren walk from the room, closing the door softly behind her. Her next patient, a young woman with an ego so fragile that her voice was barely loud enough to transmit her thoughts, was

431

already waiting, but Nancy did not immediately buzz her in. Instead, she called Merle and then Rutti and arranged to meet them for lunch. She held the phone after hanging up on Rutti as though to make another call and then shook her head ruefully. She combed her hair, applied fresh lipstick, and pressed the buzzer. She smiled at her patient and moved her chair close to her so that she would not miss a single word spoken so hesitantly in that frightened wisp of a voice.

They met for lunch in a quiet West Side restaurant and smiled when Rutti observed that it was a Friday.

"We are reverting," Merle said. "All of us together on a Friday afternoon."

"Not all of us," Rutti pointed out.

She glanced at the chair that would have been Anne's on which they had placed their briefcases, heavy with the Filofaxes that each carried. Nancy said nothing.

"Keren called me last night," Merle said. "She said you're not exactly clicking your heels over their decision to marry."

"Not exactly," Nancy replied evenly. "Should I be?"

"It's all a bit swift," Merle agreed. "But I like him, I really do."

"I don't know." Rutti looked up from the napkin on which she had been doodling. "She's known him for only two weeks. I'd be uneasy about Sarah marrying someone she'd only known for two weeks. Still, I knew Werner for years and yet I did not know him. I said that to Anne on the phone last night. . . ." Her voice trailed off.

"And what did Anne say?" Merle asked. She vested Anne's opinion with importance. It was Anne, after all, who had made the most difficult decisions and who had paid the most painful price.

"I told Anne how good they seemed together, Keren and Alan, that it was a shame they had such a brief time together. And Anne said that intuition was more important than experience. And she had faith in Keren's intuition." Rutti spoke slowly, trying to remember Anne's exact words.

"Why?" Nancy asked softly.

"Because she inherited it from you. Nancy, Anne cares about you — she admires you so much." Rutti looked at her friend. Her words were a plea.

"I know she does. But I — we — have to work something out.

Anne and I. If we can. And I'm not sure that it's possible." Regret slowed her words. Miserably she crumbled a slice of bread, shoving the crumbs about.

Rutti leaned forward. "Nancy, if Sarah came to me the way Keren came to you, I'd raise the same objections. Yes, they haven't known each other long enough. Yes, it would be good if they gave themselves more time. But I'd know that in the end Sarah would do exactly as she pleased and I'd have to accept that. Because that is what we always said to our daughters, Nancy. *Be in control of your own lives. Make your own decisions.* That was the example we set for them."

"So the blame is on us," Nancy said.

"No. The credit is on us," Merle countered. "On you. You've raised a daughter who's strong, resilient. She trusts her emotions, her instincts. She's ready to begin a new life."

"Damn it, Merle, she's giving up her life here. Her studies. Her friends and family to follow a man. She's making the same mistake I made when I married Dov, the same mistake my classmates made. All those damn alumni magazine class notes. 'Ron opened an office in Seattle so here we are starting over in the Northwest.' 'Doug's company transferred him to Florida and I'd love to hear from fellow alums in the Sarasota area.' And now Keren's doing the same thing, making the same mistake."

"No," Rutti said quietly. "She is not doing the same thing. Yes, perhaps she is marrying sooner than you would have wanted her to, although she is hardly a child-bride, Nancy. She's twenty-three. And she isn't simply trailing after Alan like a dutiful little hausfrau. She's going to work in Rome. She told me she's looking forward to writing about what it is like to begin life in yet another city. I know, as an artist, that such a move can only add texture to her work. And, yes, maybe she is making a mistake. But it will be her mistake. And she has the courage to see that."

"And what, after all, is the worst-case scenario in this?" Merle asked. "The marriage goes sour. They separate. They divorce. Keren goes back to Israel. Or maybe she comes to New York. And she's battered and she's bruised but she's still Keren and she starts over. The way all of us have started over." She herself, after all, had started over, remade her marriage, restructured her life.

"As simple as that?" Nancy asked wryly.

"No. As complicated as that. And maybe as sad as that. But not tragic. Keren has watched us all go through it."

"She will be all right, Nancy," Rutti said very softly. "No matter what. She will be all right."

The waiter arrived with their drinks — the vodka martinis that Anne had taught them to favor. They each thought of Anne now. Nancy lifted her glass. She smiled at her friends, sadness and gratitude mingling.

"To my Keren," she said. "And to her intuition."

"To her happiness," Merle added.

"And to her love," Rutti spoke in a whisper.

They clicked glasses and drank and then placed their hands on the center of the table, their fingertips lightly touching.

Keren and Alan were married at Egremont. Although they had invited only their closest friends and relatives, the Cunninghams' large living room was crowded. Anne could not come. Her schedule was too complicated.

Sarah stood between Seth and Noah under the wedding canopy and looked across the room at Abdul Nashif, who had arrived in the States unexpectedly. He had been awarded a fellowship at the Manhattan School of Music and would be spending a year in New York. He smiled at Sarah, a diminutive nymph in the gold wool dress that matched her curling helmet of hair. He watched as she moved forward and lifted Keren's gossamer white veil so that she might drink from the cup of wine, as she held Keren's bouquet so that Alan might slide the simple golden band onto her friend's finger while he intoned the ancient marriage pledge. Sarah twisted the ring on her own finger, the tourmaline set in a delicate filigree of silver. "I bought it because it matched your eyes," Abdul told her when he gave it to her.

Alan stepped on the glass and shouts of "Mazel tov!" rang out. Merle sat at the piano and played the gay klezmer tune she had first learned in honor of Rutti and David's wedding and once again the large room was filled with laughter and music.

The children encircled the bride and groom and danced around them, singing and shouting. Keren and Alan danced with his mother, with Dov and Lisa, with Nancy and Ari. The circle grew wider and wider with dancers darting into the center and then back. Song propelled them. Rutti, Nancy, and Merle danced together, their arms about each other's waists, their color high. Sarah and Keren gripped each other's wrists and whirled about in a wild *depka*, their skirts flaring, their laughter breathless.

Rutti took two glasses of champagne and gave one to Nancy.

"To our daughters," she said. "Keren and Sarah."

"The second generation." Nancy's voice was clear; her eyes bright with tears. Their glasses touched, but the small click was obscured by the song and laughter.

24

SARAH CLIMBED the steps to her apartment slowly, clutching the letters she had plucked from her mailbox and hugging the brown paper sack of groceries. She stopped at each landing to catch her breath, to shift the weight of the bag from one arm to the other. If Abdul were at home, she knew, she would ignore the weariness that had overtaken her as she stood in the apron of the stage for her curtain call. The knowledge that he was waiting would have energized her to dash up the steps, to call his name as she rapped on the door. But he was in Boston and so she submitted to her fatigue. She would go to bed at once and if she could not sleep she would take one of the small white pills a girl in the chorus had given her. "Just Valium," the girl had assured her. "It helps you wind down."

Sarah peeled off her gloves, struggled with the lock that, as always, needed oiling, and pushed the door open. The red light of her answering machine and the luminescent green numerals on her clock radio glowed in the darkness like the eyes of sly nocturnal felines. The room's silence oppressed her. She switched on the lamp, the radio, infusing the apartment with light and sound. She listened to the messages on the answering machine as she sifted through her mail.

She smiled because Abdul's voice came on the tape first. "I know you are not home yet," he said in his pleasantly inflected English. "It can only be the middle of the second act. But I want you to know that I am thinking about you, about us. There are important things I must say to you. I miss you, my Sarah. Touch my ring and think of me."

She smiled, touched the cool stone of the tourmaline, and thought of Abdul as her mother's voice replaced his on the tape. Rutti wanted to remind Sarah of her promise to spend time with the twins while she was in London. She was to leave in two days' time. She had worked for a year preparing for this exhibition and now she felt nervous, jangled. It *had* to be scheduled smack in the school year, exactly when David was doing a promotional tour for his new book, when Sarah was appearing in an off-Broadway revue. "Oh, Sarah," she said in a trembly voice, "I wish you were going with me. Or David. Or Merle. Or Nancy. Or Anne. I am so nervous. But I expect I'll manage."

Sarah shook her head. She had no doubt that her mother would manage. She would be lionized by the London art world. Already her desk was strewn with invitations to dinner parties and receptions, requests for interviews and cautious feelers from the BBC.

It would be a marvelous trip, Sarah knew, and she would have loved to join Rutti, but the timing had been all wrong. She could not walk away from her role and she did not want to leave Abdul, not at this crucial time when his fellowship at the Manhattan School was nearly over. She had not, of course, discussed that with her mother. Rutti was polite to Abdul, but Sarah knew that she was deeply troubled. It would have been astonishing if her mother did approve of their relationship. Still, Rutti was circumspect in her silence; her disapproval remained unarticulated.

The last message was from David. He wanted to buy Rutti a gift before she left for London. Perhaps Sarah could meet him for lunch the next day. He would be at his agent's all morning. Dutifully, she copied down the number. David would talk to her about Abdul; gently, he would speak of all the doubts that haunted Sarah, that haunted both of them.

She turned to her mail, tossing aside bills and circulars and slitting open the envelope with the colorful Italian stamp. A long letter from Keren written, her friend confessed in the first paragraph, when she was still a bit high from the bottle of champagne she and Alan had shared at lunch. *"Our first anniversary,"* Keren had underlined the words. "Does it seem possible that a year has rushed past?" It had been a marvelous year for Keren and Alan. They had found a wonderful apartment, large enough for both their computers. They worked from early morning until midafternoon, then wandered the streets of Rome. Keren had sent two stories to Alan's agent, who was optimistic, although he had as yet been unable to sell them. But Alan's novel was completed and he was at work on an outline for a new book.

"Don't tell my mother," Keren jokingly cautioned Sarah in her closing paragraph. "She'll think I've submerged my career in Alan's or some other feminist nonsense. Although I think she finally agrees that our marriage is OK — that I did the right thing. Just be patient, Sarah. Rutti will come around."

Sarah shook her head in silent disagreement with her distant friend. Nancy had objected to Keren's marriage because it had been so swift. It had not been Alan who incurred her doubt. But it was Abdul who bred Rutti's wariness. He was an Arab and Sarah was a Jew — a Jew whose father had been killed by an Arab bullet. He and Sarah came from different worlds, opposite worlds, warring worlds. All this Rutti had said within weeks of Abdul's arrival when she and Sarah sat opposite each other in a small coffeehouse on Amsterdam Avenue. Her voice was faint with misery.

"But Abdul is an Israeli," Sarah protested. "His family is from the Galilee. He's spoken Hebrew since childhood. Which is more than I can say for myself."

"Sarah. Be sensible. He's a Muslim. An Arab. You're a Jew."

"He doesn't go to a mosque. I don't go to a synagogue. Religion isn't important to us."

"But you don't live in a vacuum. Either of you. Read your father's essays," Rutti said, and that was the last time they discussed Abdul.

Sarah had spent a long afternoon at the Forty-second Street library reading Werner's essay, "The Children of Isaac and the Children of Ishmael." With clarity and cogency, Werner discussed the historic background of the ancient enmity and analyzed the deep race memory that brought forth a harvest of distrust. Sarah wept as she read. She wept for her father, that pale man who had held her so tightly in his embrace, who had whispered her name with such tenderness.

"You are my princess," Werner had told her.

"And you are my king," she had been taught to reply.

Together, father and daughter inhabited an enchanted kingdom, each at the center of the other's life. Rutti had loved her, had cared for her, but she was Werner's ballast, the essence of his being — as he had been hers. Werner's death — his distant death on a Jerusalem hillside bright with wildflowers — ended that. Years later, on another June morning, she and Keren walked to that hillside, gathering up bouquets of anemones and gentians. Sarah thought then of her slender, pale father; she wondered if his blood had stained the soft petals, if he had smelled their fragrance as he lay dying.

"Do you miss him, Sarah?" Keren had asked gently and Sarah had nodded. But she did not tell Keren that it was not only Werner she missed, but his encompassing love. Never again would she be as important to anyone as she had been to her father. Never again would she be the pivot of someone else's life. She had believed that until she met Abdul, until he encircled her again in the cocoon of tenderness she thought had vanished with her father's death.

She folded Keren's letter and replaced it in the envelope. She would write to Keren the next day as she had written her each week. It was only Keren who understood her feeling for Abdul, who had understood her exhilaration when Abdul returned to New York. "I felt as though I were alive again, renewed. It was as though for all those months from the time he left until he came back I'd been drifting through a dream and now I was living in a new reality. Can you understand that?" Sarah asked Keren.

"You are talking to a bride. Of course I can understand that. We're ladies in love." Keren responded with a flippancy she did not feel. Sarah's intensity troubled and frightened her. Keren had always sensed her friend's sadness, her yearning and had felt herself powerless to assuage that need.

It had seemed only natural for Abdul to move into the apartment when Keren married and left for Italy. It seemed natural for him to wait for Sarah each night at the small clubs where she sang, her cup of hot tea ready, the lemon sliced into a slender crescent. And she, in turn, attended each of his recitals, sat entranced as he practiced, listened to his new compositions. When she sang his eyes were fixed on her. When he played she studied his expressions, the grace of his fingers as they moved across the keyboard.

He wrote new pieces for her, taught her to use the leather drums and brass castanets he had brought from Jerusalem. They cooked together in the tiny kitchen, feeding each other bits of vegetables, cubes of spiced meat. They set the table carefully, lighting candles, filling small glasses with retsina. They ate in the softly lit alcove, their faces flushed with pleasure and expectancy.

They spent long evenings lying side by side on the open sofa bed, listening to music, laughing at old movies. He had a preference for the Marx Brothers. She was addicted to Humphrey Bogart films. He tried to teach her Arabic but gave up in despair. She could not manage the pronunciation. Instead he read aloud to her in Arabic, his long fingers nestled in the golden ringlets of her hair, and she lay beside him, hypnotized by the lyrical cadences she could not understand. They reveled in the insularity of their life together. They saw their solitude as strength.

Occasionally they had dinner with the Cunninghams or with Nancy and Ari. Ari admired Abdul. He had lunch with him and they discussed his relationship with Sarah.

"You know that it is a difficult situation — almost an impossible situation," Ari said gravely. "She would never be accepted by your people and you would never be welcome in her community. We are both Israelis, Abdul. We know that."

"We are happy. Just the two of us together," Abdul said. He thought of Sarah's delicate face radiant in the candlelight.

"People need other people. The most loving couples need friends. You are both performers. You cannot live in a vacuum. Not here. Not anywhere."

"I cannot imagine my life without her," Abdul replied simply, sincerely.

And he could not. Nor could she imagine her life without him.

They visited Rutti and David on family occasions: the twins' birthday, Thanksgiving. Rutti said little, but sadness creased her face. "Do you know what you are doing to each other?" she asked Sarah one day as they did the dishes in the kitchen. "You are separating him from his people. He is distancing you from those who love you."

"Mama! Don't ask me to give him up."

The pain in Sarah's voice tore at Rutti's heart. She drew Sarah to her, comforted her, comforted herself. The year would pass. Abdul would return to Israel. They would part. It would be sad but they would recover. She offered herself assurance that she tried to believe.

She spoke to her friends. Long-distance phone conversations with Anne. Long lunches with Nancy and Merle.

"Give it time."

"Nothing is predictable."

"They may tire of each other."

Their words were hollow. They did not meet her eyes.

The year passed and Sarah and Abdul did not tire of each other. They grew closer, their lives more intimately entwined.

And then Sarah, who had auditioned for so many roles, at last won a part in an off-Broadway revue and that very same day Abdul received an invitation to participate in a three-week program at the New England Conservatory of Music in Boston.

"There will be weekends," he consoled her.

But she had a performance on Saturday night, matinees on Saturdays and Sundays. She imagined him alone in a furnished apartment in a city where he had no friends.

"I worry that you'll be lonely." She toyed with the idea of giving up her part, but knew that she could not, would not do that. She had waited too long and worked too hard.

"My sister, Fatima, is coming to Boston. She's been invited to lecture at the Bunting Institute. We'll be company for each other. But you, will you be all right?"

And even before he left, they counted down the days until they could be together; perhaps she could miss a performance, perhaps he could fly into New York for a day.

Sarah wondered if Fatima had arrived yet. It was odd that Abdul had never mentioned his sister's plans. Sarah remembered the dark-haired woman, a colleague of Nancy's whom she had met more than once during her visits to Keren. She recalled a lazy summer afternoon when the four of them sat together on the terrace that overlooked the Valley of Hinnom. She and Keren, high school girls then, were giggling because two soldiers had trailed after them, calling to them flirtatiously, and Nancy and Fatima were deep in a conversation about their families.

"My family had a single aspiration for me," Nancy said. "I was to go to college, get a degree in education, and meet a medical student or a law student — maybe work a few years, then have my children and devote myself to quarreling with decorators."

"Oh Mom, not again," Keren objected impatiently. "This isn't a mother-daughter workshop or a consciousness-raising group. Enough already. We get the message."

"But this is a wonderful thing," Fatima interjected softly, "that a mother and a daughter can talk so honestly together. It is not a conversation that I could have had with my mother. Always, it was my father who made the decisions in our family."

It had been her father, the district doctor for a triangle of Arab villages in the Galilee, who had supported her desire to study psychology at the Hebrew University. Their neighbors were scandalized. Her mother, a traditional Muslim woman, wept openly. It was shameful that the daughter of a Muslim family would study with men as well as women at a Jewish university, that she would live among strangers at a distance from her parental home. Who would marry her? What kind of a life would she have? But Fatima's father stood firm. Fatima was talented and it would be a desecration of Allah's gifts if she did not use that talent. He arranged for her to live with an Arab family in Jerusalem, made certain that she had enough money to supplement the scholarship awarded to her by the university, and supported her in England where she completed her graduate work. He had given Abdul the same encouragement, the same support. He was an enlightened man who believed that there could be harmony between Jew and Arab, that young people like his son and daughter could contribute to that harmony and still retain their ethnic identity.

"Abdul, my brother, is a musician and a composer. So talented, so beautiful," Fatima said that day and Sarah remembered her words through the years. It was odd, she thought, how vagrant phrases, casual encounters, lodged in one's memory, strange that she should have remembered that conversation on the terrace so well. She even remembered that Nancy wore a long black embroidered gown that she had bought in the Arab market and Fatima was stylish in a brown linen skirt and a long-sleeved white silk shirt. A stranger might have thought Nancy the Arab and Fatima the American.

Fatima and Abdul were close. They exchanged letters each week. Abdul had told Sarah that only Fatima knew about their relationship. "And does she approve?" Sarah asked cautiously.

"Fatima is not a person who thinks in terms of approval and disapproval. She is a psychologist. She sees nuances — what is the word — yes, dimensions — that others would not be aware of. And she has strength. She herself ended a relationship with an English doctor because she foresaw the difficulties."

"Perhaps she didn't love him enough," Sarah suggested. "Perhaps she didn't love him as you and I love each other." She leaned over, kissed his eyes, the dark arrows of his eyebrows, stroked the silken brush of his mustache.

"Does anyone love each other as you and I love each other?" He surrendered to her touch. He did not hear the fear in her voice. Nor did she sing him the song she wrote the next day, a wistful ballad of lovers who come from worlds so different that they must retreat to a secret island of their own. It became the opening song for her set at the small East Village club that had booked her for three consecutive Tuesdays, but after those three weeks, she removed it from her repertoire.

"It's too sad," she told Greg, who had liked the song and wanted to hear it again. "I don't cope too well with sadness. Remember?" Greg nodded, kissed her on the forehead, threaded a finger through a golden curl. He remembered sitting beside Sarah after Werner's death. The children, he and Eric and Keren, had been charged with comforting her. But Sarah could not be comforted. She could not stop crying.

"I was in the middle of my daddy's heart," she said, her voice breaking. "And now he's gone. Now I'm not in the middle of anyone's heart." They all worried about her, cosseted her. Anne organized picnics in the park. Merle bought her gifts, small, tender surprises: a sweater the color of marigolds with ribbons to match, a recorder crafted of ivory. There was always a bed ready for her at Nancy's. She and Keren were already like sisters and Nancy listened to her patiently, spoke to her softly, comforted her when nocturnal terror wakened her from sleep. She was concerned about Sarah, but she understood that the death of a father was a trauma only time could assuage. Eventually Sarah might want to speak with a therapist, but she seemed to be coping. David and Rutti were supportive; Sarah's music offered her expression, and when sadness threatened to overwhelm her, she could always turn to her friends.

It was Greg whom Sarah phoned now but he was not at home. She thought of calling Abdul. It was late and he might be asleep, but he would not be angry with her. Still it would not be fair to waken him. He had an early practice the next day, and an evening recital.

"Come on, Sarah," she told herself firmly. "You're a big girl now. Enough of this."

She went to bed wearing Abdul's pale blue pajama top, the tourmaline ring pressed against her cheek.

The next day, it took Sarah and David a scant ten minutes to purchase a gift for Rutti. Merle had directed them to a boutique on East Sixty-seventh Street, and they agreed at once that the paisley wool shawl would be perfect. Pleased with themselves, they went into the French restaurant next door, which Merle had also recommended, averting their eyes from the homeless man in a shabby, buttonless coat who crouched near the doorway.

"Merle and Andrew ought to write a consumer's guide to New York," David said as he opened the menu.

"But Greg wouldn't buy it. All this stuff — restaurants, boutiques — really turns him off. The only thing that interests him is his teaching. And he's really terrific at it."

"And he can afford to choose it as a career because of what Andrew did," David reminded her.

"David, come on. There are lots of teachers whose fathers aren't millionaires. Give me a break."

"But Andrew's position will make life easier for Greg. And that's what we all want for our children, what your mother and I want for the twins and for you, to make your lives easier."

"It will take more than a check to do that," Sarah replied. The bitterness in her voice surprised her.

"We know that. Only too well. Sarah, we're worried about you."

"I can't help that." Her response was plaintive, resistant. "I'm not worried about myself. David, this has been the best year of my life. The revue is good and I think I'm pretty good in it."

"You're wonderful in it," David agreed. He and Rutti and the twins had been in the audience on opening night, applauding till their palms ached. "That's our Sarah," Adam told Liora excitedly, and Abdul, who sat beside the small boy, smiled at him. "And my Sarah too," he said very softly, although both David and Rutti heard him;

David took Rutti's hand in his own, massaged the fingers turned so icy cold.

"And I'm happy with Abdul. That *is* what you wanted to talk about, isn't it?"

"Yes, I want to talk about you and Abdul. Although it occurs to me that you will have thought of everything I can say. You know how difficult it will be, impossible, I think, to ever reconcile the differences in your backgrounds."

"We don't believe that," she said. "Abdul thinks that one day those differences will not seem so overwhelming."

"When, Sarah? In your lifetime? Read your own father's work."

"I have," she said. "I didn't know you had."

"Now you know." He smiled at her and she flashed him the shy elfin grin that had won his heart all those years ago. "I love you," he told Sarah just before his marriage to Rutti. "But I don't want to take your father's place — not in your heart, not in your memory." "No one can do that," Sarah replied solemnly. "We were planted in each other's hearts, me and my daddy."

He remembered those words now as he leaned toward her.

"Once you told me that you and your father were planted in each other's hearts," he said.

"And that is how I feel about Abdul now," she replied with the same solemnity, the same certainty. "I feel that we are planted in each other's hearts. Firmly rooted."

"You are speaking the language you spoke as a child," he said reprovingly.

"And I feel loved as I have not felt loved since I was a child." She saw the look of pain that flashed across his face and was suddenly contrite. "David, please. I know how much you care for me — how much my mother loves me. It's just that I never felt — I don't know — essential, I think that's the word I want — yes, essential — to either of you as I felt essential to my father, as I feel essential to Abdul now."

He was silent as the waiter placed their meals on the table. Chefs had become illustrators, he thought. Food was the obsession of the decade. Vegetables were sculpted, fish and poultry arranged as in a collage. Wealth created its own expectations. The nouvelle cuisine for the nouveau riche. He tried not to think of the homeless man crouched in the doorway. It saddened him that his children were coming of age during a time of such polarization. The rich moved swiftly past the poor. Whites and blacks stared nervously at each other. It had been years since he had heard the anthem "We Shall Overcome." The headlines screamed of hatreds: warring races, warring religions. He felt its impact on his own work. The predatory animals, the wolf and panther, that he had recently drawn for a zoological society brochure turned out too threatening, while the gentler woodland creatures, the rabbits and the deer, were too submissive. "Watch it, David," the youthful art director said jokingly, "the eighties are having their way with you."

He tasted his salmon. It was excellent. Sarah stared at her trout as though it mystified her and then removed the vegetables, piece by piece. She had always been a fussy eater. Rutti told him that when she was a child Werner cut her meat in very small pieces, carefully and intently boned her chicken. David had watched Abdul carefully measure out the sugar for her tea, butter her toast. The small gestures of love.

"Sarah, I know how deeply you and Abdul care for each other. But can you live your lives together? And where? And how? And how long will it be before one of you begins to resent the other because too many sacrifices had to be made? Sarah, your mother is worried but she didn't ask me to talk to you today. I wanted to share my thoughts with you because I love you, because I don't want you to be hurt." He spoke very gently.

Sarah covered his outstretched hand with her own.

"Please, David. You're not saying anything I haven't thought. I'm frightened. And I know that Abdul is, too. We talk about everything, but we never talk about the future, our future. Words like 'next year' and 'some day' aren't in our vocabulary. But of course all that will change very soon. Abdul's fellowship is over. This stint at the New England Conservatory is the last phase and then he'll have to make some decisions — whether he should return to Jerusalem or try for another fellowship here or maybe a teaching job. He's spoken about London. Or maybe Paris. He has all sorts of options. He'll have to decide. We'll have to decide." She was very pale. She did not deceive herself. She understood her own vulnerability. "I love him, David. I could not bear to lose him."

"We can bear more than we think," David said.

Too swiftly, he called the waiter and ordered dessert, raspberries and whipped cream for himself, an éclair for Sarah. They discussed the reception Rutti anticipated in London, the twins' new addiction to tennis, the book signing David was scheduled to do at Kroch's and Brentano's in Chicago.

"Will you see Anne?" Sarah asked.

"No. She'll be at a conference in Mexico. Apparently her marriage has given her the freedom to travel. There is always someone to look after Tommy and the other children."

"Clever Anne," Sarah said.

"They are all clever, clever and wise and courageous. Your mother and her friends. The playground sisters."

He stared hard at her and Sarah knew that he was charging her to emulate the women whose lives had informed her childhood. They had, each in turn, made painful choices. *But they had their lives and I have mine,* she protested silently.

Still, she smiled at him and they walked arm in arm as they left the restaurant. It was only after he left her on the corner and plunged across the broad avenue that she began to cry. She did not bother to wipe away the tears that streamed down her face as she walked slowly downtown.

The notice on the company bulletin board was curt. The lead singer had the flu and her understudy was not available. The next two performances were canceled. The management regretted that there had been no time to inform the cast. Alternate arrangements were being made for ticket holders at the box office. The actors and actresses, singers and dancers, milled about annoyed and grumbling.

"Hey, do we get paid if they cancel?" someone asked.

"They have to pay us. Equity rules. Isn't that right, Sarah?"

Sarah, who had taken the job as Equity representative mainly because no one else would assume the responsibility, nodded.

"Listen, it's not so bad to have two nights off if we get paid," an actress said. "Let's get out of here, eat dinner like normal people, catch a flick. What do you say, Sarah?"

"I don't think so," Sarah said.

She glanced at her watch. She could rush home, pack an overnight bag, and get to the airport in time to catch the last shuttle to Boston. Almost at once, the depression that had settled on her after her lunch with David the previous week lifted. She hurried out of the theater and hailed a taxi.

As she tossed a change of clothing into her bag, it occurred to her that she should let her family know she was leaving for Boston. But her mother was in London, David was in Chicago. The twins were staying with Merle and Andrew, and there was really no time to call — there wasn't even enough time to call Abdul, she realized. Hastily, she checked her wallet to make sure she had her credit cards and enough money. Several business cards fluttered out, and annoyed, she picked them up and thrust them into the pocket of her jeans.

Her heart pounded wildly as cab after cab passed her without stopping. She could not bear the thought of missing that last shuttle, of returning to the empty apartment. At last a cab stopped and she jumped in.

"The Boston shuttle, La Guardia," she said and sat at the edge of her seat as the driver wove in and out of the dense, early evening traffic.

"Hey, don't worry, we'll make it," he said reassuringly. "Sit back. Relax."

But she could not sit back, could not relax. The trip that she had begun on a whim was now vested with a primacy that obscured everything else.

They reached the airport at last and there was a seat available on the shuttle and time enough to get to the gate without running. Time even to pause at a phone and try Abdul's number. There was no answer. She remembered then that he had a recital that evening and she worried briefly that he would not be at his Cambridge apartment when she arrived. But that would not matter. She would sit on his doorstep and wait for him to claim her, to assure her that everything, after all, was going to be all right.

She took a cab from Logan to his address in Cambridge. He had described the apartment that the conservatory had assigned to him. He had told her it was on the second floor, its bay window facing Garden Street. She looked up. A light was on and a figure was silhouetted against the drawn shade. She smiled in relief. He was home after all. She imagined the surprise in his eyes when he saw her, the touch of his hand on her head, against her neck, his welcoming gesture of tenderness. She raced up the stairs, buoyant with expectation, and pressed on the apartment bell — two long rings, one short — their secret signal. Flushed with excitement, trembling, she waited, already smiling, poised for joy.

"Sarah!"

It was Fatima who opened the door, who took her hand and drew her into the apartment.

"What a surprise. Abdul didn't tell me you were coming."

"I didn't know myself." Speaking too rapidly, painfully aware of the nervous intensity of her voice, she told Fatima of the cancellation and her impulsive decision to come to Boston. "It seemed like such a fun thing to do," she said, surprised by the hollowness of her laugh, the use of words that were foreign to her. She would not reinvent herself for Abdul's sister. She was sorry, nevertheless, that she had traveled in jeans and a loose plaid shirt. Fatima wore a long gray skirt, a pink silk shirt, her raven black hair neatly twisted into a loose knot.

"Wonderful," Fatima said. "I think such spontaneity must be an American luxury. But you must be exhausted."

"I wouldn't mind washing up," Sarah agreed.

"Of course."

She gave Sarah a towel, directed her to the bathroom.

"Are you staying here, Fatima?" Sarah asked. *Why hadn't Abdul told her that his sister had arrived?* She felt a twinge of uneasiness.

"No. I'm at the faculty house. I have been spending a great deal of time here. It's easier to work in a flat, to have access to a kitchen. And then Abdul and I have a great deal to discuss after all these months. But let me put the kettle on. You look as though you could do with a cup of tea."

"Coffee would be terrific," Sarah said.

She intended only to wash her hands and face, but the shower was irresistible. She turned it on full force and stripped off her clothes. She washed her hair and as the hot water soothed her, she tried to imagine the conversations between Abdul and his sister. Surely he had spoken about Sarah. Surely she had spoken of their family. She imagined them talking late into the night, their voices low and troubled as they spoke in a language she could not understand. *No.* Surely

Abdul's voice had trembled with love, with joy, as he spoke to his sister. Surely he had told Fatima, as Sarah had told David, that they were rooted in each other's hearts. Yes. Yes. Of course he had. She shut the water off, toweled herself dry. Her hair, always irrepressible, was a tangle of damp gold ringlets. Because she had not brought a robe of her own, she slipped on the white terry cloth robe she had bought Abdul for his birthday. The scent of his sandalwood soap clung to the fabric and she lifted the belt to her lips and kissed it.

The front door opened as she stepped into the hallway. Abdul's smile was radiant, his eyes soft with tenderness, when he saw her.

"Sarah, Sarah. I can't believe it."

He hurried to her, and yes, he placed a hand on her head and the other against her neck as he kissed her — as she had imagined, as she had hoped. And she held him close, said his name again and again.

"Abdul. Abdul. Abdul." She had not been wrong to come. How could she not have come? They needed each other. They were essential to each other's life. Still, she was aware of Fatima's gaze. And she knew that Abdul too was uncomfortably conscious of his sister's presence. They stepped away from each other, like guilty children, surprised and embarrassed because an adult has intruded on the foolishness of their game.

Fatima eased the awkwardness of the moment. She prepared tea for Abdul and herself, coffee for Sarah. She sliced a pound cake very thin and set it on the table with small dishes of honey and jam and a bowl of fruit. And Sarah, relieved to have something to do, set out the plates and cutlery as Abdul changed from his suit into jeans and a soft shirt. They sat around the table in the small kitchen and Fatima asked Sarah about Nancy and Ari.

"They're fine," Sarah said. "Nancy has a busy practice and Ari's cultural exchange programs are effective."

"Effective?" Fatima lifted a thick dark eyebrow quizzically. Her color was high and her leonine features were frozen with doubt. Sarah understood that she had stumbled into dangerous territory, but she did not retreat.

"The musicians, the writers, the artists, Jews and Arabs, who have been touring the States, have attracted large audiences, especially on the campuses. And what Ari is particularly pleased about is the fact that many American Arab and Jewish students have come out to hear them, to see the art, to reach some sort of understanding. . . . "

"It is encouraging," Fatima said. "But just barely." The bitterness in her voice matched the bitterness Sarah often heard when Ari spoke of the smoldering hostility between Jew and Arab. So many years had passed since the Six-Day War, since her father's death, and yet the peace that had seemed so imminent in the aftermath of that war had not come.

"We thought that it would all be over in a few months," Chana had told her. "We truly believed that we would gather at a conference table, that we would give the Arabs their land and they would give us our peace. It all seemed so simple then."

But of course it had not been so simple. It had taken eleven years and the intervention of the United States for a peace treaty to be signed with Egypt. And now there was an impasse made all the more impenetrable by the war in Lebanon.

Still, they took hope from the smallest sign. It was an achievement of a kind that she and Abdul and Fatima sat together in this Cambridge kitchen, that Fatima asked with affection about Nancy and Ari. It was a miracle that she and Abdul, Jew and Arab, loved each other, understood each other.

Inexplicably, hope swelled within her. She touched Abdul's hand and smiled at Fatima. She would ambush Abdul's sister with her affection. She changed the subject and told Fatima, who knew of Keren, about her marriage and the whirlwind love affair that had preceded it.

"They knew each other two weeks when Alan asked her to marry him. And she said yes almost at once. And now they've been married more than a year and they're wonderfully happy," Sarah said.

"Yes, the speed of the courtship is extraordinary," Fatima agreed. "But it's not surprising that the marriage is a success. Two young people, working in the same field, from similar religious and cultural backgrounds, experiencing no financial difficulties — I would say that their marriage has a solid foundation."

"You make Keren and Alan sound like a case history," Sarah said, a tinge of anger in her voice.

"I'm sorry. An occupational hazard. All I mean is that Keren and

Alan did not bring any basic cultural and religious differences into the marriage that would compound tensions between them," Fatima replied. She hesitated for a moment, but remained silent, busying herself with refilling their cups.

As we do. Abdul and I, Sarah thought. There was power in Fatima's unspoken words.

Fatima gathered her papers. It was late and she had to lecture in the morning.

"Good night, Abdul." She kissed him on each cheek. "My brother." She spoke with the gentle formality of her people.

"Good-bye, Sarah."

"Good night, Fatima. Surely I'll see you before you leave."

"Perhaps. But I am here for so short a time and there is so much to do. Perhaps Abdul has told you that our mother is not well. I have brought her medical records with me. Tomorrow I will take them to a cardiologist at the Harvard Medical School."

"No. He didn't tell me," Sarah replied. "I'm sorry. I realize that you must have a great deal to do."

She wondered, as the door closed behind Fatima, what else Abdul had neglected to tell her. She turned to him, but before she could speak, he lifted her in his arms, carried her into the bedroom, and placed her on the bed. Slowly, deliberately, he untied the belt of the terry robe so that she lay outstretched upon it, a golden butterfly pinioned against the white cloth. Tenderly, he traced the contour of her naked body, his hands supple against her narrow hips, gentle upon the swell of her breasts; his fingers, moving as though they were possessed of an intelligence of their own, stroked the soft, fleshed crevice between neck and collarbone. As a blind man memorizes a text by touch, so his fingers studied the texture of her skin, the indentation of her waist.

He kissed her, his lips so soft, his tongue licking at her eyelids because she feared to open her eyes. They made love that night with measured tenderness. Their bodies moved in unison, and when at last he lay against her, exhausted, his head on her breast, she said softly, into the darkness, "You are rooted in my heart. In my heart. You give me anchor."

She fell asleep at once and although she could not remember her dream she was certain that Werner appeared in it, that he smiled and told her not to be afraid. She wakened to the elusive memory of that dream and the realization that it had been many years since she had dreamed of her father.

The scent of brewing coffee teased her and she stretched languorously, touching the sheet still warm from his body.

"Abdul," she called playfully, but there was no reply.

She shrugged into the robe and went into the kitchen. He had left her a note and a set of keys to the apartment. He had gone to the conservatory for a meeting. He wanted her to have a lazy morning. He would be back for lunch. There was fresh coffee, croissants. "Enjoy," he scrawled. He had underlined the word, but he had not signed the note. The omission disturbed her and she chastised herself for her sensitivity.

She lifted the curtain and saw that a light rain was falling. She had not brought a raincoat and the only shoes she had with her were the sneakers she had worn. She saw the rain as a reprieve. She would stay in, read, prepare lunch for herself and Abdul. She had inherited her passion for cooking from her mother and her mother's friends.

Like many women who are too busy to prepare meals regularly and rely on convenience foods or restaurants, they were, when they had the time and energy, passionate and creative cooks. The preparation of food was, for them, a celebration, a sensual adventure in intimacy. "It's remarkable how much fun it is to cook when you only do it a couple of times a month," Nancy had observed cynically, but her friends ignored her. Their faces glowed as they vigorously sliced vegetables, stirred fragrant, simmering stews, stood over a steaming wok crumbling fresh spices. They smiled with cryptic pleasure as they tasted a sauce or a fragment of caramelized carrot. Always, Sarah associated the hours her mother spent in the kitchen, moving happily through vagrant clouds of steam, with love.

She checked Abdul's refrigerator. Vegetables and eggs, a wedge of yellow cheese, a container of yogurt. The pantry was almost bare, but she found a packet of rice, a bouillon cube.

She took a leisurely bath, drank her coffee, and, propped up against the pillows, ate her croissant. She read the reviews of his recitals that had appeared in the Boston papers and in the *Harvard Crimson*. Each critic admired the originality of his composition. They discussed the atonality of the music, which did not obscure a subtle, repetitive melody. The *Christian Science Monitor* critic wrote: "Mr. Nashif's work is multilayered. The *maqamot* of Arabic music are well married to the Western influence. It would appear that the composer has stumbled onto the secret that has traditionally divided East and West and has discovered where the twain might yet have a fortunate and harmonious meeting."

Sarah smiled. Ari would like that review.

"My talented Abdul," she said aloud. She kissed a corner of the pillow to which his scent clung, found a strand of his dark hair and twisted it about her fingers into a ring.

Smiling, she pulled on her jeans and one of his wide-sleeved white shirts and went into the kitchen. She turned the radio on and energetically cut and chopped the vegetables, mixed them with the beaten eggs, as she hummed to the music. The *William Tell Overture.* The oil was sizzling when the first aria began and she sang along as she poured the mixture in and stirred it. Her face was flushed and beads of perspiration pearled her upper lip when she heard Abdul's key in the lock.

"What's this?"

"I've cooked us lunch, a wonderful lunch. To celebrate your splendid reviews." She whirled about to face him, her face lifted expectantly.

He hesitated for a split second and then kissed her on the cheek. The raindrops that had settled on his dark silken mustache were cold against her skin.

"You're not pleased?" she asked.

"Just surprised. I thought we'd go out to lunch. Somewhere near the conservatory. I have to be back for a rehearsal session with the woodwinds. They're performing my "Jericho" this weekend and there's that tricky passage. And I wanted us to have time to talk."

"We can talk just as easily here," she said. "Everything is done. You can tell me all the important things you have to say to me." She quoted from the message he had left on her answering machine, her voice playful, teasing. She was unprepared for his silence, for the sadness in his eyes.

"Yes, you're right," he said at last, "we can talk just as easily here." He spoke slowly in a voice that was unfamiliar to her. She thought of the theme and countertheme he used so often in his compositions and it occurred to her that he was using it now. Her hand trembled as she put the food on plates and set the plates on the table, as he moved past her in the tiny kitchen for utensils, napkins, glasses that he filled with water.

"You don't want wine?" She had noticed a bottle of Chablis in the refrigerator.

"No. I will be conducting. I want to have a clear head. But if you want some I'll open it."

She hesitated.

"Yes," she said finally. "I do want some."

He poured a glass for her, set the bottle on the table. They ate in silence. The radio continued to play. Arias of love's anguish, of life's cruelty.

"Wonderful," she said. "Wonderful music."

"And true."

He rose and turned the radio off. When he returned to the table she saw that there were tears in his eyes. She refilled her wine glass and lifted it.

"To us," she said. Her toast, so bravely uttered, was a challenge.

"I cannot drink to that, Sarah," he said.

She drained her own glass, and stared at him.

"What's happened, Abdul? What are the important things you have to say to me?" Her tone was brittle, defensive.

"I have been thinking about us. I have been thinking of nothing else since I came to Boston. I wrote scenarios in my head. Of how we could remain together. Of where we might live. I thought that we could live in Europe — France, Spain. I remembered hearing about a couple in Israel — a Jewish boy and an Arab girl who married and went to live in South America. Venezuela. The bride, it was said, killed herself. She could not bear the isolation, the loneliness. The more I thought about it, the more scenarios I wrote, the more hopeless it seemed. I would be giving up my family, my community, the source of my inspiration. You would be giving up your family, your friends, your home. We would be outcasts wherever we went. I would not become Jewish. I would not ask you to become Muslim. We would have neither homeland, nor family, nor religion."

"But we would have each other." Her voice was hoarse, constrained by grief. She poured herself another glass of wine, but did not drink it.

"It is enough now," he said. "But it will not always be enough. We would want to have children. What would be their religion, their nationality, their community? Our lives are our own, Sarah, but we would be visiting exile and misery on another generation. Fatima made me see that. That was why she did not marry her English doctor. She made me say the things I could not say, see the things I could not see. We must think of the future, my Sarah. I want children. As you do."

"I want only you," she whispered pleadingly. "I need only you. And you want me. You need me. Oh, God, we need each other. How many times have you said that we belong to each other, that we live in each other's hearts? And what of last night?"

She willed him to remember how he had touched her, how he had looked at her, the majesty of his tenderness, his whispered words in English — "Sarah, my darling, my sweet, my love" — his exultant shout in Arabic, *"Habibati — ya, habibati"* (my beloved, oh my beloved).

"It was wrong of me," he said miserably. "But I was so overjoyed to see you. So overwhelmed by you that I could not help myself. I was saying good-bye, you know. I was memorizing your beauty and saying good-bye to it."

She remembered how she had felt under his febrile touch, under the intensity of his gaze. Perhaps her father had looked at her like that before he left her for the last time. She had been a small girl, half asleep, but she remembered that Werner had knelt beside her bed, had touched her brow. She thought that his fingers were on fire. He whispered to her in the darkness. He told her that she was rooted in his heart, that she was his beloved. But he left her and never returned. She heard Nancy and Anne speaking softly, just outside her room, after they learned of his death. "Perhaps it is better this way. Painful but better," Nancy said. That was what they would say when they heard that Abdul had left her. *Perhaps it is better this way. Painful but better.*

No. It would not be better and she could not bear the pain.

"Why good-bye?" she asked.

"You heard Fatima say that our mother is ill. I must go back to Israel. I must see her."

"I'll go with you." She reached across the table, grasping his hands and digging her fingers into his wrists. "Abdul, what will we do without each other?"

"I don't know," he said quietly. He stroked her fingers, lifted them to his lips, kissed them one by one. "But we will survive. Fatima survived. You are a strong woman, Sarah. You'll build a new life. A good life. Your mother did it. Her friends did it."

"Abdul, I don't want a new life. I don't want to be strong. I want only to be with you."

"And I want only to be with you."

His voice cracked. He stood, came around the table, and placed his arm on her shoulder, his hand on her head. His fingers threaded their way through the golden ringlets.

"Rest now. Then go back to New York. I will call you. We will talk. You will see everything more clearly. But now I must go to rehearsal. Oh, Sarah, forgive me. I love you. You cannot know how much I love you."

She did not move. He was at the door, pulling on his yellow rubber rain jacket, hesitating. He could not leave her. He would come back to her. She closed her eyes. The old game she had played with her father. "Close your eyes and count to ten and I will be standing beside you." She counted. *One. Two. Three. Four. Five. Six.* She did not reach ten. The door closed softly behind him. She went to the bay window and saw him running down the street through the rain. He did not look back.

Slowly, mechanically, she cleared the table and washed the dishes. Exhaustion overwhelmed her and she lay down on the bed and closed her eyes. But she did not sleep. Sadness intervened. Panic gripped her and she shivered, her entire body shuddered.

"I'm frightened. So frightened." She did not know whether she had spoken the words or thought them, but the fear was palpable, terrifying.

She reached for the phone. But there was no one to call. Keren was in Italy. Her mother was in London. David was on tour in the Midwest. She thought of Nancy, of Anne and Merle, but she did not want them to repeat the words spoken all those years ago. *Perhaps it is better this way. Painful but better.* Oh, God, she could not bear the pain. She clutched her stomach, waited for a wave of nausea to wash over her, and then dialed Greg's phone number, hanging up when his recorded message came on. She wondered if there would come a time when answering machines spoke to each other, offered prere-corded messages of commiserations. She looked in the mirror and her pallor frightened her. Fumbling around, she found her blush, her lipstick, and, at the bottom of the bag, the small vial of white pills. "It helps to wind you down," her friend had said.

She shook out two pills and then a third. She needed a lot of winding down. She wandered into the kitchen. The wine bottle was still on the table and she filled a glass.

"To Sarah, all alone and on her own," she said aloud, downing the pills with the wine. Her friend had been right. Almost at once a new calm suffused her. The sadness lifted and she was afloat. She was all right and everything would be all right. Abdul had not meant what he said. He could not have meant it. "I love you," he had said. She struggled to remember the exact words. Yes. "You cannot know how much I love you." "I will call you."

Yes. He had promised to call her, but she did not want to wait for his call. She wanted to see him now, at once. She would explain to him that he was wrong. She would convince him that they belonged together. He would understand. He had to understand.

She did not walk. She floated. To the door and out the door. Down the dark stairwell and into the street. She lifted her face to the rain. It was so soothing, so clean, so cool. She lifted her arms to it. The wide white sleeves of Abdul's shirt were like wings. Laughing, she flapped them. She would fly to him. She could fly now. If she was not rooted in his heart, she had no anchor. She would float, as she had always floated — a pale moon orbiting about her family — apart from them, apart from everyone. Voices spoke to her, whispered through the raindrops. Her mother. Merle. Anne. Nancy. "You can do anything, Sarah. Your life is your own." She laughed bitterly.

"Yes!" she shouted against their chorus.

She could do anything. She could fly above the rain if she chose to, but she would not. She would follow it, listen to the messages in its rhythmic patter. It would take her to Abdul. She followed the rain into the street. She did not notice the two women, one holding a red umbrella and the other a black one, who called to her, nor was she mindful of the tall youth carrying a heavy green book bag who hurried toward her. She did not see the bright red car speeding down the rainswept street, its horn bleating helplessly as the driver tried frantically to swerve to avoid her. The student reached out to stop her, to seize the white wing of her sleeve, but she was too swift for him. She flew, her arms spread wide, into the eyes of the headlights. The oncoming car tossed her briefly into the air and then, like a wounded bird, she fell onto the sleek black asphalt. Her eyes were closed. A ribbon of blood sealed her lips and crimson stains spangled the white shirt.

The woman with the black umbrella held it over her, while the woman's companion placed her own jacket beneath the golden head. A police officer dashed across the street, knelt beside her, pressed his head against her breast.

"Ambulance!" he roared. "Get a goddamn ambulance!"

He pressed his mouth against hers, breathed in and out, again and again. He smelled the sour wine, tasted the odd sweetness. Drugs and booze. Stupid kid, he thought angrily. He had a daughter of his own. Stupid, beautiful kid. He worked harder, drenched by the falling rain and his own sweat. When the ambulance came he climbed into it and sat beside her.

"Any ID?" the paramedic asked.

She had no purse, but he found the business cards in the pocket of her jeans. A card with the name of a recording studio. Another for a club in New York. And another for an Andrew Cunningham, also in New York. It was that number he called when Sarah was rushed into the emergency room.

"Yes?" Andrew was annoyed. He had been called out of an important meeting. A police officer calling from Boston, his secretary had said. Why would a police officer in Boston be calling him?

"Mr. Cunningham." The officer's voice was apologetic. He apologized for the tragedy he was reporting. "I'm afraid there's been an accident."

He described the golden-haired girl he had carried into the ambulance, light as a small child in his arms.

"Sarah." Andrew's voice was heavy with grief.

"You know her, then?"

459

"Yes. I know her."

He and the officer exchanged information. He wrote down the name of the hospital.

"Someone will be there very soon," he promised.

He hung up, waited for a moment, and then called Merle at Egremont.

His voice broke as he told her what had happened.

"Will she be all right?"

"They don't know."

"She'll be all right." Her fierceness startled him. "We will be there. We will all be there." He knew that she was crying and he pitied her, pitied them all.

Merle and Anne, Rutti and Nancy, sat side by side on the cracked, red leather couch in the hospital waiting room. Opposite them, two children, whose parents were visiting an ill sibling, crouched on the floor and silently played game after game of Concentration with a dog-eared pack of cards. The four friends watched them as once, all those years ago, they sat on a playground bench and watched Sarah and Keren, Eric and Greg at play. Now and again one of them glanced at her watch and then at the clock on the whitewashed wall. They had each observed that the clock was five minutes slow.

"Rutti, do you want some coffee?" Merle asked.

Rutti shook her head wearily. She had not slept at all during the flight from Heathrow to Logan. Her blue eyes glittered against the parchment pallor of her face. She drew the bright wool paisley scarf, Sarah's parting gift to her, more tightly about her shoulders, pressed the soft fabric to her cheek; she had been wearing it over her rose-colored wool dress when Nathaniel Evans had knocked at the door of her London hotel room. She had been on her way to the Slade for a meeting with a group of women artists. Was it possible that she had been concerned then about her short presentation, or hurt about the single negative review her show had received? It made so little difference now. Only Sarah mattered. She closed her eyes and remembered Sarah as a baby, Sarah as a small girl, Sarah singing, Sarah laughing, the warmth of the child's body against her own — the joy of her childhood. She shivered now and huddled into her shawl.

Maternal vigilance sustained small girls, but young women journeyed alone. That much had not changed, would not change.

"I don't want anything," she said. "Except some news. Why don't they tell us something, anything?" Her voice trembled with fear and she looked at each of her friends pleadingly.

"They have told us what they know," Anne said reassuringly.

She reached out to touch Rutti's hand and her fingers brushed against Nancy's. Briefly, Rutti's small cold hand was sandwiched between them. Their eyes met and they looked at each other and then at Rutti; compassion and regret blended in their gaze.

"It doesn't seem as though they know very much," Merle murmured.

"They don't. Not yet," Anne said and lifted a finger warningly to her lips. They had to comfort Rutti, to reassure her. They could not compound her anxiety with their own.

Anne had conferred with both the emergency room staff physician who admitted Sarah and with the surgeon who operated with spectacular speed, less than an hour after the accident. They did not deceive her. Sarah's condition was serious, perhaps even critical. There had been multiple lacerations and a fracture of the right leg. But both doctors were primarily concerned about trauma to the head.

"At first we thought it was a no-go," the surgeon told Anne frankly. He was relieved to be talking to another physician instead of to the mother of his young patient. (Immediately after the surgery, he had phoned his home just to hear the voice of his own young daughter.) "But we were lucky. She was lucky. We were able to relieve the pressure against the brain without difficulty. What concerns us now is her return to consciousness. We don't want her to lapse into a coma, and of course we won't be able to discern anything until the anesthesia wears off. We did everything. Everything that was medically possible. You do understand, Dr. Richardson?"

She nodded. She knew that he was asking her to understand that he had done all that he could do. He wanted her to absolve him of responsibility, to recognize that he was not omniscient. "Of course, I understand." How soft her voice had been and how soft it was now as she spoke to Rutti again, repeating his words, explaining the implications.

461

"But Anne, what do you think?" Rutti gripped her friend's hand. Anne had never lied to her. She would not lie to her now.

"I think she has an even chance," Anne said.

The words came slowly. She had visited Sarah in the recovery room and sat beside her, so fragile in the white hospital gown, her finely shaped head swathed in snowy bandages. She checked vital signs, lifted Sarah's hand to her lips and kissed it, and watched as, releasing Sarah's hand, it fell heavily onto the counterpane. Sarah's pulse was weak and irregular, her breathing shallow, her sleep profound. Still, the anesthesia had not worn off yet. And she had the resilience of youth.

"A chance?" Rutti asked, her voice broken, tears gliding in silvery streaks down her cheeks.

Merle knelt before her, folded her in her arms. Nancy and Anne left the room, and as they went into the hallway, Andrew and David hurried toward them.

"No. Nothing. No change," Anne said quickly. The cryptic shorthand of the hospital waiting room. *We have no news. She is neither better nor worse. She is not dead.*

The men nodded, and walked toward their wives.

Nancy turned to the window and looked down at the busy Boston street. How odd it was that people were going about their daily routines, hurrying across the broad avenue clutching their shopping bags and attaché cases. A couple, running hand in hand, hailed a cab and climbed into it. She began to cry.

"Nancy, don't."

Anne was beside her. Anne's arm was about her shoulder. And Anne too was crying.

"I feel so responsible," Nancy said. "If not for us, she would never have met Abdul. This never would have happened." Her voice was hoarse with misery.

"It's not your fault, Nancy. It's not anyone's fault. Oh, we want to have control. We draw up our blueprints for life. We work and plan and we have our Filofaxes and our calendars. And then life happens. We make our choices and take our chances." Anne held out a handkerchief and Nancy took it, wiping her cheeks.

"It's terrible for Rutti. And I feel so sorry for Sarah, for Abdul. Poor Sarah."

She had not been able to reach Abdul, but she had phoned Fatima at the Faculty House. Fatima was abrupt. She and Abdul were rushing to the airport; their mother had suffered a heart attack and they were leaving for Israel at once. She would be in touch with Nancy. "I hope your mother will be all right," Nancy replied. She did not tell Fatima about Sarah. *A choice, a chance* — as Anne said.

"Poor Sarah. Our poor little girl," Anne repeated. "Oh, Nancy, I'm sorry. So sorry. For everything. Everything."

"It's all right, Anne. We'll make it all right."

They turned to each other, their arms outstretched. They embraced, balanced on a rib of pale sunlight, restored to their friendship, restored to each other. Arms linked, they returned to the waiting room.

David sat beside Rutti. The children had been claimed by their parents, and the friends now had dominion over the deserted waiting room. Anne swept crumbling Styrofoam cups, clumps of paper napkins and tissues, into the wastepaper basket. Nancy emptied an ashtray, found a card forgotten by the children: the Queen of Hearts, frayed but bravely bright. Andrew hovered over Merle holding the clear plastic bag that the nurse had handed her on their arrival. It contained Sarah's jeans, the white shirt stained scarlet by her blood. Merle stared down at the garments and traced the pattern formed by the bloodstain. A red cloud against a snow-white sky. She remembered the blood on the floor of her room, the rivulets of scarlet that had streaked the bedclothes and soaked the mattress on which Tran had died all those years ago. She closed her eyes against the memory and moaned softly. It was terrible, fearful, that young women should be so lonely, so vulnerable.

Andrew's hand closed over hers. Gently, he pried the plastic bag loose from her grasp. "Sarah is not Tran," he said softly, and she marveled that he should read her thoughts. "It is different for her. Very different."

"Yes." It was different. Tran had been alone, without support. No circle of women had gathered to keep vigil for her, not in life, not in death. "But will Sarah be all right?" she asked urgently. If Sarah was not all right — *if she died* — even unuttered the words frightened her — her story would not be unlike Tran's. She too would be remembered as a young woman who had died too soon, poised at the shallow inlet, the very shore of that vast sea of dreams.

"They must tell us something, anything," Rutti said.

Anne turned and walked down the corridor. They watched as she smiled at a nurse and showed an identification card, as she was given a white coat. How confidently she walked, although grief lined her face, blanched her skin. How authoritatively she made her way down the corridors of her own province. They remembered that she had moved that way during the early years of their friendship, calculating, confident Anne who never revealed her vulnerability. Her white-gold hair was pewter now and the change caused them to look at each other and observe the encroaching signs of age. Their friendship had weathered so many years, so many changes.

And then Anne emerged from the recovery room with the surgeon who had operated on Sarah, the bespectacled man who had been unable to meet Rutti's eyes or answer her questions. He and Anne walked slowly, deep in conversation. Their expressions were grave.

Rutti leaned heavily against David. Andrew's arm encircled Merle. Nancy stood between her friends, digging her nails into her palms. Slowly, slowly, Anne and the surgeon drew near. The others moved to the doorway.

"Rutti!" Anne reached Rutti. She was crying. She took both Rutti's hands in her own, kissed her cheek. "She's awake. She's fully conscious. Oh, Rutti, she's going to be all right."

It took them a moment to comprehend her words, to understand that her tears were tears of relief. And then they fell upon her, upon each other.

"Sarah. Our Sarah."

They repeated her name again softly, lovingly. She was Rutti's child, but she was daughter to them all. They would help her as they had helped one another. Exhausted, depleted, they sank down on the waiting room couch. Rutti leaned forward and placed her hand on the low Formica table. Each, in turn, did the same. Their fingers touched, and again formed the star of friendship made briefly radiant by a sudden swirl of brilliant sunlight.